"The theme of Steven Gould's JUMPER is, quite literally, escape. The first half of JUMPER HAS A CHARM AND BOUNCE that carry the reader past the implausibility's inherent in the premise—imagine a Holden Caulfield with the power of life or death over the jerks and phonies." —*The New York Times Book Review*

"Sprightly first novel combining revenge, growing up, lonely superman and abuse-of-power motifs centered on a classic science-fiction theme: teleportation.... An exceptionally well-organized debut, with THOUGHTFUL IDEAS, A CONTROLLED PLOT AND CHARACTERS—particularly the young protagonist—portrayed with insight and compassion." —*Kirkus Reviews*

"Gould makes an auspicious debut with this playful and moving look at a hallowed science fiction concept: teleportation.... Short fiction has earned this author a reputation in "hard" science fiction, and he applies similar logic to teleportation.... His WARM, DELIGHTFUL AND COMPULSIVELY READABLE NOVEL displays assured storytelling skill." —*Publishers Weekly*

"Gould proves once again that in the hands of a wonderful, perceptive writer, there is no such thing as an old idea. What sets JUMPER apart from other novels that dip back into the well of the masters is that Gould brings his own keen empathy and rigorous intelligence to the story, exploring what the ability to 'jump' means in the life of this particular young man.... This is a book that you won't want to miss. It reminded me of why I first came to love science fiction, and yet I didn't have to be twelve again to have a great time reading it." —Orson Scott Card

"An extraordinary first novel combining the engaging appeal of early Heinlein with a biting psychological depth worthy of the most mature author. Writing with the intense edge of today's darker reality, Mr. Gould follows the fate of a young teenage boy, whose life take a turn into the unknown when he unexpectedly teleports himself.... What more could any reader want?" —*Romantic Times*

Tor Books by Steven Gould

Jumper
Wildside
Helm
Blind Waves

Steven Gould

REFLEX

TOR

A TOM DOHERTY ASSOCIATES BOOK

NEW YORK

This is a work of fiction. All the characters and events portrayed in this book are either products of the author's imagination or are used fictitiously.

REFLEX

Copyright © 2004 by Steven Gould

Edited by Beth Meacham

A Tor Book
Published by Tom Doherty Associates, LLC
175 Fifth Avenue
New York, NY 10010

www.tor.com

Tor® is a registered trademark of Tom Doherty Associates, LLC.

ISBN 0-812-57854-6
EAN 978-0-812-57854-6

First edition: December 2004
First mass market edition: August 2005

Printed in the United States of America

0 9 8 7 6 5 4 3 2 1

For Emma and Carita,
Sequels in their own right,
But also stand-alone treasures.
(And no, Emma, you can't read this yet.)

Acknowledgments

Thanks to Sage Walker for nasty things to do with one's vagus nerve, Bob Leeds for drug info, Doc "Sully" Sullivan for Trauma talk and procedures, Rory Harper and Laura J. Mixon for first readings and gentle corrections, and to Beth Meacham for that perfect mix of standing back and stepping in.

REFLEX

ONE

"Davy was gone."

The first time was like this.

"You are the most stubborn man I've ever met."

The latest incarnation of this argument started in a little pastry shop on Sullivan Street, New York City.

His first response was light. "You probably shouldn't have married me, then."

She glared.

"I can't help it. It's how I feel. At least I know how I feel. That's better than I used to be."

She watched him push crumbs across the tabletop, herding them into a neat little pile. The busboy was leaning against the lime-colored wall, watching them. They were the last customers in the place and it was almost eleven P.M. on the East Coast.

"Let's get out of here," he said.

They threaded out between the tiny tables and into the chill air of the street. It was the first week of March. Out of sight, in a deep-sheltered doorway smelling faintly of urine, he put his arms around her and jumped them, and the argument, a time zone to the west, to the small two-bedroom condo they owned near her clinic, in Stillwater, Oklahoma.

Her ears popped and she swallowed reflexively, so used to it that she hardly noticed. She was intensely frustrated. *How can you love someone and want to kick them in the butt at the same time?* "But what about the way I feel? I'm thirty-one. I'd like to have kids while I'm still young enough to keep up with them!"

The corners of his mouth turned down. "Look at how my dad—I don't exactly have the right modeling to be a parent."

You'll never know until you try.

"And there's the Aerie. It's not exactly kid-safe."

"We can live here. We can live elsewhere if necessary. It's not as if we don't have the resources."

"And when the kids start kindergarten? 'Did you take the bus today, little Millie?' 'No, my daddy teleported me.'"

She glared at him but she couldn't really find an argument against this one. Was she to ask him to stop jumping? Jump, but lie about it to their child? Let the child know, but have them lie? She knew *that* one all too well. She'd been lying about Davy for ten years.

He looked at his watch. "I have a meeting with Brian in D.C. in ten minutes. He wants to sell me on another errand."

Oh, that's convenient! Then she recalled his mentioning it the day before and felt guilty for the thought.

"You want to wait here?" he asked.

"How long do you think you'll be?"

He shrugged. "Not too long, I should think."

She was still annoyed. "I've got clients at seven-thirty. I need my sleep. You better jump me to bed, first." *Though I'd rather you jumped me* in *bed.*

"Okay."

He paced while she changed into her nightgown and brushed her teeth. He looked at books, opened them, shut them. When she was ready, he jumped her to the cliff dwelling—their hidden Aerie in the rugged desert of far west Texas. It was cool here, but not as cold as New York City.

He turned on the bedside light and she heard the faint sound of the electrical generator kicking in from its own enclosure at the far end of the ledge. The furniture, a rough, knotty pine queen-sized bed, contrasted sharply with the more contemporary bedstead back in the condo. The walls, ceiling, and floor were all rough stone; the face of this cliff, and only the rough-mortared outer wall, made of like-colored stone, was man-made. Most of the walls, natural and otherwise, were hidden by rows of knotty pine bookshelves.

She sat on the edge of the bed and sighed. "We talked about it when we got married, you know."

He winced. "You said we could take some time, first."

"It's been ten years!"

He looked at his watch again. "Look, I've got to go, or I'll be late. We can—"

She turned her back. "Oh, just go!"

"Millie. . . ."

She shook her head. "Go, dammit!" Then she thought better of it and turned back to him, but he'd taken her at her word.

Davy was gone.

Of course she couldn't sleep.

When did I become an appendage? There was a price to be paid, being married to the world's only teleport. It was like being a Saudi wife, unable to travel anywhere unless accompanied by a male relative.

An appendage.

She'd accepted this, she realized, quite a long time ago, trading her own independence for the benefits, but she was beginning to feel that something was atrophying. *If not my legs, then my spiritual wings.*

And even Saudi wives can have children.

She alternated between blaming him and blaming herself, with brief stints of blaming Mr. Brian Cox of the National Security Agency. The real blame, she knew, if it was going to rest on anyone, belonged to Davy's father, who was an abusive alcoholic when Davy was growing up, but even he'd changed, having gone through treatment and now a decade of grumpy and uncomfortable sobriety.

Deciding who to blame wasn't going to give her a child. But she wasn't willing to raise a child without a partner's help. Davy's help.

For the millionth time she wished she could jump, like Davy, so she could go after him, to finish this argument, or at least defuse it. She regretted their decision to live here, hidden, instead of in Stillwater, where she could expose him more to her friends' kids, to family settings totally unlike his own childhood.

Instead, they commuted, Davy jumping her in and out of the condo in Stillwater, usually from the Texas cliff house, though there were extended periods of living in Tonga, Costa Rica, and one glorious spring in Paris. Still, they always came back to the cliff house. It was the only place Davy felt safe.

He'd built it shortly before the NSA first discovered him, and Davy and Millie were the only humans who'd ever been there. The surrounding terrain was incredibly rugged, a tortuous rocky desert region known as *El Solitario*. Since Davy's original discovery of the place, it had become more popular. The original ranch surrounding the area had been bought by Texas and made a state park. Still, the house was built into a natural overhung cliff ledge two hundred feet from the canyon bottom and a hundred feet from its top. Backpackers had made it into the bottom of the canyon, but since the Aerie was on the side of *El Solitario* away from the trailhead, there were fifteen miles of waterless mountain desert to be crossed just to get to the bottom of the canyon.

She groped for her glasses, got up, and put the kettle on the propane burner. While it heated, she started a piñon fire in the woodstove, then browsed the shelves for a book. Davy had covered the walls in the first five years and then added freestanding double-sided shelves later. In the last two years, though, he'd finally started culling the shelves, donating books to community libraries, but his acquisition rate still exceeded his outgoing and there were piles of new books throughout the dwelling.

It was three in the morning when she awoke in the reading nook, a cold pot of tea beside her and *The Wood Wife* fallen from her lap, she gave up and went to bed.

Dammit, Davy! You must really be pissed.

When her alarm went off, at six-thirty, he still wasn't there.

Shit! She couldn't even cancel her clients, a husband and

wife coming in for marital counseling. There was no phone—only a last-ditch 406 MHz PLB—a satellite-detected personnel locator beacon used by aircraft and ships for emergency search and rescue. It used the Global Positioning System to send its location so setting it off would put some sort of helicopter on the ridge above the Aerie fairly quickly.

She and Davy had considered a satellite cell phone for the Aerie but Davy was convinced the NSA could use it to locate the cliff house. Instead, he carried a satellite pager, so Cox could get messages to him all over the world, but it was receive only.

The Emergency PLB was just that, for emergencies. Was this one? Not yet, she decided.

He could get to the Aerie right up to seven-thirty and still jump her to the clinic on time, but her professional clothes were all in the Stillwater condo. She wasn't even sure she had clothes here.

She ended up putting on one of Davy's flannel shirts and a pair of his jeans, which were tight in the crotch and thighs, and loose in the waist. She found a pair of her own running shoes and used Davy's socks.

For a while she stared at the picture on the bedside table, a Polaroid of both of them taken at a restaurant in Tahiti. She remembered Davy's irritation at the flash. He hadn't hesitated to buy it from the photographer. He didn't like images of himself floating around. He was going to destroy it but Millie asked him to give it to her instead. Only her promise that she would keep it in the Aerie had won him over.

There wasn't much in the propane refrigerator. She ate some Wheaties dry and drank two glasses of water. The ceramic water tank atop the refrigerator was only a quarter full when she checked the sight glass.

Come on, Davy! This isn't like you.

Seven-thirty came and went.

She rehearsed speeches of anger and pounded the bed with a stick. She read more. She paced. By midafternoon the anger had turned, like the worm, and she began to feel afraid.

She was afraid for Davy. Only death or severe injury could

keep him from her. No jail could hold him, no prison bars, though, she remembered, chaining him to something solid might do it—something he couldn't jump. They'd tried that experiment once, long ago, handcuffing him to a railing. He'd nearly dislocated his shoulder. Old-fashioned manacles set in a wall would hold him nicely.

She shuddered.

A while later, she began to fear for herself.

She went outside and walked to the end of the ledge, to the door set in a separate stone generator enclosure. The emergency pack was in there, but it had been years since she'd even looked at it.

She turned and looked out at the canyon. Looking south, she could see the rocky hills. It was twenty-eight miles of rough trail with no water to the trailhead at Sauceda Ranch headquarters. There was some cactus and sagebrush and surprising amounts of grama grasses, but certainly no trees this side of the Rio Grande. Rocks cast the only shade.

Well, at least it's not August.

The backpack held the emergency PLB, several sealed bottles of water, survival rations, a light sleeping bag, a signal mirror and flares, and a plastic bag containing five thousand dollars in hundreds and twenties. The bag next to it held eighty meters of eleven-millimeter climbing rope, a seat harness, and carabiners with brake bars.

She took them back into the house.

Tomorrow morning, if he hasn't returned . . .

He hadn't.

Dammit, Davy, you are a great deal of trouble!

She drank most of the remaining water in the ceramic cistern, then dressed in Davy's jeans and shirt, and a pair of his underwear. When she stepped outside it was cold, the ledge still deep in shadow, and her breath fogged around her, but she knew that would change rapidly as the sun rose higher. She pursed her lips, then ducked back inside and took the photo from the bedside table, putting it in her back pocket.

Outside again, she shut the door carefully, making sure the

latch engaged, then dragged the rope bag over to the anchor bolt and ring. Davy had set it into a crack in the ledge with a sledgehammer, then anchored it further with concrete.

She put on the seat harness and closed the front with the base carabiner, then used a double bowline to secure one end of the rope to the ring. She tugged on it. Solid as the last time she used it, in the first years of their marriage. They used to practice the descent twice a year, as a precaution, but she hadn't done it in over five years. There were more cracks in the rock around the concrete and she tugged several more times to be sure the bolt was still solidly anchored.

She put the pack on the end of the rope and lowered it, hand over hand, seeing the excess rope coil reassuringly on the loose talus slope at the bottom of the cliff. She didn't have to worry about running out of rope.

An odd tingle went through her, almost pleasurable, and she wondered if it was fear. *Am I that jaded?* She examined it more closely and realized what she was feeling was satisfaction. After all, for the first time in a long time, she was having to do something without Davy, something difficult, even dangerous, and he wasn't there to buffer her from the discomfort and effort.

Well, one good thing comes from this.

She threaded the rope through the 'biners and snapped the brake bars closed, then took up the trailing end and brought it behind her, running it across the back of her thighs before coming back to her gloved hand. She backed toward the edge, letting the rope out slowly.

She contemplated the long hike in front of her, the fact that her ID was in Oklahoma and she couldn't fly without it, or rent a car, and she'd have to take the bus. She thought about walking a minimal distance away from the Aerie and setting off the PLB, but gritted her teeth. Not yet.

She reached the edge and sighed, letting some more rope out and dropping over the edge. She started down with small jumps, then swore as the rope crumbled a bit of the edge, showering her with gravel and a nasty piece of limestone that caromed off her shin. Sand drifted into her eyes, causing her to blink in the morning sunlight.

Oh, great!

She couldn't help picturing the condo, cluttered, friendly, sand-free, with her clothing, her wallet, and a fridge with milk in it.

*Davy Rice, you're a real pain-in-the—*Above her, there was the sound of grinding rock, and then a sharp crack. The rope went slack and she dropped backwards, watching, in horror, as the bolt and a partial plug of concrete, still tied to the end of the rope, came flying over the edge. She dropped like a stone, still a hundred and seventy feet above the rocks below, her arms and feet flailing. The cold air cut past her ears and the adrenaline stabbed into her chest like a sword.

Oh, God, ohgod, ohgodohgodohgod—

She crouched in the small living room of the condo in Stillwater, a pile of rope draped across her knees and feet. The heavy bolt and ring, with a small collar of concrete, dropped to the carpet at her side with a thud.

That was the first time.

She stopped screaming, hadn't realized she'd started, but her voice cut off into choking sobs. She sat back from the crouch, banging into the glass top of the coffee table and spilling a pile of books across the carpet.

She tried to rub her back where she'd struck the table edge. It stung—she'd scraped skin.

The trouble with being a trained psychologist is that when you experience something unreal, you consider the chance that you are experiencing a psychotic break.

Well, at least I know it's possible. Davy didn't the first time it happened to him. Her breathing slowed and some of the tension eased out of her. She felt drained, weak, as if she'd run up several flights of stairs.

Can everyone? If they've taken thousands of experienced jumps?

She wanted to talk to Davy about it but, of course, she couldn't.

Where are you, David Rice!

There were several messages on voice mail but they were all

from the secretary she shared with the other two therapists at the clinic. She'd missed seven client appointments yesterday. None of them were from Davy.

She called his pager number and punched in 911, their code for come home *now*. He didn't.

She checked her watch. It was only six-thirty in the morning. She had wanted a good start for her hike. But it was after eight on the east coast.

She started by calling the Adams Cowley Shock Trauma Center in Johns Hopkins Hospital, in Baltimore. Davy wasn't there. All the patients admitted in the last forty-eight hours had their own names. None of them were John Does. None of them had appeared suddenly, inexplicably.

It took her forty-five minutes to find the number in an old phone bill. Usually, when Davy received a page from Cox, he'd jump to D.C. and use a payphone to answer, but there'd been a time when he was sick with the flu, dizzy and feverish, and had actually called from the condo.

It rang several times before switching to the voice mail system. "Brian Cox here. Leave a message. I'll get back to you."

The voice took her back ten years, to her only meeting with the man, a judge-supervised interview when the NSA first discovered Davy. Not long after that, she'd spent several days illegally detained in an NSA safe house. She shuddered and almost forgot to speak at the tone.

"This is Millie Harrison-Rice, Davy's wife. Please call me." She left the condo's number and the clinic's, then pushed the handset cradle switch down, cutting the connection.

Shit! What had Davy gotten into?

She tore off the clothes she was wearing and took a quick shower. She ran the water hot, hoping it would thaw the frozen place in her chest, a knot of suppressed grief, fear, and anger. *I'll let it out soon. When I don't have to function.*

She put on therapist clothes, comfortable but slightly formal, a combination she'd found gave her the right mixture of accessibility and authority with her clients. Jeans, a nice blouse, a silk jacket, and flats. She put her palm against the window. It was cold enough that she started to grab her overcoat, but, at the last minute, she pulled on Davy's worn leather jacket, a bit large on her, but comforting, his smell mixed pleasantly with the leather.

There was a bulge in the inside pocket and she checked it. It was an envelope with fifty twenty-dollar bills. One thousand dollars. They were new twenties, oversized Andrew Jacksons, so it wasn't his older stash, the used bills he'd stolen ten years before, from the Chemical Bank of New York.

She shook her head. *Spy money.* A small portion of a payment from one of his "errands" for Brian Cox. Non-lethal, zero-exposure transportation—an agent inserted into Beijing, a remote electronic radio monitor left in Serbia, a dissident pulled out of Baghdad. More rarely, hostages rescued, but he kept those to a minimum, for her sake. He'd done a few jobs a month—more recently during the mess in pre-occupation Iraq. The original plan had been to pay back the million he'd stolen while still a teen, but he'd kept on going, even after it had been returned with interest. He hadn't returned it to the bank, though. He'd donated the money anonymously to dozens of shelters and drug treatment centers across the country.

He still donated heavily, now, but there was also a closet back in the cliff house with over three million dollars in it.

"What else am I going to do?" he'd said. "Garden?"

She put the money back in the jacket. She might need it to find him.

Her office was only a quarter-mile away, a five-minute walk, but she tried to visualize it, tried to *will* herself there.

It didn't work.

Dammit. Did I imagine the whole thing? Was I at the condo the whole time?

The climbing rope with ring, bolt, and concrete was still in the corner of the living room, where she'd piled them.

She walked to the office, kicking through drifts of fallen leaves, unable to enjoy the colors of the changing trees. She wanted to find him, to do something. But she had no idea where he was, where to look. Davy would come to her, when he could.

She didn't know if she was strong enough.

Waiting is the hardest role.

TWO

"That's not his blood."

Davy jumped to an alley running behind Nineteenth Street Northwest, just east of George Washington University. It was cool and the pavement was wet from recent rain, but it wasn't quite as cold as New York had been and, for once, the alley didn't smell of urine. Water dripped from fire escapes and telephone wires and he hunched his neck into his jacket as he turned toward the lighted street.

Just short of the sidewalk, where the alley widened behind a store, a refrigerator carton lay tucked against the wall, waterproofed by a layer of split plastic garbage bags. The ragged blanket that served as a door curtain was half-open and Davy saw two sets of eyes reflecting the mercury streetlamp. Children's eyes.

He paused. *Did they see me arrive?* The dim faces moved back into the shadow and vanished.

Sighing, Davy crouched down without moving any closer to the box. "Where're your parents, guys?"

There was no response.

He pulled a small flashlight from his inside jacket pocket and twisted it on, pointing it down. The two children flinched in the faint light. They were cleaner than he expected and the sleeping bag they were sharing looked fairly new. The face in front was pure Mayan, bright dark eyes and shocks of midnight hair. The second face was paler, with straw-colored hair, but the features were identical. Girls, he guessed.

"*¿Donde está su madre?*" he tried.

Reluctantly, the eldest, perhaps eight—he couldn't really tell—said, "*Está trabajando. Una portera.*"

A janitor. Nightshift work that didn't require good English.

"*¿Y su padre?*"

She just shook her head.

"*¿De dónde es usted?*" Where are you from?

"Chiapas."

Displaced. He thought about what their trip must've been like. They probably traveled on third class buses up the length of Mexico, then in some horribly crowded van from someplace like Laredo after crossing the border illegally.

The little girl, perhaps five or six, suddenly spoke, "*Papa fue desaparecido.*"

Disappeared. The matter-of-fact way she said it made Davy want to cry.

"*¿Cuándo vuelve su madre?*"

"*Por la mañana.*"

He dug his emergency cash out of an inner pocket—five hundred dollars in twenties, another thousand in hundred dollar bills, all wrapped with a rubber band.

"*Oculte esto.*" He mimed hiding it beneath his jacket. "*Dé esto a su madre. Para la cubierta.*" Give it to your mother. For housing.

The girls looked blank. He said, "*Para su propia casa.*" For your own house. He tossed the cash lightly into the box, onto the foot of the sleeping bag.

The kids stared at it, like it might bite them.

"*¡Oculte esto!*" he repeated. That amount of money could easily get them killed in their situation.

The older girl finally took it and shoved it beneath the sleeping bag.

He turned off the flashlight and stood up. As he turned to walk away he added, "*Buena suerte.*" They'd need luck, even with the money.

He heard movement in the box but didn't look back.

When Davy finished threading his way through the entrance foyer and into the side room, he found Brian Cox sitting near a front window with a newspaper open, but not lifted quite high enough to block his view of the restaurant. Davy could tell Cox had spotted him first, probably while he was still on the street.

Cox was wearing his hair longer these days, looking somewhat professorial, and the football lineman physique of a decade past had turned into middle-aged heaviness draped in tweeds. Davy dropped into the seat opposite him with a sigh.

"Something the matter?" Cox folded the paper and put it down on the table.

"Yeah. I just had a delightful conversation with two little girls from Chiapas."

"You jum—came here from Mexico?"

"No. These two little girls are living in a refrigerator carton two blocks from here. Their mother works the graveyard shift as a janitor, leaving them alone most of the night. Their father was disappeared back in Chiapas."

Cox looked at him, surprised. "How do you find these people?"

"They're all over the place, Brian. You just have to open your eyes."

"You want me to call Child Protective Services?"

"Hell, no. So they get taken away from their mother? How is that going to help? I left them some money. Enough to get off the street, I hope."

Cox grunted and looked thoughtful. "You can't save them all, Davy."

"I know that!" Davy snapped. "It's just—" A waitress with dirty blond hair escaping her barrettes, a bare midriff with a pierced navel, and a large patch of thigh showing through a ragged hole in her jeans stopped at the table. Davy exhaled. "Tea, please. Something herbal." He glanced at the list. "Lemongrass-chamomile."

Cox pointed at his coffee. "A slice of the apple pie and a refill."

She smiled mechanically and left.

Davy looked down at the tabletop. "You have kids, right?"

Cox nodded. "Two boys. And yes, I was thinking of them when you told me about those two little girls."

Davy shook his head. "No. That's not the connection I'd made." He sighed heavily. "I had an argument with Millie tonight. She's ready to have kids."

Cox raised his eyebrows. "Oh? And the argument is what? That you aren't?"

"Not yet."

"I see."

Davy winced. "What do you see?"

Cox blinked, his face mild. "That she's ready and you're not."

A different waitress, a heavily made-up brunette in a tightly knotted tie, snow-white shirt, and black slacks, brought out the tea and Cox's pie. Her hair was tightly pulled back to a severe bun. Davy shook his head, bemused at the contrast.

Cox looked annoyed. "Could I get that refill on the coffee?"

"Coming right up, sir."

Davy played with the tea bag, dipping it in and out of the water. He'd had coffee in New York only a half-hour before and hoped he wasn't in for another sleepless night. He inhaled the odor of the lemongrass and it cascaded a memory of spicy Thai soups eaten on high stools under a thatched roof in Cha-Am on the coast road to Malaysia. With Millie. He took a gulp. It felt good on his throat, a surprise, since he hadn't realized his throat hurt. "She's restless, I think. She has friends but it's hard for her to get really close when she can't be truly open with them."

Cox sighed. "I know that one—at least you guys are open with each other, right? There are things I can never tell my wife."

The brunette waitress returned with the coffeepot and refilled Cox's cup. "How's the tea, sir?"

"Good. Really good." He drank some more.

Cox stared at him then at the waitress's retreating back. "She dresses a lot better than the other servers here."

Davy said, "Probably a law student at George Washington. They need money, too, considering tuition and all."

Cox shrugged. "Seemed a bit old for that, but you never know."

"What's the job, Brian?"

Cox glanced around and lowered his voice. "You've never gone into Pyongyang, right?"

Davy shook his head. "No. South Korea, yes. I've got jump sites in Seoul and Pusan but I've never been in the Democratic Peoples Republic." He drank more of his tea.

"We have something coming up in two weeks. We'd like you to acquire a site near the Hotel Pothonggang in Pyongyang. We can put you on an Air Koryo flight from Tokyo. You can go in as a Canadian."

Davy shook his head. "If you've got something coming up, why not just insert your man? I mean, with two weeks you could probably put Madonna in place without detection."

Brian rolled his eyes. "It's not an insertion. It's an extraction. The subject is on the critical mass geometry team for their tactical nuke and is under constant watch by the Civil Security Forces."

"I thought they'd stopped development. Wasn't that part of the deal?"

Brian shook his head. "Ostensibly, yes. They shut down the factory. Research? That's unclear."

"Is he defecting?"

"His only daughter went south fifteen years ago. He has grandchildren now that he's never seen."

Davy gulped the rest of his cup. "Spell it out, Brian. Is. He. Defecting. Did *he* come to *you guys*?"

"His daughter did. Subsequent contacts were made directly with him and he was eager and willing."

"Okay. Just so it's not a snatch."

"It's not." Brian snorted. "Too bad you're so particular. You're awfully good at it."

Davy shook his head. "I may have been good at it. Didn't keep people from dying."

Cox didn't push it, shrugging instead.

"How soon does it have to be?" Davy asked.

"He's scheduled to talk at a conference in the capital on the eighteenth. We thought we'd do it from a hotel room."

Davy rolled his neck and felt muscles relaxing. His shoulders dropped as tension drained from his back. "Okay. Let's do the flight from Tokyo sometime next week. Tell me when to pick up the ticket and the passssssssporrrt." Davy blinked. The word had stretched oddly in his mouth. He felt himself smile, then he began to laugh softly.

Cox's eyes widened. "Davy?" He reached across the table and lifted Davy's chin, then put his thumb on Davy's eyebrow and lifted, pulling the eyelid up so he could see Davy's eye. "Oh, shit! Jump out of here. You've been drugged!"

This was even funnier and Davy started laughing harder. Jump? Why not? He tried to picture the alcove in the Johns Hopkins Emergency Room and it just wouldn't come. He thought about the cliff house in Texas but it just didn't stay in his mind. "I can't." He said.

Cox pulled a phone from inside his jacket and held down one of the keys. He listened for a moment then said, "Avenue H and Nineteenth Northwest. Coffee shop called Interrobang. It's a snatch."

An ambulance pulled up outside, its lights flashing but with no siren. A driver and paramedic jumped from the front doors, then two more uniformed attendants jumped from the back and pulled a gurney out.

Cox began swearing, his eyes swiveling between the door leading back to the kitchen and the ambulance attendants just now entering the restaurant's main entrance in the next room. "Can you walk?"

Davy giggled. *Why would I want to walk?*

Cox stood suddenly, picked up his chair, and threw it through the large plate glass window. Davy watched as glass floated through the air like snowflakes in a blizzard. People were screaming someplace, but he couldn't be bothered to turn his head to watch. Cox grabbed Davy's coat front and hauled him bodily to his feet, then stooped suddenly.

Davy found himself hanging over Cox's shoulder, head looking down, then the world was spinning and they were outside, crunching through the field of diamonds on the sidewalk. It was raining again. He could feel his butt getting wet through his jeans, and the diamonds were gone, and Cox's footsteps had mutated from crunching to pounding steps increasing steadily in speed.

Runs pretty fast for an old guy.

All he could see were Cox's legs splashing down the pavement. He could feel a pounding in his ears as blood rushed to his head but it was just another fact, another observation, seemingly unconnected to anything important.

Nothing seemed important.

He saw something hit the sidewalk near Cox's running feet and felt stone chips cut his face. The sound of a gunshot followed, lagging behind, and Davy's orientation changed suddenly, his head swinging wide as Cox abruptly turned a corner and increased his pace, his pounding feet hitting the wet puddles hard enough with his feet to splash water up into Davy's face.

Davy was still giggling softly with odd gasps each time one of Cox's feet hit the pavement. His head was swinging from side to side and he caught glimpses of the street in upside-down fragments, left, right, left. *Oh, it's Nineteenth.* This was the way he'd come earlier.

Cox stumbled and Davy heard the gunshot immediately after. Cox managed three more steps then went down, spilling Davy into a puddle. Davy rolled sideways through the water and fetched up against a storefront security grating facing back toward Cox and the street.

Cox tried to get up and fell again, crying out through clenched teeth. Between the water and the darkness, Davy couldn't tell where Cox was hit, but he clearly couldn't put weight on his right leg.

There were running footsteps, several pairs, getting louder.

"Can you hear me?" Cox said.

Davy managed a slight nod.

"I don't get out of this, tell Cindy she's the best thing that ever happened to me. Her and the boys." He rolled over and raised his head to look back, then reached into his jacket. Several bullets slammed into him and he fell back, his hand flopping out. His cell phone skidded across the pavement.

The waitress from the restaurant walked into view, a boxy automatic pistol held extended. Her perfect hair was mussed, now, rain-wet and coming out of the bun, and her mascara was running in dark broad streaks down her cheeks like she was bleeding from the eyes, but her tie was still tightly knotted and her steps were precise.

Cox groaned, a bubbling rasping sound, and the woman took one quick step forward and put another bullet into Cox's head.

Davy felt something wet splash across his face, but it wasn't rain. It was warm.

Three more men came into view, the ambulance crew. One of them dropped to Davy's side. "Christ, is he hit?"

The waitress with the gun said, "That's not *his* blood."

Blinding light filled Davy's eyes as a vehicle pulled up, turning the men into dark silhouettes. They took him by the arms and hauled him up and pulled him, toes dragging through the puddles, to the back of the ambulance. In the distance, the sound of multiple sirens began to grow louder.

"Let's get a move on!"

As they paused at the back of the ambulance while one of them opened the door, Davy's slumped head saw the slightest movement, across the street at the mouth of an alley. A tiny figure, a child, crouched behind a trash can, staring. *Oh, yeah. That's* their *alley.*

Then he was tumbled into the ambulance, facedown on the floor, and it was accelerating. He felt fingers on his wrist, then something stabbed deep into his left buttock—*Hey!*—rousing him *almost* enough to visualize the library in Stanville, Ohio.

Then the ambulance took a turn and kept turning, spinning, like a top, and the lights went completely away.

THREE

"Where is your husband?"

"I know Joe loves me, but, *Christ*, the things he does sometimes. Last night it was the laundry thing, again."

Millie was working through lunch, trying to make up as many of her missed appointments from the day before as possible. What she really wanted to do was run around in circles screaming but she couldn't see any way that would help.

Sheila McNeil was thirty-five and having problems with her husband after four years of marriage. From everything Millie had heard in the past two months, a large part of the problem was Joe's: a fear of intimacy that drove him cyclically between approach and avoidance. Sheila's attempts to get Joe to come in for some joint sessions had been unsuccessful to-date, so Millie's current strategy was working on Sheila's coping skills and reducing the woman's tendency to obsess on her husband's actions instead of dealing with her own.

Millie made an encouraging "I'm listening" sound in her throat.

"It's just as you said. I was trying to get him to talk about his feelings again, why he didn't want to see somebody, and, pow, instant argument because I left a load in the washing machine for two days and now it was getting mildewed."

Millie nodded. "How did you handle it?"

"I told him I'd take care of the laundry but he was avoiding the real issue."

"And?"

"He stormed out and started doing the laundry."

At least he was still in the house. In the early years of Millie's marriage, when Davy had stormed out of an argument, he was usually thousands of miles away.

"How did you feel about that?"

"Angry. Hurt. Pissed off. Then it struck me as funny, but I decided that laughing at him wasn't going to improve things."

Millie smiled. "That's an improvement."

"Yeah. Beats feeling guilty, any day."

The intercom buzzed and Millie frowned. "Excuse me, Sheila." She lifted the handset. "Yes, Loraine?"

"I'm very sorry to interrupt, but there are some FBI agents out here who insist on talking with you."

Is it about Davy? Millie looked at her watch. "Didn't you tell them I'll be done in five minutes?"

"Yes, I did."

"Tell them you told me they're waiting and that I said I'll be out in five minutes."

She did her best to concentrate on Sheila for her remaining time, but it was hard.

"Our usual time, next week, but call first to confirm, all right? My life has become a bit more hectic than usual, right now."

She followed Sheila out into the outer office.

There were four men in suits waiting in the office. The oldest of them was looking at Millie, clearly differentiating her from Sheila.

He knows what I look like.

Sheila, wide-eyed, lingered, putting her coat on slowly.

Millie sighed. "Step into my office, please."

Three of them trooped inside and the fourth one gestured for her to precede him.

Polite? Or keeping me from bolting?

She went to her desk and sat.

"Good afternoon, Mrs. Rice," said the man she'd already picked as the lead.

Yep, he knows me.

The man was slightly shorter than his companions. He had a touch of gray at his temples and he didn't quite explode with the over-exercised physique that the others had.

The *Mrs. Rice* would've normally pissed her off but right now it just made her think of Davy. "I'm not so sure it's that good an afternoon, actually. Who are you?"

"Agent Anders. Could you tell us where your husband is?"

She didn't know whether to be relieved or frightened. At least they hadn't said Davy was found dead. *I saw him two nights ago, seconds before he was probably seen in Washington D.C. And how do I explain that?*

"May I see some identification, please?" She was stalling for time, but didn't like the way his eyes widened slightly at her request.

"Certainly." He pulled an ID wallet from inside his jacket, exposing a brief glimpse of shoulder holster and gun. He held it out toward her, but pulled it back when she reached for it.

"Agent Anders? I'm nearsighted. How do you expect me to read it?"

He leaned forward again, reluctantly. The ID was not FBI, but National Security Agency.

"Well, at least your name is Anders, Thomas P. And these other gentlemen, Tom?"

Anders nodded reluctantly. "Also NSA."

"Where is Brian Cox?"

He countered with "Where do you think he is? And your husband?" His expression wasn't challenging. It reminded Millie of mirroring, a technique of therapy designed to draw out the patient, answering questions with other questions. Anders's posture was patient and still, like a benevolent praying mantis.

People give themselves away to this man willingly. In another life he might've made a decent therapist. She tried again, offering a piece for a piece. "My husband is missing. Where's Brian Cox?"

"Missing since when?"

Hmmph. More mirroring. "Two days, now." She needed to

leave it sloppy. She wasn't going to explain Davy's teleportation if they didn't know about it. She needed to leave time for him to get to D.C. by conventional means. *And there is no way in hell I'm going to talk to them about* my *little trip from Texas to here!*

Anders stared at the wall behind her for a moment, then nodded sharply as if making a decision. He took a cell phone from his belt. "One moment and I'll answer *your* question." He punched a speed dial combination then, after a moment, spoke. "Anders here. The asset *is* missing. His wife hasn't seen him for two days." He listened again, then said, "All right." He put away the phone.

Millie shuddered. *Asset?* Wasn't that the same as saying, "thing"?

Anders squared his shoulders and said, "Brian Cox is dead. He was found in D.C. on Nineteenth Avenue Northwest. He'd been shot several times, then again in the head at close range."

Millie took a sudden, deep breath through her nose. "Oh, the poor man. Did he have a family?"

Anders winced. "I'm afraid so."

You were avoiding thinking about his family, weren't you? She shook her head. *And Davy?* "Davy was meeting with him," she said, since they must've known that.

"Yes. Cox told his unit's duty officer. She took your message off the voice mail system early this morning. I'm stationed in Oklahoma City and they dispatched me."

"I haven't seen Davy since he, uh, left for the meeting."

Anders noted the pause. "Gentlemen," he said to the room at large. "Establish an inner perimeter."

Millie blinked. *Inner implies outer. How many men did they bring?*

The other agents looked briefly surprised, then trooped out, closing the door behind them.

"May I sit?" asked Anders, indicating one of the chairs she kept against the wall for group sessions.

She nodded.

He moved it in front of her desk and, well, *settled* in it. Sitting wasn't quite accurate—too much of his weight was still on his feet. He took a deep breath and said, "You probably don't recognize me—I think you saw me only twice." He pursed his lips and frowned. "I worked David's case ten years ago and was on the perimeter team when we took you into custody."

"Custody?" She said that word slowly. The NSA had kidnapped her, seeking to use her as a lever to control Davy.

Anders dropped his eyes and cleared his throat. "The point is, I was one of those agents watching your college apartment. He grabbed me and teleported me to Orly Airport, in France."

She let the old business pass. It didn't matter now. "Then you know about him. Right. Davy left me at five minutes until eleven the night before last, central time. From what I understood, he was meeting Cox at midnight, eastern time."

Anders nodded. "Yes, a coffee shop called Interrobang."

"Ah, I didn't know the name. We never went there together because . . . well, because I'd had enough involvement with the NSA. Did they meet?" She was perched on the edge of her chair now and couldn't remember shifting forward.

"Yes. The night duty officer got a distress call from Cox's cell phone at twelve twenty-five. Cox gave his location and said it was a snatch . . . a kidnapping."

"Davy?" The knot in her chest was aching.

"Probably. Witnesses say an ambulance pulled up to the front door and four men started inside. While they were in the foyer, Cox pitched a chair through the front window, threw his companion over his shoulder, and left through the window."

"His companion. Was it Davy?"

"The agency has some recent passport photos and we presented them mixed with others. Three of the witnesses picked Davy's picture. Several others didn't."

"Why wasn't Davy walking? Why didn't he jump?"

"He was drugged. Our lab found a cocktail of droperidol and gamma hydroxy butyrate in the dregs of his tea. As they took effect, it must've become clear to Cox, and that's why he scrambled the alert team. There was a waitress who wasn't a waitress at Interrobang. She bribed the manager fifty dollars to wait on Cox and your husband. Said it was part of a fraternity joke."

"That same waitress and the ambulance crew ran out of the restaurant after Cox. The witnesses heard distant gunshots and when our alert team arrived they found Cox a block and a half away, dead.

"There was no sign of your husband."

Millie leaned back again. They wouldn't have drugged Davy if they just wanted to kill him. The fear subsided slightly, then surged back. *They don't balk at killing, though.* "Who did this?"

"Who do you think could've done this?" More mirroring.

"If it wasn't the NSA, I have no idea."

"Ah." Anders shook his head. "We don't know who did this."

Millie stared out the window for a moment. "Well, it was someone with *access*. They either knew about the specific meeting or they knew Cox was Davy's control and have been monitoring him continuously until they met." She thought for a moment. "It might even be another US intelligence branch. One of those agencies that Davy provided transport for. Someone who wants those services at their disposal."

Anders frowned, started to say something, then stopped himself. Finally he shifted in the chair and dropped his hands to his knees. "You're right, those possibilities are under consideration. Everyone in Cox's unit is undergoing polygraphs right now and they're doing a major screen for electronic intelligence."

Millie looked blank.

"Bugs, wiretaps. We're also checking his family, to see if any of them mentioned the meeting to anybody. Now I need to ask you the same question: Did you mention his meeting to anybody?"

Millie shook her head. "I didn't actually know about the meeting until ten minutes before he left. We were having an argu—well, a rather heated discussion about something else."

"And that was?"

"None of your business," she said, blushing. "You'll just have to trust me that it had nothing to do with Davy's disappearance."

Anders stared at her for a moment, then nodded. "All right."

Millie frowned. "How can they hope to control Davy? The minute the drugs wear off, he'll be out of there." *Perhaps ear-*

lier, even. It hadn't happened lately but in the early years of their marriage, Davy would get nightmares and end up hundreds of miles away, fleeing an illusionary danger, jumping before he was fully awake. *Unless they chain him.* She decided not to mention this to Anders.

A deeply paranoid thought hit her. *What if this interview is not about finding Davy, but learning how to control him?* Her next thought, also paranoid, brought up a different possibility.

She opened her mouth to speak, then closed it again, licking suddenly dry lips. Finally she said, "So, if Cox's unit is compromised, then I'm also in danger. Threatening me might be one way to control him. Is that why you had them establish a perimeter? Do you expect the same people to come after me?"

Anders waited a moment, frowning slightly. Finally, he just said, "Yes." She stared at him for a moment, thinking it through. What she concluded frightened her very much.

"And you want them to. If you can catch them trying to take me, it's one way to find out who's behind this."

His eyes widened and for a moment she thought she was wrong. Then she realized the surprise wasn't about the idea of using her as bait. He was surprised that she'd figured it out so soon.

"I'm not stupid, Mr. Anders."

His nod was respectful. "Obviously not. We hadn't planned on telling you that part."

She felt herself hunch down, her neck drawing down between her shoulders. "Doesn't matter. If it stands a chance of leading us to Davy, we've got to try it."

Her last client canceled on her and she was able to go home at four-thirty but didn't actually leave until five. Anders went over the route she would walk to her condo, then deployed his men accordingly.

"I'd lose the suits if this is to go on. Your guys could pass for college jocks if they dressed right."

Anders smiled. "We're not amateurs, Mrs. Rice. The men in suits are not the only assets on site."

Ah, the inner perimeter. The outer perimeter was probably in place before Anders had ever entered the office. She had to laugh. "Obviously not. But it is *Harrison*-Rice and I prefer Ms. To Mrs."

"All right, Ms. Harrison-Rice." He bent his head to one side and covered his ear. He was wearing an earplug now that snaked up his neck on a flesh-colored cord. "Right. My men are in place."

Anders took a thin oblong, flesh-colored plastic case perhaps two inches long out of his coat pocket. He did something to the side and it opened, revealing circuit board, lithium battery, and a small slide switch that he moved before recovering it. He touched something inside his jacket and spoke. "The locator is on—are you getting a signal?" The answer was apparently positive.

He turned back to Millie. "We'd like you to wear this on your person. It's a GPS tracker, a backup should they get close enough to snatch you."

She stared at it. "On my person? That's a little vague, isn't it? Not in my purse or jacket, right?"

Anders colored slightly. "The bra is probably your best bet. Underneath, to, uh, secure it." He handed her the case.

"I'll be outside." He left the office, closing the door behind him.

Alone, the humor drained away and she felt small and frightened. She was wearing a sports bra under her blouse and when she pushed the case between her breasts it stayed there, without any telltale bulges visible, even before she rebuttoned the blouse.

Again, she put on Davy's leather jacket, taking a moment to bury her face in the lining and inhaling deeply. "Oh, Davy. What have you gotten into?"

The route she'd given Anders wasn't her usual one, but a slight detour past a city playground. She stopped at the fence, watching mothers with preschool-age kids playing. One woman under the trees was being buried in leaves by twin girls. All three of them were giggling insanely and Millie felt tears come to her eyes even as she smiled. "Oh, Davy," she muttered. "I wish you'd knocked me up before you disappeared."

Enough of that! She walked on, trying to push the thought

away but she wasn't just worried about Davy. She was scared she'd never have the chance to have his children.

She looked around more obviously, looking for Anders's men and had to admit she couldn't really pick them out. This was fairly close to the university so there were a lot of pedestrians and vehicle traffic.

Only once was she sure. A blond man in an OSU sweatshirt with a backpack slung over one shoulder passed her, going the same direction. The bright orange silkscreen of the university mascot, Pistol Pete, on the sweatshirt had obviously never been washed and there were still creases from a hanger standing up on the shoulders. The clincher, though, was a coil of flesh-colored wire trailing down his neck from his right ear.

Orange is not your color.

She halfway expected Anders to be waiting in the lobby of the condominiums but he wasn't there. There also wasn't anybody on the stairs or in the hallway. *Did they even check the building?*

She hesitated before her door. *God dammit, this was my refuge. Now it feels like a trap.* She started to turn away when it opened.

"Come on in, Ms. Harrison-Rice. It's all clear."

It was Anders.

She glared. "I don't suppose you needed a key."

He shrugged apologetically. "It was better than hanging around in the hall."

She pushed past him. There was another man sweeping an antennaed box across the far wall and a third standing beside the door to the balcony, looking outside through a part in the drapes.

"Do you plan on moving in with me?"

"No, ma'am. We've been sweeping for bugs and to get the layout. There's a unit available on the next floor up. We're arranging for its use."

She looked around. The climbing rope and plug of concrete from the cliff house was still in the corner. When she'd arrived back here, this morning, it had seemed spacious. With the three men present, it felt like the walls were closing in.

Anders must've seen this. "We'll be out of here shortly."

Millie swallowed. "Leaving me alone?" *Make up your mind, girl. Do you want them here or not?*

"We've put a camera in the hall and we'll be watching the entrances to the building. There's the three, right?"

Millie shook her head. "Four. There's a stairway from the parking garage in the southeast corner. Then there's the front and back door, and the one by the pool, though they'd have to go over the fence to get to that one." She felt her breathing slow. "Where do you monitor the camera?"

"We've got a van parked down the street." At her look of alarm he added, "But there'll be men on the premises, closer."

She didn't know whether that made her feel better or not, but she said, "All right. I'm going to take a shower and change. Um, you didn't put any cameras *in* the apartment did you?"

Anders shook his head. "No . . . but you should be aware—" He licked his lips. "Well, the tracking device I gave you has a microphone."

Before she could say anything he quickly added, "I'm sorry I didn't mention it earlier, but I realized that no matter what you thought about the invasion of *your* privacy, you wouldn't tolerate the invasion of your clients' privacy."

Her initial surge of anger subsided. "Quite right. We'll have to talk about this, but right now I want a shower."

She shut the bedroom door and stood, her back to it, her hands over her face, rubbing her eyes. *First things first.* She dug the tracker/bug out of her bra and put it on the bedside clock radio, right on the speaker grill, then turned on the news. *Hope that didn't hurt anybody's ears.* Only then did she feel like she could continue into the bathroom.

She ran the water hot and let it stream across her face. Then, like melting ice, the tears came and the sobs and the fear and grief. *Davy, Davy, Davy—you better be all right!*

The next morning she met Anders in the parking garage and followed him to a full-sized custom van with mirrored windows whose chrome roof rack barely cleared the cement beams above. He opened the door for her and she climbed in. Instead of the plush carpeting and upholstered seats the exterior led one to expect, the interior was metal and utilitarian with racks of electronics, monitors, and cable.

A man wearing a tee-shirt and shorts sat in a pivoting vinyl seat. Anders directed her to a backwards-facing bench seat behind the driver's station, and perched beside her, shutting the door behind them. It was warm in the van, despite the late winter temperatures outside, and Millie shrugged off her coat.

Anders gestured at the other man. "This is Watson. That's his first name."

Watson smiled. "I'm named after three famous sidekicks."

Millie thought about it a second, then said, "Sherlock Holmes's Watson. Uh, and Watson and Crick? Who's the third?"

Watson grinned. "The most appropriate one—Alexander Graham Bell's assistant, at the other end of listening device. 'Watson, come here, I need you.'"

Anders waved his hand impatiently. "Give us Ms. Harrison-Rice's bug on speaker."

Watson pushed a slider bar up and there was a slight hum. When Anders said, "It can pick up those around you, too," his voice echoed out of the speaker. "But, you can turn it off." He held out his hand.

Millie took the tracker out of her pocket and handed it to him.

"It comes apart like this." He put pressure on the two faces and slid them in opposite directions. The face popped off and he indicated a slide switch with a zero at one end and a two at the other. "At zero it's all the way off so don't do that. In between, it's just the GPS locator. And all the way to the right, it's a GPS locator and an audio bug." He slid it to the middle position as he was saying this and the speaker stopped echoing his voice.

Watson pointed at a computer screen that seemed to be a street map of her neighborhood with a flashing dot at the appropriate space. "But we're not getting the GPS coordinates right now, because you're in this ferroconcrete garage and can't get the satellites. That'll change when you walk outside."

Anders turned the audio bug back on. "Is that satisfactory, Ms. Harrison-Rice?"

"Right. When I'm with clients, the mike is going off. Otherwise, it'll be on and I'll just have to watch what I say."

FOUR

". . . that activity is contraindicated."

Something wasn't right.

Davy was sure of it but he couldn't put his finger on it.

There was light on the other side of his eyelids. He knew he should get up—Millie got pissed if he spent all day in bed—but he couldn't even make himself open his eyes, much less sit up. *Maybe it's a virus. Maybe I just don't want to get into the having-children argument again.*

Millie must've been listening to something on the television or the radio. A distant voice, deep, male, said, "Uh, oh, that looks like an arousal pattern."

"Where?" A tenor, or was it an alto?

"That K complex . . . and those theta waves are increasing in amplitude."

"Hit him with some more fentanyl IV. Then increase the drip on the fentanyl/midazolam." Definitely an alto, a woman.

He felt something cold *in* his arm and thought it odd that it should be *in* his arm rather than on it and then he went back to sleep.

The TV was on again. It sounded like some sort of daytime hospital soap. "—an infection?"

"Probably. Either from the IV or the catheter or when we intubated him—something from the sinuses. You can't keep someone sedated this long without depressing their immune system. I've started him on Zyvox and Synercid, and we're working him up with blood cultures, UA, and chest film for now." A man.

"Dammit—the surgery's scheduled for tonight." The woman from before, the alto.

"Well, you open him like this—"

"I know, I know. It's just that the surgical team is not in on it. Getting them together was . . . difficult." She paused. "We'll abort if his temp doesn't drop below ninety-nine five before seventeen hundred. What's his white blood cell count?"

"Fifteen five. There's some thrombocytopenia and his iron's down."

"Well, he's fighting it. Hey, those theta waves are awfully sharp. What's the fentanyl/midazolam drip? That high?"

"You can't leave him on it for days and not expect some tolerance increase."

"Well, we can't have him waking up, either. Bump it. Hopefully we can take him off it in a couple of days."

"Okay, I'm increasing it to three hundred."

"You see any sign of beta formation, you hit him with more fentanyl."

"Well, okay, but we could lose him to drug interactions."

"You've got a crash cart. We're taking that risk. You have a problem, take it up with *her*."

The man cleared his throat, but didn't say anything, or if he did, the TV must've been turned off first.

He hurt.

His back hurt, his head hurt, his neck hurt. His lips were cracked, and his sinuses burned, and he was hungry. Ravenous.

What on earth did I do last night?

He remembered going to dinner with Millie, then pastries in the village, and then he was supposed to meet—*Christ. Brian!*

Images flooded back.

Glass flying over a streetlight-lit sidewalk mixed with rain. A dizzying view of an upside down street. Brian, lying on his side in a sidewalk puddle, asking him to tell his wife something. Then the bullets and the bleeding-eyed waitress from the coffee shop shooting Brian in the face.

Brian's blood spraying onto his face.

Davy's eyes ripped open. That was the only word for it—the eyelids were stuck together. The room was dark gray and the lighting was indirect, putting puddles of light on the ceiling that hurt his eyes.

The blanket and sheet were pulled up to his neck and his head was propped slightly up, as if he were on multiple pillows or one very thick one. He tried to lift his hand to push the covers down but his hand seemed stuck. He tried the other one and though there was a bit of motion, he couldn't pull it up either. He tried to sit up and fell back, pain shooting from his shoulders.

Am I that weak?

"I shouldn't try and move just yet." The voice was digitally distorted, a cross between *2001*'s Hal and a washing machine on spin. It came from a speaker over the mirror on the wall to his right.

Mirror? Probably not, thought Davy, *They're watching.*

"Who—" Davy's voice was the barest husk and the word was completely unintelligible. He tried to clear his throat and winced. It was incredibly raw.

"Best not to try speaking, either," the voice said. "Not just yet."

The door opposite the foot of his bed opened. It was brighter lit in the hall, a painful glimpse of a wall painted white on its upper half, wood-paneled below, and then it was occulted. When he opened his eyes again, the door was shut again and there was someone standing in the room with him.

He blinked again, trying to get the afterimage of the doorway out of his eyes. He was having trouble focusing. "Drink up for Mummy," said the distorted voice.

The figure guided a straw to his lips.

It was ice water and Davy suddenly realized that he was parched, like a man lost in the desert. He sucked greedily and then broke into a spasm of coughing as some of it went down his windpipe.

The figure backed away and Davy's eyes finally focused.

It—he—was a large man wearing blue scrubs complete with a cap, paper surgical mask, and latex gloves. His eyes looked concerned as he watched Davy cough.

Davy coughed a little longer than actually necessary, using the time to look for identifying marks. The man had bushy brown eyebrows. There was a faint reflection from his eye, the edge of a contact, and his ears were flat to his skull with large attached lobes.

Davy stopped coughing and licked his lips. Another shock. His face, normally clean shaven, had a quarter inch of beard. *How long?*

"More, please." His voice was a bare husk but at least this time the words were discernable.

The man cleared his throat, as if to say something, but stopped and instead held up his hand, palm out, as if to say, "Slow." Then he offered the straw again.

Davy drank small sips this time and managed not to aspirate any more water. He was oddly heartened by the fact they were taking such care to avoid recognition. It implied they weren't going to kill him outright. It also implied they were scared of him.

When he finished, the man went through an open door to the side. Davy heard running water briefly, then the man was back, placing the Styrofoam cup on a side table.

Davy remembered Cox's blood splashing across his face. *They're right to be scared.*

He considered jumping away, immediately, even though they were watching, but he'd prefer to do it silently.

Who knew about the meeting? I'm never working for the NSA again.

Then a horrible thought occurred to him. "Why can't I sit up?" His voice sounded better this time, still an octave lower than usual, but less raspy.

The man in the surgical mask looked over at the mirror.

The distorted voice came over the speaker.

"Do. Show him."

The man reached over and pulled the covers slowly down, all the way to Davy's feet.

He was dressed in a hospital gown and his bare legs stuck out. A clear plastic tube ran out from under the gown with stretches of clear yellow fluid within. *Oh, Christ!* It was a urinary catheter. He thought about jumping with it in place and winced. However, that wasn't what was keeping him from sitting up.

They were more elaborate than the usual ICU restraining straps. The cuffs were padded but they were surrounded by stainless steel and the chains attached to them with small padlocks looked heavy enough for playground swings. The man lifted the covers a bit higher and he saw the same restraining cuffs at his ankles.

They know.

The distorted voice on the speaker confirmed this. "We were relieved to find you're restrainable. You tried to teleport several times as you were coming out from under the anesthetics."

The stiffness in his shoulders suddenly made sense. He lifted his right knee and winced. Those joints had been stressed, too.

"What do you want?"

There was a noticeable pause. "Ah. Well, we'll get to that. You rest for right now. You've still got some recovering to do."

The attendant chose this moment to pull the covers back up to Davy's chin.

Davy blinked. "Recovering? From what?"

Again, there was a pause. "Just recovering."

They brought him food two hours later. One of them was the first man, recognizable by his ears and bushy eyebrows. The other was obviously female but dressed and masked the same. The chains clanked behind him, lengthening to the point where they could crank the back of the bed up and he could lift his hands high enough to feed himself. They worked without talking and the voice from the other side of the mirror was silent, making Davy wonder if one of his attendants was the voice, or if it had been this man *or that bitch who shot Brian*. He remembered the ambulance crew and wondered how many people were involved in his capture and keeping.

The food was a surprise. The soup was lobster bisque, the bread was fresh whole-grained, the salad was baby greens. *This is not from an institutional kitchen.* On the other hand, the silverware was plastic and the plates and bowl were paper. His brain thought he was starving but his body quit abruptly after a few bites of each dish.

"What if I need to defecate?" He asked abruptly. The male held up his hand and reached under the bedside table, bringing out a stainless steel bedpan.

"Yuck. Why don't you just bring a portable toilet and put it beside the bed. Surely you could loosen the chains enough for that."

The man exchanged glances with woman, who shrugged, then they both looked at the mirrored window.

The distorted voice came on, still sounding like a cross between Hal and machinery, but, somehow sounding different than before. "We'll see what can be arranged. Do you need the bedpan now?"

Different shift, Davy thought. "No. Not now." He wondered if they'd loosen his hands enough to wipe himself or if someone else would be doing it. He shuddered and rolled his neck, trying to relieve a kink. His chest itched and he lifted his hand to scratch it but when he touched the area, just under his left collarbone, it hurt.

He pulled the gown's neck up. There was a light dressing taped to the skin, a three by two square of gauze. A line of inflammation came up from the dressing to his neck. He traced it with his fingers, a ridge of discomfort that crossed his collarbone and moved up the right side of his neck. It terminated in another dressing, a large Band-Aid really, to the right of his trachea. He poked it and winced.

"Don't do that," the voice from the loudspeaker said. The male attendant pulled his hand gently away.

"What did you do to me?" Davy asked. *Did they shoot me when Brian dropped me on the sidewalk?*

No, they cut you open and they put something inside you. He couldn't help it. He knew he shouldn't jump, that his restraints would keep him from succeeding, but he tried anyway, an almost flinching reaction.

It was bad, but, luckily, there was more slack in the catheter than the cuffs for he only had the mildest discomfort from his crotch, but his shoulders felt like they'd been pulled from their sockets.

Stop it! he told himself. *You're just giving them more data.*

As much as possible he curled in on himself, groaning.

The computer-distorted voice from the loudspeaker said, "I feel safe in saying that that activity is contraindicated, eh?"

FIVE

"Do you mean: am I crazy again?"

She reached the breaking point nine days after Davy disappeared.

She started telling her clients, "I'm going to be gone for the next three weeks. I'm sorry, but a family emergency has come up and I don't have any choice." She did her best to arrange help for the most needy, loading up the other therapists in her practice, but, still, she knew she'd lose some of them. She tried to care but it was hard.

She turned on the bug before leaving the office. *Speak into the bra.* "Anders, I need to talk to you. I'm going back to the condo. I suggest you meet me in the parking garage."

She'd driven that day. The glorious crisp days of autumn were giving way to sleet and rain. On the way back, she recognized in herself a desire to floor the accelerator, to drive recklessly, just to be doing *something*, but controlled it, traversing the slick streets with care.

Anders was waiting in the shadowed corner farthest from the stairs, his breath forming a cloud around his head.

"I'm going to D.C.," she said without preamble. "I can't sit here anymore pretending nothing is wrong."

He blinked. "What do you imagine you could do?"

"More than I'm doing here!"

He exhaled slowly, a technique Millie often used with

excited clients. It was a way of saying "easy does it" without irritating them, usually without them even noticing it consciously. Often the client would match the rhythm without realizing it and they would calm down.

This just pissed Millie off more.

Anders said, "You're doing useful things here. You're helping your clients. You're still the bait that will lure them in."

"It's been over a week. They're not biting. Either that or they've spotted you and got scared off. If I'm in D.C. they'll have even more chance at me. That's why I'm telling you—not to get your permission—but to give you time to shift your base of operations or hand off to your people in Washington. If it helps, you can make the arrangements, but either way, I'm leaving in the morning."

She took one carry-on bag—mostly underwear, toiletries, and the five thousand dollars from the emergency pack tucked under a spare pair of jeans. The forecast for D.C. was cold and wet so she wore a blue raincoat with a wool liner and the NSA locater bug in her bra.

At Will Rogers World Airport the damn bug set off the metal detector, but when they sent her to the side for a "female wand," the security guard loudly diagnosed the offending object as an underwire bra.

Her cheeks burning, Millie seriously considered dropping the bug in the nearest trash can as soon as she was away from the security station, but controlled the impulse.

Anders had made the flight arrangements, putting her on a 12:40 P.M. Delta flight into D.C. with one stop in Atlanta. It left fifteen minutes late and there was another delay in Atlanta, putting her into Reagan National over an hour late. Her appreciation for teleportation had risen to an all-time high by the time she touched down in D.C. She'd spent the flights trying to sleep but all she could do was worry. *Is he dead? Is he hurt? Where the hell is he?*

By the time she stumbled out of her taxi at the State Plaza Hotel, she was truly exhausted.

The room they gave her was on the seventh floor facing

north, away from the mall and the brightly lit landmarks of the Washington Monument and the Capitol building. She could, however, see what interested her far more: the sprawling mass of George Washington University Hospital, and the streets near it, where Davy had been snatched.

She ordered a light salad from room service and ate with the curtains open. *Tomorrow*, she promised the lighted streets.

Tomorrow.

She started early, buying a portable breakfast—egg-and-bacon-on-a-roll and coffee—then sitting on the stoop of a copy shop fifteen feet from where they'd found Brian Cox, dead on the sidewalk.

It was morning rush and she watched the crowds with unfocused eyes, trying not to filter anything, to absorb it uncritically. What surprised her were the number of homeless people out, working the crowd for change. A lot of them were women.

I thought we were getting a handle on this. She shook her head. *Maybe in Stillwater.*

The temperature dropped steadily through the morning and a thin gray fog drifted up the streets, dampening the sidewalks and the walls, and leaving drops of water hanging in her hair. She'd seen the forecast so she was wearing her powder blue raincoat. She pulled up the collar of the thick hand-knitted sweater she wore below the raincoat and sunk her neck into it, feeling like a timid turtle. She was grateful she'd chosen her Merrell Chameleon hiking boots—*even though they make my feet look like boulders.*

She kept wiping her glasses off with her handkerchief.

Traffic, both wheeled and footed, lightened, and the number of homeless on the street seemed to increase, but she suspected there weren't more of them than this morning—just fewer "normal" people on the street to hide behind.

Hide? They're not hiding. You were just looking at the normal people instead of them.

She edged closer to the balustrade, using it to shield her from the mist. She felt cold, but it wasn't from the weather.

How cold are they?

There was a group of four men talking at the mouth of the alleyway across the street, leaning against the wall. One of them had a ratty backpack, two carried bedrolls under their arms, and the fourth wore an indeterminate number of blankets, Indian style.

She could tell that most of the blankets had been brightly colored but now they were muted, the barest hint of pastels where once primary colors ruled. The man with the blankets wore old Nikes, ripped, showing bare, dirty skin beneath. He turned his head as a brightly colored BMW went by.

These people are nearly always *on the street.*

She looked in her purse at the picture of Davy she'd taken from the Aerie. She went down the street to Kinko's and had his half of the photo blown up, black and white, a little fuzzy at eight-and-a-half by eleven, but clearly recognizable.

She started to get a hundred run off, so she could post them, then stopped. *How will they contact me?*

She rejected using her hotel room. The search might leave the area. She thought about putting the number of the NSA on there, but if they hadn't found him yet, she wasn't sure she trusted them to take the calls.

She asked the clerk, "Is there someplace around here that sells cell phones?"

Forty minutes later she had a local cell phone with several hundred pre-bought minutes. And, most important, a phone number.

On the way back to Kinko's, she stopped in a hardware store and picked up a hammer-stapler and a box of staples. When she left Kinko's, she had one hundred sheets with Davy's picture and the words, "Have you seen this man?" the new cell phone number, and the place and date he had last been seen.

She started at Interrobang and worked her way west on H over to George Washington University, putting them up on the phone poles and the occasional plywood fence that blocked off construction. At Twentieth she went north, first, up to Pennsylvania Avenue, then went back and did the stretch down to G street, then east as far as Eighteenth.

Every homeless person she saw she gave two bucks and a

flyer. "Hi, I'm looking for my husband. This is his picture. Have you seen him?"

No.

Next person.

No.

She worked her way in a large square around the abduction site and the Interrobang. She'd almost completed the square, coming west on H back from Eighteenth when she tried a pair of men playing cards on a packing crate. One of them was clearly a recycler, leaning against three enormous plastic bags filled with aluminum cans. The other had a bedroll and a basset hound.

"Nah. Never seen him," said the recycler.

"Me neither," said the man with the dog as he laid down a card. "Gin. You oughta try Retarded Kaneesha. She sees everything." He tilted his head to the alleyway across the street.

Millie could just make out a woman in a maroon knee-length coat leaning against the alley wall just off the sidewalk. Her head and shoulders were in shadow.

Millie gave the men some money and walked slowly across the street. She could tell the woman *was* watching her, so perhaps she really did see everything, but Millie wasn't particularly heartened by the appellation "retarded." As she got closer, she noticed the woman's face was never still. Her lips were pursing in and out and occasionally her tongue would protrude. Her eyebrows kept rising as if she were being continually surprised. She'd blink, but it wasn't a normal blink. Both eyes would squeeze shut, then open again, on a regular basis, longer than a blink.

Blepharospasm. Millie let out a deep breath of understanding. *Retarded Kaneesha! Ha.*

"I like your coat," Millie said, and she meant it. It was heavy wool with a large hood that seemed to be lined in black satin. The rain was beaded on it, not soaking in.

The woman nodded. "Me, too."

Millie held out her hand. "My name is Millie."

The woman's face stopped twitching as she smiled slightly, but she wouldn't meet Millie's eyes. She did shake Millie's hand briefly. "My name is Sojee."

"Please excuse me for asking this, but you've got tardive dyskinesia, don't you?" *Retarded Kaneesha.*

"Got it bad. You a doctor or something? Most people see it and run." While Sojee was talking and while she smiled, the twitching went away, but while she listened for Millie's answer, it started again, sudden jerks of her jaw to one side or the other, accompanied by lip smacking. Her eyes roamed the street past Millie's shoulder, watching purposefully in a way that contrasted sharply with the random movements of her jaw.

Millie shook her head. "I'm a psychotherapist. I've studied it in school. What were you on, that caused the TD?"

"I was on Haldol for paranoid schizophrenia." She said it like "I have brown eyes" or "I'm five foot eight."

"This is none of my business, so feel free to tell me to shove off. Did you change medications?"

Sojee shook her head. "Stopped taking it. Couldn't sleep on it. Plus this—" She gestured at her face. "They say it might never go away."

"They?"

"The people over at St. Elizabeth's Hospital." Sojee's tongue lunged out of her mouth and retreated. Her eyebrows arched. "You know, where they keep Hinkley, the guy what shot Reagan."

"How did they try to treat it, the dyskinesia?"

"They wanted to up my dosage of Haldol."

Millie shuddered. Taking more of a neuroleptic drug would probably stop the symptoms temporarily—until they returned even worse.

Sojee saw Millie shake. "Oh. Do you have TD, too?"

"No. Has going off of your meds caused your, uh, symptoms to increase?"

Sojee smacked her lips several times in succession and then her lower jaw jerked to the right. "Do you mean: am I crazy again? They come and they go."

Despite herself, Millie had to smile. "You don't mince words, do you, Sojee? What do you mean by 'they?' "

"Angels. Angels and demons. I hear them both. And *sometimes* I see them."

Millie nodded. "What do they want you to do?"

"The usual. The angels tell me I'm the chosen one. I'm their human champion in the angel/demon war here on Earth. The demons talk about my ex-husband and tell me to kill myself. I hear them all the time really, but there are days where I *believe* them."

Millie couldn't help herself. "And today?"

"Oh, this is a *good* day. They're just chattering at the back of the bus. I'm not letting them drive."

It was surreal, this discussion of mental illness, yet also liberating. Here was a person whose personal travails far eclipsed Millie's. One way or another, Millie would get past this crisis. Barring a miracle, Sojee would be stuck with schizophrenia and tardive dyskinesia as long as she lived.

Millie sighed and showed Sojee the picture. "I don't suppose you've seen—" She was expecting another negative, but she couldn't help holding onto a faint hope—a hope driven by the homeless men's assertion that "Retarded Kaneesha saw everything." What she wasn't expecting was for Sojee's eyes to roll back in her head and her knees to buckle.

Millie swore and lunged forward, dropping the stack of flyers and the stapler as she tried to break Sojee's fall. The woman was both taller and heavier than Millie, but Millie just managed to keep her head from hitting the asphalt.

What on earth caused that? She stared down at the woman's face, which was suddenly different. The tardive dyskinesia had ceased with unconsciousness, and, relaxed, her face went from some caricature of madness to normalcy. *She's beautiful.* Millie wanted to weep, suddenly.

Millie snagged a discarded cardboard box from beside the recycling bin and dropped her knee on it, bursting it, then folding it one-handed. She slid it under Sojee's head.

The woman was stirring already. Her eyelids fluttered and she was moaning slightly. There were a hundred different possible causes for Sojee's blackout but Millie swore it looked like an old-fashioned faint.

Was it Davy's picture? What had this woman seen?

She heard steps behind her and turned her head. The two homeless men from across the street, the recycler and the man with the dog, had crossed the street.

"Jesus, lady! What did you do to her?"

"She fainted."

The rain was worsening, falling on Sojee's face. Millie shook her head. "Go flag down a cab. I need to get her some help."

They stared at her like she was from another planet.

"Well, can you? She lies here much longer, she'll get soaked!"

The recycler said, "Lady, cabs don't stop for people like us."

Millie blinked. "Right, then. You guys bring her. I'll get the cab." She snagged the stapler off the ground and put it in her pocket. She ignored the flyers—half of them were soaked and the others would be soon. It didn't matter. The original was back at Kinko's and she could have more made.

It took her ten minutes to find a cab. The rain was getting worse and the cabs were in demand. When she got it back to the alley, the two homeless men were helping Sojee stand.

When the woman saw Millie, though, she flinched and tried to pull away, nearly falling in the process. "Stay away from me!" Her facial motions were back, tongue thrusts and the prolonged blinks.

Millie spread her hands and tried to look as harmless as possible. "You need help, Sojee. You passed out. Let me take you to a doctor."

"No way! I was just surprised, that's all. And I ain't et today. Or slept—it's this rain."

"Well, then come with me and I'll get you something to eat. You don't have to do anything you don't want."

The bellhop at the hotel was clearly disturbed when Millie brought Sojee into the lobby. Millie almost walked her into the dining room out of spite, but instead took Sojee up to the room and ordered room service.

"They're kind of slow," Millie said. "Would you like to lie down and rest until it gets here?"

Sojee was staring past Millie's shoulder. She jerked at Millie's voice. "Sorry, what did you say?"

Millie turned around. The bathroom with its golden tile and gleaming chrome fixtures fairly glowed in the fluorescent light. She turned back to Sojee. "Or perhaps a bath?"

Sojee nodded. "Oh, yes, please. You can get showers in the shelters, but they'll steal your stuff, and the cold water's standing four inches on the floor and the water's never more than warm."

Millie nodded. "Lock the door, if you like. I don't mind."

Sojee took longer than room service. While she was in there, Millie removed the bug and turned off the microphone. The food was cooling when Sojee came out of the bathroom.

Millie was getting better at reading her facial expressions, at telling the random noise of her neurological condition from her true feelings. She was surprised at the degree of emotion. Schizophrenics were known for their flatness of affect—not too happy, not too sad. Sojee's expression seemed more than content when she came out of the bathroom.

Millie gestured at the food. "I hope you're not a vegetarian. I ordered the chicken."

Sojee inhaled sharply and licked her lips. "Chicken's great." She hesitated though.

"Go on, then. Help yourself. Please."

During the initial rush, Millie sat quietly, buttering a roll and eating it with small bites, small movements, waiting with intent. She didn't want to startle the woman.

Sojee's table manners were good—she deboned and ate the chicken strictly with knife and fork, patting her lips clean with the cloth napkin every few bites. Millie would've held it in her fingers and Millie had eaten recently. Maybe it was obsessive compulsive behavior, but Millie didn't see it that way. As she actively did things with her face—biting, chewing, drinking—the random movements and twitches stilled, until the next moment that part of her face relaxed. Then the tongue thrusts and prolonged blinks resumed.

Sojee turned to the salad and Millie said, "I didn't know your taste in dressing but there's Italian on the side."

Sojee used it lightly. "Italian is safe. I'm partial to blue cheese but I'm a little bit lactose intolerant."

Millie nodded. She itched to ask Sojee about Davy again, but was not only afraid of spooking her again, but also of finding out Sojee had never seen him.

Sojee ate slowly now, eating the salad with care, pushing the onions carefully to the side, but eating all the rest, wiping the dressing and chicken juices from the plate with delicate wipes of her bread.

When everything was gone except a small pile of diced onion, Sojee wiped her lips carefully with the cloth napkin, folded it carefully, and placed it symmetrically in the middle of the shining plate. The woman sighed and leaned back in her chair.

"I know you want to ask me something—it's written all over you."

Millie, tense, anxious, and focused, was taken completely by surprise. She laughed, a short bark that came closer to breaking her carefully maintained reserve than anything that had happened since Davy's disappearance. She turned her head to the wall and squeezed her eyes shut, breathing carefully. The moment passed and she was still in control, but her eyes burned.

"Yes. I started to ask it once, already, but you fainted when I showed you his picture."

Sojee looked away for a second and, for a moment, her tongue thrusts stopped as her mouth tightened. "Yeah. I was surprised, that's for sure." She sank deeper into the chair. "I thought he was a hallucination. I must've been breakin' pretty hard when I saw him. He kept vanishing and reappearing on me." She pointed at her coat, draped over the luggage stand by the door. "He took me to get that coat. One minute I was shivering in the snow and the next thing I know, I'm standing in Macy's, only it's not the Macy's out at Pentagon City, but the one in New York, and he's asking me which coat I like. The clerks didn't want to come anywhere near me, but he was like a cat on a rat and wouldn't take no for an answer. When I found this one, I never took it off again. He paid for it with hundred dollar bills and we walked away, but then I found myself back on the street, in D.C. I know something happened but it was all so weird, I don't know what was real and what wasn't." She reached out toward the coat. "Except for that, I guess. I keep it on too much, even when it's hot, because I'm sure it's going to dissolve sometime soon. Disappear into thin air like my Angel."

"Your angel?"

"Well, what else should I call him?"

Millie took the picture out again. "His name is Davy. He's my husband." It took her a moment to add, "And he's missing." The room was out of focus but when she cleaned her glasses, it didn't help. She blew her nose and that helped a bit. "When did you get your coat?"

"January third. It was that arctic air mass came down and froze all the Florida orange trees. In D.C. it got to three below zero. Are you going to vanish, too?"

Damn. That was two months ago.

"What makes you think that?" Millie remembered her jump from West Texas to Oklahoma and her stomach lurched. *It's possible, I suppose.*

"Well, an angel would be married to an angel, right?" She eyed Millie's blue raincoat. "Or maybe you're the Blue Lady."

"The Blue Lady?" Millie shook her head and let it go. "Is that the last time you saw Davy? When he bought you your coat?"

"He checked on me a month ago. He asked how I was doing and gave me some money."

"But not last week?"

Sojee shook her head.

The corners of Millie's mouth turned down sharply, surprising her. *Keep it together, girl! You can cry later.*

She took a deep breath and expelled it through tight lips. *Like Lamaze breathing*, she thought, and that nearly caused the tears to rise back to the surface.

Sojee was watching her, brow furrowed, eyes narrowed. "Did you just waste a good meal on me?"

Millie shook her head. "I never saw a meal less wasted." She sucked on her lower lip and looked at Sojee. "We need desert, I think."

Sojee opened her mouth, then closed it. After a few random tongue thrusts, she said, "Bring it on."

They kept it simple, apple pie à la mode and coffee—decaf for Sojee.

"What sort of name is Sojee, anyway?"

"Short for Sojourner. My full name is Sojourner Truth Johnson, but how on earth do you go around with that mouthful when you're six? Sojee is what it's always been, really."

Both woman were quiet for a moment. Then Sojee said, "I could ask around . . . check the shelters and the kitchens. Somebody probably saw something."

Millie felt her throat tighten up again. "I would be very grateful." She had to blow her nose suddenly and snatched up the room service napkin still in her lap. She felt like one raw wound. *I thought I was holding this in.* Kindness had breached her defenses where adversity hadn't.

Sojee was looking at her when she finished wiping her eyes. "I should get going, so you could rest."

Millie started to agree absently, then shook her head. "Get going where? Didn't you say you hadn't slept today." She looked pointedly at the two queen beds.

Sojee's eyes were moist now. "You sure?"

"Nobody else is using that bed, Sojee. You might as well." She smiled. "It's in my best interest to have you well rested tomorrow, when you're asking around."

SIX

"Now you can mop the floor."

The last time I spent this much time in one room was over four-teen years ago and even then I left it to go to school.

And it wasn't just being in one room. Davy lived outdoors more than most people. Weather didn't constrain him the way it did others. If it was raining or snowing or too cold in one place, he simply jumped elsewhere, usually staying in the same hemisphere but not always. Early morning in the States was always a good time for a walk down the esplanade in Brighton, Sussex or tramping in the high meadows on the Cambrian Way in the mountains of Wales. Late afternoon in Oklahoma was a great time to snorkel at Hamoa Beach on the east side of Maui or to hike up to the Puako Petroglyphs on the Big Island.

Staying in one place, indoors, was getting to him. Davy had definitely progressed into the "getting well enough to be really cranky" phase of his recovery. Coming out of surgery was bad enough when you weren't chained to the wall. When you were—well, cranky didn't really cover it.

They'd removed the catheter and brought in a bedside portable toilet, then, apparently working on the far side of the wall behind his bed, they let out enough chain so he could reach the toilet, the sink, and even as far as the foot of the bed.

He took to pacing, moving from the wall to the foot of his bed, stopping just short of the chain's reach before turning back again. The management of his chains became second nature, their rattling and slithering across the floor, background noise.

Just call me Jacob Marley.

He didn't care that the hospital gown was all he was wearing and every time he turned, he mooned the watchers behind the mirror. He suspected the pacing was beginning to bother his keepers. The computerized voice said, "Would you like to watch some videos?"

He laughed a short unfunny bark. "Yes, I'd like *Stalag 17, Chicken Run, Alcatraz,* and *The Great Escape.*" And when there wasn't any response, he added, "And a baseball and a baseball glove."

They didn't say anything after that but when lunch was served, there was a paperback novel on the tray: *The Count of Monte Cristo.*

Well, someone *has a sense of humor.* He opened the book. *On the 24th of February, 1810, the look-out at Notre-Dame de la Garde signalled the three-master, the* Pharaon *from Smyrna, Trieste, and Naples.*

He'd read it before, a couple of times, but as there wasn't anything else to do, he started it again, the first three chapters, then threw it across the room, to bounce off the mirrored observation window.

It had been some time since he'd read it and, while he remembered *The Count of Monte Cristo* was a book about a prison breakout and revenge, he'd forgotten how much, first of all, to justify the later revenge, it was a book about *betrayal.* And Davy was feeling very much betrayed.

Somebody knew about that meeting. Or at least they knew enough to follow Brian. And it wasn't Brian. Brian had cleared himself from suspicion very thoroughly.

He glared at the book where it lay. He'd meant to hurl it out of reach but its rebound had carried it back to the foot of the bed. He put out his hand and jumped.

The chains writhed like snakes, a crack-the-whip movement that moved to the wall and then back down toward him, smacking his wrists and ankles painfully, but he was standing at the end of the bed, his hand on the book.

He could still jump within range of the chains.

That is if he was willing to risk broken wrists or ankles.

Parts of the chain were being accelerated instantly, over a distance of mere feet, but the energy imparted to the rest of the chain was considerable. Plaster dust floated in the air near the wall where the chains vanished through rough holes.

He wondered if his observers had seen him do it or grasped any of the implications. He waited for a moment, but there was no reaction from the speaker. The door didn't open.

He picked up the book again. He'd gotten through the betrayal. Perhaps it was time to check out the escape.

They brought supper that night, as usual, two different men in surgical masks and scrubs.

He wasn't feeling very well. There was a persistent ache from the surgical scar on his upper chest and above, too, a tenderness that ran under the skin. Yet he had energy, too.

So he took their masks off.

One second he was reading in bed, the next he was standing at the extent of his chains, reaching out with both hands and closing on their masks just as the recoil from the chains reached his wrists. The chains, really, more than his own arms, snatched the paper masks off.

They jerked back, the one holding the supper tray dropping it with a clatter. They stopped, out of reach and stared at him, startled, perhaps even afraid.

He wasn't sure, but he thought he recognized one of them from the restaurant—one of the ambulance crew, a small-chinned man with blond eyebrows so white as to be almost invisible. The other man was a hook-nosed individual with bushy reddish brown eyebrows and freckles. Not young, though—in his forties, perhaps.

Davy stared at them, hungrily. These were his enemies, but

they were the first faces he'd seen in days, perhaps weeks. He had no idea how long he'd been drugged.

The blonde held his hand to his cheek where a line of blood was forming. Davy must've caught him with a fingernail.

"Sorry," Davy said, gesturing. The chains clanked again. "Didn't mean to gouge you."

The computer voice came over the loudspeaker. "Leave the room, Gentlemen."

They turned and left, without ever speaking.

Davy sighed.

The supper tray was lying out of reach, a small steak, baked potato, and salad, lying in a small lake of milk. Davy looked at the mirror. "Any chance of getting my supper?"

There was silence, and Davy thought they were ignoring him, or hadn't heard, when the computer voice said abruptly, "I think . . . not."

Davy shrugged philosophically and turned back to the bed. There was more plaster dust in the air and small chunks of Sheetrock on the floor. He went over to the holes in the wall that the chain ran through. He could see through to the other room, which was dimly lit, but he couldn't see where the chains went. They dropped down and vanished. When he tugged on one of them, it was as secure as ever.

He got back on the bed and picked up the book.

The next morning, things changed.

They came before breakfast, right after he finished using the portable commode, three, in scrubs, unmasked.

Two of them were the men he'd unmasked the night before. *Two thugs. And I call them Thug One and Thug Two.* The third was the brunette waitress from Interrobang.

The woman who'd murdered Brian Cox.

They stopped beyond the reach of his chains, Thug One and Thug Two slightly behind the woman. At first, Davy thought they were still cautious, wary of him because of his action the evening before, but then he realized it was more of a power dynamic.

The woman was in charge and they were afraid of her.

Wise. Very wise.

He was torn. If he were free, he'd jump. *Away? Or do I take her and drop her from the Empire State Building? And do I catch her before she hits?*

"Get off the bed," the woman said.

Davy slid to the side and stood. For the first time in days he was conscious of the open-backed gown and his bare butt. Standing felt safer, anyway. He noted that her hair was pulled back in the same tight bun and her makeup was just as heavy, though not running, this time, like it did in the rain. *If she shoots, perhaps I can jump to one side—*

The chains started clanking across the floor, pulling back into the wall, removing the slack. He had to shuffle backwards to keep up with them. When they stopped, he tugged, but they weren't just being held by someone—they'd been secured somehow, in this tighter configuration.

"Okay, move it." She wasn't talking to Davy, this time. Thug One and Thug Two pulled the bed away from the wall— away from Davy—then unlocked the casters and rolled it to one side.

Davy didn't like the look of this—being held up against the wall brought back memories of his father and a flashing rodeo buckle at the end of swinging belt. His stomach churned and he licked his lips, some part of him expecting a beating.

Then the chains loosened and he walked forward, expecting them to stop again where the end of the bed had been. Instead, Thugs One and Two and the woman backed up against the door. The chains stopped when he was two yards short of them. The arc of the chains let him walk over most of the room, excepting only the end of the room with the mirrored window and the door.

The woman said, "Get the bucket."

Again, it wasn't directed at Davy. The hook-nosed redhead stepped through the door and returned, rolling an institutional mop bucket in yellow plastic with a mop squeezer. There was a mop in it and he heard liquid sloshing. Davy caught the heavy smell of pine-scented disinfectant.

"You want me to mop the floor?" Davy asked. *I could reach you guys with that mop.*

She looked at him, eyes narrowed. "In a minute." She turned her head to the side, toward the mirror. "When you're ready."

Davy coughed. He frowned. He didn't have a cold. He hadn't been drinking or eating. *Some saliva in the windpipe?*

He coughed again, harder. And there was an odd tingling in his throat. He coughed hard enough to double him over but when the spasm was over he had no trouble breathing, no feeling of something in his throat.

"That's it?" said the woman, looking toward the mirror.

The computer voice came back. "Calibration. Just a tickle. *This* is the operational level."

Davy doubled over, vomited violently, and lost all motor control, falling to the floor. His chest hurt, stabbing pain in the vicinity of his heart, and he was having trouble breathing. He vomited again and again, though the first spasms were so spectacular that now he was bringing up just drops of bile.

Abruptly, it stopped.

He was lying on his side, in a puddle of his own vomit, his face and hair sticky with it. He gagged again, but it wasn't the tectonic upheaval of seconds before. It was mild, by comparison. He tried not to breathe through his nose.

"Oh, Christ." He became aware that he'd lost bowel control, as well, apparently as violently as everything else. The combination of smells was nauseating, but he truly didn't have anything else to throw up.

He climbed to his feet, aware of aching stomach muscles and sore spots on his shoulder, elbow, and the side of his head where he'd hit the floor. The pain in his chest had lessened though the ghost of angina seemed to linger. One of his hands was free of vomit and he gingerly touched his head. The finger came away with blood on it.

He had trouble meeting their eyes. Even though he was aware that what had just happened was done to him—not by him—he felt humiliated and ashamed.

The two men watching him were pale, the blonde, Thug One,

tending toward an actual shade of green. The woman seemed unaffected. She took the mop handle and pushed the bucket into the part of the room he could reach, letting the mop handle fall to the floor where it bounced—bap, bap, bap—three times.

Thugs One and Two went out the doorway, eagerly. The woman paused, with the door still open, and tucked a few stray hairs back into the tight bun on the back of her head. She smiled.

"Now you can mop the floor."

It took two attempts before he could climb to his feet. He was weak as a kitten and, once vertical, the room spun around him. It took all his concentration to stay on his feet.

Well, the only good thing was that, with his chains lengthened, he could actually go into the attached bathroom and use the bath. He had wanted to bathe before this incident, but now, dripping with three different kinds of bodily fluids, his want had been supplanted by overpowering *need*.

The bathroom looked like a standard residential toilet except a large mirror over the sink had clearly been removed—paint and the outer layer of some Sheetrock had been ripped out by the glass adhesive—and a smaller, plain steel mirror had been bolted to the wall instead. Davy took one look in the mirror, then turned away.

The gown nearly defeated him. It was disposable paper, but the fibers running through it made it hard to tear and, even though he managed the ties in back, the chains prevented him from just taking it off. Finally he summoned the strength to rip out the shoulders, allowing him to pull it off the chains. He wadded it up and stuffed it in the small plastic trash basket.

He didn't know if they had a camera in the room. He pulled the shower curtain closed and, with the water full in his face, let himself cry. He did his best to keep it quiet and to hide the tears with the running water, but he didn't stop until it abated several minutes later.

There was a bottle of squeeze soap in the shower and he scrubbed himself again and again, until his skin hurt. He knew he'd gotten all of it, but he still didn't feel clean.

He got soap on the bottle and it slipped through his fingers, falling to the bottom of the tub. He groaned as he picked it up, then stared at it. He turned his back on the shower and squirted soap underneath the manacle padding on his left arm, twisting it to distribute the soap all around his wrist.

He pulled and twisted, trying to relax his hand as the manacle rode up the base of his thumb. The padding compressed to a degree, but the manacle stopped short right below the accumulated bulge of knuckles at the base of his fingers—but it had slid a lot farther than he'd expected. He wondered what would happen if he soaped both wrists, then jumped.

He looked down. The restraints on his ankles weren't going to fit over his foot, no matter how much soap he used. He sighed and rinsed the soap out from under the manacle padding.

Drying off, he looked in the steel mirror over the sink and shuddered. The scar on his chest, a semicircular curve starting an inch below his collar bone, had the red, raw look of still-healing tissue. A smaller straight version, healed to the same degree, was midway up the left side of his neck. He wanted to claw through the skin and yank it out, whatever they'd put in there, but judging by the scar, part of it was very close to the jugular.

He looked up at his eyes. The scars were awful in and of themselves and also in what they concealed, but what he saw in his eyes was even more terrible, more frightening. He had to look away and it was beyond his strength, just then, to look back.

When he returned from the bathroom, wrapped in a towel, he found a pair of what looked like hospital scrubs on the bed. He held them up and found that the outside pants seams were Velcroed from cuff to waist and he could actually put them on despite the chains. On the short-sleeved shirt the Velcro was on the side seams from the waist to the underarm side of the sleeve. He could pull them on over his head and seal the sides.

He liked wearing pants again, but thinking about the forethought his keepers had put into this bothered him. It looked like they didn't expect to take off the chains anytime soon.

The room stank, and his mess and footprints were still on the floor. Like in the shower, he washed the floor several times more than necessary.

It's not the mess you're trying to erase, is it, Davy? No matter how many times you wash the floor, it won't undo it. It happened. And it's probably going to happen again.

SEVEN

"This isn't exactly what we had in mind, you know."

Millie armed Sojee with a stack of flyers and the stapler, then dropped her on Columbia, near Christ House.

"I'll make the rounds," Sojee told her. "I'll call you if I hear something."

Millie gave her some change. "Call me around five, even if you don't hear anything, okay?"

Sojee's lips smacked several times and she finally said, "Well, okay. About five."

Millie had the taxi drop her back on the street in front of Interrobang. She walked slowly down the street and around the corner, back toward what she was coming to think of as the "departure zone"—the place where Brian Cox had died and, possibly, the place where Davy might have been seen last.

Hopefully, Davy had "departed" that place in a different manner than Cox.

She'd had breakfast with Sojee, but she went into the restaurant anyway, asking for a table at the window, *the very one*, she figured.

The windows in the place were bordered with announcements of this and that performance, this and that dance studio offering classes, this or that dojo offering martial arts instruction, this and that person looking for a roommate. Even when they'd been ripped off, the layers of yellowed Scotch tape formed reefs and shoals. Except *this* window. This window must've been replaced recently. There were a few announcements on it, but none of the ancient evidence of bygone posters. This window had just been replaced.

She ordered coffee but didn't drink it.

Hopefully the management was a little more careful about letting non-employees serve food now, but this wasn't the time to test the issue.

She felt a little odd, today, like a corner had been turned. She'd looked, the day before, for the NSA watchers, but hadn't really seen anybody. She believed they were keeping back, depending on the bug and intermittent checks, hoping to lure Davie's snatchers back into the open. Their absence had been palpable after the seven days she'd spent under surveillance back in Stillwater.

Today, her back itched.

They're out there.

She laughed at herself.

You're imagining things.

The itch was still there and no matter how she squirmed in the chair, she couldn't scratch it.

She left Interrobang and walked east, but the sidewalks were so busy that anybody could have followed her without detection. A cab went by, then another. She flagged the third one, self-consciously thinking about Sherlock Holmes, and told the driver, "The Mall, please, at the Capitol end."

He dropped her at the corner of Fourth and Independence and she walked across the grass to the East Wing of the National Gallery. She headed up the stairs for the Upper Level where the huge red and black Calder mobile hung in space beneath the faceted glass roof, but when she reached the top of the stairs the elevator doors opened and a woman pushing a fussing baby in a stroller got out. Millie couldn't hear anybody on the stairs below but she stepped quickly into the elevator. The doors shut, then it continued up. She stayed in when it opened on the top floor, then she pushed the basement button and took it down and rode the moving sidewalk down the concourse toward the older West building. At the end of the walkway, she crossed to the gift shop, and browsed, standing behind one of the display shelves and watching the pedestrians coming from the East building carefully. Across the way, water sheeted down the glass wall of the Cascade Café.

Several minutes passed and she frowned. There was a cluster of Japanese tourists, a family of five, three elderly ladies practically tottering, one of them using a rolling walker, and a single man carrying an easel and wooden paints case. *They'd have to be more organized than I could imagine to come up with that outfit on such short notice.*

She was about to relax when she saw him, a man coming *from* the West Building, walking slowly, casually checking out the patrons seated at the cafe. Over half the five hundred seats were full and he was pausing often to examine a particular grid of tables, then moving to another.

He'd actually walked past Millie already, but hadn't seen her as she'd been blocked by a shop display. She moved around that same display unit and positioned herself to peer over it, between two large coffee-table art books.

He was average height with blond hair cut very short around a large bald spot—*like a monk's tonsure*—and wearing a dark blue windbreaker and slacks.

He could be looking for his wife. His kids. His grandmother.

She looked at the way he stood and something made her doubt his innocence. She pulled off her blue raincoat and rolled it, white liner out, into a compact bundle. There was a lull at the counter and she stepped up quickly and purchased a scarf, a fabric printed with a reproduction of Mary Cassatt's *Children Playing on the Beach*. She paid quickly, with cash, and asked for a larger bag than the one the clerk initially offered her. "For my coat," she explained, smiling.

The clerk shrugged and gave her a paper bag with plastic handles. "Thank you *so* much."

The "monk" had stopped at the edge of the café, where the walkways terminated, his eyes directed toward the East Wing.

Millie ducked into the restroom, right by the Gift Shop, and hurriedly tied the scarf around her head, gypsy style. Wrapped and tied, it transformed the kids on the beach to just another abstract pattern in tans and blues with the cheeks of the girl a pink highlight above the knot. She exited slowly and walked across to the Espresso and Gelato Bar.

He was still standing at the end of the walkway but now he was talking on a cell phone.

Is he NSA? They said they'd keep clear.

She was trembling and, she realized, afraid, but it didn't make her want to run. It made her want to break things. She focused on the man's bald spot. *Or heads.* Fight or flight. She was surprised which side of the divide she came down on.

If I could only hear what he was saying. Unconsciously, she was leaning forward, even though he was over sixty feet away, at the other end of the restaurant, straining to hear with her entire being.

"—sign of her. We picked her up at the hotel. She dropped the black woman on Columbia then came to the National Gallery." The accent was vaguely British, but not—perhaps Australian. "Hyacinth followed her into the East Building and her team is staking out the ground floor exits while I'm covering that underground walkway to the other building."

Millie nearly screamed, but managed to contain it. Her knees wobbled and she sagged heavily to the right, clutching at the waist-high barrier that separated the Cascade Café from the walkway.

She was standing right behind the Monk. She turned her back on him, breathing deeply.

I jumped?

I jumped.

I jumped!

Immediately on the other side of the barrier one of the diners, a woman, was staring at her with her mouth open, a glass of water lifted halfway off the table, but frozen. Her companion, a man facing away from Millie, was saying, "What's the matter, Paula. You look like you'd seen a ghost."

Millie tried to reassure her with a smile but she was still shaky and the expression on her face felt strange. Apparently it looked strange, too, for the woman flinched and dropped her glass on the floor. It wasn't a loud noise among the din of the diners but the Monk turned his head just as Millie turned back to check on him.

His eyes widened slightly and he turned back away from her, casually. "Would you give my best to Portia and the gang and tell her I can't wait to see her?" He listened for a second. "That's right." He was walking away as he talked, moving across the concourse toward the gift shop.

Millie fought back an urge to plant her toe firmly up his ass and turned, walking as quickly as she could toward the West Building. If she understood the Monk's conversation, there wasn't anybody covering this end of the concourse. Well, not yet. There might be someone running across, at the Mall level, right now.

She paused at the end of the shop, just before she turned right toward the stairs. The Monk had turned and was walking briskly after her, still back by the restaurant, but closing. He was talking on the phone again.

She ran up the stairs but shied away from the door at the top. It was straight across to the East Building and she could see a figure sprinting toward this door but still quite a ways away. She ducked into the gallery at the top of the stairs and stopped, unable to move, before Whistler's *The White Girl*.

"Oh my God." She said it out loud. The girl, clad in a long white gown and standing on a wolf skin, was life size, the painting itself almost seven feet tall. White drapes behind, shining with light, an oriental carpet below the wolf skin. The woman's eyes, her dark brows, her dark brown hair, and red lips stood out against a sea of varying hues of white conveying a surprising amount of detail, but the thing that stopped Millie in her tracks, that captured all of her attention, was her stillness. Not an artificial stillness, but a calm stance.

Serenity. She's serene.

She wasn't running away from strangers. Whatever she was doing, she was facing it calmly, with poise.

I can do this. She reached into her blouse and pulled out the tracking bug. Since talking to Sojee she'd disabled the microphone pickup but now she slid the back off and pushed the slide switch to its full-function position.

There was a museum guard standing at the entrance to the next gallery, but she was watching a group of children instead of Millie. Millie turned and said conversationally, "I'm being tailed, guys, and, unless it's you, you better get your ass over here. I'm going to stay in the National Gallery, West Building, main floor, but going from gallery to gallery."

She tucked the bug back into her bra and took the scarf off her head, then knotted it loosely around her neck like a tie. She took one more look at *The White Girl* and summoned resolve. *Share some of that serenity, please.*

There were steps in the east foyer, at the head of the stairs, and she left, moving to the next gallery. Her head twitched as she passed five Winslow Homer paintings. *This is that sort of place. Get over it.* She summoned mental blinkers and moved on.

Many of the galleries had multiple doors leading from them, making the place a maze. She worked her way toward the middle of the building, settling in Gallery 56 before a six-foot-high portrait of Napoleon in his study. There were four entrances to the room and two museum guards.

She thought it was time to settle, to let her chasers find her, but Napoleon was staring at her a bit too directly. She moved around the bench in the middle of the room and studied instead *Portrait of a Lady* by Vigée-Lebrun: a woman portrayed by a woman. While this subject wasn't as serene as *The White Girl*, she seemed to know what she was about. When she looked out of the frame at Millie it was as if they were sharing something. Millie didn't feel studied and judged as she did by Napoleon. The scale helped, too. *Portrait of a Lady* was only three-and-a-half feet high. She didn't loom over Millie like the Emperor did.

She stood and moved close enough to read the note card. "—was under threat of the guillotine after the revolution. She was forced to flee Paris in disguise in 1789."

Maybe that's what you have to share with me—you are another woman pursued. Millie licked her lips. *And you survived.*

Next to *Portrait of a Lady* was another work by the same artist, two woman sitting next to each other while two children hung on one of the women. *The Marquise de Pezé and the Marquise de Rouget with Her Two Children* read the card. They watched Millie kindly, even the very young boy with his head in his mother's lap.

My allies are everywhere. Millie laughed quietly, causing the female guard to look her way. Millie smiled at her, then looked up, at the security cameras. *And not just in the paintings.*

She thought about her jump on the concourse level. Was she under the eye of a security camera then? Would anyone check it if she was? She shook her head. What mattered for now was that her followers were walking past countless video cameras as they searched for Millie in the museum. If the NSA couldn't get access to the recordings, then she would be very much surprised.

She nodded at the two women in the painting and moved on, out the west door, to consort with several more allies, several portraits by Goya, particularly *Señora Sabasa Garcia.*

Here, finally, they seemed to catch up with her. The Monk passed by the door to the East Sculpture Hall, and moved on without pausing, but shortly thereafter, a brunette, her hair pulled tightly back in a bun, wearing heavy makeup, a tailored jacket, jeans, and knee-high boots came in and began studying the *Still Life with Figs and Bread* on the wall behind Millie.

Millie smiled at *Señora Garcia* and left by the north door, moving west through the main hall and into the rotunda where a bronze Mercury dominated the center. She eyed the main entrance to the south but wanted to stay under the eyes of the security cameras, near the museum guards, in the public eye.

She moved into the West Sculpture Hall and took the second left, chosen because it was empty for the moment, except, of course, for the ever-present guard.

She stopped, blinking. *Why is no one here?* It had to be an abnormal ebb in the tide of patrons—the room was filled with Rembrandts. She turned slowly in the middle of the room, then froze opposite another ally—*Saskia van Uylenburgh, the Wife of the Artist.* Millie felt the connection again, the sense of shared problems, of shared strengths.

A couple came in through the east door and started moving around the gallery, studying a gorgeous rendition of a European man in turban and robe. Millie eyed them. They weren't very convincing. The woman hung on the man's arm but her posture was wrong, not relaxed. If they'd walked into her office like that she would've thought, *impending divorce, they're going through the motions.*

Now she gave it another interpretation. *They don't have an existing relationship that calls for touching each other. That's camouflage, for me.*

Millie took the west door and turned sharply, to put her out of sight of the couple. She counted to three, then stuck her head back around the door. The couple was moving toward her, walking apart, no longer touching. The instant they saw Millie they each swerved toward the other, then paused to study another Rembrandt.

Gotcha.

Millie turned and walked. She was scared but she was also smiling. *Come on, guys, it's time for the NSA to put in an appearance.* She moved through the gallery, a roomful of Dutch painters who were *not* Rembrandt, and into a roomful of Flemish work, notably, Rubens. She paused before a giant painting over ten feet wide and seven feet tall.

Ouch—that's a little too close to home.

It was *Daniel in the Lions' Den* and, while Daniel's eyes were on heaven, several of the life-sized lions looked out at Millie with startling intensity.

She only had one other exit from this room, besides the direction she came in. She took it and found herself in a smaller room with more Rubens. She cut through it into a larger gallery and paused before yet another Rubens, *The Assumption of the Virgin.*

She paused again. "That's the ticket," she muttered. Angels and cherubs carried the Madonna toward heaven while onlookers either stared up in awe or touched the discarded shroud. *Where are you, Angels?*

She took deep breaths and turned from *The Assumption* to *Marchesa Brigida Spinola Doria*, the only other Rubens in the room. The woman wore an enormous Elizabethan collar but she looked out at Millie with impish merriment.

Right, another ally. If she can look amused in that collar, perhaps I can relax under these circumstances. She decided to settle for a moment, to let them present themselves again, to give her someone to point at, when the NSA finally showed up. Fifteen minutes went by while the *Marchesa* and she communed, during which the only people to enter the room were a woman shepherding seven pre-teen girls.

Her phone rang and Millie jumped. The guard glared at her and she scrambled to silence the ringer.

"Hello?" It was the first time the phone had rung and she seriously expected it to be from someone who'd read the flyer.

"Millie, do you recognize my voice?"

It was Anders, the NSA agent.

"Yes. Thought you were still in the Sooner State?"

"We can gossip later, girlfriend. Right now we'd like you to leave the building on the Sixth Street and Constitution Avenue side. By the north door—the one that faces away from the Mall? There'll be a white cab waiting. The driver is wearing a red baseball cap. He's one of ours. Get in."

"What about my, uh, companions?"

"We'll be watching and recording. Trust us. This is what we do."

"All right." She stared at the impish face of the Marchesa. "Now?"

"Now."

"On my way." She hung up the phone and put it in her purse. The fastest route was through the Main Gallery to the Rotunda, then down the stairs. She walked quickly, looking straight ahead, fighting not to stare into every doorway she passed. She continued to hold her allies in her mind, the images of women throughout the Gallery.

Serenity. That's the ticket.

It was raining again, with a nasty wind that ripped at her

clothes. Her raincoat was still in the bag, but she didn't want to take the time to put it on, so she held the bag over her head and sprinted for the street.

The cab was there, as promised, but she felt a stab of dismay as she saw someone sitting in the back. *Did someone grab it first?* In this rain, cabs would be eagerly sought. But the person in the seat handed the driver something, then opened the door and got out as she approached, leaving the door open for her.

"Thanks," she said as she ducked into the cab, but the man was walking briskly away, toward the museum. The car left the curb before she'd finished shutting the door and turned hard across two lanes of traffic to make the Sixth Street turn. She twisted in the seat to watch the museum door, but parked cars already blocked it, and then buildings as the driver whipped right onto Pennsylvania.

"Where are we going?" She dabbed at her glasses with her handkerchief.

The driver grunted. "We're meeting up with my boss but first we're feeling for ticks." He continued on down past the reflecting pool and entered the traffic circle near the Capitol building. He stayed in the circle three times around, then spun off south on First, spun around the next traffic circle twice, then took Maryland Avenue toward the south side of the Mall.

The traffic circles made Millie carsick and she leaned back and closed her eyes, taking deep breaths. When she opened them again, they were running down the far side of the Mall, behind the Air and Space Museum on Independence Avenue, south of the National Gallery but out of sight.

"Looks like we're clear," the driver said.

Millie looked at him for the first time. He was bearded and looked somewhat middle-eastern, though his accent was pure Boston. He was wearing dark glasses despite the gray rain.

"I'm going to stop in a second. There'll be a Verizon phone van. Hop out and into it, quick as you can."

He turned sharply on Seventh, north again. The phone company van was parked illegally on the corner, orange cones set out, front and back. One of the van's back doors swung open as the cab braked and she was out the door and inside. She heard the cab's tires squeal on the rain-slicked pavement as it accelerated away and then the van door was slammed behind her.

The inside of the van smelled of ozone and mildew. It was like the surveillance van they'd used in Stillwater, cabinets of electronics and monitors and a pivoting workstation seat. Anders was the one who'd opened the door for her and he moved back, now, threading his way between the operator in the workstation chair and the sliding door. He sat in the backwards-facing bench seat behind the driver's seat and gestured her forward.

The console operator, a woman with short gray-streaked hair, moved, too, and patted the console seat. "Here, dear. We'd like you to look at some pictures."

Millie set the bag with her coat in it on the floor and edged onto the chair. It was warm in the van but she'd gotten wet in her run for the cab. She unknotted her scarf and pulled it across her shoulders, like a shawl.

"This is Becca Martingale," said Anders, indicating the operator. "She's our liaison with the Bureau."

"FBI?"

Becca nodded. "Yes, Counter-Intelligence."

Millie groped for something polite to say, but settled for a tired nod. She looked at Anders and bit her lip. "Is she *fully* briefed?"

Anders said carefully, "She knows that Davy was one of ours and was kidnapped. She doesn't know what Davy *did* for us."

Becca was watching this interchange with interest. When it didn't go any further, she leaned across and pulled the mouse to her end of the narrow counter running under the monitors. "Here. We've got a short clip of your exit from the Gallery." She clicked a control and video-in-a-window began running on the right-most monitor.

Millie watched herself exit the building and run up the sidewalk, the bag held over her head, splashing through puddles she didn't remember. The camera must've been in a car on the street for she angled past it, but the view stayed on the Gallery stairs. The first person exiting the Gallery after her was the heavily made-up brunette in the knee-high boots who'd sat with her in the room with the Goyas. She started down the stairs at a good clip, then stopped suddenly and took out a phone. The camera zoomed on her. The woman said something on the phone, then retreated back into the shelter of the overhang, still holding the phone to her head. A man entered the frame, coming from the street, but paused there, in the shelter, clutching his tweed jacket together at the neck.

"He's the one who held the cab for me."

"Yes," said Becca. "What about the woman?"

"She was in the Goya gallery with me, but that's the only time I saw her. However, it was after the Monk found me, so I think he passed me to her."

"The Monk?" asked Anders.

"Blond man, blue windbreaker, large bald spot." She used her finger to draw its size and placement on her own head. "Like a tonsured monk. I lost him once and doubled back close enough to overhear a phone conversation." She closed her eyes for a moment. "He said, 'We picked her up at her hotel. She dropped the black woman on Columbia then came to the National Gallery. Hyacinth followed her into the East Building and her team is staking out the ground floor exits while I'm covering that underground walkway to the other building.'" Millie opened her eyes and shrugged. "Then he saw me and cut the call."

Becca blinked and turned to Anders. "You didn't say she was in the game."

Anders looked mad. "She's *not*. Why'd you do that? Sneak up on him, I mean."

Millie cheeks warmed. "I had to know if they were really following me."

Anders kept staring at her as if he wanted more.

She bit her lip. "This has been stressful enough. I wanted—I needed—to rule out paranoid delusions."

Becca opened her mouth—a silent "ah." "You *are* a mental health professional, aren't you. And the black woman?"

"She's pretty much a mental health professional, too, in her own way." Millie smiled to herself. "She's a homeless mental patient who knows Davy. He's helped her several times in the past few months. She's asking the street people she knows if they saw anything the night of the abduction." She gestured at the screen. "Did your man hear anything?"

"No, she finished as he came up. But **Becca** recognized her," Anders said.

"You're kidding."

"I've been in Counter-Intelligence my entire career." Becca was fiddling with the mouse again. She enlarged another video window. It was the same scene, with the woman still waiting, but the window title said *Live Feed A*. "She was a freelancer—a deniable asset. I worked with her once, fifteen years ago. Her name—her full name—is Hyacinth Pope. Couldn't forget a name like that. She had just started doing some contract work for the CIA then, but the wall came down, and most of her career since has been in the private sector."

"What does that mean?"

"Corporate security and espionage."

"And kidnapping?"

Becca shrugged. "Or worse, but she's never been indicted, much less picked up. But this affair may be compartmentalized."

"You guys don't like English very much, do you?"

Anders said, "Means that her group could be involved but that a different cell did the snatch."

On the screen Hyacinth Pope left the shelter of the overhang again. The camera tracked her to the street where she got into a late model Dodge Caravan. The camera zoomed on the driver.

"That's the Monk," Millie said.

Anders leaned forward. "Ah. Padgett. Well, that tells us something."

"And that is?"

"Padgett was with Executive Outcomes, but now he works for the BAd boys."

Becca whistled. "Bochstettler and Associates." To Millie, she added, "They're a 'consulting' firm."

"What do they do?"

Becca said, "Well, ostensibly they're international commerce specialists, helping to develop and maintain markets in foreign countries."

"And is that what they do?"

"It's exactly what they do," said Anders, with a grim face.

Millie must've looked puzzled, because Becca added, "They aren't too picky about how. Like Executive Outcomes, before the South African government shut them down, we suspect the BAd boys of toppling whole governments to arrange a more favorable business 'climate.' That's rare. There's also a couple of questionable deaths. Usually, though, they tend to work through bribery and blackmail."

"Who do they work for?"

Becca shrugged. "That's harder to figure out. There's usually multiple benefactors to their various operations. Whenever a big business project goes through, no matter who it hurts, it usually benefits multiple parties—is it the primary company? One of the junior partners? The local vendors? The international vendors? Specific local politicians?

"Their overt client is the World Trade Study Group here in D.C., a PAC funded by several multinationals. WTSG promotes 'streamlining' international business practices, but the overt work the BAd boys do for them is legit—simple PR stuff, pushing the benefits of international trade to foreign governments."

Millie nodded slowly. "WTSG I've heard of. Streamlining means removing as many regulations and laws as possible, right?"

Anders nodded. "Right."

"Why aren't they in prison? BA, I mean."

Anders looked uncomfortable. Becca laughed, but there was no humor in it.

Anders said, "Primarily, evidence. There's circumstantial links but nothing incontrovertible."

Becca added, "However, there's also no pressure to go get harder evidence. 'It's about the economy, stupid.' Big international deals benefit our economy. That's been the bottom line for the past several administrations. In fact, past attempts have been actively discouraged and in the post nine-eleven economy, it's even more so."

Again, Anders looked uncomfortable, but he didn't gainsay this.

Millie frowned. "And now they may have kidnapped my husband—wait . . . let me put it another way. They've stolen a U.S. Intelligence Asset. Isn't that worth getting concerned about? Seems like they've gone from illegal actions against foreign governments to illegal actions against their own, doesn't it?"

Anders held his hand out palm down and wiggled it. "We still don't know if the BAd boys did the snatch. As Becca said, it might be compartmentalized. But there's some sort of connection, all right."

Millie pushed. "And you're going to follow up on it?"

Becca and Anders both nodded.

"Oh, yeah," said Becca.

The rain had stopped by the time the white cab dropped her at Martha's Table, the famous soup kitchen on Fourteenth Street Northwest. She walked past the yellow building face, past the long line of people waiting to be fed, and found Sojee right where she'd said she'd be, near the corner at the end of the block, sheltered in the doorway of a boarded-up store. She seemed relieved to see Millie. "What took you so long?"

"Sorry." Becca and Anders hadn't wanted her to go at all, but they'd really insisted that she wait until they'd put "support in the environment." Millie was trying hard not to examine every face she passed. At least she hadn't seen the Monk yet.

Doesn't mean he isn't here, though.

"This way," Sojee said, heading south. "I found someone who saw my angel the night he disappeared."

Millie's skin itched. She felt like hostile eyes surrounded her. "Are they sure it was Davy?"

"Matthew, chapter seven, verse twenty: By their works shall you know them."

"What works?"

"Well, they said, *'Un ángel nos dio el dinero.'*"

Millie forgot about the eyes for a moment and tried to switch mental gears. Finally she managed, "An angel gave them the money?"

Sojee's smile was twisted, overlaid by something dark. "Yeah. Looks like seeing angels is contagious."

"How much money?"

"She didn't say. My friend, Porfiro, says her and her two kids went from living in a refrigerator carton in an alley off Nineteenth to subletting a room from a family in his building. They've agreed to meet us at The Burro. The one down on Pennsylvania." She looked sideways at Millie. "You're buying."

Millie smiled briefly. "Of course. My Spanish isn't very good, though. Are you up to translating?"

Sojee shook her head. "No. Porfiro is coming, though. He'll do the job. Smartest crazy person I know."

"Uh, and Porfiro is . . . ?" She looked away. The gyrations of Sojee's face were making it hard for Millie to concentrate.

"Porfiro was in St. Elizabeth's with me. Bipolar—but lithium's got him smoothed down. He's the super in the building this family moved into."

"And what's their name?"

"Ruiz."

Sojee swung west on T Street and Millie, caught by surprise, scrambled to catch up. Her phone rang.

"Yes?" She kept walking.

It was Anders's voice. "They're up to something. They're moving in force, but so are we. We'll be right there if . . . if they do anything."

Millie felt a sinking feeling in the pit of her stomach. She struggled hard to keep her voice calm, neutral. "You want them to, don't you?"

Anders hesitated for the briefest interval. "Do you want to find Davy?"

"Ah . . . all right." Millie licked her lips. "Bring it on." She disconnected.

She started to look around, then stopped herself. *What about Sojee?* Was it fair to involve her in this? "Sojee, there's something I should tell—"

The Dodge van from the Museum made a hard right into the

mouth of the alley some twenty feet in front of them and stopped abruptly, blocking the sidewalk. The driver reached back and slid the side door open. It was the Monk.

At the same time, Millie heard footsteps on the pavement and turned her head. Two men rushed from the open door of a bodega and there was a screech of brakes on the street. Two more men were crossing the street at a run. A cabby, who'd had to brake for them, was shaking his fist and cursing in Farsi.

The two men from the store reached them first, walking fast, their arms coming out from their sides, palms forward. *Like someone herding sheep.*

Millie started to move forward, to put herself between the men and Sojee, when Sojee pulled Millie back and stepped forward, instead. Sojee held her fist out, thumb up, and waved it back and forth at the two men, who swore and recoiled from a sudden cloud of red mist.

Pepper spray, Millie realized. The two men's faces were streaked with an orangish red. *Dyed pepper spray.*

Sojee pivoted, moving toward the two men who were threading their way through a narrow gap between two parked cars. The one in the lead had seen what happened, and he was hesitating, but his partner bumped him from behind, forcing him forward. He ducked below Sojee's spray and charged forward, going for her legs. The cloud caught the second man full in the face.

Sojee went over backwards onto the wet sidewalk as the first man grabbed her legs.

She's trying to protect me. Millie took a step forward. The man was scooting quickly up Sojee's body in a horrid parody of sexual assault, trying to get up to her arms, to get the pepper spray away from her.

Millie's fear, predominate, gave way to sudden rage. She took another step and kicked him full in the face with the toe of her Merrell hiking boots.

He fell to the side, his nose a sudden red fountain, and Sojee, cursing loudly, emptied the last of her pepper spray into his face. The man rolled over, clutching his eyes and wheezing.

One of the men who'd come from the store had dropped to

his knees, his breath coming in wheezes, but his partner was rushing back at Millie, his red-streaked face contorted with rage, blinking water from his eyes. He came at a rush, to propel her toward the open door of the van, but suddenly dropped to the pavement.

Sojee had hooked his ankle and held it now with both hands. He hit the pavement hard, only partially breaking his fall with his arms. Sojee, screaming and cursing, pulled her way up the back of his legs. He tried to get back up, but she grabbed his belt at the small of his back and heaved him down again. He balanced on one hand and raised the other, to swing a hammer fist back at Sojee, so Millie slammed her boot down on the out-spread fingers of his supporting hand.

He screamed and Millie felt bones crunch under her boot.

Millie heard racing engines and screeching tires followed by the sound of pounding feet.

Not more of them?

In the van, the Monk looked wildly around, then accelerated the vehicle into the alley, disappearing between the buildings.

The running figures wore FBI baseball caps and windbreakers. They focused on their attackers, instead of the two women.

Not *more of them.*

Sojee was pounding her opponent with the empty pepper spray container, punctuating each blow with, "You! Got! My! Coat! Dirty!"

Millie caught her hand. "That'll do, girlfriend. That'll do."

Sojee stared up at Millie, her eyes wide. Then her face twisted and her tongue stuck out of her mouth to the side and she had a blepharospasm, a prolonged blink. "Oh. Right." She pushed off the back of her opponent and stood awkwardly. Millie pulled her to the side, out of the way of the large and healthy-looking men with the shotguns.

There was the sound of distant screeching tires from the alleyway followed immediately by a loud crash. Millie, seeing that the four men in her immediate vicinity were under control, poked her head cautiously around the corner.

The florist van was twisted at the far end of the alley, the windshield starred with bullet holes. A large cloud of steam was billowing from its front end. There seemed to be another car across the far alley.

"Don't do that."

It was Anders, standing on the sidewalk on the other side of the alleyway. Becca was right behind him.

Millie pulled her head back. "Why?"

Three rapid gunshots suddenly boomed down the alleyway and Millie jumped back. "Oh."

Anders, not taking his own advice, was looking down the alley. "Hmmm. Okay." He stepped across the alleyway, moving briskly. He looked at the four men who were now handcuffed and being frisked. "This isn't exactly what we had in mind, you know. We thought we'd actually let them start the snatch before we moved in."

"I wasn't going to resist. I didn't have time to warn Ms. Johnson."

Anders tried to frown, but he couldn't. He covered his mouth, then laughed outright. "I can tell I'm going to need a personal copy of this videotape."

Millie stared at him. "You videotaped it?" She looked around, wondering where the camera was. "Of course you taped it."

Becca was looking around the corner, then squeezed her coat lapel and said, "Roger that." Millie noticed the earplug. Then the FBI agent jerked, her eyes going wide. "Agent down!" she said loudly, and tore down the alley, drawing her gun as she went. Three agents followed her.

Anders, his eyes narrowed, gestured for them to cross the alleyway. He drew them further down the sidewalk.

"You and Ms. Johnson will find Curtis at the end of the block in the same White Cab. He'll take you to The Burro for your appointment."

"We don't have to make statements?"

"Later. The video will do for now."

Sojee was staring around her, her lips smacking, her cheek twitching. At the mention of her name, she stared at Anders specifically, then asked Millie, "Are these friends of yours?"

Millie hesitated for the briefest interval before saying,

"Allies." She brushed some beaded water off of Sojee's coat. "Are you all right?"

"I'm gonna need some more pepper spray."

Millie nodded. "I may get some myself." She linked arms with Sojee and started walking, wondering what had happened at the end of the alley. When they'd gone several yards, she said, "Thanks, Sojee, for protecting me back there."

Sojee snorted. "Looks like you didn't need no protectin'. Those assholes who jumped us sure did, though. They better stay away from me, I'll whup their asses again." Then she smiled. "You *nailed* that man in the nose. You pretty hot with that can of whup ass, yourself."

"You hold 'em, I'll kick 'em."

EIGHT

"I like a man in chains."

Thug One, the blond man with the nearly invisible eyebrows, put the lunch tray down just inside the door, then slid it within chain reach.

Davy was ravenous for lunch. He'd not had breakfast and the involuntary purging of his stomach worsened matters. He ate slowly, though. His throat was still raw from the bile and he didn't want to risk repeating this morning's experience—with or without outside help.

After finishing every crumb, he used the bathroom. On the way back the chains started retracting through the wall again.

Oh, great.

When he'd been pulled up to the wall again, they came back, the blond Thug One who'd brought breakfast, the brunette who'd killed Brian, and the hook-nosed man with the reddish brown hair—Thug Two.

What now?

They ignored him. The woman held a small plastic meter of some kind, with a stub antennae. She was watching a digital readout closely as she walked across the room. When she was in the middle of the room, about three feet out from the foot of Davy's bed, she crouched and began moving it from side to side. At several points she made marks on the floor with a felt-tipped pen, then, after about ten minutes of this, she waved at the other two.

"There. As marked."

Thug One held a roll of two-inch-wide gaffers tape in fluorescent green. He put long strips of it on the floor, forming a square four feet across.

While they were doing this, the woman was working farther out, again, looking closely at the meter and making marks on the floor. When the men had finished the square, she said, "Yellow tape here."

When the men were done, they had a yellow square with truncated corners eight feet outside the green square. They didn't bother completing this larger square near Davy or the bed, but when they were finished, the woman ran her meter around its perimeter both inside and out, then checked the green square again.

"Right. We're good to go." She handed Thug One the meter and jerked her thumb to the door.

Both of the men went to the door. Thug One turned right before he went through the door and looked at Davy, then, for the first time since entering the room. "Be a good dog," he said, his mouth twisted oddly.

When the door was shut again. The woman backed up, outside the line of yellow tape. Almost immediately, the chains went slack again and Davy sat down on the edge of the bed, just inside the larger square.

"You'll not be staying there," she said.

"Great. I'd love to get out of this room."

She shook her head. "Not my meaning."

"Who are you, anyway?"

She didn't answer him.

"Well, I might as well call you *something*. Murderer is accurate, but it just . . . well it lacks something. I believe I'll call you Miss Minchin."

The woman looked intrigued, despite herself. "And this refers to?"

"Miss Minchin's Seminary for Select Young Ladies." Davy wasn't sure he wanted to get into the plot of *A Little Princess* with this woman, especially detailing what a cast iron bitch Miss Minchin was. "She liked little boxes, too, and people to stay in them."

"I don't have time for sweet talk. Get in the green square."

Davy stayed where he was.

She lifted a hand toward the mirror and snapped her fingers.

Davy doubled over, coughing violently. He was nauseated, on the edge of throwing up, his forehead covered with clammy sweat. He pushed off the bed and, bent over, still coughing, shuffled toward the green square. Almost immediately the coughing and the nausea lessened. When he stepped over the green tape, the urge to cough and the nausea ceased completely.

She went on talking. "Outside the green box, you'll feel it. Just outside the yellow box, you get a repeat of this morning's ride. You do remember this morning, don't you?" She looked over at the empty mop bucket and mop, leaning in the far corner.

Davy wanted to wipe the sweat from his forehead but he forced himself to stand there, unmoving, watching "Miss Minchin" with eyes cold and distant.

She continued. "You go outside the yellow box and the convulsions will probably kill you."

Box is the right word.

"Do you intend for me to live here? In this four-foot square? Are you going to bring the portable toilet back?"

She shook her head. "Your body will let you know when you need to be in the square."

"If you turn this on while I'm taking a shower, I could crack my skull and die. I'm pretty sure you guys don't want me dead."

"There are a lot worse things than dying, darling. You'll get a warning, sort of like being in the yellow square. If you're not in this big square," she indicated the outer yellow boundary, "within two seconds, it'll be like this morning and worse. You won't be, ummmm, 'symptom free' until you're all the way inside the green square."

"Miss Minchin was the right name."

"I really must look that up. We're going to leave the zone on for a few more minutes. *You* figure out when you can leave it."

She turned. As she walked away she swung her hips. Davy watched her ass sway from side to side. In the doorway she paused, blew a kiss, and let the door swing shut behind her.

Nice legs.

I'd like to break them.

He stuck his hand over the edge of the green tape. Nothing happened. He sat down and stuck his feet over the edge. Again, nothing happened. *Did they already turn it off?*

He scooted up to the line. As his torso edged over the tape, he coughed lightly and felt a mild wave of nausea. He scooted back again. The coughing and nausea ceased. He lay down on his back and started inching out of the square, feet first. He didn't feel anything until his upper chest crossed the line.

No surprise there. That's where the scar was, where they'd put the device, whatever it was. He stood back up inside the square.

He experimented, leaning out into the larger square. His stomach heaved and his coughing was rough but he could walk two thirds of the way to the yellow line before he had to stagger back in defeat. He thought he could probably push it even further in an emergency, but they were watching and there was no reason to let them know his limitations. He believed them about the far edge. The memory of flopping on the floor like a freshly caught fish was still strong in his mind.

He was testing the border again when the sensations cut off abruptly—the coughing and nausea dropped away—and he staggered. He felt like someone who'd been shoving at a stuck door, when all of a sudden the door is opened from the other side.

He wanted to wash the sweat from his face and rinse his mouth but it took a definite act of will to step over the yellow line on the way to the bathroom.

Two seconds, he told himself. *Two seconds is lots of time.*

They started testing him an hour later. He was lying down, reading *The Count of Monte Cristo*, when he felt a tingling in his throat followed almost immediately by a wave of nausea, then the inevitable cough. Then it stopped and he wondered if it was a fluke.

Then he doubled over, coughing and throwing up, getting vomit on his sheets and covers. He scrambled for the end of the bed and the safety of the green square.

Shit! Shit! Shit!

The scrambled voice over the speaker said, "Two seconds—we meant it."

He felt like crying when the wave of nausea quit but he couldn't stand the thought of giving them the pleasure. He stood slowly. He'd gotten vomit on the pants of his scrubs. He ripped the side seams open, pulled them off, used the unsoiled section to wipe his mouth, then bundled them up and threw them into the bathroom.

He tried the border but felt the telltale tickle in his throat. He stepped out far enough to snag the railing at the end of the bed, coughing heavily, and then dragged it toward him, backing into the safety zone. He stripped the soiled sheets and threw them into the bathroom as well. The still-clean blanket he wrapped around his waist, sarong-style.

Then he dragged the bed farther, until the head was in the green square, and lay down, his chest centered over the green square.

He tried to read, but couldn't concentrate. For a while, then, he counted slowly to twenty and turned pages as if he was—a defiant form of meditation. Then he made a show of yawning largely and, putting the book down, he rolled over on his side facing away from the mirror, and pretended to sleep.

This is not going at all well.

He was awakened by movement, disorienting, as he hadn't been aware he'd fallen asleep. He sat up in time to see Thug One backing away, again. Looking around, he found that they'd moved his bed back out of the square.

Why? Oh. They can't train me *if I'm not out of the square when they turn it on.* He hopped back out of bed, swinging his chains clear automatically, and started to drag the bed back.

The blonde shook his head and started back toward him. "You've got to leave the bed against the wall."

Dammit!

Davy jumped, not toward the man, but toward the mirror, to the full extent of the chains. Almost immediately the chains began reeling through the wall, slowly pulling Davy back as his unseen jailers realized he was closer to the door than the blonde was.

Thug One looked frightened and his hand went up to the scab on his cheek, left over from when Davy had snatched the mask from his face. He started back toward the door.

Davy jumped, before the chains were pulled up too short, past Thug One, across the man's path to the door, and braced himself.

The chains moved so fast you could hear their passage through the air. They caught Thug One at the shin, knee, hip, and stomach.

The pull on Davy's wrists and ankles pulled him forward two meters but it *threw* Thug One across the room and into the wall with a dust-raising crash. The man hung there for a beat, like a cartoon character, and then he crumpled to the floor. Where he'd hit the wall the Sheetrock and paint were caved in.

The slow reeling of the chains continued and Davy shuffled back, keeping up with them. He felt ashamed of himself. *Show some control! Don't show them what you can do until you can use it to get free.*

When he was all the way up against the wall the door opened and they came for Thug One. They used a backboard and a cervical collar and they carried him out like he was made of glass.

Davy expected the chains to loosen again, but they didn't. They were too short for him to reach the bed, too short, even, for him to lie down. He could sit with his arms hanging in the wrist cuffs, level with his shoulders. He couldn't reach the bed, or the book, or his Styrofoam drinking cup.

He coughed twice and a wave of nausea passed over him. *Oh, Jesus!* He pulled on the chains but they were unyielding. He was just outside the yellow line.

It was the worst yet and it went on and on and on until he finally passed out.

He woke up slumped in a pool of vomit and feces, still dangling from the chains.

Miss Minchin was standing there with the mop and the mop bucket. She was watching him closely, her head tilted to one side. "Was that fun?" she asked.

Davy didn't say anything. His throat was raw from bile and, even though the device wasn't activated, he was nauseated.

She persisted. "Was your little chain trick worth the result?"

Davy looked at her steadily, doing his best to ignore the fluids and the smells.

She stopped smiling. "Don't mess with us. You'll regret it every time."

Davy spit to the side, trying to get the taste from his mouth. "Do you know what aspiration pneumonia is?"

She shrugged. "We've got airway suction, antibiotics, oxygen—hell, we've even got a crash cart to restart your heart. You won't get out of it that easy." She threw the mop down before him. "Now clean up your mess."

He took a shower, first, then, a towel wrapped about his midriff, cleaned the floor. When he'd flushed the water and cleaned the mop and bucket, he took another shower.

He coughed twice, under the shower head, and the wave of nausea began. He didn't bother trying to run or walk. He jumped and found himself standing in the square, naked and dripping, automatically bracing to avoid being pulled off balance by the recoiling chains.

Should've at least grabbed the towel.

He had pushed the bed aside, to clean the floor, and it was at the limits of the yellow square, too much for him to try. Even the thought of reaching for it was enough to make him gag. He did his best to squeegee the beads of water off his body with his hands, then sat, his knees pulled to his chest to conserve heat while he dried. He counted slowly to a hundred, then tried the border. The device was off again.

He went back into the bathroom. There were deep gouges in

the door frame and the shower curtain had ripped edges where the chains had slashed through it. He dried off and walked back out into the room.

They'd brought him some clean sheets for the bed, but they hadn't brought him any new scrubs. He'd rinsed the worst of the bodily excretions out of the soiled scrubs earlier during his first shower. Now he held them up before the large mirror.

The computerized voice was silent.

Like that, is it?

He washed the scrubs in the tub, in water as hot as he could stand, using the shower gel from the dispenser on the wall as detergent. When he'd wrung them out he hung them and the towel across the rod.

Petty punishments are as nasty as the big ones when they go on and on. He had been regretting hurting Thug One, but the regret was fading fast.

His stomach muscles hurt from the prolonged vomiting and coughing, as if he'd been doing sit-ups. *Might as well do the rest.* He spent the next thirty minutes doing mild calisthenics and stretches. He did the exercises naked after rejecting the thought of wearing a damp towel or worse, a blanket toga. *If it was good enough for the Greeks . . .*

He couldn't help thinking about the observers behind the glass, or *her*. *Is she watching?* He didn't find that thought at all erotic. At least it kept him honest. He didn't cheat on the number of push-ups or deep knee bends.

There were several exercises he rejected when they tugged on his healing scars. On others, it became clear that the flailing of the chains interfered too much. On a few, the weight of chain was a help, like leg lifts.

Near the end of his workout, they turned the device back on and he had to move abruptly, three feet to the right. He pivoted two steps and continued his hamstring stretches inside the square with hardly a missed beat. After some seated quadriceps stretches he tried the border again. There was no telltale nausea.

He considered staying where he was. *They won't stand for that. They can't train me if I don't feel it.* He went to the bathroom and drank water. It felt good on his raw throat but he couldn't help but think, *if you've got to throw up, might as well make it as innocuous as possible.*

His stomach rumbled, hungry again. He wondered if they'd feed him or whether they were still in punishment mode.

He went back to the bed and picked up the book.

There were no device activations during supper. He was ravenous, but his raw throat made eating painful. Still, frequent applications of ice water allowed him to get the entire meal down.

They still hadn't brought him fresh clothes. He left the tray by the door, sliding it across the floor for the last yard his chains would not reach. The scrubs he'd washed were finally dry except for some dampness at the seams. He folded them neatly and set them on the foot of the bed, then went back to reading, reclining on the bed.

Fifteen minutes later they were at it again, but he found he could stroll, still reading, into the square, even though he was coughing. He started to leave, after the usual minute, but found the field was still on. He sat, cross-legged, on the cold floor, and continued reading. At the end of the chapter he checked again but the coughing and nausea still waited outside the tape.

His butt became too cold to keep sitting. He put the book down and began some dynamic stretches, to warm up. His abdominals still hurt from the coughing and vomiting, but not as much as they had earlier. He credited the stretching exercises.

Nicely warm, he checked the border again. Still on. He read some more, standing, checking the border after every page. Another chapter passed and the field was still on.

Oh, come on!

He did some more stretches. The cold was concentrating water to his kidneys and he was beginning to feel it in his bladder. He thought about peeing on the floor but he'd had enough involvement with bodily fluids already today.

The bed had been moved into the corner while he was unconscious and it was well outside the yellow square. *Do they want me to wear clothes? Are they telling me that I shouldn't have paraded around without something warm on?*

He froze, suddenly. *Maybe they turned it on and just left? Went out for supper. After all, why should they watch me when they've got this device?*

He had a mental image of Miss Minchin and the redheaded Thug Two in some clinic or hospital visiting the blonde he'd injured, while all the other staff were bowling, a team in a local league, their scrubs and masks their team uniform.

He tested the border again, but it was still active.

Next time I keep the blanket with me.

He wondered what would happen if he jumped past the yellow zone entirely. *Would I get the two-second warning if I avoided the middle zone? Would that be like when they first turn it on?* He froze in place.

He could do a lot with two seconds.

He remembered Miss Minchin working the meter across the floor. *Signal strength. But was it a zone of low or high signal strength?* He touched his chest. *Does my little friend here "tickle" me when it gets to a higher signal strength or when it loses it altogether?*

He no longer felt cold at all.

They knew he could teleport. That's why they'd grabbed him in the first place. So, a border of a stronger radio field was right out—unless they could blanket the entire planet, he would always be able to jump past it.

But he couldn't jump away from this gadget in his chest. That could mean they were broadcasting some low strength, focused field at the green square. As long as the device received this signal at a sufficient field strength, it stayed off. This would imply that the yellow zone was an area of leakage before the field attenuated completely below some detectable limit and the device adjusted its level of punishment accordingly.

So what are they doing when the device is "off?" When I can wander at the limits of my chain?

Perhaps they broadcast a less focused signal, one that covered the entire suite, perhaps the entire building.

Christ, I hope they've got some sort of battery backup! He pictured a heavy spring thunderstorm knocking out power lines and him dying an ugly death in a pool of mixed bodily fluids.

Suddenly he felt the cold again.

He leaned across the green tape.

It was off. *Or it's just on more.*

He put the scrubs in the middle of the green square along with the blanket from the bed, then took a hot shower. They waited until he was drying himself before he felt the painfully familiar double cough. He walked briskly out, still toweling, and into the square.

While he dressed, he thought about the warning—the brief spate of nausea and the coughing. Was it the device's reaction to no radio field or were they doing a brief dip in broadcast strength of the larger field, then waiting two seconds before turning it off?

If it was an automatic feature, it gave him some latitude—if he could get out of these chains. For someone like Davy, a lot could be accomplished in two seconds.

He wanted to experiment, to test the limits, but he also wanted to do it without an audience. He did not want them to know what he was and wasn't capable of.

He checked the border. It was still on. He was still "in the box." He stepped back to the center of the square.

The copy of *The Count of Monte Cristo* was still lying on the bed, beyond the yellow border. If his theory was right, it should be in the zone of no signal.

They were working up to a way to control him without chains. Like the NSA, they wanted to use his abilities, but they couldn't do that if they couldn't unchain him. And if he jumped away and the device came on full force, as if he'd forced himself past the yellow line, there was good chance they'd lose him and his abilities altogether.

You go outside the yellow box and the convulsions will probably kill you.

Would they? If he went directly to that zone?

He gritted his teeth and jumped to the side of the bed. The

chains sang through the air and he felt the warning cough, but *only* the warning level. He took the book and jumped back. It took slightly more than a second because he'd paused, by the bed, to feel the effects.

Quickly he checked the line of green tape again. No—they hadn't turned it off (or on, as the case may be). The cough and nausea was still there. He'd been worried the warning cough by the bed was psychosomatic—expected and therefore experienced.

He actually felt like smiling, but hid it, turning away from the mirror and sitting on the folded blanket. He pretended to read for a while, his mind racing. Had they noticed?

The chains started reeling through the wall and he quailed inwardly. Are they punishing me again? He checked the border before the chains dragged him across, but they had turned on the larger radio field and he felt nothing unpleasant. He strolled with the moving chains and positioned himself, back to the wall, as they pulled up short.

The door opened and Miss Minchin came in. Behind her was a masked man in glasses and surgical scrubs pushing a cart with a computer on it. He rolled it to the wall and plugged it in. While it was booting up, he said, "Here's the wand." He handed Miss Minchin a flat plastic box on the end of a telephone cord. It was about the size of a television remote control. The other end of the cord was plugged into the back of the computer.

She examined it closely. "Left side, yeah?"

"Yes. I'll need another moment, to finish booting."

That the man spoke surprised Davy. Until he'd unmasked the blonde and redhead, all the staff had kept quiet in his presence, using the voice scrambler to communicate. Maybe the staff didn't care anymore. *Maybe they think they've achieved enough control over me so it no longer matters.*

Miss Minchin walked slowly toward Davy, tapping the box against her outer thigh with each step. When she was a meter short of Davy, she stopped and looked back over her shoulder, toward the technician.

He was still watching the screen. "Oh . . . kay. We're up."

She reached out with the "wand" and Davy flinched.

"Relax, little boy. If Mama wanted to spank, she could've done it from the other room—with a *button*." She rested the flat side of the box over Davy's left pectoral—where the newly formed scar was. "How's this," she asked.

The masked man said, "Negotiating . . . connection established. Right. Give me a minute to upload the new parameters."

Miss Minchin smiled, her eyes on Davy. "Take your time. I like a man in chains." She traced her free forefinger across Davy's collarbone.

Davy looked at her and said earnestly, "I'm going to throw up."

Miss Minchin stepped back slightly looking alarmed, then said over her shoulder, "Should he be feeling anything?"

The technician said, "Nothing from the device."

Davy said, "Right. It's not the *device* that's nauseating me."

Miss Minchin chuckled softly. "You are *such* a tease."

Davy wondered if he pulled her hair out of its bun if her brains would drop out on the floor. It was a thought.

The man at the computer shook his head. He was watching the computer monitor. "Oh . . . kay. I've changed the parameters. Let me run a checksum to verify the upload and we'll be done." He clicked a few more keys, shifted the mouse. "And . . . there. Confirmed." He accepted the paddle back from Miss Minchin and stowed it while the computer shut down, then unplugged the unit from the wall. While he was coiling the power cord he said, "You should tell him."

Miss Minchin shrugged, still watching Davy.

"Tell me what," Davy finally said.

Miss Minchin pointed at the yellow line. "We've shortened the grace period before it activates. It's a *lot* shorter now. I wouldn't take any chances if I were you. No more experiments, right?"

Davy pictured dropping her into the quarry pool near his home in West Texas. At this time of year the water was a nice chilly fifty-five degrees. The temperature wouldn't kill her since she could get out pretty quickly, but the impact after the sixty foot drop would be severe and she'd be pretty miserable until her clothing dried.

"What's so funny?" she asked.

He blanked his face. He hadn't realized he was smiling.

"No, really. I could use a good laugh."

He shook his head.

She shrugged and vamped across the room, holding the door while the technician pushed the cart out. "Sleep well," she said and let the door swing shut behind her.

He didn't.

Before breakfast, they'd put him "in the box" over twenty times. He lost track sometime after number eighteen.

He tried to sleep in the green zone, curling up with the blanket and pillow on the floor, but they reeled in the chains when he did that, pulling him out. He was afraid they'd leave the chains short and turn off the field, a repeat of his last punishment, so for the rest of the activations he stood near the green line swaying in and out of the field until it went off, then stumbled back to bed.

By the end of the night, he wasn't sure if he was actually waking up during each incident. Not that this earned him more rest—it felt like some continuous nightmare.

They left him alone while he ate breakfast, but they started up again when he was showering, leaving him lathered, dripping, and naked in the middle of the green zone. They kept him there a token thirty seconds before he was able to go back and finish. Once dry, it was on again, off again, right through lunch.

He always jumped to the square. He didn't want to take any chances with the newly shortened grace period. Or, to be specific, his body didn't want to. He tried more than once to stroll nonchalantly back to the square, but it was always too hard, and he'd flinch before he could complete the walk, and then he'd find himself standing in the square, bracing from the recoil of the chains.

Operant conditioning. A reflexive response.

Just what they want.

NINE

"I've still got blood on my boots!"

The Burro was in a cluster of other restaurants at the corner of Pennsylvania, where it angled through the intersection of Twentieth and I Street Northwest. The family Ruiz and Porfiro was sitting across the street in a small triangular park.

Sojee waved to them. "Get in line for a table," she said. "I'll fetch them over."

Millie obediently joined the small group waiting outside the door. The couple beside her said, "They're taking names," so she stuck her head in and told a harassed young man "Six, please. Non-smoking."

"Right." He stared at her like she was completely insane but she could tell several people were ready to leave and that tables would be opening up soon. "What name?" he asked.

"Rice," she said.

"I'll call you."

She went back outside. The group was moving across the street with Sojee on one side of the stocky, mustached Porfiro and the Ruizes on the other. The children, two girls in parochial school uniforms, were clinging to their mother, who was trying to get them to walk faster before the light changed.

When they reached the curb, Sojee came ahead and said, quietly, "Kids are scared of me—of my facial twitches."

Millie shook her head and spontaneously hugged the woman. "That's gotta be hard."

Sojee looked surprised and her eyes were suspiciously bright when Millie let go. "I just wanted you to know why they were freakin'. Maybe I should wait out here."

Millie shook her head slightly. "No." She turned to Porfiro, just coming up. "Hello, Porfiro, I'm Millie," she said, holding out her hand.

"Thought so," he said, smiling. He shook her hand and then introduced the Ruizes. "This is Señora Ruiz and her daughters Juanita and Nuk."

Juanita, the older of the two, had lustrous dark hair and dark brown eyes. The two girls' facial structure and eyes were identical, but Nuk's skin was much lighter, and she had pale straw blond hair.

Albino. Millie smiled and said, "*Hola. ¡Con mucho gusto! Me llamo* Millie."

The children hid behind their mother who nodded slightly and said, "*¿Que soñaste?*"

Millie wrinkled her brow and glanced at Porfiro. "I'm afraid my Spanish isn't very good."

"It means—well, it's a greeting where they come from," the man said.

"Ah." She wanted to scream at them, *What do you know about Davy!* She took a sudden shuddering breath of air, exhaled, and tried to smile again at the girls, who were peeping out from behind their mother's dress.

She thanked them for coming. "*Gracias por venir.*" She groped for more words. She'd about reached the end of her Spanish from her stay in Costa Rica. "*Yo realmente aprecio su ayuda.*" *I really appreciate your help.* Millie saw understanding in the woman's eyes, and pain. *This woman needed help once,* she decided, *and* didn't *get it.*

"Rice—party of six!"

She gestured for Señora Ruiz and her children to precede her. "*Vayamos.*" She rubbed her stomach. "*Tengo hambre.*" She pulled Porfiro aside and said quietly, "What happened to their father?"

Porfiro glanced ahead at the woman and her children before looking back at Millie. He made an abbreviated motion, his thumb across his throat, then whispered, "With most of their village. Taken. No bodies found—blood everywhere. She took the girls into the rain forest when the first truck pulled into the village." His mouth twisted. "She'd had a dream."

Millie stared for a second, then nodded. They caught up with the others. Two older men were arguing with the receptionist. "We've been here longer than they have!"

The young man was patiently explaining, "We have large tables and small tables. A large table opened up. I'll have a table for two in just a minute, swear to God." When he was inside, and leading them to their table, Millie heard him mutter to himself, "What an A-two hundred."

Their table was a largish corner booth with bench seats on three sides. Millie slid in and took the far side, which put the girls on one side with their mother at the end, and Porfiro and Sojee on the other side.

With Porfiro's translation skills they got the drink order in fairly quickly. After the waiter left, Millie asked, "I understand you saw my husband." She took one of the photocopied pictures from her purse and unfolded it.

Señora Ruiz looked briefly at the picture and then at the girls who became excited.

"*Si, si, nuestro ángel en la noche!*" said Juanita.

Porfiro translated, "Their angel in the night."

"*¿Por qué llámelo eso?*" she asked, surprising herself. The Spanish was coming back. *Why call him that?*

"*Él apareció fuera nada,*" said Nuk.

"Out of nothing, you say." Millie blinked. "When was— ¿*Cuándo? ¿Qué día?*"

Señora Ruiz said, "*Cinco de Marza. Cerca de medianoche.*" She looked at Porfiro.

"Yes. They moved into the building the next day—the sixth."

The very night. The very time.

The drinks arrived and Millie forced herself to be still, to wait, which was tested even more when the waiter wanted to take their food order. She ground her teeth and insisted the family Ruiz order anything they wanted, no matter the cost.

When the waiter had finally departed she fixed her eyes on Señora Ruiz. "*¿Qué usted vio?*" *What did you see?*

"*Nada. No estaba allí. Eran.*" She tilted her head to her girls. *You weren't there?* She took a deep breath and tried to find that utterly calm, non-threatening place she sought when she did family therapy. She stacked her hands one upon the other, then lowered her head until her chin rested on the back of the hands and her eyes were on the same level as the children's. "*¿Qué vieron ustedes?*"

She depended on Porfiro to translate. She couldn't understand what they were saying half the time and even Porfiro had to clarify several times, asking *Señora Ruiz* the meaning of a phrase. Millie was sure several of the phrases the girls used were not Spanish.

The story, told mostly by Juanita, started, "We couldn't sleep. It had been raining and the fire escape was dripping on our box, our refrigerator carton, bap, bap, bap. No one was there and then he was there, like he fell from the sky or grew out of the ground. Nuk gasped and he heard."

"Juanita made the noise."

"Nuk did."

"Juanita."

"Nuk."

Millie smiled. "*No importante. ¿Y entonces?*"

"He talked to us in English but we didn't answer. He bent down and light came out of his fingers. He looked at us but he stayed back. He talked to us in Spanish. He wanted to know where our parents were. Because we're not supposed to talk to strangers, I didn't say anything but Nuk did."

"What a lie! I never!"

"You did!"

"Did not!"

Millie said, "What did he learn from whoever it was that talked?"

"That Papa is disappeared and Mama is a janitor. That she

works at night. Then he gave us the money and told us to hide it. For a place to live, he said. I didn't want to take it but Nuk said we should."

"I never!"

"He gave us his blessing then and he left."

Millie blinked. "He blessed you?" *That didn't sound like Davy.* "What were his exact words?"

"*Buena suerte.*"

"Ah. How did he leave?"

"He walked away. We could hear his footsteps down the street. We got out of the box, then, and hid the money under the loose brick in the wall of the alley, so no one could take it from us."

Millie was disappointed. It was the sort of thing Davy would do—give the kids the money—and she was glad to hear the story. There was really nothing here that would help, though.

"And you didn't see him after that?"

Both girls looked at each other then back at Millie as if she was being incredibly thick. "When *La Llorona* killed his friend and took him away, we saw that, too."

Millie jaw dropped and she stared. With a manifest effort she closed her mouth and said, "You saw that. That's horrible. That's *wonderful*—don't translate that. What did they mean, *La Llorona.*"

Porfiro said, "The weeping woman. She's the ghost of a woman who drowned her own children and she takes other children in an effort to replace them. Sometimes they call her Bloody Mary."

"Why did they think it was her? Scratch that. Just ask them to tell me what happened."

The story continued.

"There were gunshots on the other side of the street and we got out of our box and hid behind the trash cans, so to stop the bullets better than the cardboard. A man carrying our angel is running up the street. Others are chasing them. He is shot in the leg and he falls, spilling our angel, whose eyes are open but cannot move.

"The man who is shot reaches into his coat and they shoot him some more. He drops a telephone. He is all over blood.

"Then *La Llorona* comes. Her empty eyes are dripping black blood and she carries a large gun. I was more scared than even the night the paramilitary came to the village. I was afraid that she would kill our angel but she shoots the other man, instead, in the eyes so he won't be able to find her in the afterworld.

"Then the ambulance comes and they put the Angel in and drive away. They left the other man lying on the sidewalk."

Nuk added, "The rain washed his face."

"The different ambulances and the police came then and before they found us, we took our sleeping bags and the money and ran through the alley."

"Different ambulances? How were they different?"

"They didn't have the angel."

"What? Davy—my angel?"

"No. The angel on the door. *Un angelito.*"

"There was a little angel painted on the door?"

"Yes."

"Which door?"

"On the driver's door. Maybe the other door, too, but we did not see."

"Were there any other differences in the ambulance?"

"Maybe the words on the side but they weren't *Español*. I don't know."

"The colors were the same?"

"Yes. White with an orange stripe." Juanita drew a horizontal line with her finger. "The snake on the stick in the blue . . ." She dipped her finger in her lemonade and sketched the EMS Star of Life, an X with a vertical line through it on the tabletop. " . . . *como un asterisco.*"

A waiter and waitress appeared bearing trays and Millie sat back as their food was presented with the standard mantra: "Careful—the plate is very hot."

Millie was eating the fish tacos, grilled mahi-mahi filets wrapped in a soft corn tortilla and topped with lime-cumin slaw and salsa fresca. The Ruizes were having *carnitas* burritos.

Porfiro said, "They don't eat meat very often. It's an exotic luxury for them—they lived near a lake and occasionally would get fish and they kept chickens for eggs. Usually it's beans and corn. Or sometimes they would eat venison to keep from losing their crops."

Millie felt confused and must have looked it, too, for Porfiro said, "If they don't kill the deer, the deer would eat their crop. And once killed . . ."

"Ah. *¿Está bueno?*" Millie asked, indicating the food.

"*¡Si!*" said Señora Ruiz. She gestured with her fingers, for Millie to try some.

Millie cut a section of her fish taco, transferred it to the edge of the woman's plate, then cut a small chunk off the uneaten end of Señora Ruiz's burrito and popped it in her mouth.

She shook her fingers and said, "*¡Delicioso! Muy sabroso.*"

Señora Ruiz smiled shyly, then her expression became serious. She began talking again, gesturing to Porfiro to translate for her. "I am glad you have money because it is hard for a woman when her man disappears, but I would understand if you would like the money back that your man gave us. When they took our village we had nothing—they took even the chickens—and it was very hard."

Millie held up her hands. "*Yo no quiero dinero. Tengo bastantes.*" Her Spanish failed her and she said to Porfiro, "Tell her I'm just trying to find my husband."

Señora Ruiz nodded vigorously when Porfiro translated.

"I know what that is like, too. I hope God will return him to you. Since you have money, it is to be hoped that they will ransom him. Alas, in our case, they only wanted our land, and if I hadn't gone into the jungle, we would be dead, too."

"Why did you come here—to Washington? Was there no place in Chiapas?"

Señora Ruiz tilted her head to one side, considering. She said something that Porfiro translated as, "I go to my family in Naha." Then she said something that he didn't understand at all. She rephrased it and he said, "God wanted her to come here first. On the way." He shrugged.

Then she said something to Porfiro that caused him to look

uncertain, but she repeated it. It was the phrase she'd used when they'd been introduced, *¿Que soñaste?*

Porfiro said, "She asks, what did you dream? It is the way her people greet each other." He fingered something below his neck, under the fabric of his shirt. Almost reluctantly he added, "They believe dreams are about what has happened or will happen."

He doesn't like this. She saw the gleam of a silver chain around his neck. *A crucifix?*

She thought about some polite evasion, a white lie denying any dreams. She hadn't slept well at all since the night Davy left. With Sojee in the room with her the previous evening, someone who wasn't Davy, she'd tossed and turned most of the night.

Still, there was that weird sequence just before the dawn and she wanted to give them something back, something for the clues they'd given her.

"I had trouble falling asleep, but when I did I dreamed the same thing. I was trying to sleep but every time I rolled over to get comfortable, I would land on a pin. It would poke me and I'd throw it out of the bed, but the bed was full of them, and I didn't get to sleep until I laid a red bedspread over them."

Porfiro translated for her and Señora Ruiz questioned the man about his choice of certain words, narrowing the meaning to more specific choices. She looked back at Millie and asked another question.

"What color is your bedspread—the real one?"

"At the hotel? Green, with yellow orchids."

Señora Ruiz nodded, then asked another question.

Porfiro apparently didn't understand and Señora Ruiz rephrased it. He turned back to Millie and said, "She wants to know your *onen*, your clan—your totem. She says foreigners often don't know what their totem is." He made a very abbreviated sign of the cross and touched his shirt again.

Millie blinked. "I have no earthly idea."

Porfiro translated this and Señora Ruiz nodded and began talking again.

"She says to interpret your dream it would help to know. She thinks, from the symbols in your dream—the way you present the blood and snakes, that you are a female spider monkey, which makes you a distant relative of her clan."

"What snakes? What blood?"

He asked Señora Ruiz, then translated the explanation. "The pins. Thorns, pins, needles, a rope are all symbols of snakes. The red blanket is blood."

Millie shuddered. She felt the queasy fascination of a rational person for the supernatural. *I know there are things in this world I can't explain. Look at Davy.*

"Does this predict the future?"

Porfiro checked. "She says it warns. A bad thing can be avoided through advance notice in a dream. It isn't unchangeable. I told you of her going into the jungle when the paramilitaries came? The night before she had a dream."

Señora Ruiz talked again and Porfiro resumed his translation. "If you're of the monkey *onen*, she thinks your dream tells of danger coming at night, when you would sleep, a danger waiting for you."

Considering the events of the day, this wasn't the most unlikely thing she'd ever heard. Gravely she asked "What does she suggest?"

"Do not sleep in that bed tonight. Go somewhere else."

Millie sent Porfiro and the family Ruiz home in a cab, paying the driver in advance.

Just before they drove away, Señora Ruiz had said, *"Ki'we-nen tech. Ki'i ba' willik."* Millie, puzzled, looked at Porfiro, who shrugged. Señora Ruiz, seeing their confusion, said, *"Tenga cuidado para el qué sueña."*

Porfiro made the sign of the cross, then translated, "Be careful of what you dream."

Millie stared after the cab long after it had turned out of sight.

Sojee said, "You off your meds?"

Millie shook herself. "Not on meds. Just distracted. Wondering, really."

Sojee looked around, her head twisting and turning. She

grumbled, "It's bad enough being a paranoid schizophrenic without having actual people following you around and attacking you."

Millie turned west and began walking up the sidewalk. Sojee fell into step with her but looked over her shoulder often. The streets were busy both with cars and pedestrians.

Sojee said abruptly, "I've been asked to check back into St. Elizabeth's. I guess Hinkley misses me."

"Why? Do they want to treat your schizophrenia?"

"No. My psychiatrist got me a place in a drug study to treat my twitches. They're—" She switched to an exaggerated pompous academic voice. "—checking the efficacy of a combination regime of vitamin B-6 and tetrabenazine in the treatment of tardive dyskinesia and other hyperkinetic involuntary movements of the face." A man came out of a doorway and Sojee jumped, but he turned and walked east, the opposite direction.

Millie patted Sojee's arm. "When do they want you to check in?"

"They want me tonight or tomorrow."

"Ah. Do *you* want to?"

"Well, I wasn't too thrilled about it."

Millie raised her eyebrows. "Is there a chance of worsened effects? Dystonia?" Tardive Dystonia would expand her involuntary movements from her face to the rest of her body.

"Nah—and what side effects they've seen are controlled by reducing the dosage. Tetrabenazine seems pretty safe that way, but it's the hope/disappointment thing."

"If you don't try it, it won't not work."

Sojee nodded. "Yeah, but frankly it's looking better and better, now."

"To get off the street? Or to get away from my enemies?"

Sojee looked around again. "Well—you spend a night in a real bed, a safe bed, and it ruins you for a while. Makes it hard to stay up all night. Even in the shelters you've got people trying to steal your stuff or feel you up. You may be warm but you don't really want to sleep." There was a loud bang down an alley and she jumped.

Millie looked, but it was only a door flung open by someone carrying out garbage.

Sojee was holding her hand to her chest. "All right. I'm nervous about those guys who jumped us, too. Especially after hearing about Bloody Mary and your dreams."

"Ah. Not your usual story, was it?"

Millie's cell phone rang and she fumbled it to her ear. "Yes?"

"We'd like to meet." It was Anders.

"Hold on a minute." She looked at Sojee. "Would you like to go to St. Elizabeth's tonight?"

Sojee nodded.

Millie talked into the phone. "Ms. Johnson needs to go to St. Elizabeth's. I thought I'd take her in a cab, then I could meet you?"

"All right," said Anders. "Curtis will pick you up where you are. Just keep walking until you see him coming down your side of the street, then flag him."

Millie looked down the street at the cars, dim shadows behind glaring headlights. "It's quite dark now. It'll be hard to identify the right cab."

"His off-duty light will be on but he'll blink it, then switch over to on-duty as he nears you."

"All right. Please make it so."

After they dropped Sojee at St. Elizabeth's, Curtis took the white cab in a long circuitous route out past the National Zoo and then back again, toward the Mall. Millie closed her eyes and tried to rest. At least he wasn't whipping around traffic circles again and again.

Eventually they ended up at the Willard Inter-Continental Hotel. He pulled up to the side entrance and said, "They're in the Round Robin Bar."

"No tags?"

He snorted. "Puh-lease."

She felt severely underdressed as she threaded through the columns and furniture of the lobby with its elaborately carved ceilings and mosaic floors. She found Anders and another man sitting at a corner table of the bar where, a small placard informed her, Henry Clay introduced the Mint Julep to Washington in the 1820s. Both men stood when she came in. Anders pulled out a chair for her.

"Ms. Harrison-Rice, this is Dr. Henri Gautreau."

A waitress approached in a tuxedo shirt, cummerbund, black tie, and miniskirt.

Millie waited until her pencil was poised before saying, "Glenlivet, double."

Dr. Gautreau said, "Another Sam Adams." He had a very slight French accent.

Anders said, "I'll switch to coffee." When the waitress was gone he looked at Millie and raised his eyebrows. "A double?"

"I've had a hard day. *You* should know exactly how hard." She looked down at her feet. "I've still got blood on my boots!"

His glance flickered sideways to Dr. Gautreau. He held up his hands. "Acknowledged. It's just not over, you know."

It? The day, or the whole mess? "Then you'll have to keep me safe, while I'm 'impaired.' " She turned to Dr. Gautreau and said brightly, "And what is Dr. Gautreau, when he is at home?"

He smiled. "I'm an anthropologist."

Anders added. "It was quite a coincidence, really. Our Mexico analyst pool has a couple of indigenous language experts but none of them knew more than a few words of Lacandon. Dr. Gautreau was attending a symposium at the Smithsonian this week."

Millie's eyebrows raised. "The Ruizes? When they weren't speaking Spanish?"

Dr. Gautreau nodded. He was dressed in a rumpled suit and his tie had clearly been removed earlier—bunched, it stuck out of the breast pocket of his jacket like a distempered cabbage. He had a tightly trimmed beard and long, wild hair pulled back from his face by a knotted piece of Guatemalan cloth.

"I hope I am able to help. I would not, though, if I hadn't been assured that Señora Ruiz and her family weren't the subjects of this investigation, but only witnesses."

"That's certainly my understanding, Professor." She looked

at Anders. "The FBI isn't going to turn them over to the INS are they, because of their immigration status?"

Anders shook his head. "The FBI doesn't know about the Ruizes. They're helping us, but we're not giving them access to our raw ELINT."

Millie frowned and opened her mouth to speak.

He held up his hand. "Don't worry. We've already passed the datum about the angel on the ambulance door and they're scrambling. But they don't know about the Ruizes per se. We'll pass all the useful info."

Millie subsided. That had been her concern.

Dr. Gautreau frowned. "There are less than five hundred of her people in existence. Before I leave here, I'm going to offer to take them back with me."

"Was that five hundred before or after her village was wiped out?"

"Both. Señora Ruiz's second husband wasn't *Hach Winik*, but *Nahuat*. It was a *Nahuat* village that was destroyed when she fled."

"How do you know this?"

"I divide my time between the Museum of Anthropology in Mexico City and Chiapas. It's where I live. I'm painfully aware of each and every known atrocity in Chiapas. I've also met Nuk before."

"Her youngest daughter, the albino?"

"No. Nuk is also Señora Ruiz's first name. She originally came from Naha, the northern Lacandon community."

Millie looked at Anders. "Just how much of the conversation did you record?"

"There were a few words lost to ambient noises. Dishes on the table. Other diners. Not many. Signal processing is, after all, what we do."

"So what were the Ruizes saying, when they spoke in Lo— Lacandon?"

"Yes. Or, *Hach Winik* is what they would call it."

The waitress brought their drinks and Gautreau waited until she was gone before saying, "What was really interesting to me was the differences between what they said and what your translator said."

"He wasn't translating them correctly? Deliberately?"

"Oh, no—not deliberately. Most of it seems to be religious bias. For instance, every time he said God, Señora Ruiz or her daughters had either named a particular Lacandon god or said gods. The translator—Porfiro?—kept suggesting *La Madonna* for anything feminine, but she wouldn't have it, and he just fell back on God, finally."

"Was that during the interchange when she said that D.C. was on the way to Naha?"

"Yes. What she really said was that in a series of dreams it was revealed that she couldn't go home unless she came here first. That all her other choices were bad. She also said that now she could go home." He shook his head. "Obviously, this is where I'm meant to come in." His expression was matter-of-fact.

"Like she knew you'd help her home?" Anders snorted. "That's pushing things, isn't it?"

Millie stared at Dr. Gautreau, bemused. She pursed her lips, then said to Anders, "You're the one who said 'it's quite a coincidence, really.'"

Dr. Gautreau just smiled and sipped his beer.

Millie turned back to the anthropologist. "I heard them actually say *La Llorona*. Porfiro didn't make that up, right?"

"Yes, and no. The girls suggested *La Llorona* but first they suggested *U Na'il Kisin*, the wife of the god of death and earthquakes." He laughed. "At another point, their mother even suggested that their journey to D.C. was due to the intervention of *Hesuklitos*, but Porfiro didn't recognize that this is actually the inclusion of Jesus Christ in the Lacandon pantheon. They consider Christ the son of *Äkyantho*, the god of foreigners, and therefore a very *minor* deity." He shrugged. "They're quite open minded about other religions. Almost the Unitarians of Mesoamerica."

This is all very well but . . . She took a large swallow of her Scotch, almost grateful for the burning sensation in her throat. "Is there anything they said, that we don't know, that will help us locate my husband?"

"Hmmm. I'm not sure if I'm the best judge of that. There were several things they did say that didn't get translated or weren't translated correctly. There was a speculation that your husband was actually one of the assistants to the rain god, *Mensäbäk*, who are the *Hahanak'uh* or "Water House Gods." In particular, they were thinking he might be *Xämän*, who also represents north. The *Hahanak'uh* create thunder when *Kisin* exposes his buttocks to them, making them angry." He frowned. "I've been around the *Lacandon* for fifteen years but I've never heard them talk about a living person this way."

Anders lifted his head. "They're just children, after all."

Dr. Gautreau looked at Anders with a level, skeptical gaze. Finally he said, "In fifteen years I've talked to a lot of Lacandon children, too. It's *still* unusual to me."

Millie shook her head. *If you only knew.* "*Kisin*? Is that the god they thought the woman was? *La Llorona*?"

"Her husband. To the Lacandon, the gods are like people. They have spouses and children and one parent, *K'akoch*, who made the flower that all the other gods were born from, and doesn't care at all about the affairs of humans. They are subject to a lot of the same constraints, too, that people are."

He looked at the outspread fingers of his hand. "Hmm. There was an additional description of *La Llorona* as possibly being *N'ail Äkyantho'*, the wife of the god of foreigners, but they rejected it immediately. The Lacandon describe *Äkyantho'* as a light-skinned man carrying a gun, as foreigners carry a gun, so it was probably her weapon that made them consider this."

That reminded Millie of something the children had said. "They said her eyes were bleeding black, or at least Porfiro translated it like that. Do you have a take on that?"

Dr. Gautreau pursed his lips. "The kids pretty much said just that. It was raining though. Mascara?" He traced his fingers down his face like tears.

"Perhaps."

Anders said, "She's probably the fake waitress from Interrobang—the one who drugged him. The description was of a young woman with heavy makeup. We tried to do a composite, but the different witnesses came up with wildly varying images. Lots of makeup, though. That they did agree upon."

"Ah. Is there anything in the description of the ambulance that didn't get translated? Or the people."

He shrugged. "The facts are pretty much all there. The interpretations that the Ruizes gave it were quite different."

Millie took the last of her Scotch and swirled it in the glass before swallowing it. She was starting to feel the alcohol now, a glow in the stomach and a relaxation in the shoulders. "I wonder," she posited, "if I should ask Señora Ruiz where to find Davy?"

Dr. Gautreau shook his head. "It doesn't work like that. Ninety-nine percent of all Lacandon dream interpretations are, uh, negative—not informational. The depiction of danger, sickness, or bad luck to come. As Porfiro and Señora Ruiz said, it's not fixed. Forewarned is forearmed, but finding things or people is not part of the tradition. When she left you, she said, 'Sleep well you. Be careful what you see.' Dream, in other words. It's the traditional goodnight, but it shows what they think about predictions. Not only can dreams of trouble help you avoid it, but there's an implication that controlling what you dream also keeps you from trouble."

"She did tell me not to sleep in my room tonight."

"I was once warned by a Hach Winik not to travel to a particular village because of a dream I had. Because it was late in the day, I stayed with my hosts overnight. The next day, when I drove that road, bodies were everywhere. There had been a battle between the paramilitaries and the EZLN." Dr. Gautreau tilted his head down and looked at Millie intently. "If she had said that to *me*, I would change hotels immediately."

Anders looked uncomfortable. "I don't believe in dream warnings, but it might not be such a bad idea, after all. Especially considering Mr. Padgett is still at large and—" he looked down "—the blood on your boots."

TEN

"Tantrums, you know."

There were four blank end pages in the last signature of *The Count of Monte Cristo*. Davy tore them out carefully, under the covers in the middle of the night. Initially, he hid them in his pillow case, but in the morning he slipped them, folded in tight creases, next to the roller of the toilet paper dispenser inside the cardboard tube.

He wanted a pen or a pencil, but if worse came to worst, he could improvise something using food or, he shuddered, other substances he'd been seeing too much of lately.

What he wanted, really, was to send a message to Millie.

Dearest Millie. Have been kidnapped and wired for electricity. Hope you are well. Davy.

He laughed to himself, but felt his eyes sting suddenly and took a shuddering breath. *Too close?*

He'd been avoiding even the thought of Millie. If he even started thinking about her, there were too many things to worry about.

Did she get out of the Aerie safely? Does she have any idea what happened in D.C. or did she just think I abandoned her after our fight? If she did find out about my kidnapping does she realize I'm alive? Is the NSA watching out for her and is that a good thing? Is she actively looking for me and, therefore, in danger of being found by these psychopaths?

And that was the biggest worry of all.

His hands hurt and he looked down, surprised. His finger-nails had left a series of curved lines across the palms of his hands. He consciously relaxed his fingers, then rubbed at the marks with his thumbs. *Could use some fingernail clippers.*

Could use a lot of things.

He shook the chains. *Freedom to leave this place. Freedom from observation. Freedom to go to Millie.* He felt his hands clenching into fists again and grabbed the chains, instead. He jerked heavily on them, an up and down motion, and they cracked against the wall, chipping the paint. He took all four chains in his hand and jumped ten feet back, still facing the wall, to the extent of the chains' reach. The chains jerked rigid, but did very little to the wall. Instead, Davy was yanked forward onto his hands and knees.

Oh! He froze, staring at the floor, hammered by a sudden realization. It wasn't the grief he'd been avoiding by not think-ing of Millie, of the things taken and kept away from him.

It's rage.

He jumped to the bathroom door, bracing automatically as the chains whipped around and cracked into the wall. Then to the opposite side, by the bed. Sheetrock cracked and paint chips dropped to the floor under the impact. The noise was awful.

The noise was wonderful.

He jumped again, alternating sides, accentuating the effects by timing his leaps to correspond with the sinusoidal waves running down the chains. His wrists and ankles were being wrenched painfully and he was aware of this, on some level, but on another, it didn't matter at all. Sheetrock was exploding away from the edges of the hole. Entire foot-wide sections were cracked, hanging off by the thinnest shreds of paper lam-inate. Sheetrock dust hung in the air, dancing eddies of parti-cles stirred by the whipping of steel links through the air.

And then he was standing in the square, in the green box, his throat tingling from the aftermath of the warning signal.

He rocked on his feet, surprised. He hadn't been conscious of a cough. He wondered if he'd mistaken some physical reaction—the dust in the air would make anybody cough—and had jumped in response, but when he leaned over the green tape, it was there. The tingle in his throat, the incipient nausea.

He stepped back to the center of square, blinking, his nose suddenly itching from all the dust in the air. He surveyed the damage. The hole from which the chains emerged was three feet high, exposing upright two-by-four studs and a smaller hole in the Sheetrock on the other side of the studs, the wall of the adjacent room. That room was as unlit as ever, but there was enough light coming in through the newly enlarged hole that Davy had high hopes of actually seeing what lay beyond when the field was shut off again. But the wall was a real mess.

Hmmm. They're not going to like this.

They kept him "in the box" for hours. They did not bring him lunch.

His first awareness that he was no longer "in the box" was the computerized voice. "You have two minutes to use the restroom."

He didn't need telling twice. For the past hour he'd been considering peeing on the floor. When he'd finished, they reeled the chains in through the now larger hole in the wall. He crouched and looked through, keeping to the edge to allow light through.

It took him a minute for his eyes to adjust. It was a small room with a bed and dresser stacked against one wall, crowded, as if they'd been pushed out of the way to make room for the large drummed marine electric winch that had been bolted to the middle of the floor.

The door opened and Davy turned around, suddenly very nervous. *Of course, if they wanted to punish me, they could've just turned off the field.*

Miss Minchin led in two men, dressed like maintenance staff, though they did wear the ubiquitous paper surgical mask, as did Miss Minchin. She pointed to a spot just inside the yellow square about halfway between the green box and the bathroom door. "About here, I suppose. Make sure and straddle one of the floor thingies. The beams." In addition to the masks they were wearing rubber gloves.

"The joist," said the first man, thumping a half-inch-thick, foot-square steel plate onto the floor.

"Whatever!" Miss Minchin snapped. More calmly she said, "Keep your masks on. Believe me, you don't want to catch his disease. And keep your tools in the hall unless they're in your hand."

She walked across the floor to Davy and said quietly, for his ears alone, "I'm going to be in there—" she pointed at the mirror "—with my hand on the button. You say one word to them and you'll be puking and coughing all over the place." Then she leaned forward and added, "And I'll have to kill them." She jerked her head minutely back toward the middle of the room. "Got it?"

Davy considered head-butting her in the nose. He took a deep breath and said quietly, "Got it."

He couldn't see her lips smile but he saw it at the corners of her eyes and her cheekbones.

"That's Mama's little angel." She turned back to the men and said to the two workmen, "Quick as possible. We'll be getting you the chains in a moment."

She exited the room without looking back.

When the door had shut, the man closest to the door said, "Now thaaaat's what comes from keepen your dildo in the freeeeezah."

The other man laughed nervously. "Don't. I helped wire this room for sound."

The man grunted. "Ah." He began tapping the various spots on the floor with his hammer until it made a less hollow sound, then slid the plate to that point. "There. Take the other plate downstairs—I'll drill the holes and drop the bolts through and you can get the nuts on, eh? Then you can bring the welder when you come back." He tapped the floor. "And a fire extinguisher. Just in case."

I know that accent. It was an extreme New England accent, only different. *I've been where they speak like that.*

The man who stayed behind used a long-shafted half-inch drill bit to drill through the floor, using the corner holes on the plate as a guide. In less than fifteen minutes, they'd bolted the plate to the floor, presumably anchored to an identical plate in the ceiling below. The two ankle chains were cut with an abrasive wheel in the room behind him, and Miss Minchin came back into the room to pull them through. They measured the distance from the plate into the bathroom, and then trimmed the chain back.

One of them took a U-bolt out of his pocket. It had been bent so that the open end was at a right angle to the closed loop. They threaded last links of the chain onto it and began welding it to the plate.

Davy coughed. His throat tingled. He jumped, even before he thought, but slammed back against the wall, his shoulders flaring with pain. He stared wide-eyed at Miss Minchin. "Did you turn it off?"

The two workmen looked up. They hadn't seen him try to jump but they heard the sound of his back hitting the wall.

Miss Minchin frowned and looked at the mirror.

The computerized voice spoke over the speaker. "It's the arc welder. It's jamming the signal. It'll be all right if they keep their arcs under one second."

"We can do that," said the welder.

"No!" Miss Minchin said. "The conditioning will be compromised." She pulled the welding unit's plug from the wall socket. "Wait," she told the welder. "He's got an electronic prosthesis. You could kill him." She left the room at a run.

One second? Is that the new time limit between warning and full-out convulsions?

Miss Minchin came back carrying a plastic box with a short, stubby antennae. She walked right up to Davy and held it out, toward his chest. Davy started to reach for it and she slapped his hand. "Hands off, vomit-boy." She turned a dial and said to the welder. "Try it."

He tapped the electrode to the plate and there was a flash, but this time there was no tingle, no cough.

Miss Minchin held her thumb up. "Looks good."

They started to weld in earnest and the overhead fluorescent lights went off and a small emergency light, mounted in the corner, came on.

"Sonofabitch," said the welder.

His partner voice said, "It's just the breaker. I'll get it." He left, propping the door open. Distant sunlight showed dimly in the hall.

Miss Minchin backed away from Davy and looked at the mirror. "What's the status on the primary?"

There was no reply.

Hmmmm. Are they out over there, too? He stared at the box in Miss Minchin's hands. "Would I be puking if you didn't have that here?"

She looked at him, apparently thinking it over. Finally, she clicked it off. There was no tingle. "See? The primary is on a battery backup. The green square is always safe."

The lights came back on. When the workman came back, he said, "It's a thirty amp breaker, but there's a lot of other equipment on the circuit. You'll have to keep the welding current down."

"Can't they shut down the other stuff?"

"No," said Miss Minchin. She turned the box back on.

They shrugged and went back to work at the lower setting. It seemed to take forever.

Miss Minchin kept her eyes on Davy, but her hands relaxed a bit and the device tilted forward enough that Davy could see the faceplate. It was a gray plastic prototype enclosure of the sort you could buy at RadioShack. Its only features were the antennae, an LED power indicator, and a rotary switch marked OFF, 2m, 10m, 30m, 100m, and 500m in magic marker. The switch pointed to 500m.

Meters?

They kept pouring water on the plate, to keep the floor from catching on fire. Davy was sorry to see the resulting weld looked quite solid.

Miss Minchin turned off the box and put it in the hallway.

"We'll just go get the plywood now?" the workman said, half telling, half asking.

Miss Minchin nodded. Then, to Davy's surprise, as soon as they'd left she took a key from her pocket and unlocked the padlocks on his wrist restraints using the same small key.

He eyed the key thoughtfully.

She said, "Don't even think about it. You'd be in convulsions before you could get it into the first lock."

With the cuffs off, his wrists showed raw and red, almost scaly. He rubbed them carefully, resisting the urge to scratch until he bled. Miss Minchin backed away to one side, clear of the chains, and said, "In the box."

He didn't wait for the warning cough, jumping immediately. He braced, from habit, for the pull of the chains on his wrists, but they weren't there anymore and he fell over backward, his feet jerked out from under him.

Miss Minchin laughed.

Davy sat up gingerly, keeping his face impassive, but he could feel his ears heat up. He checked the border, out of curiosity. He was indeed "in the box."

Miss Minchin coiled the now unused chains and wrist restraints, and tossed them through the hole into the other room. After a moment, the workmen came back with a sheet of half-inch plywood, which they fastened to the wall over the broken Sheetrock, anchoring it to the studs with two-inch screws.

"You want us to clean up this stuff, Ma'am?" They indicated the broken Sheetrock scattered on the floor.

"No."

They nodded and left.

Miss Minchin tore the mask off her face. She turned to the mirror. "Let him out."

Davy tested the edge of the field, then stepped out. His arms felt unnaturally light without the chains. Still, the chains on his ankles pulled as heavily as ever on his legs. *And on my spirit.* He touched the scar on his chest. *But the real chains lie here.*

Miss Minchin said, "Better see if you can reach the bathroom."

He found that he could sit on the toilet if his legs were extended. He tried the shower. "I won't be able to stand in the tub." The chains were too short. They'd measured into the tub but hadn't accounted for the angle up and down over its edge.

Miss Minchin came to the door and looked. "Take baths. Let your legs hang over the edge." She went back to the door. As she went out she said, "It's your own fault. Tantrums, you know."

She hadn't said, "Clean up this mess," but that seemed the implication. On his new shortened leash, he couldn't walk up to most of the walls but he could reach them. Since they'd removed the wrist restraints, he could get down on his hands and knees and stretch out to pick up the chunks of Sheetrock.

While he was piling them together he found the screw, one of the two-inch Sheetrock screws that they'd used to fasten down the plywood. It was up against one of the pieces of Sheetrock and half-buried in Sheetrock dust.

He palmed it and continued to clean up. While the mop bucket was filling, he used the toilet, then slipped the screw into the toilet paper roll, with his scraps of paper.

Unfortunately, it looked too large to get into the key holes on the padlocks of the ankle restraints, but he would check, in the night.

They put him in the box ten times before supper, then several times through the night, on some random basis. He wondered how they decided. Did a computer program tell them, using some random number generator? Or was it scheduled weeks in advance? Or did they just wait until he was fully asleep, to maximize his confusion and thoroughly disrupt his rest?

He pictured them behind the mirror. Sometimes he imagined them watching intently, some savage smile lingering on their lips, laughing each time they sent him to the box, drinking his misery with eager eyes. His other image was much worse—a man not even watching, bored, reading some magazine or book, and only reaching out to poke the switch when some timer went off. Then, glancing briefly through the window to make sure he was actually in the box, before turning back to his book. Oh, yeah—and yawning.

This second image chilled him because he thought it more likely. How could someone do this to another human without mentally placing him in the category of "thing" first? Passion implied involvement. He suspected Miss Minchin of some form of involvement. But the others?

Under the covers, in the night, he tried the screw on the padlocks of the ankle restraints but his earlier suspicion was correct. It was too thick.

It was sharp, though. For one bleak moment he thought about using it to pop his jugulars, covers pulled up to his chin. They wouldn't find out until they put him in the box or noticed the blood dripping under the mattress. It wasn't a serious thought, though.

Not yet.

Of more serious consideration was a bit of surgery, on his chest or lower neck, to see if he could disable the device. *With a sharp screw, no antiseptics, and no anesthetic. Sounds like fun to me!*

He shoved the screw beneath his pillow and turned. A mattress coil creaked as he shifted his weight.

Hmmm. There are other things that can be torn by a sharp screw.

He didn't rip the cloth cover of the mattress. He was pretty sure what he wanted to do would take a lot longer than one night, and he would need to conceal the effort. So, his first session he settled for painstakingly opening the bottom seam of his mattress, near the corner next to the wall. Left alone, the weight of the mattress held it closed. With the fitted bottom sheet in place, it was undetectable.

Unless they look.

He left the screw tucked inside the mattress.

An hour later, after two turns in the box, he resumed his work. His goal was the wire from a coil spring—one of the interior coils to avoid a detectable sag in the edge. It took him the rest of the night to cut his way between two border coils and through the pocket of one of the interior coils. The fabric didn't rip, even when he'd started a good hole with the screw. He had to saw, roughly, with the threads, then tug, then saw some more.

Everything was one-handed, as he had to work without apparent movement, lying on his stomach, face buried in the pillow, only one arm over the edge of the bed.

Then they put him in the box and he nearly tore open his arm pulling it out between the coils as he jumped. Another time he didn't let go of the screw and nearly dropped it on the floor in the box. He sat on the floor quickly, back to the mirror, and hid it between the stainless steel band and the inner padding of his ankle restraints.

By morning, he had the coil completely exposed, but the tops and bottom of the spring were fastened to the wire frame by crimped metal clips and they eluded his initial efforts to wrench it free.

He left the screw inside the mattress and gave up for that night. This time, he was ready for sleep.

After breakfast, Miss Minchin entered the room. She was dragging a chain that went around the edge of the door and she carried a pair of felt slippers and a heavy bathrobe.

"In the box."

He complied immediately, from choice—not reflex. He wanted to give her an impression of cooperation for the moment.

She walked forward and stopped five feet from the edge. "Lie down—stick your feet out to me."

He did, keeping his upper chest inside the green tape. She unlocked his left ankle restraint but, instead of removing it, she switched chains, locking the padlock to the new chain that ran out the door. Then she unlocked the right ankle, but this time she completely removed the restraint, dropping it on the floor and leaving the small padlock beside it, still open.

She straightened back up and took a radio from her pocket—not the plastic box she'd had before, but a scrambled handheld transceiver. "We're ready here. You?"

"Switching on. On," said a voice from the radio.

She slid the bathrobe and the slippers across to Davy. "Come on, boy. Walkies."

He scrambled to his feet staring at her.

She walked to the door, then paused. "Well, I suppose you can stay here if you want."

He threw on the robe and tested the border. They were

broadcasting a larger signal, apparently, for there was no warning tingle at the green tape or the yellow. He pushed his feet into the slightly large slippers and walked forward, coiling the chain as he went.

It felt very odd, going through the door—surprisingly difficult.

He'd been expecting some sort of institutional setting—some sort of clinic, but the hallway was clearly not that. It was manorial—old and elegant. Carved or molded accents decorated wainscoted walls. There were small dark, satin-finished side tables adorned with bowls of fresh flowers. At the far end of the hall there was an actual window, framed by heavy drapes, where bright sunlight puddled on the thick carpet and made his eyes tear.

The outside.

The chain ran the other direction, away from the window, and ended, Davie saw, just down the hall. A heavy furniture hand truck stood there and strapped to it was an upright cylinder, one and a half feet across and two feet high. He took a step closer and saw that it was concrete cast in an iron pipe. The end of the chain was secured to a U-bolt projecting from the cement.

Miss Minchin led him toward it. "You'll need to push this along."

Davy eyed it and tried to remember how much concrete weighed per cubic foot. The pipe itself was at least a half-inch in thickness, a significant weight even without the concrete. He tried to tilt the dolly back on its wheels but didn't succeed until he'd braced one foot and leaned far back. The little plate on the back of the dolly said it was rated to 700 pounds, but the way it creaked, he strongly suspected it was overloaded. He balanced it carefully, looping the coil of chain he'd been gathering over his arm.

If I jumped, I bet it would come with me—all seven hundred pounds. He remembered moving entire loaded bookshelves—not huge ones, but weighty enough—and once a small refrigerator when he and Millie had purchased the condo in Stillwater.

And where would I be, then? Flopping on the floor and vomiting? Perhaps going into cardiac arrest? And when I try to jump back "in the box" I won't have the coordination to bring the weight with me.

He looked at Miss Minchin and raised an eyebrow.

She pointed down the hall, the direction he was facing. "There's an elevator."

They passed a door on the right and Davy made himself ignore it. The doorway was in the right place to lead to the observation room on the other side of the mirror.

The elevator was on the left, at the end of the hall, wood-paneled doors, wood-paneled interior, a cut glass insert, a small mirror. There was barely room for Miss Minchin, Davy, *and* the handcart. Miss Minchin took the opportunity to stand a little closer than necessary. Davy found his body reacting to her warmth and scent.

He shuddered.

Remember Cox. Remember she put a bullet in his head and she'd do the same to me if they ever decide I won't cooperate.

The elevator controls showed four levels, basement through third. They were apparently on the third floor now, for Ms. Minchin had pressed One and they'd passed another floor. They exited into another, taller hallway—grander—opening on a hotel-lobby-sized living room, a parlor, and a large, formal dining room with runway table.

Miss Minchin diverted him down a smaller hallway, to his right, and they passed a large kitchen, a laundry room with multiple washers, dryers, and a heavy duty commercial ironing station.

This is somebody's grand house—a mansion, really.

"Servants' day off?"

Miss Minchin didn't respond and he concluded that they'd cleared them out before bringing him through.

At the end of the smaller hallway there was an exterior door, white with rows and rows of four-inch beveled glass panes, and beyond that, a porch overlooking a walled expanse of brown grass bisected by a walkway that ran straight across to a cast iron gate in the far wall. An undulating border of evergreen plants ran beneath the walls and a dry stone fountain decorated the corner. The air was cold but the sun was up and the walls blocked what wind there was. Davy took a moment to tie the robe shut.

"To your right," Miss Minchin said, from behind him.

There was a wheelchair ramp, running down beside the building, then turning into a down-sloping path that curved through winter-mulched flower beds where the barest tips of early tulips or irises were poking up through the straw. The hand truck wanted to run away on the slope and it took all of Davy's concentration to keep it under control. This curving path rejoined the main walk back near the porch.

Miss Minchin led him to the center of the yard.

"There." Miss Minchin pointed. Someone had dug a hole beside the walk, roughly the size of the cylinder. She stepped up beside Davy and tilted the hand truck forward. The cylinder bounced down hard on its base, then fell forward with a thud that could be felt through the ground. She rolled the cylinder until its end was over the mouth of the hole, then pushed down with most of her weight, to tip it on into the hole.

She had to pull her foot back quickly to avoid getting it caught when the cylinder dropped, but she managed, just in time.

Too bad.

He swore at himself. *I should've jumped to the Adams Cowley Shock Trauma Center.* If any one place could've kept him alive and figured out what was causing his convulsions, it would be them. Now, cylinder down in the hole, there'd be no moving it.

Miss Minchin wheeled the hand truck back toward the porch and dropped it on the brown grass just short of the steps.

Well, maybe I would've survived.

Davy took a deep breath and blinked. *The sea?* There was a whiff of salt air and the more pungent odor of low tide. As if to confirm it, he heard the cry of a single seagull, *lonely and haunting solo and raucous in company.* He thought back to the workman's accent. *Martha's Vineyard?*

Or maybe Nantucket? He'd never been on Nantucket but he'd spent several days bicycling around Martha's Vineyard once. He didn't *stay* there, but had jumped daily, right before Memorial Day. He'd tried it after Memorial Day, too, but it was far too crowded. The accent, once heard, was unforgettable. He'd heard that the accent on Nantucket was similar, only more so.

And there are mansions.

It would explain all the seafood.

He pushed on the top of the concrete cylinder with his toe. It didn't budge in the slightest, as if it were part of some massive rock outcropping reaching up from the bones of the earth. He was puzzled. It would take a crane to get the weight back out of that hole, but its placement looked deliberate and long-term. *Are they going to leave me out here in the open to graze upon the grass?*

The brick walls enclosing the three sides of the yard joined the corners of the house and were at least eight feet high. The cast iron gate at the far end had gaps between the bars, but all he could see was a distant garage door framed by leafless shrubbery at the end of a gravel path. The house, as he'd noticed in the elevator, was three stories above ground, but there were big dormer windows jutting from the roof, hinting at substantial space in the attic. The basement was clearly evident, too, both in the windows peeking above window wells and the stairs opposite the wheelchair ramp, leading down to a door under the porch.

His eyes were slowly getting used to the light, and now he lifted his eyes to the sky, bright and blue and cloud-free. He took a deep breath. There were contrails high overhead and, after a moment's searching, he spied a lower jetliner. *Hmm. Bound for Logan?* If so, the house was north of him, and the gateway south. This certainly matched the sun's position.

Unless I'm totally wrong about where I am.

Miss Minchin was sitting on the porch steps watching him. He decided to ignore her. The chain allowed him a forty-foot circle that kept him pretty much on the grass, five feet short of the walls' border shrubbery and twenty feet from the gate and porch.

He shivered. To warm up he walked the perimeter—counter-clockwise since his left ankle was constrained by the chain. *I'll wear a groove in the grass if they leave me here long enough. Like a dog on a chain.* He swung his arms and scuffed his feet as much as possible in the short grass. A circle would be visible from the air, from satellite. *Like a dog on a chain—and that's what they would think.* He stopped scuffing.

After fifteen minutes of this, Miss Minchin talked into her radio. He heard the static and a voice in reply, but couldn't make out what was said. She stood and came up the walk, halting where the arc of his circle crossed the cement. She tossed something shiny onto the ground and, curious, he approached.

It was a key, presumably the key to the padlock. He looked at her. She was holding the radio to her mouth and watching him.

He crouched and took it, still watching her. When she didn't say anything, he moved it toward the padlock.

"Now," she said, into the radio.

He felt the tingle in his throat and coughed. The key wouldn't go in, but then he turned it one hundred and eighty degrees and it slipped in, twisted, and the lock popped open. He got it out of the hasp, pulled the restraint open, and jumped.

He was in the box, gasping.

He had tried to go to Adams Cowley. He had pictured Adams Cowley.

He'd ended up here.

The computerized voice said, "Put the manacle on."

He jumped—not to Adams Cowley, not home to the Aerie, not to the condo in Stillwater. He jumped to the hallway, right outside the observation room, and opened that door. Even as he did so, he coughed and his throat tingled, but he managed, for one instant, to look at the three men inside the room, before his body flinched back to the box.

He closed his eyes, trying to eke everything he could out of the one glimpse. He'd seen a darkened room with a counter under the tinted window, a microphone, video monitors, a video camera, and three men.

Three startled men, staring back over their shoulders at the open door, their eyes wide open with surprise. One of them was Thug Two, the red-haired, hook-nosed man, and another was Thug One, the blonde he'd thrown against the wall. The blonde was still wearing a foam cervical collar, souvenir of his last encounter with Davy. Davy hoped it had hurt when he'd been compelled to twist to face the door. He hadn't seen the third man before. He was older, with a white lab jacket, dark hair gone mostly gray, glasses, sharp long nose. One of the video monitors had shown the bathroom tub and toilet and a rim of the sink, bright and clear, even though the bathroom light was off and the door shut.

Darkness will not hide me.

The computerized voice said, "Now! No more tricks. Put the manacle on."

Davy coughed and felt the tingle in his throat

But I'm in the box!

He considered, for the barest instant, not obeying. It would counteract some of the conditioning, if they sent him into convulsions "in the box." It would be a grave mistake, on their part.

But he couldn't make himself face that—not now.

He crouched and put the padded restraint over his ankle, threaded the padlock shackle onto the last link of the chain, and put it through the hasp on the restraint. He twisted the padlock shackle into alignment and pretended to push it shut, using the motion of his hands to rap the body of the padlock against the stainless steel of the outer cuff with a muffled click.

Weirder things had happened. They might not check.

The tingle stopped and he exhaled a breath he hadn't realized he'd been holding. He checked the border—he was still "in the box." So he dropped to the floor cross-legged with the unlatched padlock hidden beneath his calf.

They left him "in the box" for forty-five minutes. He imagined them talking to Miss Minchin and plotting a new punishment for him, but now that they'd removed the winch, there was nothing to pull him physically out of the box.

He imagined them doing it directly, muscle against muscle, maybe sending Thug Two in, but they probably remembered what had happened with Thug One. Davy looked over at the wall—the depression from the blonde's shoulder and hip were still visible.

Let them come. He wasn't feeling that manageable just yet.

Miss Minchin entered the room and he tensed. He could slip off the manacle and jump behind her, drop her in the pit in west Texas, and be back in the box before the full convulsions kicked in. *But I'd still be in the box at the end of it.*

Miss Minchin said, "Stick out your foot."

He extended the one without the manacle.

"Ha, bloody ha. The other foot." She raised her hand to the mirror, three fingers extended. She retracted one of them, waited a beat, and retracted the other.

Reluctantly, he extended his foot.

She looked at the open padlock and sighed, then looked meaningfully at the mirror. "Do I have to do *everything*!" She gestured at Davy. "Shut the padlock, vomit-boy."

"Shut it yourself." He pulled it from the hasp and tossed it across the room, followed by the ankle restraint. He stood up.

He didn't think he could lose this one. If they went ahead and sent him into convulsions, in the square, it would counteract the conditioning. He was visualizing the trauma center at Adams Cowley, ready to jump.

She looked down at the lock and manacle, then back up at him. "Don't mess with me, vomit-boy. You'll regret it."

He slapped her in the face, starting the swing before jumping. The impact swung her head around. She lashed out but he was already back in the box, his arm dropping to his side. The cough and tingle were momentarily there but fading already.

Miss Minchin had dropped back, eyes wide, hands raised, body flinching into some sort of martial arts stance. Davy's handprint was vivid on her cheek.

"Probably." Regret it, he meant. Davy held his breath, waiting, expecting the warning buzz. It didn't come. *What's a boy got to do?*

He jumped, swept her rear foot from behind and was back in the square before she hit the ground. She rolled to her feet again, her hand held palm out to the mirror, as if to say, "wait."

He slapped the top of her head, hard, from behind, and she kicked back, cobra fast, but he was back in the square and she was dancing on one foot, off balance. She turned and reached for the doorknob but he knocked her spinning away with a body slam.

She scrambled up. This time, instead of going for the door, she came at him. He walked toward her slowly, despite the cough, and, when she committed herself to a front kick, jumped behind her, reached out and grabbed her collar. Both feet went out from under her and she landed hard, on her back.

This time, back in the square, he coughed again. An odd mix of dread and relief coursed through him. He waited—he wanted to be in full convulsions when he arrived, hopefully unable to jump. If he could survive anywhere, it would be in the Trauma Center.

He . . . jumped.

He blinked as the lighting changed and he was on hospital tile, doubled over, vomiting, coughing, defecating. His vision was tunneling down but he saw a pair of legs in scrubs turn toward him, a voice saying, "What the—"

No!

He was back in the box, on all fours, the vomiting stopped, weak as an infant *and soiled like one*. He saw movement out of the corner of his eye and turned his head just as Miss Minchin kicked him in the face.

ELEVEN

"A cup of tea."

Curtis took her out into the Virginia suburbs and said, "Pick one. I'm pretty sure we're clean and our escort says the same."

Millie blinked. *Escort?* She swallowed. "Right." She didn't waste any time watching for the watchers. The cab was cruising a strip of hotels and stores. She saw a Comfort Inn with the vacancy sign lit beside a twenty-four-hour drugstore. "That one," she said. "Drop me at the drugstore, first. Need some things."

He pulled up. "Use the bug if you need help, or when you're ready," he said. "We'll be around."

"Sure," she said. *If I need anything I'll just talk to my bra.*

At the drugstore she picked up a toothbrush, toothpaste, deodorant, and a package of cotton underwear decorated with cartoon characters. *Davy would like these*, she thought. *Well, he'd like to take them off . . .* It was one of his favorite lines. "You know, that sweater would look *marvelous . . .* on the bedroom floor."

She felt an ache of desire, of longing, of anger. *Damn you, Davy. Get your ass back here. I need to get laid.*

She paid cash for her purchases, then cash again at the hotel, using a false name on the registration card. When she was in the room, a second floor unit unfortunately close to the ice machine, she tried to relax.

The evening before, she'd been unable to sleep because Sojee was in the room. Now, she wanted Sojee back. Being hunted through the museum and attacked in the streets certainly changed the tenor of things.

Yesterday her search had been colored with feelings of hopeless desperation, of a search conducted for a needle lost in a limitless sea. Her motions and efforts had been driven by a need to be actually *doing something*. Now, when the hopeless scope of her search had revealed the faintest narrowing of possibilities, it was almost more painful than the previous abject hopelessness.

But the desperation is still there. She laughed at herself. *At least* some *things remain the same.*

She got into a hot bath, trying to relax as much as she could, but she couldn't come close to unwinding until she had climbed out and, dripping, leaned one of the room's two chairs against the door to the hallway and the other against the connecting door to the adjacent room. They wouldn't stop anyone capable of defeating the locks and bolts, but they'd make noise.

Then she sank back in the tiny tub and let the heat work on her neck and upper back muscles.

The second year of their marriage, Davy had taken a six-week massage course. The thought of his hands on her neck and back brought tears to her eyes. She sank back in the water, to let the tears wash away, but when she came back up, her nose had started to run. She could reach the toilet paper, but it disintegrated and stuck to her wet hands, useless.

She was stretching up for the thin hotel towel when she heard a heavy impact and the sound of splintering wood followed almost immediately by someone swearing and stumbling heavily. She heard the chair kicked violently forward, crashing against the dresser and then—

It wasn't a conscious thing. Her heart gave a tremendous thud and adrenaline surged through her, and she was sitting naked on the living room floor in her condo in Oklahoma with a surprising amount of water soaking the carpet.

Oh. My. God.

She scrambled through the dark room, to *her* bathroom, in a daze, surprised to find the old familiar towels and even Davy's ratty terrycloth bathrobe. She buried her face in it, clutching the robe like a drowning woman grabbing at a life buoy.

Jumping.

The damn thing was a pain but thank God it was there when she really needed it. Not wanted. She hadn't had time to *want*. She'd heard the circumstances of Davy's first jumps, but the sheer emotional force—well, she suspected she understood a bit more, now.

Here, a time zone to the west and slightly farther south than D.C., bright twilight still showed through the blinds, but it was dim in the apartment. She put her hand on the bathroom light and then jerked it away, as if it were hot.

They think I'm in D.C. but it doesn't mean they're not watching the condo for Davy. And it didn't have to be whoever snatched Davy and attacked her and Sojee. If the NSA were still watching, they might move in thinking her one of the kidnappers or even a returning Davy.

And then they'd know she could jump.

She took a deep breath. She deeply regretted not having her wallet and her cell phone and, most of all, her glasses, but *thank God I was naked. That damn bug didn't suddenly go from D.C. to Stillwater and report its GPS-determined position.*

Her spare glasses were in the top drawer of her side table, though finding them was a matter of groping and muttered swearing. Finally, wearing them, the room went from a dark blur of shadows to a sharply delineated network of dimly lit outlines. She took the comforter from the bed and wrapped it around her, bath robe and all, then sat down on the floor, propped against the walls in the corner of her bedroom.

Our bedroom.

Our besieged bedroom.

She tried to close her eyes momentarily, just to calm her breathing and the thudding of her heart, but the slightest distant creak in the building caused her to start and stare frantically at the balcony and bedroom doors.

How did they know?

Either they *had* followed her to the hotel, despite the assurances of Curtis and escort, or Curtis had reported back and the leak had occurred above him. The timing would work for either scenario. She didn't want to think that Curtis, himself, was the leak, but her current level of paranoia was such that she couldn't discount the possibility.

I've got to get out of here.

She went to her dresser and pulled whole stacks of underwear, socks, pants, and shirts. She found Davy's hard-sided suitcase in the hall closet and dumped the clothes in, adding shoes, toiletries, and Davy's old leather jacket.

I don't have my keys, I don't have any money.

She looked at the door to the apartment. *And I'm not going out that way.*

She took a firm grip on the suitcase handle and lifted it.

What do I do now? Raise my fist and say, "to the Aerie"? Might as well say, "to the Batmobile!"

She tried to imagine the sheepskin-strewn rock floor of the cliff dwelling, its dark shadowing corners, and knotty pine furniture with legs cut to odd lengths on the uneven floor. She *willed* her self to be there, gritting her teeth as if the clenching of her jaw muscles would push her through space and time.

She didn't move.

Dammit! What does a girl have to do—throw herself off the balcony? She turned angrily, and the suitcase knocked loudly into an end table.

She twisted, looking back toward the door, her heart thudding. *Did they hear—*

She was standing on cold stone, in the dark interior of the Aerie.

This is ridiculous.

She made tea.

There was just enough water for that and no more, and it was a horrid waste of water when one is in the middle of a mountainous desert. Even the local oasis was out of her reach—the rappelling rope was back in the condo.

But tea is comforting. Tea is soothing.

Of course I don't seem to be able to jump unless I'm scared to death, so maybe soothing isn't the way I should be going.

It wasn't quite true. She remembered the time, in the National Gallery, that she'd jumped to eavesdrop on the Monk—what had Anders called him? Padgett. That time she hadn't been afraid for her life.

She wandered aimlessly while the kettle warmed on the propane burner.

But I wasn't thinking about jumping *either. That's probably the ticket.* It was a regular defense among her clients—intellectualizing. They'd examine a problem with all the sharp focus of intelligent minds, dissecting and analyzing everything—anything to avoid an actual *feeling*. Well, feelings often hurt, didn't they?

So maybe this is a feeling *thing.*

She felt pretty sure that if she jumped off the ledge outside with a destination in mind—someplace safe—that she'd actually jump.

She was also terrified at the thought of trying that. What if she didn't jump? Must she risk her life every time?

The teakettle began to whistle at the far end of the dwelling and she turned to walk back to it—then stopped herself, well short.

*You've got to solve this. Maybe it's not so dramatic as flinching away from death. Maybe it's as simple as wanting to overhear someone far away or—*She licked her lips and looked at the burner. She'd have to do something quickly or the very last water would boil away.

Maybe it's as simple as wanting a cup of tea.

She didn't try to jump. Instead, she thought about the sound the tea kettle made—its piercing whistle, the frantic vibrations of thousands of bubbles shaking the container, making it rattle slightly on the burner. She thought about the feel of vapor, the sense of air heavy with moisture, the rich, almost tropical dampness when you stood near a boiling kettle. She thought about the smell, the promising fragrance of a dry black pekoe tea bag as you opened the paper envelope, the wetter, heavier scent when the boiling water floods the cup and soaks the tea.

And she was there, standing in front of the burner, twenty

feet crossed in the beat of a single heart valve. The hairs rose on the back of her neck and she turned off the burner.

There's nothing like a good cup of tea.

She seemed to have got the hang of it.

For the condo in Stillwater it was the vanity in the master bathroom: a potpourri of smells ranging from perfume to toothpaste to baby powder; the feel of broad Mexican tile on bare, often wet, feet; the rasp of a toothbrush across lips, gum, and incisor.

For the Aerie there was the smell of stone, of old piñon wood smoke, the feel of thick-napped sheepskin wool pressing up between toes, and a sense of solidity that the floor in her second floor condo did not have.

There was a visual element as well, but it really took more than just picturing a place. She had to use other senses, to imagine herself already at her destination, already engaged with the environment.

And imagining makes it so.

She made three quick trips to fill the ceramic cistern, running the water cold from the bath tap and hoping the condo wasn't bugged for sound.

It was getting easier now that she'd done the same trip a few times. The scents, the textures, the colors weren't being recalled piecemeal. Now it was a flicker of sensory memories that abruptly solidified into the real thing.

She refilled the kettle. She hadn't made that cup of tea yet and she really felt she deserved an entire pot.

It was only fifty-five minutes after she'd fled the D.C. hotel bathtub. She thought about Anders and the NSA and the FBI.

There was a leak. Either there was a mole or a bug. How else did they find her there? She couldn't believe it was a random break-in.

It can't be Anders—he's had all the opportunity in the world to snatch me. But that was as far as she could be sure.

He'll be worried sick.

She wrapped her arms around herself. The damn kettle was

taking forever to boil and the Aerie was cold. She built a fire in the wood stove, bone-dry pine needles, resinous pine cones, split piñon kindling, and a twisted piñon log atop all. One match and it took easily, bright yellow flames and crackling ignitions of resin. The heat was palpable and she crouched down before it, opening Davy's robe to let it fall on her bare skin until the tea kettle whistled again.

She jumped back to the kettle. It was less than five long steps away from the fireplace, but she wanted control of this thing and felt practice would bring it.

She set the teapot, warmed, emptied, refilled, and now brewing, near the wood stove. There was no milk in the place. The last time she'd been stuck here, when Davy had initially disappeared, she'd made do with creamer. That wasn't necessary, now, if she could get this thing under control. There wasn't any milk in the condo, either. She'd given the kitchen spoilables to a neighbor before flying to D.C.

Where could she buy milk? What places did she know so intimately that she could jump there? She looked down at the terry cloth robe she was wearing. She could think of a few places but none where she would be comfortable in a bathrobe. *Except Mom's kitchen. There's probably milk there.* But her mother had heart trouble. Seeing Millie suddenly appear would probably kill her.

Millie dressed in a warm, long-sleeved dress from the hard-sided suitcase and slipped her feet into a pair of flats.

Money was no problem. She went to Davy's chest. Davy Jones's Locker, she'd called it. It was an antique wooden steamer trunk at the foot of their bed, draped with a spare comforter. The ancient lock had rusted open long before Davy ever bought it. She pushed the comforter aside and lifted the lid. It was half-full, mostly hundred dollar bills, but there was a small tray of "spending money"—bundles of twenties and tens—on top.

She didn't want to think about it. Last time they'd seriously checked, there was over two million dollars in the chest but the level looked higher now. She took a rubber band off of a bundle of ten-dollar bills and used it to pull her tangled, still damp hair back into a ponytail. As an afterthought, she took one of the tens and closed the trunk again.

She needed to get the milk before the tea over-steeped.

There was one place, on the corner of Houston and Sullivan streets in Greenwich Village that she knew intimately. Five of their favorite restaurants were in that area and Davy always jumped to the shadowed basement steps of St. Anthony's of Padua Catholic Church. She thought about it, the dampness of the old limestone, the nearly constant smell of urine—dark doorways had that danger in New York—with the eclectic mix of exhaust fumes, cooking, tree blossoms, and garbage that was also New York.

Her ears popped and she jerked in surprise as she found herself on the steps, forgetting momentarily the purpose of her recollection. It was darker than she expected, quite damp, and near freezing. The traffic on Houston was still heavy, but remote, distanced by wet fog.

Directly across the street was a small corner store, more of a stand, really, selling a mix of candy, news, lottery, and drinks. She paid for and received two quart cartons of whole milk. When she turned around again, she looked up through the swirling fog at the Church and the floodlit statue of Saint Anthony.

A memory of childhood came to her, a Catholic friend's rhyme. She thought of Davy and said it aloud. "Saint Antony, Saint Antony, please come around. Something is lost and needs to be found."

The clerk, one of the local, olive-skinned, Italian-Americans, said, "Ya gotta say it on Tuesdays. That's his day. It might work but ya gotta bettah chance on Tuesday."

She turned back to him and nodded solemnly. "I'll remember that."

He shrugged as if embarrassed.

She went back across the street to go down the stairs, but the clerk was still watching her so she headed down the street, instead, past the meat market before ducking into the entrance of an apartment building nestled between the steel-grated fronts of a balloon shop and a drop-off laundry.

She jumped from there, back to the Aerie.

The warm tea and the fire were very good after the cold air. She polished her glasses on the hem of her dress and thought about the events of the night.

How do I get in touch with Anders?

The bug, her surest way, was in the hotel room, maybe taken by whoever entered. Her cell phone was also there and he could hardly call her that way if she didn't have it. On the other hand, the bug, with its GPS locator, would betray her position and, therefore, her newfound ability. And she was pretty sure the cell phone would be useless in the Aerie.

But she still wanted Anders to know she was all right.

When the tea had been consumed and the resulting bladder pressure dealt with, she put on Davy's old leather jacket and tried to decide how to contact Anders without putting her at risk.

Two risks.

First, there was the issue of whoever wanted to kidnap her, probably as a means to control Davy. This was a big risk, but oddly enough, not the one that scared her the most.

If they find out I can jump, I'm as likely to be sought by the NSA as whoever grabbed Davy. She would be a backup "intelligence asset." They might even stop looking for Davy if they knew they could preserve this "capability."

Where to jump?

Again it was a matter of intimate acquaintance with a place. She thought she could probably return to the hotel room, but that would bother her.

The drugstore. When she'd bought the underwear, the deodorant, the toothpaste at the drugstore next to the hotel, she'd been struck by the smells from the cosmetic department. She'd blinked in the bright fluorescent lighting. There'd been a large rubber-backed rug at the doorway, for the wiping of feet. That's when the smells had hit her.

And she was there. She heard someone gasp and blinked in the bright fluorescent lighting.

It was the cashier who'd gasped. "I didn't hear the door chime," she said, holding a hand to her chest. "So when I looked up and you were standing there—I mean, it almost looked like—" She broke off. "Surprised me."

"Sorry," said Millie.

Davy had talked about this phenomenon. "When people know a thing is impossible, they *know* it. They can be looking directly at you when you appear out of thin air and they'll come up with a *logical* explanation before you can even open your mouth."

She glanced behind her. There were several cars in the parking lot of the hotel that hadn't been there before—large SUVs and one police car with a broad green stripe on its side framing the letters "Alexandria Police" across both doors. She moved further into the store.

"What's happening next door?"

The clerk's eyes widened and she said, "An FBI agent came in and asked me if I'd seen anything suspicious next door, but he wouldn't say what had happened!"

"My goodness." She smiled and asked, "Where's the shampoo?"

"Aisle ten, dear."

"Thank you." Millie turned, trying to be casual about it. She went back and stared blankly at the shampoo bottles, then picked her usual brand.

She paid for it with the change from her milk purchase, then walked out the door, across the parking lot, and into the hotel lobby.

"There she is!" the clerk said, stabbing his finger toward her. The two FBI agents—they wore the windbreakers with the large letters across the back—swiveled their heads around.

She raised her eyebrows. "Has something happened?"

Anders wasn't happy with her.

He didn't believe her story about running a bath, then deciding the little plastic bottle of hotel room shampoo was woefully inadequate and that she'd gone out with the cash only, forgetting her phone, the bug, and even the hotel room key. She accounted for the time by saying she'd decided to walk a bit, once out, to clear her head, before buying the shampoo.

She, in turn, wasn't very happy with Anders.

"Who leaked? How did they know where I was?"

They'd apparently left as soon as they'd come, once she turned out to be absent. They'd looked at the bug, apparently, and her phone, for both were suspiciously free of fingerprints, even Millie's.

Anders said, "They probably thought it was a trap when they saw the bug, if they understood what it did."

On the bright side, she had her wallet back, and her phone. She refused the bug. "They looked at it. It may be encrypted, but they still might be able to track it." She looked around the room. "In fact, who says that's not how they found me?"

They were talking down the hall in the hotel's tiny Laundromat. Anders had put quarters in the washer, and turned it on, empty, for the noise. Now that the FBI had finished their forensic search, one of Anders's men was sweeping the room for bugs.

"Not that you'll stay here, of course."

Millie, still angry, still defiant, snapped, "You've got that right."

Anders frowned. "The question is, what to do with you now?"

"You guys aren't doing anything with me. You're leaking like a faucet and I can't trust you."

Anders winced and she added, "That's a second person plural. I don't doubt *you*, Mr. Anders. But something is not right with your organization."

"You still need protection," he said.

He didn't deny it. She narrowed her eyes. "Indeed I do, but who from?" She licked her lips. "I'm going to ground."

He looked at her, frowning. "Go into hiding? Alone? No support?"

"Isn't that what 'going to ground' means?"

"Well, that's what it means in intelligence circles. Among dog fanciers it can refer to dachshunds or terriers going into a burrow, after a badger or rat—in the dark, teeth against teeth."

"Are you crazy? Going after them? That's your job. I just

want to find Davy. Are there any results, yet, about the ambulance with the angel on the door?"

He blinked. "Yes, actually. There's a medical transport firm outside Baltimore that uses ambulances of that description. The FBI is knocking on doors tonight to account for each unit's location and use on the relevant day." He tugged on his chin. "Would you keep the phone—I mean if you go to ground? It's a national account. That way I'd be able to reach you."

"How did you know it's a national account? Never mind—I don't think I want to know. I'll set up an anonymous e-mail account at Yahoo. You do the same. Don't let anybody else know about it."

He frowned. "What names? Anything you can think of has almost certainly been used."

"As I'm going to ground, I'll be rat8765. You can be terrier8765. That should be safe enough. Don't expect quick replies."

"I wouldn't send sensitive material across the nets."

"Just general progress, then, phrased generically. Some things are meaningless without context. If you've really got to talk to me, send a time and a clean telephone number—something totally unconnected to you. My phone will be off. I've heard about those cell tower simulators that can page and locate a phone without ringing it."

He frowned at her. "How would you go to ground?"

She looked at him and didn't say anything.

He laughed grimly. "Okay—when would you?"

She began to get angry. "You talk as if it's still undecided. The last time I was actually kidnapped it was the NSA that did it! Do I have to go to a federal judge again?" She exhaled a deep breath. *This time he's not the enemy.*

She didn't want him to suspect that she could jump. He might already, but she didn't want to add any more evidence. "Give me a ride to Dulles and drop me. Just you. Don't tell anybody else. Don't wait after you've dropped me."

He frowned, opened his mouth to speak, then closed it. For a moment he stared at the ratty suspended ceiling before saying, "Okay. Your way."

She blinked, surprised. He'd given in more easily than she'd thought, and that scared her. *He thinks their security is compromised, too.* Grudgingly, she considered the possibility that he hadn't been that proud of his involvement, ten years before.

She jumped to the Aerie from a woman's toilet stall outside security near the A and C shuttle gates. With security being what it was in the nation's airports after 911, she couldn't swear there wasn't a hidden video camera in the toilet, but she risked it anyway.

The fire had burned down but the embers still glowed in the stove. She added another log and some pine needles for encouragement, closed the tempered glass door, and went to bed.

The sheets were cold at first, and faintly musty. She slept well for the first time since Davy had been taken.

She breakfasted in New York. The same shadowy basement stairs she'd used the night before put her on Sullivan Street and she had a huge pear-ginger muffin and coffee at Once Upon a Tart. She'd been in D.C. long enough to shift her circadian rhythms to the east coast, but had slept late enough that the restaurant was less than busy.

After eating, she took a long walk up to Twentieth on Sixth Avenue and ducked into Kinko's where she paid cash for enough internet time to set up the e-mail account rat8765. While she was logged in, she sent a test message to terrier8765 letting Anders know the account was active.

DOG-BREATH,
ACCOUNT ACTIVE. WILL CHECK DAILY, WHEN POSSIBLE.
YOURS TRULY,
RATTY

After sending it she browsed the news at CNN and ABC, waiting fifteen minutes before going back to Yahoo to see if her message had bounced. It hadn't.

The talks were off again in Palestine. More fighting in India. In the midst of a terrible drought, Afghanistan was now flooding. Successful expansion of International Space Station. Rioting in Zimbabwe, Argentina, and Islamabad. Five more car bombs in Baghdad and two in Falluja.

When she went back, not only had her message not bounced, there was a reply from terrier8765.

DEAR RATTY,
NEWS OF MEDICAL TRANSPORT AND BAD BOYS. AND
OTHER.
SINCERELY,
DOG-BREATH.
PS. 703-345-2818 AFTER SEVEN EASTERN.

Millie jumped to D.C. before making the call, managing, after some thought and imagination, Sojee's alleyway off of H Street, where Sojee had fainted in the rain. She huddled there, hidden behind a garbage can, and hit the send button on her cell phone.

The alleyway had a streetlight opposite its mouth, but slightly down the street. A great swath of the other side of the alley was awash with light, but Millie's side was deep in shadow. While the phone connected, she pulled a bundle of recycled cardboard over and sat on it, leaning back against the brick building. The was a ring on the line and Anders answered.

"I'm impressed."

A small rat, or a large mouse—Millie wasn't sure—ran along the far side of the alley. Millie pulled her feet in closer and watched it distrustfully. "What has impressed you?"

"A team of our guys went into Dulles after you but you lost them. They were watching all the ground transport within minutes of you being dropped but you slipped past them."

She stiffened. "We had a deal!" The rat looked toward her, balanced on its hind feet and sniffing the air.

"I didn't send them! Apparently I'm not completely 'in the loop' on this thing. They LoJacked my vehicle." He paused. "They nearly fired me off the case because I let you go to ground."

"Now that's the NSA I know and love. Why didn't they fire you?" *If that rat comes one foot closer, I swear I'll throw the phone at it.*

"Because I stood my ground, I suspect. I pointed out that we were clearly still compromised and that I wouldn't give you up to anybody until we'd cleaned house—so, if they wanted to lose contact with you, they could go right ahead and fire me."

The rat turned back to the far wall and continued to an open trash can. "Good for you. What makes them think I didn't fly out?"

"You aren't on any of the passenger manifests and you aren't on any of the security cameras. How *did* you get out of there?"

The rat poised itself and then jumped vertically, all the way up to the top of the can. The sudden movement made her jerk. *I jumped, just like the rat.* She had no idea rats could jump so high.

She had prepared an answer for Anders's question. "Parking garage. I paid a woman three hundred dollars to drive me out. I said my abusive alcoholic boyfriend was after me and he was watching the taxi and bus stands. I hid on the floor in the back seat." She bit her lip. She hated lying.

The rat was out of sight but she could hear it rustling through the trash.

He laughed. "Very nice. Not the sort of thing one would report. You have someplace safe to stay? You're not using your plastic, I hope?"

"Give me some credit—I mean credit for sense. What was the other news?"

"At bed check, Ms. Johnson was unconscious, blood pressure very low and heartbeat very fast. They transferred her to D.C. General but she never turned up. Shortly after the ambulance left, another city ambulance showed up, responding to the call."

She forgot about the rat. "The first ambulance was a fake and somebody drugged her!"

"Looks that way. We'll know soon enough. Before they transferred her, St. Elizabeth's drew blood."

"What on earth could they want Sojee for?"

Anders was slow in answering.

"Tell me!" Millie said.

"They could want intelligence on how much we know. Considering how effective Ms. Johnson was in defeating their attempted kidnapping, they may think she's an operative, someone in the know. Or, if they assume she's your friend, they may want her as a lever, to influence you."

Poor Sojee. "I don't suppose the first ambulance had an angel on the door?"

"Not that anyone saw. You call for a D.C. ambulance and an ambulance with the right colors shows up—people see what they expect to see."

Millie thought about the drugstore clerk the night before. "Yes, don't they just."

"However, Angel of Mercy Medical Transport in Ellicot City, Maryland, is missing another ambulance. They're the company I mentioned last night, with the angel on the door."

"Another? Did they lose one last month?"

"As a matter of fact, they did. Last month's vehicle turned up in a parking garage at Logan airport. Four days after *that* night."

"Boston? They took Davy to Boston?"

"I seriously doubt it. These people aren't stupid. We're checking on it, though, and cross-checking the movements of Mr. Padgett and friends at Bochstettler and Associates."

"You said you had news of them. Padgett?"

"Not Padgett. The FBI agent he shot is stable and expected to recover. The Bureau is not happy.

"It turns out your friend from the National Gallery, the woman that Agent Martingale recognized, has been associated with BA in the past. Miss Hyacinth Pope flew from Logan to BWI two days after the snatch."

"Where is she now?"

"We don't know."

"You guys didn't follow her from the Museum?"

"Yes, but we only had one vehicle tailing Padgett's van and he dropped Ms. Pope before moving in on you and Ms. Johnson. The tail followed orders and stuck with Padgett. That's *how* we discovered they were up to something more active than surveillance."

"Do you think she was the one who left the ambulance at Logan?"

"It's possible. Or it could've been the last leg of a longer trip—we haven't finished tracing possible flight connections. Her originating city might be where they really took Davy."

"What are you and the FBI doing about Sojee?"

"Everything in our power."

Millie touched her tongue to her upper lip, then said impulsively, "It's just that I have my doubts that a homeless mental patient would command their full attention."

The rat appeared again, at the rim of the garbage can, and hopped a foot horizontally to the next can.

Anders cleared his throat before saying, "Perhaps not usually, but remember our interest in this. Whoever took Ms. Johnson also took, as you so cogently put it, a national intelligence asset. In addition, the Bureau takes a *very* dim view of their agents being shot. Mr. Padgett definitely *got* the FBI's attention."

Millie shuddered. She was struggling with the unpleasant sensation of being *grateful* that an FBI agent had been shot. Three more rats were moving along the base of the far wall. *Ugh. Time to go.*

"Any other news?"

Anders said, "No."

"Find them! Both of them."

"We're working on it."

The rats swiveled around, looking at her. One crept out into the middle of the alley.

"Gotta go."

She jumped, not bothering to disconnect the call. "Rats! Yuck!" Her voice echoed off the Aerie's rock walls and she shuddered again. The phone beeped and displayed "Signal Lost" and then the "Searching for Service" message. She powered it down.

Rats.

Going to ground would *never* have that meaning to her.

TWELVE

A cup of tea, *redux*.

Davy's head felt several times too big. It throbbed. He took a deep breath of air and his stomach heaved. He stank—all the old familiar odors—and he was in danger of vomiting in reaction.

He tried to push himself into a sitting position but something was awkward—wasn't working right. His right eye did not want to open, but his left eye showed him that he was in the box and that his wrists were now joined by handcuffs. One of his old chains was padlocked to the links between the wrist cuffs. The other ran to the ankle restraint now back on his left leg.

He used both hands to roll to a sitting position. His head throbbed heavily in response. He touched his closed eye briefly. His cheek and brow were swollen and there was a crust of blood where the skin had split under his eyebrow.

His ribs hurt, too. He lifted his shirt and found a dark purple and blue bruise on his left side. *She kicked you more than once.*

He checked the tape border and found he wasn't in the box. He nearly fell the first time he stood but managed to stagger to the bathroom door in a kind of controlled perpetual forward stumble. Lean forward to the point of falling, step, repeat, repeat, repeat.

He found that with only one ankle manacled, he could stand in the shower as long as he kept the confined foot up on the bathtub edge.

He didn't try to undress until he was under the streaming water, then he ripped the Velcro side seams apart and rinsed the worst of it away. Washing in handcuffs was a problem especially when he lifted his arms to wash his hair and face. His ribs screamed and he managed to wash his head only by hunching it down to the hands rather than raising them.

With the blood washed away, his eyelids came unstuck on his right eye and he was able to open it, though narrowly. He washed carefully, working over every inch of his body. He left the clothes for later. Even though his usual sense of pollution was still making him want to scrub and scrub and scrub, his head and ribs would not support the activity.

He toweled dry carefully, especially around his head, but despite the light touch, the towel came away bloodied. When he looked in the mirror his face was lopsided, the right brow and cheek puffed out. The split in his brow had reopened under washing but only seeping blood. He took a wad of toilet paper and held it there as he shuffled to the bed and lay down.

He thought about the screw in the mattress but knew that the handcuffs would make it very difficult to retrieve. *And what good would it do me, anyway?*

Well, I could cut my throat.

It seemed that every time he fell asleep, they'd put him in the box. Despite the discomfort of his ribs, he started to pull the bed over but the computerized speaker said, "No. Hold it. We have a reason for doing this."

Davy paused and stared impassively at the mirror.

The voice went on. "We're trying to make sure you don't have intracranial bleeding."

"A little late to be taking so much care, isn't it?" For a second Davy felt guilty, because he'd started the current conflict, but he stopped himself quickly. *Don't go there.* They *started it when they snatched me. When they killed Brian. When they stuck this thing in my chest.*

"Perhaps," said the voice. "Since vomiting is often a post-concussion symptom, we're concerned."

"Did I vomit again, after she kicked me?"

"Ah. So you remember her kicking you?"

"Oh, yes. And she kicked me again after I was unconscious."

The voice was silent.

Davy lifted his shirt and showed the bruise.

"Well, yes, she did," the voice admitted. "But not in the head."

"You're lucky I can still teleport. You should consider that the next time you turn her loose. All this effort would be wasted, wouldn't it?"

The voice was silent for a moment. When it came back, the computerized scrambler had been turned off. "Yes, it would be very aggravating. Get some rest. We won't bother you before morning." The voice was a mature baritone. "Perhaps it's time we had a little chat."

They brought him fresh Velcroed scrubs, an icepack, ibuprofen, and the key to the handcuffs. After he had dressed, the hook-nosed, red-haired man came in and supervised two women as *they* mopped the floor and changed the bedding and towels. They talked to each other in what Davy thought was Portuguese and as they departed with all the dirty laundry, including the soiled clothing from the bathtub, he said the only phrase he knew, "*Muito obrigado.*"

They looked at him owlishly, ducked their heads, and said, "*De nada,*" before scurrying out. The redhead backed out the door in their wake, still watching Davy until the door completely shut.

As well you might.

The floor was barely dry when a butler in black tails, gray waistcoat, and pinstriped trousers pushed a silver tea service into the room. Two maids, in knee-length gray dresses with white eyelet collars and cuffs, carried in a table and a starched white tablecloth. They left and two footmen came in, each carrying a heavy formal dining chair. The table was set up at the limit of the chain, one chair inside that circle, the opposite chair beyond.

As the footmen left, they held the door for a man Davy had never seen before.

"How do you do?" The man's voice was the unscrambled one from the loudspeaker, the voice that had suggested a "chat." He was wearing a suit that was so clearly not off-the-rack that Davy couldn't begin to estimate its price. His shirt was so white that it hurt Davy's eyes. He was in his late forties or early fifties, clearly very fit. His dark brown hair was simply cut, his temples receding somewhat. He cocked his head as he waited for Davy's answer, and his nose and chin and large, slightly lined forehead made Davy think of a vulture. For all of that, he was a handsome man.

In answer, Davy touched the swollen side of his face. "I've been better," he said.

"I expect so. Do sit."

The butler held Davy's chair from the left, so it wouldn't tangle with the chain. Davy sat and thanked him before facing back to his host. "And you are?"

"Lawrence Simons, Mr. Rice. This is one of my houses." Simons sat before the butler could get around to that side of the table, so the butler turned to the tea service instead, placing cups, plates, cloth napkins, and silverware on the table.

"And is Miss Minchin also one of yours?"

He looked puzzled for a second. "Ah, you mean Hyacinth." He chuckled. "Hyacinth was not amused when one of her colleagues explained Miss Minchin's role in *A Little Princess*. Ms. Pope *does* work for me. For certain jobs she's invaluable." He gestured at Davy's face. "Not all things, though."

Davy narrowed his eyes. "She's a murderer."

Simons raised his eyebrows and said mildly, "Well, yes. Why did you think I employ her?"

The butler didn't miss a beat. "Lemon or milk, Mr. Rice?"

Davy sat still, chilled. "Milk, please," he said after a beat. "Two lumps."

"Three or four if you count your face and ribs," said Simons, laughing briefly.

The butler handed Simons his tea without asking his preference, a thin slice of lemon floating in the cup. He put the three-tier dessert tree within reach of both and said, "Will there be anything else, Sir?"

Simons shook his head. "No thank you, Abney."

Davy held his cup between his hands, savoring the warmth.

The door closed behind the butler and Davy said, "What do you want, Mr. Simons?"

"Ah. Where to begin?" He looked meditative and touched his tongue to his lips, a quick darting motion. He tilted his head again. "The scones, I think." He took a pastry from the bottom tray. "May I recommend the clotted cream?"

Davy's head still hurt abysmally but he'd also emptied his stomach recently. *Little Mr. Bulimia.* He tried an unadorned scone, chewing slowly and carefully. "I wasn't referring to the tea, Mr. Simons."

"Of course you weren't. Just my little joke. As to what I want, well, I want your services—your unique and undivided services."

Davy observed, "Normally these sorts of arrangements are handled with an offer of salary . . . not surgery."

"You'd be surprised, Mr. Rice. Quite surprised. In my sphere these things are often handled by ways other than salary. Addiction, for instance. Fear of exposure. A favor for a favor. Sexual gratification." He held up one hand and flipped it over, palm up. "Gunpoint."

Davy put his cup down. "Clearly we move in different circles." He wasn't hungry or thirsty anymore. "Surely money is easier, even cheaper in the long run? Why didn't you try me with money?"

"Several reasons, but the biggest one is that I didn't think it would work." Simons crossed his legs. "I know how much you're already paid by the NSA, and with that very comfortable compensation you have set very specific limits as to what you'll do for them. You don't have enough . . . need. Yes, enough *need* for money to work. Your scruples are too fine, your needs too small. After all, what's to keep you, with *your* abilities, from taking anything you want?" He smiled pleasantly. "We needed something more compelling."

Davy did not reply to this. He had better manners than Miss Minchin but he was *much* scarier.

"This is not to say that I'm unwilling to compensate you for cooperation. We don't have to use *just* the stick. There's room for carrots, too." He gestured around. "Your quarters, to start with. I see lots of room for improvement. We have a private beach, too. I don't see why you couldn't have access, provided certain measures were taken."

"What sort of measures?" Davy said.

"Well, I've been quite busy and my involvement in this project has been at a remove. But now that I'm on site, I don't see why you need more than two-tenths of a second to react to a warning. I've timed several of your reactions—you don't need much time at all. And, without so much time on your hands, you're less likely to get into . . . mischief."

"You mean my encounter with Miss Minchin—that is, Hyacinth?"

"Yes, Hyacinth. No, that's not the mischief I had in mind." Simons shook his head. "I appreciate that encounter. It gives me a *much* better idea of your capabilities. But scaring the boys in the booth—" he turned and gestured at the one-way mirror— "that's mischievous." He faced Davy again. "And companionship. We could arrange for some sort of conjugal visit from your wife."

What about my wife? Davy thought about denying Millie's existence but if they knew how much the NSA was paying him, they knew about Millie, too. "I think not. You'd have tried to use her as a control, already, if you had her. And I'm not doing anything that would put her in your power."

Simons eyes crinkled. "Delightful. I deal with so many stupid people—you wouldn't believe it. So refreshing. Well, the visits don't have to be from your wife—someone of the same physical type, or perhaps *not* the same type, since you've been together, what, ten, eleven years? You might want a change."

"I'll pass."

"Well, there's Hyacinth. She has a bit of a crush on you."

"You are *too* kind. Really. No, thank you."

Simons chuckled. "All right. Perhaps her sexual attentions can be saved for the *stick* side of the equation. However, access to video, books, television, anything within reason—I'd be willing to provide these things for a little cooperation."

"And what would that involve, this cooperation?"

"Just some tests, initially. Nothing invasive. We'd like to know something of what you can do. I know, for instance, that distance is not an issue—you've been know to jump people all over the world for the NSA. And that you can transport anything you can pick up."

Davy didn't correct him. He could take almost anything he could physically *move*, he didn't necessarily have to lift it from the ground. "I can hardly travel when this—" he tapped his chest—"keeps me here."

"That device keeps you where we choose. But we can choose other places—even an entire range of places."

We? Curious choice of pronoun. Perhaps he isn't the top of this food chain.

Simons raised his voice. "Would you come in, Dr. Conley?"

After a moment a gray-haired man wearing a lab jacket, glasses, and flannel slacks came through the door. He was the older man from the observation room, the man Davy had seen only for an instant.

Dr. Conley nodded to them both and said, "Good afternoon, sir. Mr. Rice."

Ah. He had been the man in scrubs who'd come in with Miss Minch—Hyacinth, when they'd reprogrammed the implant. The glasses were the same, the voice was the same.

"Dr. Conley would like to do some evaluations of your ability. Some—what did you call them, Dr. Conley?"

"Benchmarks, sir."

"Yes. Benchmarks. They don't involve anything more exotic that letting him take some measurements and watching you exercise your talent. In return, I'll improve your living conditions."

Davy blinked suddenly, his eyes burning. *Gratitude? I'm feeling* gratitude*?!* He deliberately recalled Brian's face in the rain, the horribly neat round hole over Brian's unseeing right eye. *This man aimed Hyacinth the way Hyacinth aimed the gun.*

He poured more tea from the pot, concentrating on keeping

his hands steady and his face still. He added the sugar and poured the milk and clamped his teeth together behind a slight smile.

I won't kill for you. I won't put others in your grasp. And, at the first opportunity I get, I will destroy you and your entire organization.

He stirred the tea in the cup. "All right. I suppose we can give it a try."

Two hours later Davy felt like Sara Crewe in *A Little Princess* when, after being reduced to months of servitude by the perfidious Miss Minchin, she awakes one morning to find that someone has turned her cold, bare, drafty loft into a luxurious palace.

And look what trouble that *caused.*

He sat off to one side, still wearing the ankle restraint, while a series of liveried servants removed his hospital bed (and the hidden screw) and replaced it with a king-sized four poster. In quick succession they also brought a large Turkish rug, a standing wardrobe, a bureau, a leather recliner, and an elegant writing desk with chair. Most of the furniture was satin-finished oak with heavy brass pulls and was maneuvered with the difficulty of very heavy furniture.

The headboard of the four poster and the drapes from the canopy hid the sheet of plywood screwed to the wall. An entertainment center and a wall-mounted flat-screen TV covered most traces of the broken and dented Sheetrock where Davy had flung the blond man into the wall. And the rug and the bed covered most of the taped lines on the floor. The table from the tea service had been cleared and set with its pair of chairs against the wall by the bathroom door.

The resulting transformation was completed by the hanging of four framed prints: two large landscapes, a watercolor by Winslow Homer, and a flat print of Wesselmann's *The Great American Nude*.

He'd seen the Homer before, in a book. It was one of his Key West paintings, three black men hauling the anchor up on a schooner, sails ready to hoist. He'd also seen the molded plastic original of the *Nude* at the National Gallery. It was an odd work, very few colors depicting a very tan blonde with extreme patches of white skin around her breasts and hips, two-tone nipples and a slight cluster of pubic hair. There was the barest hint of a belly button and the head was a simple oval outlined in yellow, a brief line to define the chin, and two red lips around an area of undefined white teeth.

The nipples, the mouth, and the groin were the most detailed parts of the work. Even the tan line screamed, "usually covered." Yet there was no personality, no real individuality, no sense of person.

Great American? Typical *American male view.* He wondered if Wesselmann had intended this a reflection on objectification or if the piece merely displayed the artist's own views. He hoped it was intentional but thought the piece dated to the midsixties when sexism was more part and parcel of the world's fabric.

When the staff had finished, Dr. Conley came back in, rolling the computer station they'd previously used to reprogram Davy's implant. He left it outside the radius of Davy's ankle-constrained range and handed the plastic paddle on its telephone cord to Davy.

"If you would be so kind as to hold this over your—that's right. You remember." He plugged the unit in and began whistling quietly to himself.

Davy wanted very much to see the monitor's face, but it was not only turned away from him, it had privacy flaps extending forward along its sides and top, screening its contents from anyone not directly before it. *What's the parameter range? Could I set the delay to so high a value that I'd have time to jump away and get the damn thing surgically removed? And I wonder where they keep the computer when it's not right here? And finally, where do they keep that portable transmitter that Hyacinth Pope (aka Ms. Minchin) used when they were welding? With that in his possession, he should be able to go anywhere.*

Dr. Conley completed his adjustments, shut down the computer, and accepted the wand back from Davy. He said, "Excuse me, please. I'll be back in a moment." He rolled the computer to the door where it was taken by somebody unseen. Dr. Conley returned and sat down at the table. Davy joined him, kicking the chain across the floor pointedly.

"Since you've shortened my 'leash' you'll be able to unlock this, won't you?"

Conley looked at his watch. "Another fifteen minutes should do it."

Davy frowned. He'd expected a yes or a no—not this delay. "Does the device take time to accept your programming?"

Conley explained, "Mr. Simons will be airborne in fifteen minutes. He is a very cautious man. When he is on site, you will wear the restraint. And—" He paused, pursing his lips. "We want the implant programmer off site, too."

Shit! Davy sat back and tried not to let his disappointment show. "What's my new interval on the pukometer?"

Conley tilted his head down and looked at him for a moment, silent, over the frames of his glasses. He pursed his lips and said, "I think this will work if I'm as direct as Mr. Simons. There are things I can't tell you but I won't lie to you. If I can't answer a question, I'll just say so—I won't make something up. I'm a scientist and as such, I'm uncomfortable with lies."

Science without virtue . . . He thought about asking Conley how he felt about vivisection.

Conley pushed his glasses back up and continued. "First of all, you should know that I've completely removed the delay interval. You leave the range of the field and the governor will go full on, no warning, immediate convulsions. You've shown us that you can do much with little. In fact, that's why Mr. Simons has decided to remove himself. Even with no interval, he's decided you are too dangerous to be in striking range."

Now that *is too bad.* Davy smiled, pointedly. "Aren't you worried? For yourself, that is."

Conley licked his lips. "Frankly, yes. But I accept the risk."

"Because of the pay? I forgot—Mr. Simons deals in all sorts of motivations, doesn't he? What is his hold on you?"

"You are correct that it is not my salary," Conley said. "Among other things my motivation is this chance at new science. Because of the phenomenon—your ability has no precedent and its implications for physics are staggering."

Now why doesn't that reassure me said the guinea pig? "Is that your religion, then? Physics?" Davy felt a reluctant tug of curiosity. He'd read everything he could of speculations as to how teleportation would work. There'd been a surprising amount of work done on it for something that most people were sure was impossible. The recent physics of the past decade involving quantum teleportation did not seem to apply. He was fairly sure that his being wasn't destroyed and recreated every time he jumped. If that were the case, then why would manacles restrain him? "And what do you make of this phenomenon?"

Conley opened his mouth for a moment but nothing came out. He shut it and licked his lips. "I don't know. That's the short answer. I *suspect* a great deal, though. What have you decided?"

"Berthold rays," said Davy, with a serious face.

Conley raised his eyebrows. "A simple, 'I don't know' would suffice."

Davy went on. "Poincaré non-Euclidean pocket universes. Zero-point vacuum holes. Quantum tunneling. Enthalpic reversal. Gravitational distortion by strange matter stars. Violations of causality. Imaginary rest mass. Scarlet women. Ragtime. Jungle instinct. Mass hysteria."

Conley looked over his glasses at Davy again. "Just so. Do you always babble like this?"

Davy said impassively, "The idle brain is the devil's playground."

"How do you teleport? Not the physics of it—the act of volition—what do you do that causes the displacement?"

I'm certainly not telling you. He lied. "I struggle very hard to stay where I am . . . and fail."

Conley looked back over his glasses. "Is *this* cooperation?"

Davy relented slightly. "I don't really know how I do it." He pointed across the room. "If you were to go across the room to the light switch, you wouldn't think about it—you don't think about all the individual movements necessary. In fact, if you actually tried to micromanage all the actual muscles, you'd probably fall right over. You just do it, correct? You don't think about it. It's something like that."

Conley stood up. "Wait a moment, please." He left the room and came back almost immediately with the key to the padlock which he put on the table before Davy.

Davy picked it up slowly. "Mr. Simons must be airborne."

"Quite. You may wish to get dressed. We'll take a walk."

Davy unlocked the ankle restraint. "Dressed?"

Dr. Conley walked to the wardrobe and opened it. There were hanging shirts, pants, two suits. He walked to the bureau and pulled open the top drawer revealing briefs, socks, and pajamas.

"You've lost a little weight, I believe, but if anything doesn't fit, tell Abney, the butler. He'll take care of it."

"Not Ms. Pope?"

Conley shook his head. "Hyacinth is reserved—how did Mr. Simons put it? She's the stick, but hopefully, she'll remain unused. She's accompanying Mr. Simons on other business." He held his hand out. "The key, please."

Davy put it on his palm and started to give him the lock as well. "No. Not the lock. Keep it open, with the restraint. You'll be needing it. But rarely, I hope." He went to the door. "Ten minutes?"

Davy nodded and Conley left.

He thought about jumping again—to Adams Cowley, but the last attempt was too fresh in his mind. He gagged reflexively and closed his eyes and breathed deeply. When the nausea had passed, he tore off the Velcroed pajamas and threw them into the bathroom trash can.

The bureau seemed to be stocked from a Lands' End catalog and yielded a pair of jeans, new, yet washed several times to softness, crew socks, gray briefs, and a white polo. He added a navy oversized crew sweater and was trying to choose between the leather deck shoes and a pair of white court tennies when Conley stuck his head back in, his lab jacket gone and a fleece sweater over his arm.

"Where are we walking?"

"The beach. And on the way back we might try an experiment."

Davy picked the tennis shoes. They'd gotten the size right, even accounting for his triple-E width and high instep. *Well, they had the shoes I was wearing when I was snatched.*

Moving without chains felt odd and, again, he had trouble at the threshold of the door, but Dr. Conley walked on without pause, and Davy caught up in a few strides.

This time they turned away from the elevator and found, at the end of the hallway, a broad stair with carpeted steps and an elaborate oak railing leading down two flights to the next floor.

"First I need to show you something." Conley led the way to a room that must have been right below Davy's quarters. He opened the door and gestured Davy to precede him into the room.

At one point, Davy supposed, it had been an elegant bedroom, but the furniture was gone and the once-pristine oak floor was scuffed and gouged. What dominated the room was a column, four feet on a side, of gray, rough-finished concrete, going from floor to ceiling.

Conley spoke. "So, the transmitter and a battery backup are encased in the middle of that, though there are wave guides that project above. It's on house power and it's radio controlled from *off site*. You manage to interrupt the power supply and a day or two later, when the battery runs down, your implant is going to activate. You interfere with radio transmission or reception by messing with the wave guide and the implant will activate. The concrete is reinforced with a triple grid of one-inch rebar and you couldn't get it open without explosives. And that would probably wreck the transmitter and—"

"My implant would activate." Davy felt his stomach clench. His tentative plan had been to find the transmitter, take it, and escape. "I'm surprised the floor supports the sucker."

Conley pointed down and drew an imaginary line across the floor. "There's a load-bearing wall that cuts across, right beneath it. That's why they chose your particular room." He studied Davy's face. "I'm not trying to rub your nose in it or anything. I just think it's important for you to understand the situation, so that you don't do anything . . ."

"Stupid?" suggested Davy.

Conley's lips twitched. "Ill-advised." He led the way back out of the room.

They went down another floor and then they were walking down the hall and turning, again, past the kitchen, past the laundry room, to the courtyard.

The sky was cloudy and the glare was worse than no clouds as the brightness came from all parts of the sky. He blinked as they stepped off the porch but the crisp, salt air felt wonderful in his nose. It couldn't have been more than sixty degrees Fahrenheit.

The chain was still there. Someone had coiled it neatly upon the top of the concrete weight, but the padlock and restraint were gone. Davy had no doubt they would appear again if his captors thought it necessary.

Conley pulled his fleece on without stopping, pushed open the iron gate at the end of the courtyard, and walked out. Davy followed. Beyond the shelter of the walls, the wind was brisk.

"Did they just push the output up?" he asked.

Conley glanced at him sideways. "You refer to the radio signal?"

"Yes."

"We've changed things a bit. We won't be using that device you saw Ms. Pope use. Unrestrained, you could snatch it and go. But, no, we haven't just increased the gain." He licked his lips. "That signal is a relatively simple digital key transmitted redundantly on three different frequencies to minimize the chance of accidental signal loss. To prevent you from being able to take a transmitter and run, we've split up the key between two different synchronized transmitters."

Davy saw the garage he'd glimpsed earlier and a gravel drive that led around the house to his left. Conley turned to the right down a gravel path that led away from the garage, driveway, and house to a raised boardwalk snaking into tall sand dunes.

Conley said, "So, to our east, we have a transmitter, and to our west." He stopped and stepped off the boardwalk, crouched, and drew two intersecting circles, like a Venn diagram, in the sand. Conley rested his finger in the common lens shaped intersection. "We're here, where the two signals overlap in sufficient strength and the key is—" he meshed the fingers of both hands together "—complete. If you were to go toward either transmitter, you'd enter a zone with only a partial key." He dropped one hand, leaving the other out with gaps between the fingers. "And the implant would trigger."

Well, scratch that *notion.* Davy felt a reluctant admiration for the arrangement. *These people are not stupid.* "How do you know we're not about to walk into a V-zone?"

Conley frowned. "V-zone?"

Davy opened his mouth and mimed sticking his finger down his throat.

The corners of Dr. Conley's mouth jerked up briefly. "Ah. The *Veeee-*zone. We had someone out here with a meter, checking. If we stay on the boardwalk, we're fine, and I'll show you the limits and bounds, once we're on the beach."

"Will I still get a boundary warning, when I approach the edge?"

Conley pursed his lips. "We *think* so."

The boardwalk rose on pilings now, lifting over to the tops of a dune, then stretched over an expanse of salt marsh and open estuary. Their feet thumped hollowly on the planks.

"That is, we're not sure what the device will do since you will be moving toward a region of *stronger* field strength in one key, even as the other drops. We think, however, that you'll have the same incremental increase in nausea and perhaps the tingle in the throat. We hope so."

Davy couldn't help saying, "How very reassuring."

Conley added, "Perhaps it would be safest if you didn't test it."

They reached another dune on the other side of the marsh. Davy could see the sea, now, and the wind was dead offshore, in their teeth. His hair, longer than it had been in years, whipped about in the breeze. He looked left and right. There were other houses in the distance but none closer than half a mile.

"How did you know?" Davy asked Conley. "About the nausea and the throat?"

Conley scratched his chest and looked at Davy. "Did you think we'd risk untested technology on you?"

"Ah—so there were trials. FDA-approved, no doubt."

Conley turned his head away without answering and Davy, left to his imagination, shuddered. He felt sure the trials had been more aimed at effectiveness than at safety. And if Simons and his people had been interested in figuring the upper limits of punishment, he supposed at least one person to have died.

They passed the last dune and descended a flight of shallow stairs to the beach proper. The tide seemed out and the surf was heavy. Large dark rocks rose from the wet sands and deflected pounding waves high into the air. The water's edge was at least another hundred and fifty feet but the wind carried spray to Davy's face. The beach was deserted as far as Davy could see.

"See those flags, there?" Conley pointed at a pair of sticks with fluttering fluorescent orange bits of plastic fastened to their tops. They were stuck in the sand, near the dune, to their left, perhaps sixty feet away. "Line them up and they define the eastern border." He pointed at another pair to their right, roughly the same distance. "The west. You can go right down to the water's edge without a problem. Don't go in, though. The water is sure to degrade the signal."

Davy shivered, this time from the wind and spray. "I should think hypothermia would be of greater concern."

"It's not always so cold or windy. Lots of people swim during the height of the summer."

I don't plan to be here then. "Can we go back now?"

"Certainly. In fact, why don't we teleport?"

Davy looked at him. "Is that the experiment you had in mind?"

"Yes. Thought it might yield some insights."

Davy nodded. "Okay. Watch out for a brightly lit tunnel. If you see it, stay *away* from the light."

"Oh, very funny," said Conley, but he looked a bit unsure.

"We can walk back, you know." Davy gave him the choice.

"No, I want to experience this. What do I—"

Davy jumped behind him, lifted him slightly, and jumped back to the "box" in the room.

"—do." Davy released him and Conley staggered, dropping to one knee and catching himself with an outstretched arm on the foot of the bed.

Davy sat in the desk chair and spun it around to watch Conley stand back up, an abstracted look upon his face. "Did you see any light?" Davy asked.

Conley looked up, an irritated look on his face. "I wanted to use a stopwatch."

"Surely you've timed my jumps with the video."

"Not over that distance. Besides, a watch being teleported might show some discrepancies."

"Time dilation?" Davy shook his head. "I wear a watch normally. No matter how often or how far I jump, it keeps the same time as the U.S. Naval Observatory, more or less."

"Ah," said Conley. He looked at the mirror on the wall and raised his voice. "We're done with the beach for now." He turned back to Davy. "Well, must go make some notes. This room and the bathroom are currently safe for you, but anywhere else in the house and the governor will kick in. Abney will be bringing your supper up."

He started to leave, but turned back at the door. "One last thing—about the governor." The look on his face was an odd one—almost compassionate. "You should know that it has anti-tamper features. It's booby-trapped. You try to remove it—to cut it out—it'll kill you."

THIRTEEN

"Come away from the edge!"

At one end of the Aerie, framed, as most things were in the dwelling, by overloaded bookshelves, stood an entertainment center with a ten-year-old Sony TV, a standard VCR, a DVD player, and a specialty player for 8mm videotapes. Davy and Millie watched the occasional rented movie there, but its main purpose was as a repository of Davy's jump sites.

Early in his jumping career, he'd discovered that, unless he used a site on a regular basis, he couldn't recall enough detail to return there without some sort of memory aid. The result was several racks of thirty-minute 8mm videotapes with labels such as *NYC: Central Park West by Museum of Natural History*, *Western Australia: Kalgoorlie-Boulder Train Station, San Francisco: Metreon*, and *Moscow: Tabula Rasa Night Club, 28 Bereshkovskaya Naereshnaya*.

She was busy working her way through the places she had been, especially those in New England—those that might help her in the search for Davy. There was never more than a few minutes at the start of each tape—Davy didn't want to search through an entire tape when he wanted to recall a jump site and thirty minutes was the smallest commonly available tape size.

The image on the tape showed a classic Greek revival building in white stone with four Doric columns. Large golden letters adorned the frieze: QUINCY MARKET. The plaza before the building consisted of alternating ten-foot sections of flagstones and old brick. Bright blue market umbrellas stretched down one side of the building and people walked around in shorts. On the audio Davy's voice said, "Faneuil Hall Marketplace. The overriding impression is baking bread and other restaurant smells with a whiff of traffic exhaust."

This was enough to recall her last visit, an evening walk, idly browsing the stores. Davy had eaten a cookie from Kivert and Forbes and she'd bought a beeswax taper at Yankee Candle. It was last September and they'd been comfortably cool there when it was suffocating back in Stillwater.

She stopped the tape and jumped, appearing behind the column in the teeth of a cold wind that whipped around the corner of the building. The market umbrellas were gone for the season. She shivered and hurried inside the colonnade where she bought a calzone from North End Bakery.

This was the pattern. Watch a tape. Once she recalled a place well enough, she took the jump, then sat in that place—sampled it—until it was firmly fixed. This often involved food, perhaps a regional specialty: Italian in Boston, a street vendor hot dog in New York, a pretzel in Philadelphia, a polish sausage in Pittsburgh.

I'm going to get fat. But in truth, she merely tasted a few bites before it would cloy in the mouth. There was nothing wrong with the food but, ever since Davy went missing, she had had no appetite.

After acquiring several sites, she jumped to the Manhattan Kinko's, where she checked her e-mail. Anders had sent a message requesting a call. "And don't use your cell." He left a number. She jumped to Union Station in D.C. and used a pay phone.

"The second ambulance was found abandoned in Tiverton, Rhode Island, a small town across the Sakonnet River from Portsmouth. It sat for two days in the parking lot of the local hospital. Those who remember seeing it, thought it was there for a transfer, in or out. Finally a State Trooper put the FBI's bulletin and the ambulance's Vehicle Identification Number together and phoned it in."

"Northeast, again," Millie observed.

"Yes. The FBI went over it. There were no unexpected prints and several smudges made by fingers wearing rubber gloves, but, since latex gloves are routinely worn by emergency response personnel, this isn't conclusive. No one saw who had left the ambulance. They're widening inquiries, to see if the ambulance was spotted anywhere else in the state, but nothing, so far."

Millie replied thoughtfully. "But it was northeast, again, like the ambulance found at Logan, and it's not unreasonable to assume that it indicated at least a general direction."

Anders agreed. "But that's not the main reason I called."

"No?"

"I'm being watched—within the agency. And someone way above me is clamping down on the search for Davy. They've reassigned resources and discouraged continued monitoring of Bochstettler and Associates."

"Are you being monitored now? Are they listening?"

"No. This is a prepaid cell phone I acquired with cash and fake stats months ago when I was working a different case. It was a contingency phone that never got used. They've got your phone, though. You put the number on all those flyers so they'll have the ESN from your service provider. That's why I told you not to use it."

"Don't knock the flyers. They got me Ms. Johnson. They sucked in Padgett and Hyacinth Pope."

"I'll grant you Ms. Johnson. We can't be sure that Padgett and Pope weren't pulled in by other means. Whoever knew Davy was meeting Brian Cox probably knew we'd moved my surveillance of you from Oklahoma to D.C."

"More leaks from the NSA." She did not make it a question.

Anders didn't hesitate. "It might not even be leaks. The way this is going down, it might even be another part of the agency."

"The NSA kidnapped Davy?"

Anders was silent for a bit. "If not them, then someone with so much pull, they can influence the agency."

Millie returned to Boston—this time the unmarked circle of cobblestones to the east of the Old State House. She didn't need a videotape. It was her imagination that recalled the spot—not so much its actual appearance—a vivid visualization of the event it marked: the Boston Massacre. She'd read a biography of Crispus Attucks as a child and visiting the spot with Davy had fixed it forever in her mind.

She appeared in the midst of a tour. Several tourists gasped and one stumbled. She said, "Excuse me," and walked on.

She heard a voice behind her say, "Where did *she* come fr—" before it faded into the traffic noise.

She took a cab to the Boston South Station and caught a MBTA commuter train to Providence. She didn't think it was necessary to travel to Tiverton. She thought, like Anders, that it was just a place to dump the ambulance. But she didn't have a jump site in Rhode Island. Davy did, but she'd never been there so his tape was useless.

The train she took stopped seven times before pulling into Providence, but only took an hour and three minutes, total. She could've flown much quicker or rented a car, but these things required identifying herself, and she didn't want to be plugged into the system. The very thought of it made her feel as if electronic fingers were running through her hair and tugging at her clothing.

She shuddered.

In Providence she took a cab to the harborfront and drank coffee while walking briefly through the old buildings of the east side. She found an alleyway with a unique view of the waterfront and chose it as a site. She tried it a few times, jumping back and forth to the Aerie, then dispirited, found a bench overlooking the water.

It was perhaps fifty degrees but the sun was out and there was very little breeze. She settled in Davy's old leather jacket and scowled at the seagulls that settled expectantly before her.

What am I doing? Would any of this running around really help?

Well, it keeps me from going crazy.

She dropped the coffee cup in a trash barrel and walked west along the waterfront, toward the Radisson. A man turned the corner and ran toward her and she flinched before realizing it was just a jogger.

For a moment she'd thought—*Well, I don't know what I thought. Maybe that they'd recognized me, even if this isn't where they supposed me to be.* If she kept working the areas where Davy was likely to be found, someone, the NSA or BAd Boys or FBI, would recognize her.

Have to do something about that.

She went back to the Aerie and pawed through the tapes until she found a jump site in London. It was four P.M. there, but she found a hairdresser in Kensington High Street who was available and would do what she wanted *and* for U.S. currency.

She left, two hours later, her shoulder-length, straight brown hair gone, replaced by ash blond hair cut mannishly short. The stylist, a young woman with blue hair and several piercings, asked for Millie's phone number but was told, gently, "Tourist. Going back to the States today."

She then made it true by jumping to Albuquerque and visiting an optician on Eubank and Comanche. She knew the place because of time spent with cousins who'd lived in the adjoining subdivision—not because it was one of Davy's haunts—but she recalled it well enough to jump. She took the precaution of jumping first to the Aerie, to equalize her ears, before jumping to Albuquerque, a mile above sea level.

It was well she'd come west to the mountain time zone. She had to wait a hour for the optician to see her without an appointment and, as the woman insisted on dilating Millie's eyes, she had to sit in the waiting room with her eyes covered before her pupils recovered enough to try the contacts.

They had obviously improved the technology in recent years. The last time she'd tried contacts, in her teens, she'd been unable to insert them without epic struggles, or endure them, once they were in. She'd given up in disgust.

Now, a few blinks, and it was as if they weren't there. She agreed to the doctor's suggestion, continuous-wear disposables, designed to be worn for two weeks, day and night, then thrown away. They were green-tinted and when she looked in the mirror, she didn't recognize herself.

When did I lose so much weight? The past weeks had taken their toll. She'd noticed the loosening of clothing but, with her long brown hair framing and partially concealing her face, the extent of the change had gone unnoticed. Now, with cheekbones more pronounced and chin sharpened slightly, as well as the changes to hair length, hair and eye color, she looked like someone who *might* be related to Millie Harrison-Rice . . . but not closely.

Which is both good and bad.

One more level of change, she decided, was needed. Ala Moana shopping center in Honolulu was her next step. She looked up at the sun, shining down through the palm trees, still quite high above the horizon. *I am in a perpetual afternoon.* She shook her head and yawned. She was tired, her internal clock was still set six hours to the east, and though it was four o'clock in Honolulu, it was ten at night in D.C.

She hit the boutiques, buying things she didn't ordinarily wear: dresses, formal skirt and jacket combos, and pants suits. She tried to avoid anything too striking. Her goal was not to be noticed. But she wanted to *not* dress as she had in D.C.

At Hino's Hairstyles & Wigs she purchased a brown wig and had it shortened slightly, until, wearing it, she looked pretty much as she had before the attentions of the blue-haired stylist in Kensington High Street.

Her last purchase, from LensCrafters, was a pair of glasses right off the display rack, no prescription. "I know it sounds a little strange but I wear these frames when I'm not wearing my contacts." She showed them her prescription glasses from the purse. "But my clients trust me more when I wear glasses and I'm in long-wear contacts, now. I want a pair I can use over them."

The clerk assured Millie that she'd heard much stranger reasons. "There are people who want to look intellectual but are cursed with good eyesight. Also, actors. Women with older husbands. And then there's safety glasses."

These are *safety glasses.* She paid cash, jumped back to the Aerie, and slept.

She had the cab drop her after they'd passed the address.

The offices of Bochstettler and Associates were not, as she had originally supposed, in D.C. proper. Instead, they occupied a small, two-story office building off Interstate 395 in Alexandria.

It was a two-story brown brick building surrounded by a high wall of matching brick with a manned gate. Like alien flowers, bouquets of video cameras adorned the corners of the roof or stared down over the walls on thin pylons. The windows were narrow slits of mirrored glass and, combined with the wall, made Millie think of arrow loops set in the side of a castle keep.

She studied the building again from the roof of a six-story medical professional building a block over.

She'd taken the elevator up to five, a floor the directory showed had an internal medicine clinic, two oral surgeons, a chiropractor, and an acupuncturist. The waiting rooms were not combined and she had no problem following the exit signs to a stairwell door. The door to the roof had one of those electronic latches brightly labeled "Alarm Will Sound," but also contained a wire-reinforced glass window, so she'd been able to jump past without opening the door.

Now she could tell there was an interior atrium at Bochstettler and Associates that seemed deeper than it should be and that what the building lacked in windows on the outside, it more than made up in the interior courtyard, those walls being all glass, floor to ceiling. There was a single row of parking around two sides of the building that held sixteen cars and three limos.

The medical professional building she stood atop was the tallest structure in the vicinity so she felt confident of her privacy. Even the small bull's-eye window in the roof access door was on the other side of the elevator machine shack, so if someone looked out that window, they wouldn't see her.

She looked at the sun. The medical building was southwest of Bochstettler and Associates, so the sun was behind her and to the right. *Binoculars are called for.* Behind her she heard the whining of elevator motors in the machine shack and the massive ventilators, thankfully on the other end of the building, kicking in. She looked down at the gray pea gravel covering the rooftop tar. *And a chair.*

At B&H Photo in New York, she bought a pair of twelve-hundred-dollar binoculars—Canon 18 by 50 All Weather IS. The IS stood for image stabilization. The binoculars made the distant security guard, sitting in his glassed gate booth, look like he was just across a city street, and the slight whirring of the stabilization prisms held the image rock steady despite her unsteady hands. The binocular salesman, a nice Hassidic gentleman in black suit, hat, and long curling sideburns, warned her she'd need a tripod to hold it steady if she let the batteries run out, so she had extra double-As in the pocket of Davy's old leather jacket.

She felt guilty for spending so much on the binoculars so she only spent six bucks on a green plastic patio chair.

Three hours later, her butt aching, she wished she'd spent more on the chair.

She was careful to note that the sun was above and behind her, so the lenses of the binoculars wouldn't give off any tell-tale reflections. She also stayed between the roof's edge and a large rooftop ventilator, keeping her silhouette off the skyline.

The BAd Building, as she was thinking of it now (BAd Building, no biscuit!), had at least one floor underground. The atrium was one floor deeper than the surrounding grass. At this angle, Millie could see into both of the aboveground floors in the atrium and about halfway down the glass of the subsurface level as well. She cursed the angles. She was getting too much reflection from the windows to see more than occasional movement and too little reflection to see the bottom of the atrium.

There'd been some coming and going, as she watched, and now there were seventeen cars in the parking lot and the same number of limos as before, but one had left and another arrived. The security was tight. The gate wasn't opened until the security guard had inspected the passengers of the car and, once, he'd made one driver open his trunk before letting them enter.

When the new limo arrived, it stopped at the front door and

a pair of security guards had come out to flank the car while its occupant, a tallish man in a nice suit, walked quickly inside before the chauffeur could get around the car. The chauffeur was left to shut the door before he got back in and drove the limo around to one of the parking places.

She cursed the man for not looking around as he'd walked in. The only distinctive feature she'd noted was slightly receding temples—nothing extreme—and the perceptible elegance of his suit.

The guards, still looking outward, backed toward the doorway and, only when the man was inside, did they turn and follow.

This was a big shot.

She wondered who he was and what he knew.

"What are you doing up here?"

She hadn't heard the door over the sound of elevator motors and she didn't catch the sound of the footsteps on the gravel roof until the voice was already talking.

She stood quickly and turned, nearly jumping away, but stopping herself in time. *I'll have time to jump if I must.* She stood slowly and looked around.

There were three people standing there. A tall black man in a gray suit, an older guy in maintenance overalls, and, in the lead, a well-dressed woman with short gray-streaked hair.

Millie blinked. It was Becca Martingale, the FBI counterintelligence agent.

Millie was wearing sunglasses and a baseball cap, jeans, and Davy's leather jacket. Since her hair was now blond and very short she wasn't surprised when Becca didn't recognize her. This was a *good* thing.

Time to go.

She turned her back on the agents, took a step toward the foot-high parapet, and looked down at the evergreen shrubbery clustered thickly at the bottom of the building seventy feet below. She froze. *Fingerprints.* The green plastic chair would certainly have hers, where she'd carried it from the store.

Becca misinterpreted her hesitation and said, "That's right. There's no place to go. Come away from the edge!" Millie glanced back at them. They were only ten feet away now.

She took a sliding step to the chair, hooked her arm through the armrest, and stepped back again, away from the agents.

"DON'T!" yelled the black agent, his arm reaching out reflexively.

She jumped, meaning to clear the foot-high parapet, but the chair threw her off balance and her heel caught. Instead of dropping, like she'd planned, feet first, she flipped over and plunged into the open space backwards.

It was remarkably like the first time, at the Aerie, when the anchor bolt broke free of its hole and she'd plunged toward the rocks.

She flinched back to the condo, too flustered to choose a destination. The chair banged into the carpeted floor, wrenching her arm, and she swore out loud, then shut her mouth hard. There was still the possibility of listening devices here.

I hope I was out of sight when I jumped.

She jumped to the Aerie before putting the chair down.

"What were they doing there?" she said aloud. "Could they have followed me?"

To get there she'd taken a cab from Dulles and she supposed they could've spotted her at the airport, but she really doubted it. She didn't look anything like the Millie they knew.

But they do *know about Bochstettler and Associates.* She nodded. That made sense—they'd gone to the roof for exactly the same reason Millie had. To watch the BAd building.

Well, that wasn't so scary, then. They were just following the case and they'd chosen the same surveillance spot. She'd been half afraid they were psychic.

And that means they *weren't called off.* She wondered if the FBI was less vulnerable to pressure from above. *Or if it's inside the NSA and therefore not over the FBI.* She had a chilling thought. *Or they* have *been called off, but* I'm *now the object of their investigation.* She bit her lip for a second, then shook her head. No, that went a bit too far toward paranoia.

But now they'd be wondering what on earth happened to the strange blond woman after she went off the edge of the building. She pictured them rushing to the edge, expecting to see and/or hear her impact the ground below, and then the surprise at seeing and hearing nothing. With any luck, they would think Millie's body hidden by the shrubbery and would waste more time poking through the bushes looking for it.

Next time I do something like that, I must see what I can do to provide a body to be found.

She was back in the medical professionals' building within the hour, wearing a long red wig and a knee length sweater tunic in green and black. The red wig went very well with her green contacts and she felt confident that she no longer resembled either the old Millie or the figure who'd dropped off the building.

On the sixth floor there was a pediatric neurologist whose suite of offices was on the side of the building facing Bochstettler and Associates. The waiting room held several children in powered wheelchairs and a few more in leg braces and crutches. Millie almost flinched away from so much pain, but stopped herself. There wasn't really any noticeable pain in the room—the pain was in her reaction.

Several of the kids were playing a board game, albeit with the aid of attending parents or home health aides to move markers, spin the pointer, and turn over cards. Two of the kids with crutches were giggling in the corner.

Just kids, she admonished herself. If they couldn't walk or even move from the neck down, they were still kids.

There was a reception window but the woman seated there had her back turned, talking on the phone while she flipped through a stack of medical records. Millie walked to the corner of the waiting room hidden from the receptionist, and picked up a magazine.

A girl, strapped into a standing wheelchair operated by a puff/sip switch backed away from the board game which she had been watching, and rolled over to Millie. She brought the chair to a halt with the front wheels inches from Millie's foot.

She had black bangs cut straight across the middle of her forehead and enormous blue eyes which, combined with the silver framework of her chair, made Millie think of a Margaret Keane big-eyed waif painting in a chrome frame.

"Hello," Millie said.

A woman, seated on the other side of the waiting room and reading a book, looked up. "Come away, Maggie," she said mildly.

Millie held out her hand and shook it side to side. "She's not bothering me." To the little girl she said, "My name's Millicent. And your name is Maggie?"

"Like the Rod Stewart song. Though I'm more of a pain in the neck than that woman was. And I don't pick up younger men." Maggie was able to move her head but her arms hung down, strapped to cushioned pads on the frame. "I don't pick up anything."

Millie had thought the girl seven or eight, but now considered revising that upward. "Why do you think you're a pain in the neck?"

"Well. What do *you* think?"

Millie tilted her head to one side and narrowed her eyes before finally saying, "Maybe you think your parents have to do too much to help you. Maybe you lose your temper sometimes and won't cooperate. Maybe you feel ungrateful, sometimes, despite all the stuff you have to have done for you. Maybe you feel no one can possibly understand what you're going through."

Maggie, who'd been smiling, frowned at this. "You're a psych, aren't you?"

"A family therapist," Millie laughed. "And you *are* a pain in the neck."

Maggie nodded, solemnly. "Told you."

"May I ask how old you are?"

She considered this for a moment, finally saying, "You may."

Millie waited for a second, then smiled. "Okay. How old are you?"

"Ten . . . in two months. How old are you?"

"Thirty-three . . . in one month." *And ticking.* "Why the wheelchair?"

"So I don't lay around like a throw rug."

Millie snorted, half involuntary laugh, half sob. "Did I say pain in the neck? I must've meant another portion of the anatomy."

"All right. Swimming pool. Deep dive. Shallow end. I was seven."

Now Millie wanted to cry, but all she said was, "Ouch."

"Could be worse. I can breathe by myself. Look at Christopher Reeve."

The door to the hallway opened. A man stuck his head in and looked around the waiting room. Millie tried not to freeze—it was the large black FBI agent who'd been on the roof with Becca Martingale. He saw him look toward her corner, then pass on. He spent more time studying Angie's mother than anybody else in the room, but then she was sitting by herself and she had brown hair, like Millie's real hair color. He pulled his head back into the hall and let the door shut.

Millie exhaled.

Angie eyed her. "Was that man looking for you?"

"What makes you think that?"

"Well . . . you smiled but you held your breath all the time he was here."

Perceptive. "Ah. Well, I'm not sure who he was looking for." *Which really is true, if disingenuous.* "I wish I had a kid like you."

Maggie looked startled. "What? Broken?"

Millie shook her head. "Smart. Beautiful. Funny."

Maggie wrinkled her nose.

A nurse came to the door and said, "Maggie Peterson."

Maggie blinked her eyes. "Gotta go." She turned the wheelchair with the sip/puff controller.

"Nice meeting you, Maggie." She watched her roll to her mother, then both of them follow the nurse back into the clinic. She pulled out some tissue from her purse and blew her nose. She sighed deeply and asked herself if she was sure she wanted children. The answer was a resounding affirmative *even if they're* broken.

She lifted her magazine and pretended to read again, checking the room. Another woman eyed her before going back to helping with the board game. Just curious, Millie judged. A man, seated by the children with leg braces and crutches, eyed her more circumspectly with most of his attention to her stockinged legs, where they crossed at the knee. *A different kind of curious.* But not one she had to worry about.

Millie ignored both of them and instead checked the office hours posted on a small plastic sign on the reception desk. Today the clinic would close at five. If they took appointments all the way up to closing, she could hope the last of the staff and patients would be out the door by six-six-thirty at the latest.

She was tempted to wait until Maggie came back out. *She'd be leaving, anyway.* Instead she memorized the corner she sat in, then walked back out into the public hallway in the manner, she hoped, of someone seeking a restroom.

She was back at seven, appearing in the corner where she'd talked with Maggie. She was dressed in what she thought of as ninja chic: black tennies, black jeans, black turtleneck, black gloves, and masked, á la ninja, with a black tee-shirt, her eyes peaking out through the neck hole, the tee-shirt's sleeves tied behind her head.

She felt absolutely ridiculous.

"And so, Sheila, is Joe responding to your requests for more emotional connections?"

"No, and I must tell you that I'm having trouble trusting a therapist who wears a mask. Why are you wearing it?"

Why indeed? Well, the answer was video cameras. She wasn't expecting any here in the neurologist's office but from what she'd seen of Bochstettler and Associates, there were more cameras around than tie-dyed tee-shirts at a Grateful Dead concert.

She went looking for a window and was surprised to see that most of the examination rooms, even though they were on the outer wall, didn't have windows. She finally located a floor to ceiling glass wall in a staff break room and found herself with pretty much the same view of the BAd building as she'd had on the roof above.

She lifted the binoculars.

The scene was the same but the video cameras stood out now. They weren't really any more visible. She was just more sensitive to them, now.

There were two at each upper corner of the building. There were four pylons set eight feet inside the fence corners with two cameras each. On two of the inner corners of the atrium, at the roof line, two more cameras tilted down into the courtyard.

But there really didn't seem to be anything surveying the rooftop.

That I can see.

Couldn't be helped. If she wanted to get into the building, she'd have to risk it. It wasn't as if they could stop Millie, even should they spot her.

Don't get cocky. Davy had a lot more experience with this than you and they caught him.

It was this thought that led her to check for *other* observers on a different roof. The one directly above her. *The FBI had a reason for being on that roof.*

She went up the stairs quietly. She found the door shut completely with no sign that the alarm had been disabled. Its little LED was shining brightly. She jumped past it and peeked around the elevator machine stack. No figures crouched or sat at her old watch post but there was something. She walked closer and laughed to herself.

A weatherproof video camera mounted on a sandbag-anchored tripod pointed down at Bochstettler and Associates. A coaxial cable snaked from the camera housing to an antennaed box sitting back from the edge.

They *were* watching. Just not in person. It took her only a few minutes of scanning with the binoculars to find the Verizon phone van parked in an alley a half a block away from the BAd building.

What to do? What to do?

If she jumped onto the roof, she'd be in clear view of the FBI camera. It was dark over there, but she'd bet the camera was low-light capable. They wouldn't be able to tell who it was, but they'd be able to tell that *someone* had appeared on that roof out of nowhere.

She studied her intended destination again. Then bent down and unscrewed the video cable where it entered the antennaed box.

All they can tell is that their camera went dead.

She jumped into deep shadow, crouched on the gravel against a dormant air-conditioning unit. She stayed there, moving only her head, trying to see if any of Bochstettler's cameras were pointed across the rooftop.

She figured she had at least ten minutes easy before the FBI could get back up on the roof and see what happened to their camera. Longer if they had to hunt up someone with a key.

She duck-walked to the edge of the roof overlooking the inner courtyard. At night, with the interior hallways lit and shining through the open doors into the offices lining the top floor, she could see through the reflective glass easily. She picked one of the offices on the opposite side, top floor, and studied carefully, through the binoculars.

This was a harder jump. It was one thing to jump from one gravel rooftop to another. The temperature and wind and slightest whiffs of distant exhaust were the same. There was something about the world on the other side of the tinted glass that seemed unreal. She exercised her imagination picturing her own clinic back in Stillwater as a model for the hushed feeling of a controlled-climate building. Her first attempt, however, put her there, in her own office, and she heard the receptionist, on the phone, in the other room, clearly working late. She returned to the roof. Her next try succeeded.

She was in a large office that actually wrapped around one of the interior corners. Clearly a power office, with almost a living room suite of furniture at one end of the L-shaped room, a large conference table at the bend, and an isolated massive teak desk at the other end. She took a deep breath through her nose and noted some of the details of the carpet and the three abstract paintings on the wall, then looked at her watch.

Only four minutes had passed since she'd disconnected the camera. She jumped back, to the rooftop of the medical building, and reconnected the cable loosely. *An intermittent.* If anyone diagnosed the unit, they might think it a simple loose

connector and not active sabotage. She heard the elevator
motors whine and jumped back to the big corner office, her
heart pounding.

Out of the frying pan . . .

She settled against the wall, in the darkest corner, and listened to the sounds of the building.

There'd been four cars in the parking lot and she would bet
at least two, if not more, belonged to security guards. Probably
more—someone had to be monitoring all those cameras. There
was also the possibility that those cameras outside the building
might have some brethren within. She heard the distant sound
of a vacuum cleaner.

All right. They aren't all security.

She looked around the room, checking, in particular, the
corners at the ceiling, searching for cameras and motion
detectors.

*But, they can't have the staff cleaning and the alarms active
at the same time.*

Millie did not like the contents of the desk. They were laid
out with a geometric purity that was almost sterile. *Or anal.*
There were no files in the desk's file drawers. The only papers
were blank stationery. There was a networked computer, a
sleek black thing with a large flat screen, and a matching key-
board and mouse underneath on a silently sliding shelf.

She turned it on but found it password-protected on the hardware level, not even proceeding to boot. She considered just
taking the entire thing with her.

Surely someone could get at its contents?

The distant vacuum cleaner had stopped and started several
times but now it sounded louder. She gave up on the desk and
tried the two doors at the end of the office. One led to a smaller
office, possibly an assistant's, and the other was a large coat
closet, two umbrellas and dark raincoat hung from the rod and
on the shelf above was an attaché case in gold anodized aluminum, a Halliburton case, the kind that screams "steal me!"
Her heartbeat, slowly settling after the tension of her initial
arrival, shot up again. But the case wasn't locked and it was
empty except for a crumpled sticky note stuck in the corner.

She unfolded it but there was only a ten digit phone number in the 508 area code followed by the letters "egc tt 9/2 2:30."

She stuffed the note deep into her jeans pocket, carefully, making sure it didn't stick to her gloves as she withdrew her hand. She peeked carefully outside the door. The vacuuming came from a lit office three doors down. Each of the doors had a nameplate set beside the door. She glanced at the wall beside her. The plate said, "N. Kelledge, CEO."

The vacuum cut off and a small Hispanic woman in green coveralls backed out of the lighted office carrying a trash can. Millie jerked her head back into the office and jumped away.

She returned to the Aerie tired and frustrated and in need of a bath. Since her unknown enemies had kicked in the hotel room door in Virginia, she'd been making do with sponge baths in the cliff house and, of course, the stylist in London had washed her hair when she'd cut and dyed it.

Dammit! Are they or aren't they monitoring the condo?

She felt like arriving there on foot, unlocking the door, and seeing what happened. *Who would arrive? The NSA, the people who kidnapped Davy, or are they the same?* She still believed that Anders had nothing to do with it but she wasn't confident that it wasn't some other part of the agency.

The thought of another bath interrupted decided her against the attempt. She looked through Davy's site tapes until she found one labeled *Ten Thousand Waves*.

It was an hour earlier in Santa Fe and her ears popped painfully hard—the spa was at eight thousand feet. She walked up to the spa from the lower parking lot, following the footpath through the Japanese landscaping.

She'd brought a swimming suit since she'd expected to be using the non-reserved communal tub, but the last hour bath was starting in ten minutes and one of the smaller private tubs was available due to a cancellation. She shampooed and washed in the woman's shower room and wore the provided kimono to her assigned bath, an acrylic hot tub surrounded by shoji screens, except for its uphill side, which faced on scrub piñon trees trained by nature and twenty years of judicious care, into bonsai-like perfection. The New Mexico sky was studded with brilliant pricks of light and there was snow, in spots, under the trees.

She was glad not to use the bathing suit but the hot water and icy cold air made her long for Davy. The last time she'd been here with him they'd used the Ichiban room—which had included an indoor mattress. She ached at the thought. When she climbed out of the tub she was grateful for the cold air for more than one reason.

She checked out and jumped back to the Aerie the minute the receptionist's back was turned.

Underwear. She had clothing enough in the Aerie because of her shopping, but her underwear supplies were depleted. There were clean panties and bras in Stillwater.

She jumped to the living room of the condo and looked around, nervously. It was quiet, as usual, but there was a strange tickle in her throat. She sniffed deeply through her nose. Again, she felt something odd in her throat. She thought that the weekly cleaning lady, Lonnie, must've changed the furniture polish she was using. Millie didn't like it.

The room was quite dark, only lit by the diffused glow of a streetlight shining through the drapes, but she could tell something was different at the front door. She took a step toward it and the room lurched, tilted oddly. She dropped to her knees, her robe opening where she'd been holding it shut.

The door had been taped shut, long strips of duct tape running around the sides and top and triple wide at the gap between door and floor. She twisted around and saw plastic sheeting over the fireplace.

That's odd, she thought, almost dreamily. Her lungs felt heavy. Convulsively, she stabbed her nails into her bare thigh, raking, knowing the feeling of calm was an artifact. It was the lack of sensation, the lack of response from her nerves that finally awoke in her a sense of urgency.

Inhalation anesthetic.

She flinched away.

She felt the gritty limestone texture of the bare rock of the Aerie floor on her knees, then her cheek, and then nothing.

FOURTEEN

Mugu Man

For two days Davy let the servants wait upon him, jumping down to the beach twice a day, and losing himself in the DVD collection. He tried not to think. Not of Brian Cox, not of escape, not of his captors, not of Millie. For a period in the morning and in the afternoon, he performed for Dr. Conley, jumping to and from specific locations in the courtyard as Conley measured, recorded, and speculated.

He was not surprised to learn that there was no increase in local radioactivity when he jumped. Nor any other electromagnetic fluctuations. However, an Infrared Imaging Camera, when he jumped from the shade of a wall to a sunlit portion of the courtyard, showed a slight increase in temperature at his departure site and a slight drop at his destination. It was the barest tenth of a degree change.

"The difference in temperature between the two locations is over six degrees. There must be some sort of leakage when you jump."

Davy nodded. "Perhaps." His own experience told him he wasn't disappearing one place and appearing another, but that a gate opened ever so briefly. He'd captured it, once, on video tape, and wondered if Conley had. He didn't ask, though. He didn't want to give Conley any ideas.

The next day, when he appeared in the courtyard at Conley's

request, he found a strange apparatus consisting of a large, transparent four-foot cube made of one-inch-thick sheets of plastic and held together by a framework of pipe clamps. Davy went closer and smelled acetic acid. He saw that the joints had been heavily sealed with a translucent substance and the smell confirmed silicone caulk.

The chamber's only other feature was a pair of plastic pipe nipples threaded through the top. One went to a large pressure gauge with a range of 800 to 1200 millibars and the other went to a rubber hose that went off to a small air compressor.

Conley was waiting.

Davy stared at the chamber with disfavor. "Do you know anything about diving physiology?" Davy asked.

"A little." He pointed at the gauge. "The reading is absolute. I don't expect to work in differences of more than 20 millibars, so I don't think we have to worry too much about popping your lungs or your eardrums."

Davy stepped closer. The gauge read 1002 millibars but Davy had no idea how close that was to normal pressure at sea level. "Is it pressurized right now?"

"Not a bit." Conley pointed to a valve manifold mounted on the compressor. "It's open to the outside."

Davy crouched down and jumped into the box. It was warmer inside, catching the sun, but the pressure, as Conley had said, was the same. He jumped back out.

"All right. What's your plan?"

"Well, why don't I start by pumping some air into the box, about twenty millibars. Then you jump into it and we'll see what happens to the pressure. If your volume just appears out of nowhere, we should see a slight increase in pressure as the air in the chamber is compressed into a smaller space."

"How much is twenty millibars in pounds per square inch?"

A true physicist, Conley pulled out a calculator. "Uhm, point-two-nine-oh-oh. A little more than a quarter of one psi."

Davy said, "I can live with that."

He watched the gauge carefully as Conley switched valves and added a little air into the chamber. The gauge climbed much faster than Conley expected and he had to bleed some off to get down to the designated 1022 millibars. He shut the valve and said, "There. Barely half an inch of mercury. Just an afternoon high pressure zone."

Davy worked his jaw left to right to ready his eustachian tubes, then crouched again. He opened his mouth wide and jumped into the chamber but didn't really notice any pressure difference in his ears, though he felt air move through his hair for an instant. Davy glanced at Conley through the plastic and saw that the physicist's jaw had dropped.

"What?" he asked Conley, reappearing beside him.

"The second you appeared the pressure dropped back to atmospheric. It *didn't* increase."

"Umm." Davy didn't comment.

Conley frowned at him. "You suspected this, didn't you?"

"Not really. My ears pop all the time when I change altitudes." *But I'm usually not changing to and from sealed chambers.*

"Let's reverse it. Get in. Then I'll increase the pressure and we'll see what happens when you jump out."

"No more than twenty-millibars, right?"

Conley held up his right hand, palm out. "Swear."

Davy jumped back into the cube.

Davy's ears popped as the compressor ran. By craning his neck around, he could just see the gauge through the top of the chamber. Conley got the pressure right, 1022, first time, without having to bleed it back down.

Conley shut the manifold and backed away, his eyes on the gauge.

Davy jumped. His ears popped again. He looked at the gauge on the chamber. It read 1002. As he'd suspected.

"I think your gauge must be broken," he said to Conley.

"Tunneling. So that's it. It must've been warm and cold air that carried the temperature difference. When you jump, air flows through the hole."

Davy didn't say anything.

"Go put on some shorts."

"What?"

"Shorts. No socks. No shoes. Please."

Davy returned before Conley had completed his arrangements. Conley carried two plastic dishpans out of the back door of the house and behind him came one of the footmen, carrying a bucket.

Davy stood on the grass, which was cold, but not as cold as the sidewalk. Conley put the two dishpans down and directed the man carrying the bucket to fill one of them. The water steamed slightly in the cold air and Davy was relieved. At least they weren't using cold water.

Conley dismissed the footman and turned to Davy. "All right. Let's see what else passes through the hole." He stuck a ruler into the full dishpan. The water filled three quarters of its volume and the ruler showed five and a half inches at the waterline. "Stand in that, please."

"I'm going to catch my death, traipsing about in shorts with wet feet."

Conley smiled grimly. "Catching your death may be a real problem, but it won't be from a cold."

Davy stepped into the warm water. It rose slightly over his ankle.

"Good," said Conley. "Please teleport into the other dishpan."

Davy obliged. He looked down. There was a good inch of water in the previously empty dishpan he was standing in.

Conley, back at the other pan, was measuring the depth again. "Well, that's interesting, isn't it? Is it flowing through the hole or just clinging to you, a sort of surface effect, when you jump?" He motioned Davy to step out of the tub and measured the water depth. "Three quarters of an inch. Back in please."

"The full one?"

"No, this one," he pointed at the mostly empty pan. When Davy had done this, he motioned Davy to jump back into the filled tub. "Teleport back, will you?"

Davy did so.

"Conley stooped and measured the water in the mostly empty tub. "An inch and a half. The water is not clinging to you. It's flowing downhill, from deeper water to shallow, through the hole—the gate." He stared at Davy, not as a person stares at a person, but as a person stares at an annoying mystery. "You're folding space," he said, accusingly.

"We'll need a gravity gradiometer."

They put Davy in the back of a cargo van.

"You're scaring me, you know," he said to Conley.

"It's just like the beach. We've got two split keys, one in a car ahead of us, one behind. You'll be fine."

Davy tapped the door of the van. "Metal. Faraday cage. Electromagnetic interference?"

"Ah." Conley pointed at a loop of wire hanging in the middle of the van ceiling. "I've run an antenna. It conducts the signal quite well. We had a test run this morning over the same route. I sat inside with the meter and there wasn't the slightest dip in signal strength."

"You could have traffic problems," said Davy.

"During the off season? Don't worry. You're not secured. You can jump back to your room at the slightest hint of nausea." Conley shut the door.

Davy sat at the front of the compartment, his back against the bulkhead dividing the cargo compartment from the driver's cab. They hadn't given Davy a watch but he counted off the seconds. There were five minutes of bumpy gravel road, then they turned onto pavement. There were a few stops, as if for a stop sign, and once a stop-start-stop-start that was clearly a few cars waiting to go through a stop sign.

He'd counted out fifteen hundred seconds before he felt the van turn tightly, then reverse. Conley opened the rear door and Davy blinked. It wasn't as bright as he expected. The van was inside an airplane hangar.

It was pretty obvious. An airplane, a single engine utility craft was parked right in front of him. There was a weird boom extending aft from the bottom of the tail section and the letters on the pilot's door said, "BHP Falcon Survey System."

Conley smiled. "We only have this for an hour. It's not the expense, but the fact that there are only a few of them and they're heavily scheduled."

"What is 'this?' " Davy asked.

Conley led him around to an open cargo door in the side of the craft. "It's an airborne three-D gravity gradiometer. They're using technology declassified a couple of years ago—a navigation tool used by nuclear submarines. They use it to locate ore bodies and map hydrocarbon reservoirs."

"How sensitive is it?"

"Perhaps too sensitive. At one meter it can detect the gravity generated by a three-year-old child."

Inside the plane a man sat at a console. A squat black rounded disk was mounted on the floor. Wires led out of gold-colored connectors and snaked down the side.

"I'm surprised you didn't just buy one," said Davy.

Conley sighed, but before he spoke the technician at the console said in a thick Australian accent, "So, that vehicle will be here during the test?"

"Yes."

"Very well. They've set up your screens," he gestured toward the side of the hangar where Davy saw the sort of standing panels used to make cubicle farms in big offices. They were set up in a long row.

"Right," Conley said. "When can we start?"

"I've got to do a calibration run with you lot at least a hundred meters away. It'll take ten minutes."

"Very well. We'll be back in fifteen?"

The tech nodded and Conley led Davy toward the end of the screens and around one end. On the other side, a standard doorway was set into the much larger hangar door. When they were at it, but before he opened the door he said, "Jump back to your room, right? Someone will tell you when to come back here." He pointed at the floor right in front of the exterior door. "Can you do that?"

Rather than answer, Davy just did it, appearing next to the four poster bed back at the mansion.

The clock on the entertainment center showed fifteen minutes elapsed before Abney, the butler, came in to tell him his presence was requested back at the hangar. Davy jumped in front of him. He didn't know how "trusted" Abney was but he hadn't been told to avoid his talent in front of the servants. He had a morbid feeling that they'd all be killed after this.

Conley was waiting for him. They walked back to the end of the screen. Conley pointed out a series of chalked circles on the concrete behind the screen. "All we want you to do is, first, simply walk from this circle to the far circle. Slowly. After that, teleport back to this first circle, count to five, the next circle, count to five, the next circle, count to five, etc."

He had Davy do a dry run while he watched. "Right. I have to clear out so my mass doesn't interfere, but the technician will give you the go-ahead, all right?"

"Understood."

"After the last jump, count to five and go back to the house. Don't come back here cause I'll have turned off the keys." Conley left by the door. As it shut, Davy jumped to it and looked through the rapidly closing gap. All he saw was a stretch of concrete and then low green brush beyond. In the distance, he saw a barn silo. It didn't tell him much. He returned to the first circle. After a moment, the Australian accent called out, "Ready when you are!"

Davy did the slow walk to the far circle, then the series of jumps with the five-second pauses. He waited the additional time before jumping back to the house.

And what did that prove?

There were heavy winds and thunder that night. The rain had stopped by dawn, but the waves thundered still onto the beach the next morning and Davy spent a good hour watching them pound the sand. It was therapeutic. He didn't know which he identified with more—the surf, raging against the immovable stone outcroppings, or the rocks, taking enormous punishment without being able to strike back.

Without thinking about it, he realized the beach faced south. It was the sun's movement across the sky and his memory of its position other times he'd been there. *That fits Martha's Vineyard.*

Conley hadn't bothered him after the test in the hangar. Nor had he shown up that morning. Davy was torn—curious about the results, yet happy to be left alone.

They kept a watch on him, when he was on the beach. Not to prevent him from fleeing or wandering out of bounds—obviously the governor did that—but to keep him from communicating with anyone.

Before they gave him clearance to go to the beach, they would send someone out to sit on a tall rock outside the safe zone with a view up and down the shore. If the beach was empty of people, they switched on the key transmitters and told him Davy was clear to jump.

The beach was private, without public access, but there were people in some of the neighboring houses, caretakers and stubborn winter residents surf casting in hip waders, but he'd only see them in the distance. If they looked like they were coming down the beach toward Davy, his watcher would speak on his radio and blow a whistle to let Davy know they were turning off the keys in the next two seconds.

Davy disliked the whistle almost as much as he did the earlier waves of warning nausea. In fact, at the whistle's shrill call, he'd feel nauseated but without the telltale tingle in his throat.

Only when he was back in the box did the sensation leave off.

This morning they blew the whistle before lunch when there wasn't anybody visible on the beach, near or far.

He stood in the box, breathing deeply. The door opened.

It was Hyacinth "Miss Minchin" Pope.

He almost didn't recognize her. She was dressed in a black tailored suit that conformed tightly to her figure. The skirt was short, mid-thigh, and the stockings were patterned lace ending in high-heeled pumps.

And her hair was down, falling past her shoulders in shining waves.

I guess her brains don't fall out. He felt that familiar tug of desire mixed with fear, but he managed to keep his face impassive.

"Miss Pope."

"Mr. Rice." She sauntered into the room, the heels making

her hips roll even more than usual, and perched on the arm of the recliner. "You've come up in the world, I see."

Davy couldn't help himself. "It's my reward for throwing you around. I wonder if I could work up to my own bungalow?"

She laughed at him and crossed her legs. The skirt inched up and Davy saw the tabs of a garter belt suspender hooked to the top of the stocking. She leaned forward, causing the skirt to inch even higher.

Davy swallowed. "What may I do for you, Miss Pope?"

"I've come to fetch you for lunch. In the dining room. Do you want to change first?" She eyed his Dockers, tennis shoes, and sweater.

"Is this a formal event?"

She shook her head. "No, just thought I could . . . help." She licked her upper lip, a quick motion from one corner of her mouth to the other.

"I'll wash up," Davy said. He took off the windbreaker and hung it in the closet, then went into the bathroom, washed his hands and face, and combed his hair.

For a second he stared blankly at his reflection in the mirror. *What does she want?* He wondered if she was back in charge and Dr. Conley was no longer involved.

When he came out of the bathroom, she was in the lounger, sideways, looking like a lingerie ad. Her back was against one chair arm, left leg over the other, right leg straight up in the air. She was smoothing her stocking and her skirt had ridden so high Davy could make out black lace panties.

He swallowed hard and jumped past her to the door. Holding it open politely, he said, "Shall we?" Thankfully the back of the lounger blocked the more salacious parts.

She swiveled and stood, demurely smoothing her skirt as she passed him.

He didn't walk beside her but proceeded by jumps, first to the head of the stairs, again waiting politely until she'd reached him, then jumping to the landing below, then the second floor hall, next landing, ground floor hall. He even held the chair for her.

I'm not with *you.*

She was looking at him warily by the time he sat himself.

They were the only diners. Lunch was served by two foot-men supervised by Abney the butler. Abney presented a wine bottle to Davy and he forestalled the ceremony by saying, "Per-haps Miss Pope would lend her expertise."

Abney didn't blink but changed to the other side of the table, presenting the label to Miss Pope instead. She nodded, tasted, and eventually approved a white Spätlese to go with their clam chowder and pasta with lobster, tomatoes, and *herbes de maquis*.

When Hyacinth asked, Abney explained that the *Maquis* was a thick underbrush that covered parts of Corsica and the herbs that grew there gave the island its nickname, "the scented isle."

The round loaf of hard-crusted bread was hot from the oven and wonderfully suited to soaking up the sauce. Davy concen-trated on eating. Finally, he asked, "What has become of Dr. Conley?"

Hyacinth patted her lips with the linen napkin. "The good doctor has gone off to consult with colleagues. Apparently his little experiment with the very expensive gravity thingie pro-duced results. Lots of 'em. He is in analysis mode for the time being."

She held up her wineglass and one of the footmen stepped forward and poured. She didn't even look at him. "Which leaves time for *us*."

Davy didn't like the sound of that. He raised his eyebrows.

She took a plastic prescription pill container from her suit pocket and pushed it across the table. "Take one."

"What is it?"

"Doxycycline. We're going to take a little trip."

He looked at the label. It read, "Doxycycline, 100mg. Take Once Daily, for the prevention of Malaria."

"The tropics. Just the two of us?"

She shook her head. "Not exactly."

Too bad. Not that he had any romantic intentions. If he were traveling with just one, they would have to use the complete signal transmitter and he might be able to grab it. Instead, they were probably going to do that roving split key thing, half in front, half in back. If it were just Hyacinth and himself, he could consider possibilities.

"Where are we going?"

"Nigeria."

They made the jump in the middle of the next afternoon.

"It'll be dark there, now," said Hyacinth, checking her watch. She'd changed into khaki pants, hiking boots, and a photojournalist's vest over a cotton polo. She carried a shoulder bag and her hair was back up in its usual tight bun.

Davy'd stuck with jeans, tennies, and a white cotton buttondown with the sleeves rolled to the elbows. They both reeked of DEET. There was always malaria to consider in Africa and Nigeria definitely had the chloroquine-resistant *P. falciparum*, which was why she'd given him the doxycycline.

"You're sure the keys are in place?" He hadn't meant to ask—it was almost convulsive—but the fear of jumping into an area without a safe zone was uncontrollable.

The bastards had done their job well.

"I told you. They called. They've bracketed the terminal building. You *said* you could do it." She put an edge of derision in her voice.

Mr. Simons, Hyacinth informed him, had sent the team out two days previously.

"All right, then," Davy said.

For Davy it was routine, but he felt Hyacinth stagger as he set her down in the terminal. He steadied her automatically as she reacted to the environmental changes: light to dark, winter central heating to an air conditioning system not keeping up with the humidity, and the total change in smells.

The dark nook off of baggage claim, normally empty, was occupied by three Hausa women and a child, watching a violent thunderstorm through the glass doors of the terminal. Davy had appeared just behind them and set Hyacinth down before the women noticed.

After her initial start, Hyacinth stood quietly. Then a bright flash of lightning striking outside the terminal followed immediately by a window rattling thunderclap caused them all to jump, Davy included.

The women gasped, almost screamed, when they noticed Davy and Hyacinth standing directly behind them and they scurried away, dragging the surprised child, and casting frightened looks over their shoulders.

Hyacinth gave a half-laugh then asked, "Where is ground transportation?"

Davy thought about directing her to the long line of small pickups, some with shells on the back, that crowded fifteen or twenty locals aboard for fifty Naira each. Instead he pointed at a set of doors across the broad hall and they started around the edge of the room, avoiding the crowds waiting for luggage or passengers. He'd been here several times and was prepared when a large, heavy local man dressed in jungle camouflage battle dress stopped in front of them and demanded their papers.

Hyacinth was reaching into her bag, probably for a bribe, Davy thought. "Don't," he said conversationally. "He's not a real official. It's an extortion scam."

"Are you sure?"

"He doesn't have rank insignia. I'm sure."

The man, who heard all this, raised his voice. "Your papers! Now!"

Davy shook his head. "Perhaps you could show us *your* identification," he raised his voice almost to a shout, "Mr. *Barawo*."

People turned at the word.

The man looked around and swore, then snatched at the strap of Hyacinth's bag but missed when she took a step back out of reach. He made the mistake of following.

She kicked him in the shin, then broke his nose with the heel of her hand. He staggered back, dripping red.

There was a stir from the other end of baggage claim and the real thing arrived: uniformed and armed National Police.

Davy gestured at the man holding his bloody nose. "*Barawo*. He tried to steal her bag."

"Ah," said the sergeant in charge. He gestured. "Take him."

A bystander, another local dressed in a cheap suit, said, "No. She attacked him!"

Confederate. Davy shook his head, then looked at the man with the bleeding nose still blinking tears from his eyes. He must've weighed twice what Hyacinth did. Then pointedly back at Hyacinth.

One of the NPF said, "*Abokin barawo, barawo ne.*"

The man in the suit gulped, then backed away. "Perhaps I was mistaken."

Davy asked the policeman, "What is that you said, about a thief?"

The sergeant in charge translated, "The friend of a thief is a thief also."

"*Usema.*" *Thanks.* Davy turned to Hyacinth. "A gift here would keep us from having to go to the local NPF precinct to make a statement."

She nodded and took her hand out of the bag, something folded within. She held it out to the man in charge, as if she were going to shake his hand. "We are late for an appointment, Captain. We really appreciate your help in this matter. Would it be all right if we went on?"

The sergeant didn't correct her about his rank but glanced surreptitiously at the wad of Naira notes she'd handed him. They were each of the five-hundred denomination, about $3.80 U.S. each, but the wad was half an inch thick, folded. He stuck the money in his pocket, then stepped back and saluted. "Quite all right, Madame. We will deal with this *mugu* man."

"*Na gode,*" said Davy.

They went through the doors. There was a tan GMC SUV sitting at the curb with two guards huddled against it, the shapes of their assault rifles showing through their ponchos as the rain streamed off the plastic.

The rear door opened as Hyacinth stepped out, and she and Davy dashed through the downpour, then scrambled into the rearmost bench seat. A gray-haired occidental in khakis, seated in the front passenger seat, watched them as they climbed in. The two armed guards followed them, taking the center bench seat and resting their gun stocks on the floor. "Go," the white man said and the driver gunned the engine and the SUV moved out with a jerk that rocked Davy in his seat and swung the door shut.

Davy twisted and looked back through the rain. A few of the NPF were coming out onto the sidewalk, perhaps to try a separate shakedown of their own or just to see where they were going but they flinched back from the rain.

Hyacinth said, "What did he call that guy? *Mugu*?"

Davy leaned forward and asked one of the guards.

"*Mugu*?" the guard replied. "Bad. Evil."

Davy shivered. The AC was on and he was wet from the rain, but it wasn't the cold. Yes, the man in the terminal had been evil, but it was a small evil, lowercase. He stole and bullied and extorted "let me go" money from insecure people.

He looked at Hyacinth: her hair was back in the tight bun he'd only seen her without once. She was evil. Her boss was even worse.

They passed the airport sign. Murtala Muhammad had been a pretty good leader, for a dictator. He'd cut way back on corruption and seemed to be steering the country into some form of prosperity when a bunch of sergeants and low-ranking officers killed him in 1976. Still, they named the airport after him.

Davy hated coming to Nigeria.

He'd been here several times before the death of Sani Abacha, the last dictator. Once it had been for the NSA and other times for himself, removing a few Amnesty International personnel thrown in jail by the late regime. Nigeria was the sixth largest producer of oil in the world, yet it had the most appalling poverty and violence. Abacha's family got over three billion U.S. out before he died of his "heart attack" and, while some of the money had been recovered from the Swiss banks, the bulk was still missing.

The SUV didn't head into Lagos. Davy was glad. He'd heard that the roadblocks were nowhere near as bad now, but in the old days you never knew if you'd be stopped by the police, the army, or a local gang intent on robbery and murder. Instead, the vehicle rounded the airport on the perimeter road and turned into the guarded gate at the commercial air operations terminal, where the charter and oil company air services were.

He wondered where the keys were. He hadn't seen any cars preceding or following them, so they couldn't be very close. They must be broadcasting a fairly strong signal. *Or they hid both keys in this car and just aren't telling me.*

One of the hangar doors was open, a ten-foot gap, and the SUV pulled straight in, the headlights throwing sweeping shadows across the walls as the pounding of the rain on the SUV's roof stopped with an abruptness that was almost shocking.

He saw three helicopters and a single-engine airplane. A series of small offices had been partitioned against the rear of the hangar. The driver cut the headlights and it got even darker as someone shut the hangar door and they all got out.

The rain was even louder on the hangar roof—more area, less insulation—an oppressive wall of noise. Nobody tried to talk but someone switched on the overhead lights. They were weak fluorescent fixtures and the result, even after they flickered completely on, was inadequate, as if there was a film over the eye.

At the front of the hangar the local who'd pushed the hangar door shut waved, picked up a spindly, misshapen umbrella with a few broken ribs, and ducked out into the storm through a small door set in the greater hangar door.

The man from the front seat looked at the guards and said, "Gentlemen," and pointed at the doorway. One of the men said, "We are here to guard, not to stand in the rain. We will stay inside."

The man in khaki said something in Hausa.

The guards looked surprised, then laughed.

"And you will be paid," added the man.

The two guards pulled up the hoods on their ponchos and moved out into the storm.

"What did you say?" Hyacinth asked.

"A Hausa proverb: It's a new thing for a thief to knock at the door before entering. This way." He pointed to one of the small offices, the corner one. He unlocked it with a key, reached in and flipped a switch.

The lights inside were brighter than the poor ones in the hangar and it was air-conditioned. Even before he felt the air, he saw the moisture-laden air of the hangar condense as it mixed with the air in the office, a swirl of fog. It felt good, though, when the three of them were inside.

Hyacinth introduced him. "This is Davy. This is Frank."

Frank's accent was an odd combination of Brit and American. His skin looked like worn leather and the wrinkles at the corners of his eyes spread out like the Niger River delta. He shook hands with Davy.

Back at the mansion Hyacinth had said, "He's just a pilot. He doesn't know anything about us, or you. You tell him anything and I'll have to kill him and get another pilot."

Frank worked for International Aid. He'd been loaned to them at the request of Mr. Simons, a favor bought from the board of trustees by a very large donation.

"I didn't realize the weather was so bad," Hyacinth said.

Frank said, "Not a big deal. These are just the usual afternoon thunderstorms lasting a bit late. The MET forecast is clear after midnight."

"Is that when you want to go?"

"Oh-one-hundred."

Hyacinth looked at her watch. "What's local time?"

He looked at her, clearly puzzled. "It's seventeen twenty-eight. Didn't you change your watch on the flight?"

Hyacinth began setting the local time into her wristwatch. "No."

Frank asked, "How long were you at the terminal?"

She narrowed her eyes. "Why?"

He held up his hands, placating. "Sorry. None of my business, but, what with the weather, every international flight in the last five hours was diverted into Abuja."

"Ah," said Hyacinth. "Well we didn't come by that, um, mode of transport. We'll be back at oh-oh-thirty, for the flight, all right?"

"You want the car and the guards? We didn't book them for a trip into town but they'll be glad of the work."

"Where do you get them?" Hyacinth asked. "Is there an agency?"

He laughed. "You might say that. They're National Police. Approximately half the force in Lagos is on hire as bodyguards while the other half runs vehicle checkpoints to scam 'let me go' money out of people with improper papers."

Hyacinth made a silent "Oh" with her mouth. "Don't worry about the car or the guards. We'll make our own way."

"I wouldn't go into town without them," Frank said.

Davy didn't blame him for being worried. It was fourteen miles into Lagos proper, not that the city hadn't spread out to the airport—there were more people in the area than in Los Angeles.

Hyacinth shook her head. "We won't."

She left the office and walked along the row of the doors, toward the aircraft. Frank was staring at them from the doorway, but she ignored his comment, "There's no exit back that way."

Hyacinth turned, and when she turned to pass behind the larger of the three helicopters she glanced back at Davy. "Okay?"

"Let me get my bearings." Davy took a deep breath of tropical flowers, aviation fuel, and distant smell of rotting trash. "Okay."

He picked her up from behind and she deliberately rubbed her butt against his hips. He jumped back to the square—the room in the mansion—and pushed her away, blinking in the better lighting.

She stumbled forward to regain her balance then turned, looking down at his crotch. "Do you have something in your pocket?"

He jumped past her, to the door, and opened it. "We should both get some rest if we're going back in three hours."

She raised her eyebrows and sauntered toward him. "We could lie down for a while, sure."

He considered jumping her downstairs to the dining room and immediately returning to the room alone, but there was no lock on the door. He sighed. "Leave me be." After several beats he added, "Please."

She lifted a hand and put it on his chest, just over the scar, and smoothed Davy's shirt with her fingertips.

"Or I'll jump you back to Lagos and leave you to wait in the airport terminal."

This got to her. "You can't. The keys aren't on."

He shook his head. "You're lying. You haven't communicated with your team. You didn't hear the weather report until I did. You couldn't have planned it in advance. There were too many dynamic factors."

"You're right. I better see to that." She took a cell phone from her bag and pushed a button. "Excuse me."

She left.

Davy thought about jumping back to Nigeria, before she had a chance to communicate with her team, but what good would it do? As soon as she reached them, they'd shut down the keys and he'd be forced back here.

Wait.

FIFTEEN

"Don't be stupid, Mr. Padgett."

Millie's cheek, where it had rested on the stone, was numb, and there was a pool of saliva sticking to her chin.

Gross. She wiped it with her sleeve and checked her watch. She'd been down for ten minutes, but she doubted she would've woken up at all, if she were still in the condo. The numbness in her cheek was wearing off and with it came a stinging. She checked her face in the mirror by the bed and found she'd scraped her cheek when she'd passed out.

Life is entirely *too interesting.*

She threw on clean jeans and a dark tee-shirt, running shoes without socks, and Davy's dark leather jacket. Then she grabbed the binoculars and jumped to Stillwater but not the condo. She appeared in the city park a block from her place, next to the merry-go-round. A streetlight shining on the playground equipment cast stark, elongated shadows across the dead grass and dirt.

She stood still for a moment, listening, panning her head slowly. A dog walked briskly by on the street, anointed the base of a signal light, then trotted on. She heard cars on adjoining streets and saw their distant headlights reflecting off buildings.

She went into the stand of trees that bordered the park and moved down the chainlink fence that separated the park from a convenience store and the back end of the subdivision that contained her condo. She jumped to the other side of the fence and then to the roof of the gas station. An extra-large facade on the front of the building was lit by the bright lights and illuminated signs over the pumps and, as a result, cast a deep shadow across the gravel and tar roof. Millie put the binoculars to her eyes and studied the two sides of the condo visible to her.

She could make out the entrance to the parking garage, but not the main walk-in entrance. A minivan arrived as she watched but she recognized it as one of the families from the first floor.

She thought about the gas in the condo. *What could they have used?* There were the gaseous anesthetics but she didn't know much about them. *Except many of them depress respiration. Rather dangerous thing to administer* without *careful attention.* Hopefully there were people close at hand and some sort of motion sensors.

How did they tape the inside of the door and get out of the apartment? The apartment was moderately airtight. Sheetrock walls and ceiling with taped joints, plywood floor covered in carpet or tile. Davy had used expanded foam at the wet wall where the pipes entered the dwelling in an effort to keep the neighbors' cockroach problem from becoming theirs. So, that left the door to the hall, the windows, the fireplace, and the balcony's sliding door. The windows were tight, double-paned, with rubber seals.

She nodded to herself. *The patio door.* The sliding door had a good seal—they made sure all the windows were shut, sealed the front door and fireplace, and left by the balcony.

She jumped back into the trees and went wide around the block. There was a tree two streets away from her patio that she'd always been curious about. She'd seen a girl and a smaller boy playing in it after the leaves fell. While the leaves were still up, it was screened, but now, the leaves were just budding. She found the appropriate yard and, after several attempts, jumped into the tree, from lower branch to upper branch, and finally climbing over the low railing onto the small wooden platform.

Squatting down, her back braced against the trunk, she

thought she could avoid silhouetting herself against the city lights, at least as seen from the condo. She focused the field glasses on the apartment and frowned. The curtains were drawn and there didn't seem to be any lights behind them. She sighed and wondered if they'd even known their trap was sprung.

If I had left that trap I would be monitoring the place with low-light video.

Maybe they didn't need to come check it.

There was a flicker of darkness—not light, but as if the white curtains had shifted slightly. Millie thought she'd imagined it but then she saw it again, the swirl of the curtain pushed aside, then a figure moved between the curtain and the glass door. The reflection on the door changed slightly as the door slid quickly open and shut. There wasn't much light on the balcony but Millie could tell the figure wore a full face respirator, like the ones used by firefighters, complete with a backpack-slung air tank.

For one second she thought the person might *be* a local fire fighter, perhaps from the city HazMat team. *Right. Where are the lights? The trucks? The crowd of onlookers being held back by police?*

The figure pushed his mask up onto the top of his head, the supply hose jutting forward and down like the trunk of an elephant trumpeting. As the figure peered over the rail, looking down, and swiveled its head left and right, the light from the corner street lamp shined on *his* face.

Millie blinked, surprised. *What is* he *doing here?* It was the Monk, Padgett, who'd shot an FBI agent while escaping from the site of Millie's attempted kidnapping. *Well, it's not D.C. The FBI are probably not combing* this *vicinity as vigorously.*

Her mouth felt odd and she realized she had pulled her lips back from her teeth which were grinding together. She couldn't help thinking of the day Padgett had harried her through the National Gallery.

She expected him to climb down, to drop onto the grass below, but instead, Padgett reached up, to climb toward the balcony above—the third floor. He was struggling a bit and she thought it was the SCBA pack.

Perhaps he will fall, she thought with a slight degree of hope. She pursed her lips and studied the dwelling above. There wasn't anyone else on that balcony and the door was shut completely. *Perhaps he could be* made *to fall.*

It took Padgett several tries to swing his leg up to the edge of the third floor balcony. He pulled himself up and had just achieved a standing position, feet on the lip of the balcony, hands on the railing, when Millie appeared on the balcony and yelled in his face.

Padgett recoiled, a natural enough reaction when one is suddenly confronted with a figure and noise appearing before your face out of nothing, but he probably wouldn't have fallen if not for the weight of the SCBA pack. He twisted as he lost his grip on the railing, and Millie, suddenly conscious of the consequences of Padgett landing on his back, the air tank beneath his spine, felt her stomach lurch.

Fortunately Padgett twisted in midair, managing to face outward and remain upright, but the sound of his impact with the ground was bad enough.

She turned and glanced into the condo through the sliding glass door. There was a glow against the wall, like the light from a TV or computer screen, but there didn't seem to be anyone else within. *If he had a partner, they would've helped him up, wouldn't they?*

She jumped to the ground, her way, Davy's way—*not* Padgett's way. It was dark below, for the distant streetlight that had lit the balcony above was blocked at ground level by a tall evergreen hedge.

Though Padgett had avoided landing *on* the air tank, its weight had slammed him to the ground. His mouth gaped as he strained to breathe, but he wasn't getting any air. She felt enormous guilt wash over her and hoped he'd just had the wind knocked out of him. She pictured broken ribs puncturing a lung or a crushed trachea blocking his airway.

She hovered, wondering how to get him breathing, when his

eyes focused on her. Still gape-mouthed, his right hand clawed across his stomach to where a gun hung in a clip-on cross-draw holster. The memory of the FBI agent he'd shot came as she stepped forward and kicked at the reaching hand. She missed, but the toe of her sneaker caught him in the stomach and the gun, half out of the holster, fell to the ground as he doubled over.

Besides knocking the gun out of his hands, the kick in the stomach had apparently jump-started his diaphragm. Padgett's fish-like gaping had gone to a labored, asthmatic wheezing that did seem to be moving air in and out of his lungs. Millie darted forward and scooped up the gun, a blocky automatic, then stepped well back out of range. She looked at it and shuddered. She didn't even know where the safety was or whether it was cocked or chambered.

I can always hit him over the head with it. She looked back at Padgett. Her eyes were adjusting and she made out a pair of handcuffs in a loop on his belt. Hoping again that there weren't broken ribs, she walked around him and pushed him flat onto his face, leaning down onto the airtank. He tried to struggle back over and she pressed the muzzle of the gun into the back of his head.

"Don't be stupid, Mr. Padgett." She wasn't going to tell him that her finger was nowhere near the trigger.

He froze at the gun's touch and she fished the handcuffs from below his hip. These, at least, she knew how to work. She'd done an internship during college at the county jail— psychiatric evaluations on incoming prisoners. They hadn't been responsible for handling cuffs but the guards had shown them what to do in an emergency and had let them play with the cuffs. Once she had both of his wrists secured behind Padgett's back she double-locked them with the key she'd found in his pocket.

She still didn't feel in control, though. The man probably knew a dozen ways to turn the tables on her, handcuffs and all, so she snaked his belt out of his pants and hog-tied his ankles.

That's better.

She was surprised that they hadn't been disturbed by a

neighbor coming to see what the noises had been about—either her scream or the sound of Padgett hitting the ground. The nearest condo's windows were lit, but through the closed window she could hear a television blaring. *Ah.*

Still, they could be interrupted at any minute.

She took the air tank off of him. She had to unthread the shoulder straps completely because of the handcuffs but was able to unbuckle the waist belt. She jumped it to the Aerie and put the tank and facemask on the bed. After a few seconds' thought, she put the gun on top of the propane refrigerator.

What do I want to do with him? She thought about dropping Padgett in D.C. and calling the FBI but she wasn't sure that would help get Davy back. There were certain things that the FBI *couldn't* do when interrogating a prisoner. Of course, legally, nobody could do those sorts of things, but Millie, at this point, was willing to break the law—she just wasn't sure she *could* hurt anybody.

Well, she wasn't sure she wanted to struggle with the injured Mr. Padgett, even if he was bound hand and foot. She thought about the inhalant in the apartment. *Right.*

She gave up on the respirator pretty quick. Padgett's face was larger and a different shape than hers and no matter how hard she clinched the mask straps, it still leaked.

"Okay," she said aloud. "Better not to have to carry the weight, anyway."

She jumped back to Padgett and found him wiggling across the lawn.

Can't be that *injured.* She took hold of the belt around his ankles and tugged.

He yelled.

Oops. Perhaps he is.

"Ankle?"

He swiveled around and bared his teeth at her. "Bit of trouble with my knee." Almost as an afterthought, he added, "Bitch!"

She looked around to see if anyone was responding to his yell. No one yet. "Really, Mr. Padgett. Language!" She stooped and grabbed him by his upper arms. He was too big for her to pick up, but she thought if she held on hard enough . . . She took several deep breaths, then jumped into the condo.

He yelled again when he found himself on the floor of the living room and she wasn't sure if it was surprise or she'd wrenched his knee again. She wasn't going to open her mouth to ask, either.

Padgett shut his mouth almost immediately and she could tell he was holding his breath. Even without breathing, the harsh reek of the anesthetic reached her nostrils. She doubted that Padgett could hold his breath very long after yelling as he had. She released him to slump onto his side.

Millie felt the need to breathe herself, nothing desperate, yet, but she'd known her destination. She reached across Padgett and tapped his upper stomach with the heel of her hand in the same place she'd previously kicked him. The air left him in a spasmodic gasp and he began wheezing again, then coughing.

She jumped back to the Aerie and took a deep breath, but the anesthetic that swirled around her was still strong enough to make her dizzy. She took several steps away from where she'd appeared before breathing again.

So, how much oxygen is in the condo? Had Padgett displaced all the air or was the anesthetic mixed in? She wanted him unconscious but she didn't want him dead.

She looked at her watch. When she'd entered the condo unaware of the gas, it had taken less than a minute to render her unconscious. *I'll give it three minutes.*

She jumped to the swimming hole. That's what she called it, anyway. It was a deep pit a few miles from the Aerie with a spring-fed pool in its bottom, a small island in the center. In the beginning of August, when the sun beats down on El Solitario like a hammer upon a forge, Davy would jump her there to swim. The water was cold and clear even in the hottest afternoons.

Davy had mixed feelings about swimming there. His first use for the pit had been to deposit aircraft hijackers. One of them had been wearing a bomb and blew himself to chunks, which Davy had laboriously removed. Later, Davy had imprisoned Brian Cox and Rashid Matar, the man who'd killed his mother, on the island. It was also here that he'd finally stood up to his father.

But, then again, that was ten years past, and since that time there'd also been many lovely summer afternoons, swimming naked and doing things that had very little to do with swimming and everything to do with being naked.

It was cold in the pit and dark, the high rock walls cutting out the moonlight. You could hear the wind blowing above, whistling though the rocks among the rim, but down here the air was still. There were hard, glinting stars directly above, and the western lip of the mouth of the pit caught a sliver of moonlight, but down on the bottom it was like the poem by Henley: *Out of the night that covers me Black as the pit from pole to pole.*

She took several deep lungfuls of air, then held her breath before returning to Padgett at the condo. He was limp, his mouth slack, drool dripping down his cheek. She put him on the island in the pit and, using a flashlight, emptied his pockets, and patted him down. She found a thinner automatic pistol in a second holster inside his waistband at the pit of his back. She stared at it like it might bite her, then searched him all over again, before unlocking the handcuffs.

In the light of the flashlight, lying slack-jawed on the cold sand, he looked pathetic.

She covered him with an old sleeping bag. *Oh, well. I can always give him to the FBI if this doesn't work.*

Back in the Aerie she popped her lips percussively as she examined her booty. "P–ilfering P–adgett's P–ockets Pr–oduces P–ossible P–ath to . . . to—" *Well, clues and shit.*

His pockets contained a very sharp serrated single-bladed knife; a set of keys, which included an Enterprise Rent-A-Car key, a Schlage key of the kind commonly installed in the residential doors at her condominiums, and the handcuff key she had already used; six hundred and seventeen dollars in cash held together by a money clip; assorted loose change totaling sixty-three cents; and a thin leather wallet containing a Great Britain photo driver's license bearing Mr. Padgett's face but not his name, an American Express Card, a bank card, and a health insurance card. All the cards bore the name of one Robert Maurice Burke.

Well, Mr. Padgett, I suppose if I'd just shot an FBI agent, I'd avoid using my own name, too.

There was also a cell phone that had three telephone numbers stored in the recent call activity and nothing in the programmed memory.

Two of the numbers were in the 405 area code that included Stillwater, but she didn't recognize the exchanges. The 405 also included Oklahoma City, too, though. The first phone number had a 508 area code.

Where did I see that recently?

She scrambled back to where she'd dropped her dirty clothes on returning from Ten Thousand Waves. The yellow sticky she'd taken from the briefcase in Bochstettler and Associates was in the front pocket of the jeans. The area code was also 508. In fact, the area code and the exchange of both numbers were the same.

It was now after midnight on the east coast. She yawned and thought about Padgett, lying on the cold sand. Once the anesthetic wore off, which had probably already happened, he'd be pretty uncomfortable. If his knee truly was injured, it would be difficult for him to sleep.

Good.

She blinked, surprised at herself. *I had not thought myself such a* wicked *person.*

But she must be for she fell asleep within minutes of putting her head on the pillow and not a thought was spared for the discomforts of Mr. Padgett.

She briefly checked on her prisoner in the early morning, peering at him through binoculars from above, on the upper rim of the pit. Sometime in the night he'd stirred himself enough to climb into the sleeping bag and zip it shut. The sandy island was poorly lit by reflected light, but she finally determined that, though his eyes were closed, the sleeping bag rose and fell with his breath.

She sighed with relief and put the binoculars back in the Aerie.

Her next stop was an internet café on the upper west side of Manhattan, where, by doing an area code/exchange search, she found out that the phone numbers in question were for Edgartown, Massachusetts. A query at a mapping website showed her that Edgartown was one of the townships on the island of Martha's Vineyard. *Oh, yeah. Davy and I bicycled there once. We had fried clams at that clam shack, uh, The Bite.* That was in Menemsha, on the other end of the Island.

She zoomed way out on the map until both Cape Cod, Nantucket, and a large chunk of mainland Massachusetts and Rhode Island were visible. *The two ambulances were abandoned in New England. One at Logan in Boston. One in Rhode Island.* Each was only a few hours from the Vineyard, though there was the ferry to consider. But they could've used a private boat or a private aircraft. *Or stuffed him in a car trunk.*

On the chance that either of the numbers was a commercial listing, she searched on the entire ten digit number. The one from Padgett's cell phone came up nil but the number she'd found on the yellow sticky belonged to the Edgartown Golf Club. She looked at the sticky again. "egc tt 9/2 2:30." EGC-Edgartown Golf Club. Her father had golfed. TT-Tee Time? September 2, 2:30 P.M.

She felt a stab of disappointment. A golf date eight months previous. Why should it mean anything.

When all you have is straw, you clutch at straws.

She called from D.C., using her cell.

She got a voicemail system telling her that the course was closed for the season and would not open until the first of June and, as the course was a members-only facility, guests must be accompanied by a member. Then it gave her the option to talk with the facilities manager by pressing one.

"Tom here."

"Hello, my name is Nancy Burquist. I'm a bookkeeper assisting Mr. Kelledge's tax accountant."

"And who might Mr. Kelledge be?" Tom's voice was pure Yankee Vineyard. She hadn't heard the accent in years but it came right back to her.

"Mr. Kelledge is the executive director of Bochstettler and Associates in Washington D.C. I'm trying to straighten out some of his expense reports." She sighed loudly. "He's being audited by the IRS."

The voice sounded mystified and mildly irritated. "And what would that have to do with the Edgartown Golf Club, Miss?"

"He played golf there, apparently. I've a record for a tee time last September the second for two-thirty in the afternoon. Don't know if you keep records that far back, but I need to know who he was playing with so my boss can justify the greens fee and cart rental to the auditing agent."

"Well, I might be able to find that. It won't be under Mr. Kelledge's name since I'm sure he's not a member. Can you give me a few minutes? I'll have to get last year's binders out of the cabinet."

"Take as long as you need. You're really doing me a favor."

Tom was back in two minutes. "You're lucky. We've already thrown out the first half of last year. You said September second?"

"Yes. Two-thirty."

She heard him flipping pages. "Here we are. Two-thirty—a foursome. Simons. Oh, my. Mr. Simons. Mr. Lawrence Simons."

"I don't recognize the name."

"Uh." Tom's voice changed, became more breathy, jovial. "Ah, I was mistaken. That was three-thirty. The two-thirty slot is for Jones. Hmm. Don't know which one, we have several in the club."

She frowned. "Could you fax me that page?"

The joviality drained from Tom's voice. "I'm afraid not. I should've remembered that it's against club policy to reveal this information. A violation of member privacy. You'll just have to ask your Mr. Kellog which Mr. Jones."

"Kelledge."

"Whatever. We're very busy here. Good-bye." He hung up without waiting for a response.

She went back to the Aerie and searched the tape archive for a jump site in Edgartown but the closest she could find was that spot in front of The Bite in the tiny village of Menemsha, on the other end of the island, almost as far as you could get from Edgartown and still be on the island. She went back to Manhattan and bought more computer time. A simple internet search revealed hundreds of Lawrence Simons but adding the search term Martha's Vineyard or Edgartown came up blank.

Still, it's an island. How far could it be?

MapQuest told her—15.21 miles.

She bought coffee and a bacon-and-egg sandwich at a deli around the corner from the internet café before jumping back to West Texas. Padgett was awake. He was seated at the water's edge, wrapped in the sleeping bag, and one bare leg stuck out from under the bag and lay in the water, wet to above the knee.

Millie shuddered. It must be like ice. She fetched the binoculars from the Aerie. The knee was definitely swollen, even without the distortion of the water. She returned the binoculars and fetched a bottle of ibuprofen.

She jumped down to the island, a good ten feet behind him, and put the coffee and bag down silently. She jumped to the rim again and, judging the distance, she tossed the plastic bottle of ibuprofen down. It hit the water two feet in front of him, splashing spray across his shirt and face.

Padgett jumped and swore as his leg splashed water into his lap. He looked up, but Millie had jumped to the far side of the rim and was now watching through a gap between two rocks.

Padgett picked the bottle out of the water and was peering at the label. He dumped several onto his palm and sniffed it. He put one of the pills on a rock and used another rock to crush it into powder, then used a wetted fingertip to taste the powder.

Millie tossed a rock, this time, to thud onto the ground behind him, near the Styrofoam cup and the foil-wrapped sandwich.

Padgett jerked his head around, his hand going to a fist-sized rock beside him. Millie wasn't sure, for a moment, that he'd spotted the food, but then he began scooting gingerly across the ground on his good leg and his arms, and she was satisfied.

On Martha's Vineyard, The Bite was closed for the season, and the wind eddied down Basin Road and cut through the sweater and button-down-shirt she wore like they weren't there. It really was above freezing, she assured herself, but the air was damp and harsh. She went back for Davy's leather jacket, gloves, and a hat.

Back on Martha's Vineyard she took the Route Four bus to West Tisbury. She had to wait almost an hour, there, to catch the Number Six down-island to Edgartown.

Here, the wind was worse than in Menemsha, fresh off Nantucket Sound and buffeting her as she walked. Looking across the mouth of the harbor toward the Chappaquiddick side, she could see good-size waves pounding onto the beach there. Where she stood, on Water Street, the wind whipped between buildings and carried stinging droplets that tasted of salt.

She consulted her map and headed inland. It took her twenty minutes to reach the clubhouse of the Edgartown Golf Club. It would've taken her less time, but once, head bent to avoid the vicious wind, she'd missed her turn and had to backtrack. As she expected, it was closed and locked, but a man was doing something with a tractor in the distance. She knocked loudly and when there was no answer, she looked in the large picture window overlooking the putting green and jumped within.

I could come back at night, she thought, then shook her head. At night she'd have to use a flashlight or turn on the lights and she'd be even more noticeable.

She found the member records in the back office in a gray filing cabinet. Simons, Lawrence was a member in good standing having bought his two hundred and fifty thousand dollar membership over twelve years before. The address his monthly statements went to was in New York City, but his qualifying address—members had to have a residence on the Vineyard—was listed as being Driftwood Hall, Great Pond Lane. The listing was for Edgartown but that street was not on the small map Millie carried. There was no local phone number listed but she wrote down the address and phone number of his place in New York, a 212 area code—*Manhattan*—and put everything back as she'd found it.

She took a careful look out the window. The man on the tractor was headed this way. She thought about the nasty wind swirling down Water Street among the restaurants and the gray and white whaling mansions, and she jumped.

"That's down by South Beach," said the expatriate British woman who waited on her at David Ryan's Restaurant. The fancy dining room upstairs was still closed, but the pub on the first floor was warm and out of the wind and this woman gave her Earl Grey in a pot properly warmed. "It's west of that big resort hotel, the Winnetu. There's quite a few expensive homes down there. I mean, even expensive by *Vineyard* prices."

"How come it's not on my map?"

The waitress bent over the paper and tapped a line leading toward the shoreline. "That's it. The one marked 'private drive,' though there are several different homes off of it. But the fire department insisted they slap a name on it so they can know where to go."

Millie wrapped her hands around the teapot. "How far is it?"

"From here? Three, four miles. You don't want to go down there without an invite—it's gated and they run private security. Them what lives there likes their privacy. More hot water?"

In Manhattan, the winds and temperatures were less severe, and Millie, warmed by the tea and comfortably full of a bruschetta steak sandwich, finally stopped shivering. She briefly stopped in an internet café and sent an e-mail to rat8765:

WHO IS LAWRENCE SIMONS?

She walked across Central Park to get to the East Side.

Mr. Simon's billing address was on East 83rd between

Madison and the hulking mass of the Metropolitan Museum of Art. The house was a four-story townhouse faced with gray stone, wrought iron window bars, and security cameras. She swallowed hard and kept walking. The house was three times as wide as the adjoining brownstones and included two street-level garage doors.

She half expected the doors to rise up and squads of white armored stormtroopers to come pouring out.

She turned south on Madison without looking back. She wasn't worried about the cameras. With the museum just down the street they must get thousands of people walking by. And she hoped, with her short blond haircut, that she looked nothing like the Millie Harrison-Rice they'd hounded through that other museum.

She reached 81st and looked west, back toward the museum. She'd never look at any art museum again in the same way after that time in the National Gallery. And, surprisingly, the associations weren't all bad. Her imagination (and the masters' work) had provided her with a host of allies. She'd learned something about her inner reserves.

And what would my allies do about one Lawrence Simons?

She checked on Mr. Padgett, midday.

He was trying to make a fire by the bow drill method in the old fire pit still marked by blackened stones. *It does give him something to do.* Still she was worried about him. It was probably her very recent experience with the nasty, cold winds on the Vineyard that put her in sympathy with him.

She jumped to the Aerie and took four piñon logs from the woodpile and, using string, bundled them together with some old newspaper and a long-tipped butane fireplace lighter. Back at the pit, she picked a spot well to Padgett's rear, jumped down, held the bundle out at arm's length, and released it as she jumped away.

Watching from the rim, she saw Padgett jerk around as the logs clattered to the ground, a startled look on his face.

The next time she checked, he was crouched close to the burning fire.

Her next delivery was a portable toilet and a roll of toilet paper. After that, a set of crutches purchased from a thrift shop. Last, a bucket of fried chicken and a six-pack of bottled water.

In each case, she waited until he was settled and put the items quietly down some distance behind him and left before he noticed.

Examining his face through the binoculars, she thought, *Haunted. He looks haunted.*

Good.

SIXTEEN

"Good eating."

It was the most terrifying plane ride Davy had ever taken.

He'd wondered how they were going to do it. He didn't think they'd put a plane ahead and behind him with the keys. Instead, Hyacinth gestured him into the Cessna Grand Caravan and, when he was in his seat, she cuffed him by the ankles to the base of the seat before him and covered the chains with a sweater from her shoulder bag.

He broke into a cold sweat. He'd flown into all sorts of remote areas in all kinds of small aircraft but the knowledge that, in the event of a crash, he could teleport away, made the flights more like amusement park rides—the illusion of danger, not its actual manifestation.

She spoke into a radio after pocketing the key to the cuffs. "Romeo is fixed in space. Bring 'em in."

A few minutes later two more SUVs pulled up on the concrete apron. Two guys, each with shoulder bags, got out and walked across to the plane. Frank, the pilot, doing his walk around, asked them to put their bags in the cargo compartment and then take the two seats most forward. "Behind the pilots' seats."

The plane was configured for mixed duty, the rear cargo section was separated from the front by a barrier of nylon webbing and the front had the two pilots' seats and six passenger seats.

Frank shut the cargo door and walked around to the passenger door. He crouched and pulled up the lower half of the door, with the steps. Before he shut the top, he said, "You may take the co-pilot's seat, if you like, Miss Pope."

She accepted, threading forward between the seats. Frank walked around the plane and entered from the pilot's door.

They were airborne fifteen minutes later and out over the dark stretch of Lagos Lagoon, outlined in lights. Lagos Island blazed, and then they were past the shoreline and out over the Bight of Benin. They climbed southeast, bound for the Niger Delta. The half-moon, low on the western horizon, cast a long bright finger on the sea below.

Davy had never been to the Delta. His previous trips to Nigeria had been to Lagos and the Federal capital, Abuja. Below five thousand feet the turbulence was severe, but they reached a level of relative calm above. The AC finally caught up with the humidity and Davy's breathing slowed as he became convinced death was not *immediately* impending.

Fifty-five minutes later they crossed back over land and began the descent. The turbulence began again shortly thereafter and Davy started sweating.

Ahead, the Delta was on fire. He knew what it was, but it still looked hellish. They landed along a stretch of asphalt road lit entirely by one of the gas flares. It towered into the sky, several hundred yards away, a massive pillar of flame reaching fully two hundred and fifty feet into the air. Davy could feel the radiated heat through the window. Frank turned on his landing lights though he didn't really need them. As soon as all three wheels were bumping across the road, he reversed the pitch on the prop and the shoulder strap bit into Davy's chest.

They were expected. A trio of Toyota Land Cruisers were parked in the grass, short of the mangroves. Frank taxied past them, then reversed pitch again and backed the plane off the road.

Davy looked curiously behind him. He could see water at the base of the mangroves and wondered if Frank would back it right into the swamp. He tried to remember the position of the landing wheels. He knew it was a tricycle configuration but he couldn't remember how far back the rear two wheels lay.

It wasn't as if they'd drown. The water couldn't be that deep and the mangroves would keep the plane from sinking in. And, provided he could get these cuffs off, *he* didn't need the plane to get back home.

The turbine died and Frank ran through the shutdown quickly, before dropping out of the pilot's door and walking over to the Land Cruisers.

Hyacinth pivoted in her seat and said, "You'll have two armed guards with each of you. Settings as discussed." She had to raise her voice almost to a shout to be heard over the roar of the flare.

The two key holders threaded back past Davy, fished their bags past the cargo netting, and opened the airstair. As the first one went down the stair, Davy heard a squelching noise and a muffled curse.

"Watch it. We're right on the edge of the marsh."

By stepping off the bottom of the stair toward the front of the aircraft, the second man avoided the mud. The two men went around the front of the aircraft and joined Frank at the Land Cruisers. Frank directed them each to one of the vehicles and they climbed in. Both Land Cruisers started up and moved in opposite directions down the road. Their passage raised dust at the edge of the road.

It hasn't been raining, here.

Davy, already sweating from the heat of the gas flare, felt a surge of adrenaline. What if one of them drove out of range? He was still cuffed to the plane.

Slowly, Hyacinth moved down the aisle. She sat across his lap and leaned her chest toward his face. "Hot in here, isn't it?"

"You're pushing it, Miss Pope," he said through gritted teeth.

"And *it* pushes back," she said with a twist of her hips. But she relented and stood, rubbing against him, then knelt to unlock the cuffs. Davy jumped to the shadow cast by the flare at the rear of the remaining Land Cruiser, out of sight of the cluster of men near the passenger door. He saw Hyacinth swivel her head around sharply, looking for him. He moved out of the shadow and leaned against the vehicle.

She saw him then and climbed down the Airstair. He was hoping she would step into the marsh, but she'd been watching, apparently, and jumped lightly forward from the stair and avoided the mud. Davy saw now that the rear wheels of the plane were a good six feet away from the marsh's edge. In fact, they were forward of the airplane's midpoint and he figured the engine and fuel tanks must move the center of mass toward the front of the craft.

Hyacinth gestured to Davy and they arrived at the front of the Land Cruiser together.

Frank was talking to an African in creased khakis in one of the local languages. Davy didn't recognize any of the words so he thought it might be Yoruba, Ijaw, or Ibo.

"Right," said Frank. "This is Reverend Ilori of the ECWA mission on the Dado River. He is the contact."

Reverend Ilori was a middle-aged man. His closely cut cropped hair was shot with gray. He nodded politely and said, "May the blessings of our Savior be with you."

Davy smiled and with just a twinge of hypocrisy said, "And may Jesus Christ forever watch over and guide us all." He'd met members of the Ecumenical Churches of West Africa before, near Abuja. They were mostly good people, trying to help, but more concerned with salvation in heaven than improvements here on earth.

Frank watched this interaction, a look of mild amusement on his face. "The exchange is for dawn, at the mission itself, but if we want to be in place, we had better go."

Reverend Ilori sat in the front seat with the unarmed driver and Davy sat in the back with Frank and Hyacinth. Hyacinth kept the bag on her lap.

"We can put that in the back, Miss Pope," Frank offered.

She tightened her hold on it. "I don't think so."

"Ah. The ransom. Don't blame you."

Davy, who knew otherwise, remained quiet.

The road curved around the flare, then headed east, toward

the coast. They entered a section of grassy brush and a large, rabbit-sized animal scuttled off the road, eyes shining in the headlights. Reverend Ilori said something over his shoulder and smacked his lips together.

Frank translated. "Cane rat. Good eating. Surprising to see—they've been hunted hard around here."

Hyacinth, seated between them, shuddered. "Yuck."

Davy offered, "It's not a true rat. It's taxonomically closer to the porcupine."

Reverend Ilori turned again. "Porcupine! Also good eating." He smacked his lips again.

The asphalt road turned to dirt and the ride became much rougher as the Land Cruiser bounced over ruts and dropped into potholes. Fortunately this track ended at a wharf, sticking out into a narrow channel threading between the mangroves.

A solitary boy rose from the dock, slight, dressed only in shorts, hand held up to shield his eyes. He looked sleepy. Reverend Ilori, stepping out of the car, called to him. When the boy approached, the Reverend handed him something.

Hyacinth said, "What's that about?"

Frank took a pair of binoculars from the driver. "He was guarding the boat. Wouldn't have done us much good if someone had stolen it while the good Reverend was away."

The driver turned off the headlights but made no move to get out of the vehicle. The night seemed to close in but after a moment, Davy began to detect the distant glow of gas flares all around the horizon. The moon had set while they were driving but after a bit he could make out the brighter stars, too, through a low haze that owed more to the gas flares than local weather.

Reverend Ilori was walking out onto the dock. "We must go. It will take most of an hour to reach the mission." He climbed down into the unseen boat and turned on a flashlight.

It was a square-bowed aluminum john boat, perhaps fourteen feet long. It was seriously underpowered with a two-horsepower outboard. There was a single pole, as long as the boat, tied to one gunwale, if the motor failed. The Reverend directed Frank to take the flashlight and sit in the bow. Davy and

Hyacinth took the center thwart with the bag between them. Ilori cast off his single line and started the engine.

Things splashed into the water as they approached, and once Ilori pointed out two bright red spots reflecting the flashlight from back under the mangroves. "Crocodile." He smacked his lips. "Good eating."

Their route twisted back and forth, following the channel which varied in width as much as it did in direction. At times it seemed they were in a broad lake and other times it narrowed until they could reach out and touch the mangroves on both sides of the boat. As they crossed one wide section he felt the boat tremble, pulled slightly sideways by a current.

"River?" he asked.

"The Dodo," said Reverend Ilori.

Fully fifty minutes had passed by Davy's watch when they pulled up to an area of higher ground, cleared, with three white buildings constructed on piles, a crawl space visible below. There was no dock. Ilori pointed the bow at the mud bank and gunned it briefly before hitting the kill button and tipping the motor up. Frank shifted back toward Davy, allowing the bow to rise higher, and then the boat shuddered to a stop. Frank, first out, squelched through mud, but he seized the bow and pulled the boat farther up the bank, allowing the rest of them to step out on dry ground.

"Good, we are early," said Ilori. "Though we were probably watched as we came. They would not come if there were more of us. Or guns."

"What do we do now?" asked Hyacinth.

"Wait."

The dawn broke with the suddenness typical of equatorial regions and Davy could see that there was water on three sides of the Mission's bit of land. Several different channels wove off through the mangroves. There was a grove of palm trees clumped together on the land behind the mission, ending, abruptly, in the ever-present mangroves. The buildings were silent.

"Where is everyone?" Davy asked. "I mean, those who live here?"

Reverend gestured to the south. "Last night I took them to the village. These *mugu* men, they are without God. They killed several palm oil farmers just last week who would not pay the leave-me-alone. I do not want them to kill any of my flock."

There was the distant sound of a motor, much more powerful than the clergyman's small outboard, and then another. Two Jet Skis came out of a canal and peeled to the left and the right. Each one had two men on it. They slowed their engines and settled into the water, idling some fifty feet away from the mud bank. They were armed with SIG 540 assault rifles, probably stolen or bought from the army, and they were dressed in ragged shorts, athletic shoes without socks, and brown tee-shirts that may have been a different color once. They scanned the small group standing on the mud bank, then pushed in to the shore.

Hyacinth eased her hand into her bag, which still hung over one shoulder.

The two passengers splashed off the Jet Skis and up the mud bank. They bypassed the small group and ran to the chapel, flattening themselves by the doors, then ducking in, assault style. After a moment, they came back out, then repeated the inspection with the other two buildings. When they were done, one of them shouted, "Clear!"

One of the Jet Ski pilots lifted a plastic-wrapped radio to his lips. The two men who'd checked the building walked toward the small group. They stopped ten feet away, their assault rifles pointed at the ground between them.

"Give us the bag," said the larger of them, jerking his head.

Reverend Ilori stepped away from Hyacinth, his eyes widening.

Hyacinth shook her head. "That is not the agreement. Bring Mr. Roule."

They lifted their guns now, pointing the muzzles directly at Hyacinth. "Give us the bag, now!"

Hyacinth held up her free hand, the one that wasn't in the bag. Between her thumb and forefinger she held a dull black ring connected to an equally dark pin. "Do you see this?"

The big man narrowed his eyes. "I do not care. Give me the bag!"

Hyacinth said, "You should care. It belongs to this." She brought her hand out of the bag, slowly. She was holding a black grenade with yellow markings, the lever held to the body with her fingertips. The pin was not in it.

Davy nearly jumped away, but controlled himself. Even if she let go, there would be at least two seconds before it detonated—plenty of time.

Reverend Ilori backed briskly away from the group, praying audibly.

The two men lowered the muzzles of the assault rifles again. One of them said something, almost spat it, and Davy saw Frank's eyes narrow.

"An insult?" Davy asked quietly.

Frank nodded. "Potty talk. They don't like having to listen to a woman."

Hyacinth waved the grenade gently back and forth. "Bring Mr. Roule."

The "mugu" men retreated to the waterline.

Frank said, "You frighten me, Miss Pope."

Wise man, thought Davy.

Hyacinth laughed, a high-noted trill that carried to the armed men. In a whisper she added, "It's a training grenade. It was repainted to look like the standard H-E. Would they have stolen the ransom? After agreeing to the exchange?"

Frank shrugged. "Stealing ransoms before the drop is big business here in Nigeria. But the way we flew in, the secrecy, we avoided it. They might have released Mr. Roule if you'd given it to them, or they might have claimed the people who took the money were not the same people who had the hostage. Then there would be another demand for money."

Another motor sounded in the distance, deeper and stronger than the Jet Skis but hard to locate, diffuse. Davy scanned the mangroves and then saw it, a small boat—radar and VHF antenna just sticking above the mangroves, moving right to left before turning the corner in the channel and coming into view on the west-most canal.

It was a nine-meter rigid inflatable, fiberglass hull with a surrounding flexible pressure chamber. There were massive twin outboards at the stern, a pilot station amidships with a rigid hard bimini shading the helmsman and mounting the antennas already seen.

There were five men aboard: the helmsman, two men armed with SIG 540s at the stern, a man with a holstered sidearm in the bow, and, seated before him on the deck, a man with his arms tied behind and a sack over his head.

The helmsman reversed thrust and came to a stop at the mouth of the channel where it opened onto the water around the mission.

Davy used Frank's binoculars.

The man in the bow was dressed somewhat better than his compatriots in intact camouflage fatigues and a New York Yankees baseball cap. He unholstered his sidearm, a black and blocky automatic, and pointed it at the covered head of his captive. "Show us the money!" he shouted across the water.

Hyacinth looked at Davy and moved her eyes sideways toward the boat.

Quietly, Davy said, "It may not be him. And we need to make sure he's not chained to the boat." He studied the bow carefully, as a jump point.

Frank stepped forward and yelled, "How do we know that's Mr. Roule? Show us his face."

"Show us the money!"

Frank spread his hands apart, palm up. He shouted slowly, "I. Do. Not. Believe. You. Have. Him. This is some tourist you've stolen. We are not paying for a tourist."

"I will *kill* him!" said the Yankees fan.

"Show us his face. Show us that he is alive," Frank said reasonably. "You told Reverend Ilori he was unharmed. Was that lies?"

For a very tense moment, Davy thought the man would pull the trigger, but he finally reached over and pulled the hood off of the prisoner.

The captive was dirty, his gray hair matted, two weeks of

beard on his cheeks. He blinked against the sudden light, looking frail and scared. Frank took the binoculars from Davy.

"It's him."

Hyacinth said, "You're sure?"

"Yes. I was his personal pilot for two years. I know the son-
of-a-bitch. That's why you guys wanted me, remember?"

Davy winced. *So she lied when she said she'd kill the pilot if
I talked to him.* But while that may have been a lie before Frank
identified Roule, she probably wouldn't hesitate to kill him
now that he'd completed his job.

"Okay." She handed the grenade to Davy, who carefully
clamped his hand over the lever. Then she zipped the bag all
the way open and tilted it toward the boat. It seemed to be filled
with bundled American currency, but Davy knew better. The
two outer bills of each bundle were color xeroxes and the stuff
between was plain newsprint.

She shouted to the boat. "Can he walk?" Davy watched
closely. He didn't need Roule to walk but they wanted to make
sure the man wasn't chained to the boat.

The Yankees fan must've been feeling generous at the sight
of the ransom. He reached down and pulled the captive up.
Roule sagged but when his captor let go of his arm, he managed to stay on his feet. Davy couldn't see any chains or ropes
connecting him to the boat.

The plan was to do the swap at the shoreline. Davy said conversationally, "You're sure the keys overlap the Cessna."

"Definitely. We were covering a larger area when we did the
Lagos airport thing."

Davy inhaled and exhaled. "Right. I'd better remove Reverend Ilori first."

Hyacinth snarled. "Don't deviate from the plan."

Davy looked at her impassively. "Not appreciably."

She zipped the money bag closed, then walked down to the
shoreline and set it down where the mud was dried and crusted.
She backed away and the two men on shore ran lightly toward
it. By the time they reached it, Hyacinth was back with the
group.

Reverend Ilori had returned to the group after Hyacinth's little hand grenade incident was over. Davy edged slightly behind him as Hyacinth reached into her journalist's vest for her gun.

The men reached the money bag and both knelt beside it. One tugged on the zipper, but it seemed stuck. He pulled harder.

The flash-bang went off with the smoke grenade, throwing them both back, stunned, singed. Davy, expecting it, still flinched. He grabbed Ilori, jumped to the Cessna, where it was parked near the towering, roaring gas jet, and pushed the Reverend staggering away. Then he was in the bow of the big boat, body-slamming Mr. Yankees fan sideways, away from Roule. He dropped the grenade, the lever flying before the round black and yellow metal ball bounced on the deck. Davy heard the Yankees fan yell "Grenade!" right before Davy grabbed Roule. As Davy jumped, he saw the Yankees fan dive out of the boat.

When Davy let go of Roule beside the plane, the man fainted, dropping with slack knees to the ground. Reverend Ilori was dancing from one foot to the other, staring at them and muttering "Jesus protect me!" again and again.

"Untie him!" Davy said, gesturing at Roule, and returned to the mission. A huge cloud of torn paper and yellow smoke was spread through the air, settling slowly across the water and clearing. Barely seen through it, on the other side of the waterway, the shattered hulk of the boat was burning.

She also *lied about the grenade.*

There was splashing in the water near the boat, so he hoped the crew had gotten overboard before the grenade had exploded. Someone was firing an assault rifle and Davy saw bullet holes trace across the wall of the church and smash a glass window. He dropped to the ground. He heard Frank call to him and looked around. Hyacinth and Frank were under the chapel, sheltering behind the cinderblock steps under the front door.

He jumped to them, lying on the dusty dried mud at their side.

Hyacinth was talking on a small handheld radio. "Yes. We will be completely clear of the area by the time you get here." She held her big, blocky automatic in the other hand and she'd replaced the clip with one that stuck a good five inches out of the bottom of the grip. She stuck the gun around the corner of the cinderblocks and pulled the trigger.

"Jesus!" said Davy, covering his ears. The gun fired continuously as she held the trigger down for half-a-second. "What the hell is that?"

Hyacinth looked like she was enjoying herself. She turned toward him and said, "It's my Glock Eighteen. Cool, huh? Thirteen hundred rounds a minute. Too bad I could only get thirty-one-round clips." She turned back toward the water.

"Who was she talking to?" Davy asked Frank.

Frank was staring at him, breathing heavily. He managed to stammer, "Army. Seventh Amphibious Battalion. They're closing in and they're probably going to shoot anything that moves." He gestured in the general direction of the shooter. "Looks like their eyes went come-down-sad." At Davy's look of incomprehension he said, "They've realized they've been conned."

"Ah." Davy grabbed Frank's belt with both hands and jumped him back to the airplane.

Reverend Ilori was helping Roule to sit up, fortunately facing away from where Davy and Frank had appeared.

Frank struggled to his feet and Davy rolled away from him before also standing. Frank was looking at his airplane, then at Ilori and Roule. "Son-of-a-bitch."

"Takes people like that. Or did you mean *him*?" Davy looked at Roule. He lowered his voice. "You called him that before. Why don't you like him?"

Frank shut his mouth abruptly.

"Don't want to say, eh? Okay. Hope I didn't rescue a monster."

Frank licked his lips, then decided to speak, his face contorted. "Well, you *did*. Whole villages. Fisheries. Farms. Gone. Only he wasn't the one who got his hands dirty or took the blame. He's only the one who pointed his finger and said 'do it.' In the name of oil. For obscene profit."

Oh, shit. For one brief moment Davy considered putting Roule back at the mission, in the hopes that the army assault team would kill him.

Davy's expression looked so bleak that Frank recoiled from him, blurting, "I won't tell."

Davy shook his head. "You have nothing to fear from *me*. I wish you *would* tell. Tell the whole world!" He sighed. "You can leave when your other passengers come back. Miss Pope and I will not be riding back with you."

"You're the guy, aren't you, who stopped those hijackings ten years ago? Those airplanes and that ship in Egypt."

Davy shrugged. The conclusion was obvious. He'd been captured on video appearing on the wing of a 727 during the Cyprus rescue. Over two hundred passengers and crew saw him jump during the *Argos* ship rescue.

"What do I tell them?" He gestured toward Roule and Reverend Ilori.

"Shock. Angels. Hallucinations. Whatever you want. I better go get Miss Pope before she pops a blood vessel."

"Or the army does that for her."

"I *wish*." Davy jumped.

He reappeared under the center of the church, well behind Hyacinth. One of the shooters on the Jet Ski had figured out where she was hiding and had rounded the island, flanking her. Dried mud was flying as bullets tore past the stairs and Hyacinth was pressed tight against the back of the cinderblocks, barely in cover. Apparently she'd run out of ammo for she wasn't returning fire and she no longer looked as if she were enjoying herself. Between the shots Davy heard the distant noise of helicopters.

He would be in danger of being hit if he jumped directly behind her. She pretty much filled the only sheltered space in her vicinity and the way she flinched as the bullets set showers of dried mud flying she probably wasn't considering it much like shelter.

He looked at the Jet Ski. It was drifting, idling, and the pilot was twisted on the saddle, shooting three-round bursts.

Davy jumped and appeared with both feet on the rear starboard edge of the Jet Ski. The Jet Ski promptly rolled over, dumping the shooter, but Davy jumped away before he'd sunk more than knee deep in the estuary. He appeared directly behind Hyacinth, a large amount of water puddled around him, turning the dried, cracked dirt to mud.

One of the crewmen from the large boat had climbed into the mangroves and was now shooting at the steps, but his position didn't allow him to shoot directly at their position. Davy ignored him.

He wanted to just grab Hyacinth and jump, but the way she flinched every time a bullet slammed into the mud steps or plowed into the mud gave him an idea.

"Back to the Vineyard?" he asked.

She twisted around and said "Yes, dammit!" Almost immediately, her face changed, anger replacing fear. "How did you—oh just get us out of here!" A chip of flying debris had cut her forehead and blood ran down into her eyebrow, but she seemed unaware of it.

He allowed himself a small smile as he jumped her back to the mansion. *A mansion*, he mused, *which is on the south shore of Martha's Vineyard.*

They appeared in his room, in the box. Mud splattered on the Turkish rug. They were entwined, still lying prone, and Davy tried to roll away but Hyacinth pulled him back, twisted on top and straddled him. She dropped the radio and her Glock on the floor.

I'll jump away, he thought, but he didn't. Instead he felt her pelvis grinding against him and then her mouth on his and his body responding. He let his hands come to rest on the small of her back, just where the swell of her buttocks met her waist.

Oh, god. It's been so long . . .

Her tongue ran across his lips and she pulled his shirt apart, literally, buttons flying and cloth ripping as she tugged. She lifted up again astride him as she tore off her photojournalist's vest. He found himself lifting the tail of her polo and running his fingers over the skin of her back as she pressed her chest down on him again. He encountered her bra strap but there was no clasp at the back so he moved his hands around, under the shirt, encountering her breasts beneath stretch lace, hard nipples, and then the front closure. Hyacinth lifted to give him access and the bra separated, dropping her full breasts into his hands. She groaned and sucked on his lower lip.

Davy ached for her, even though a tiny voice in the back of his head was screaming that this woman shot, killed, murdered Brian Cox in front of him, was one of those who made him a prisoner, tortured him, kept him away from Millie. His body didn't care. *Shut up! It's not about* love.

He pushed her up and tugged at her shirt, pulling and pushing it up. Hyacinth sat up and pulled it over her head in one quick motion, shrugged off the unfastened bra, then shifted back along his legs. She straddled his knees and put one hand on his crotch as she fumbled with her other hand at the buckle of his belt.

He watched her, frozen in agonized anticipation, drinking in the motion of her breasts, the play of hollow and swell around her collarbones and the base of the neck—then he jerked his head up and raised himself to his elbows, staring.

A semicircular scar, old and faded to the merest white line, graced Hyacinth's chest an inch below her collarbone. He searched with his eyes and saw another, the thin straight line on the side of her neck.

His hand reached out, probed her skin, and felt the lump, the flat hardness below that matched his own implant. He jerked his hand away as if burned. He felt nauseated but it wasn't accompanied by the tingling in his throat. It was pure, visceral revulsion.

She reacted to his jerking away as she hadn't to his probing touch, looking up from where she was unsnapping his jeans, her brows raised. He recoiled, a jump that left him standing on the other side of the room from her.

She jabbed a finger in her mouth and swore around it. "Dammit, you might warn a girl! You nearly tore my finger off."

She stood up, her breasts swaying. Objects of desire only seconds before, Davy hardly saw them. His eyes were drawn to the scars, barely visible from across the room yet burning, to Davy's eyes, like lines of fire.

"What's wrong?"

Davy tapped his own chest, where they'd put the device. He ran his finger over the scar tissue there and on his neck.

She raised her hand to touch her own skin above the breast. "Yes? What about it?" She cupped her own breasts and lifted them. "What does that have to do with *this*? With what we were doing?"

He looked away, ashamed of himself. "It brought me back to my senses. I don't know what I was thinking." He looked back. "When did they do it to you? And why?"

She crossed her arms over her breasts. "What does it matter?"

Davy felt like he'd been drenched in ice water. His stomach was roiling and though his arousal had vanished he could still feel her on his skin. "Because you went through this yourself, you *felt* what it was like, and *you let them do it to me!*"

"Ask yourself *this* my boy: What choice did I have?" She let her hands drop again. Her mouth, so soft and yielding before, was a tight line. "I spent my share of time lying in my own shit and vomit. Not that mine works like yours. They didn't use it to keep me from running—a locked door does that just fine in my case. But they did use it to compel my . . . loyalty."

Davy shuddered. *We're all victims here.* "What did you do to piss them off?"

She turned away. "You don't understand. You probably can't understand."

"I understand more than I *did*. They turned you into a killer, didn't they?"

She stared at him, frowning, like he'd just said the stupidest thing she'd ever heard. She picked up her clothes and her gun and walked to the door.

He was upset and he found he didn't want her to leave. "What did I say?"

She laughed at him, but there was very little humor in it. Her eyes glittered as she jerked her shirt on. "You don't get it. They didn't make me into a killer—that was why they hired me in the first place." She opened the door and touched her upper breast. "This wasn't inflicted on me—it was a requirement for promotion, a necessary condition to work at this level. It was something I *chose*!" She looked at Davy with narrowed eyes, then shook her head. "I should've known better." She slammed the door hard enough that the Winslow Homer print bounced off of its picture hook and fell to the dresser top.

Davy stared at the door, his mouth open. His hands shook and his mouth was dry. He thought about her skin, her breasts, and the way his body had responded to her touch.

Then he went into the bathroom and threw up.

SEVENTEEN

"Where is my husband?"

After an afternoon spent watching Lawrence Simons's New York address from a rooftop in the next block, Millie had a bad evening and a worse night.

In New York there'd been one delivery of groceries and the mailman had stuffed several envelopes in the slot but that was all. She was using the cheap plastic chair she'd used in D.C. and it still hurt her butt.

Later she'd bought takeout for herself and Padgett, dropped his off without being seen, and eaten her meal crouched before the wood stove in the Aerie.

Her dreams had been awful. They varied from being caught by Padgett's employers to finding Davy's lifeless body, his face frozen and frost crystallizing his eyes.

In the morning, she finally gave up the struggle and crawled out of bed, bleary-eyed, at five. She made tea and dressed warmly.

Time to talk to Padgett, she decided.

She brought him a mug of tea and placed it near the head of the sleeping bag. He was snoring, apparently having slept both soundly and well. Millie returned to the Aerie for an old, weather-beaten director's chair and set it down some fifteen feet from the sleeping man. She was wearing her Millie wig and her regular glasses without the contacts. She didn't know if she was going to give Padgett to the FBI or not, but if she did, she didn't want him telling anybody about her changed appearance.

She took a deep breath and settled herself into what she called her counselor self, the persona she used to do therapy.

"Good morning, Mr. Padgett."

The snoring cut off with a glottal catch and his lips smacked together. He was still asleep apparently, but she could tell he was surfacing.

"Time to wake up, Mr. Padgett."

He pulled the rim of the sleeping bag down and peered at the gray sky, then at her. "Sod off," he said and pulled the sleeping bag back over his face.

She blinked. It was bad enough that she hadn't slept. Why should he? She got a bucket from the Aerie and, after thinking for a moment, jumped to the waterfront in Edgartown. The wind had died but the air hovered at freezing. The salt water she dipped from the harbor was fresh from Nantucket Sound and very cold—around forty-five degrees Fahrenheit.

She stood five feet back from the head of the sleeping bag and swung the bucket with a will. The icy water splashed into the opening, spreading the bag open and soaking Padgett's head, arms, and upper torso. He struggled with the wet bag, trying to fight his way clear of the cold, sodden cloth.

Millie returned to Edgartown and took another bucket from Nantucket Sound. She jumped back to Texas, to the rim of the pit well above Padgett. The man had stripped off his shirt and was huddled over the coals of the fire trying to stir them to life. He had more firewood than she remembered, then she saw that the chair she'd carried down to the island had been broken up.

I liked that chair.

She put the bucket down on the ground and jumped to the island below, again, about fifteen feet away. "Are we awake, now?"

Padgett snarled. The canvas seat and back of the director's chair had caught afire and he was arranging the chair legs carefully atop the flames. He was shivering and he reached out to take one of the crutches into his hands but he didn't use it to stand. He held it like a club. "Keep away from me, bitch!"

Millie flinched from the intensity of his voice, then steadied. *What can he do to me?*

"Do you want me to leave you alone? All you have to do is answer two simple questions." She jumped to his rear, still twenty feet away from him. "One: Where is my husband, Mr. Padgett? Two: Where is Ms. Johnson."

Padgett nearly fell into the fire as he jerked his head around, tracking her voice.

She jumped back to her original place across the firepit. "Well?"

Padgett jerked back. He lowered his eyes to the fire and he ignored her.

She jumped back to the rim and retrieved the bucket of water. She appeared across the fire from him and he jerked away, rolling sideways as she swung the bucket, but Millie ignored him, and all the water splashed into the fire pit. The fire went out in a billowing cloud of steam and ashes. She jumped to the fireplace lighter and picked it up. Belatedly Padgett grabbed for it but she'd jumped back again, twenty feet away. Swinging the bucket back and forth, she said, "Back soon. Need more water."

She didn't go back to Edgartown. Instead, she bought a large cup of coffee in Manhattan. She retrieved the cheap plastic lawn chair from the roof on 82nd Street and returned to the island.

Padgett had unzipped the sleeping bag and had wrapped the third of it that was still dry around his upper body. He was visibly shaking.

Millie placed the chair on a stretch of sand and gravel and crossed her legs, making a show of removing the coffee cup's lid, sniffing deeply at the hot steam, and cupping the sides to warm her hands. She sipped and said, "Ouch. Still too hot." She put the cup down on the ground in front of her feet.

"I don't suppose you're willing to talk to me, yet?"

He was glaring at her. His teeth were chattering. There was a distinctly blue look around his lips, but he didn't speak.

"I see. Perhaps later, then."

She jumped up to the rim, behind the boulders, where she

could look down upon him from concealment. Padgett sat there for a few minutes looking around, then he used the crutches and pulled himself to his feet. He was still shivering and physically awkward. His leg was clearly still a problem. He started across the sand toward the coffee she'd left on the floor.

She had to steel herself for the next step. *Remember what he has done. The FBI agent. Davy. His attempt to capture me.*

She jumped back to the island when he was still ten feet away from the coffee. He flinched and staggered, shifting the crutches to keep from falling.

She bent over and picked up the cup. "Forgot my coffee," she said. She took a sip. "Ahhhhhh. Just right." She smiled brightly and wiggled her fingers. "Toodles!" She jumped away.

The shadow of the pit's rim crept across the water as the sun rose higher. Using the binoculars, Millie could tell that Padgett had stopped shivering some time earlier but he must be quite cold, still. He waited on the tip of the island closest to the shadow's edge seated in the cheap plastic chair, waiting for the warmth of direct sunlight.

"Where are they, Mr. Padgett?"

He was seated with his back to the water's edge where the island narrowed, so she couldn't appear behind him. She stood there, comfortable in a bulky sweater, twenty feet away.

Padgett's mouth tightened but he did not speak.

"Shall I go get the bucket?" she asked in a light conversational tone.

He shook his head, then broke off, as if he hadn't meant to do that much. "Fuck off. I've taken much worse."

"Well, I believe you've certainly *done* worse to others. I'm not going to 'fuck off,' though, until I learn what I need to know."

"I hope they killed the kaffir bitch. You have no idea who or what you're fucking with, little girl."

Millie's eyebrows raised and she said mildly, "And you do?"

She jumped, appearing three feet away, not directly in front of him, but at an angle off to one side. Her swinging right foot caught the chair arm and Padgett toppled back, teetering for a moment at the point of balance, then over, splashing back into the water. By the time he'd thrashed his way back to the shore, dragging his bum knee, he was completely soaked.

Millie was back at her original post, twenty feet away. "That looks *refreshing!*"

Padgett swore, snatched up a fist-sized stone, and threw it at her.

She flinched away, back to the Aerie.

Leave him, she thought, trembling a little. *He's like a tea bag. Let him* steep *a while.*

She dabbed at her sweater with the dish towel. When Padgett had hit the pool's surface some of the spray had splashed her arm. It seemed every bit as cold as the water from Nantucket Sound.

What I'm doing is illegal.

She was already guilty of kidnapping. What she'd been doing today in the pit was the sort of thing Amnesty International asked people to write letters about.

Millie shuddered.

Where do I draw the line?

She watched him from the rim. Padgett was shivering violently. Wet again, his only recourse was exercise, for both his clothing and the sleeping bag were soaked. Millie watched him strip naked, then wring as much water out of the clothes and sleeping bag as he could, before he spread them across the low mesquite bushes in the center of the island. Then he circled the perimeter of the island briskly, swinging the crutches savagely forward.

He can't keep that up for long. He doesn't have the calories.

She took no pleasure in watching the naked man. He was attractive enough if you discounted an incipient potbelly and liked balding men, which Millie generally did, but she couldn't forget who he was and what he represented long enough to enjoy even the tiniest bit of titillation. Right now, she just wanted him to be as miserable as she was and the only way she knew to do that was through physical discomfort.

I'm turning into one of them, she thought. *If I ever get Davy back, he won't want me.*

She considered taking Padgett's crutches away.

You are *in a pissy mood, aren't you?*

The plastic chair was still in the water, half submerged two feet from the water's edge. While Padgett was at the far end of the island, she fished it out and shook it. She swiped most of the remaining moisture off with the edge of her hand, then sat facing him. He looked cold, still, but the major involuntary shudders had stopped and he didn't look as blue around the mouth.

He slowed as he rounded the far end of the island, when he caught sight of her, but he still continued his circuit. As he neared her, he cut across the island to avoid her.

"Hot coffee, warm blanket, dry clothes, food. Yours in the blink of an eye."

He ignored her.

She waited until he had passed and was turning away from her before she added, "Ice water is also an option."

He faltered, one crutch tip slipping slightly through the sand, but he continued on his way.

She pictured herself with a bullwhip, laying the lash across Padgett's bare buttocks. *Might as well put on the leather corset and the thigh-high boots while I'm at it.* She jumped away, disgusted with herself, angry with Padgett, and on the edge of tears.

She went back to the cyber café in Manhattan and started an e-mail to Agent Anders. She was going to ask about Lawrence Simons but then remembered Anders's comment about the security of unencrypted e-mail, so she changed it to a simple request for a phone appointment. A half-hour later, just returned from throwing a bucket of Nantucket Sound salt water onto an unexpecting Padgett, she read his reply.

CALL LAST NUMBER AT 1300 PRECISE.

She used a pay phone in the Dupont Circle D.C. Metro station, watching the second hand sweep to the top before pressing the last digit.

Anders answered on the first ring. "Hello," he said neutrally, but when he recognized her voice, he said, "They've pushed me completely aside. I'm ordered back to Oklahoma City and when I protested, they said it was that or suspension. My boss didn't like it either but he said it came from so far up that it gave him vertigo just thinking about it."

She thought about that. "Even though you're the only contact with me they have? It sounds more and more like they know where Davy is or who has him and that they're happy with it!"

"I don't know. Perhaps. I'd like to think whoever did this actually has a good reason for what they're doing."

He's not contradicting me. "Is this phone still clean?"

"I *think* so. As I told you, it's an anonymous prepaid cell. I'm in the locker room of a neighborhood gym. I've never been here before so they sure didn't bug it on the random chance I might drop by."

"Good. Who is Lawrence Simons?"

There was a perceptible pause before he said, "Pretty common name, isn't it?"

"I'd be glad to narrow it down. Do you want some addresses? Some phone numbers?"

"No!"

"So you know who he is?"

"I know who he *could* be. Give me a minute, okay?"

She put a couple of more quarters in the phone while she waited, to avoid any later interruption.

When he spoke again his voice was tentative. "First of all, don't say that name again, okay? It is a common name but one of the computers at Fort Meade might twig to it and flag this conversation for human review. Understand?"

She licked her lips. "Yes."

"How do you know that name?"

"Divergent paths led me to him. One from the man I call the Monk—remember him? Another from that firm of consultants the Monk seems to work for."

Anders said, "Have you seen the Monk recently or did you remember something you haven't told me?"

"Your turn, I believe. First tell me about Voldemort."

"Who? Ah, got you. He-who-must-not-be-named. Sinister but possibly apropos. We'll call him that."

"Is he in your organization—say, so high up you'd get vertigo thinking about it?"

She heard him take a sudden breath. "Well, he's not in the Agency. He's not in the government at all, but he is, hmmm, well, if the rumors are true, he's a man who whispers in ears. But only stratospheric ears, if you get my meaning."

Way up where the air is thin. Vertigo land. "Ah. Why do these ears listen?"

"What I know is based on rumors over the years, right? I did see something on paper once but it was pulled and shredded almost as soon as it hit the file drawer. I'm not going into it over the phone but the reasons he is listened to range from money to fear. But there's no doubt he *has* influence and it's been exerted, in the past, in directions not unlike those favored by the BAd boys."

"Ah. The profit-no-matter-what school."

"What makes you think he is concerned in this?"

"Well, your reaction, for one. But I've linked him to the—to that firm. And other . . . reasons." She didn't want to tell him about the Vineyard. She had high hopes for the Vineyard, but she didn't want the slightest breath of her suspicion to reach the people who had Davy, lest they move or kill him.

She felt a stab of cold panic. *I shouldn't have mentioned his name at all.* She didn't know to what degree the NSA mainframes monitored random phone calls (which this hopefully was) and she didn't want to ask Anders for it was exactly the sort of phrase the computers might be scanning for—a trigger to record the entire message and flag it for a human to listen to it.

Anders asked, "How did you get your clue from the Monk?"

"Is Becca still looking for him or was her organization *also* discouraged?"

"I don't think they've been called down. It's hard to put pressure on that branch when one of their own has been, well, inoculated."

She furrowed her brow for a moment. *Shot.* "I understand.

Push that group too hard and we'll all be reading about an attempted cover-up in the papers?"

Anders agreed. "It's happened."

"Well, I have a line on the Monk. Can you give me her cell number?"

He gave it to her. "You better call her right away before you lose him."

Millie thought about the shivering, naked Padgett stumping around the island at the bottom of the pit. "He's not going anywhere."

And he wasn't.

Padgett was curled in a ball, wrapped in the damp, matted sleeping bag. Sand clung to the side of his face where he'd lain on the ground and his eyes were clenched shut. He was still shivering so she knew he was alive.

She didn't talk to him but instead built a fire, bringing in charcoal starter and two armfuls of dry piñon logs. The crackling whoosh of the rising flames got Padgett's attention. By the time he'd dragged himself over to the fire, she'd returned with a twenty-ounce Styrofoam cup of hot chocolate and a brand-new sleeping bag, still sealed in plastic.

She set them down near him and jumped away. She didn't think he had the strength to swing or throw a crutch, but she didn't want to find out. Twenty minutes later, she brought a large container of Thai soup, shrimp with lemongrass, plus a box of pad thai.

She didn't watch him eat. It was hard enough even looking at him. *Hard enough to be both good and bad cop.*

She used a computer in the Oklahoma City Public Library to locate the street where Lawrence Simons's home on Martha's Vineyard was. As the waitress had told her, it was on the South Beach, the ocean side, a mile away from the Winnetu Inn and Resort, down toward the wild area around Great Edgartown Pond.

She was pleasantly surprised to find the weather much warmer in Edgartown than on her last visit. The chill north wind had become a gentle southerly breeze and, though it was still below sixty degrees, the sun beat down warmly. The jacket she'd worn over her sweater was superfluous so she put it in the small suitcase she'd brought. She mixed with the small crowd of people who came off the ferry from Falmouth and, when the Winnetu shuttle showed up, she asked the driver if there was room at the inn.

"Some," the man said. "Off season and all that, but there's a radiology symposium starting tomorrow—they've got half the hotel. You don't have a reservation?"

"No," she said. "Got time off at the last minute. Spur of the moment thing. Hopped the ferry on impulse."

"Well, I'm sure they can find you some room."

He put her bag in the back with the others and she got into the half-full van behind assorted radiologists and a young couple on their honeymoon.

At the hotel she wandered the lobby waiting for the guests with reservations to check in first. Twice men asked her if she was attending the conference but she didn't think it was radiology they had on their minds. When the last doctor wandered off behind their bellman she approached the desk and made her inquiry.

"Seven nights? So you're not here for the conference? I'm afraid all the smaller rooms are taken but I can put you in one of the two-bedroom suites." He lowered his voice and added, "I can give it to you for the same rate." He looked around to make sure none of the other guests were in earshot. "Please don't mention it to these doctors, though."

Millie said, "Waiter, there's a fly in my soup! Keep your voice down, sir. If the other customers hear you—"

"—they'll all want one, too," finished the clerk. "Yes, exactly. Which credit card do you want to put this on?"

"I'm weaning myself off of plastic. I'd prefer to pay cash."

"That's over a thousand dollars, Ma'am!"

"Good thing you're giving me the *cheap* rate. How much over a thousand dollars?"

He punched some numbers into the booking computer. "One thousand, fifteen dollars, Ma'am."

Millie laid ten hundred-dollar bills and a twenty on the counter. "There you go."

"Yes, ma'am. If you'd fill out the registration card, please."

She registered as Millicent Jones and used the address of a home in Waltham, Mass. The house was real so the address was valid, but it was empty, for sale. She'd found it on a realtor's website. The phone was in the right exchange, too, but was the listing for the realtor.

She'd taken some pains to memorize both, so she could fill the card out naturally. Paying cash was unusual enough. She didn't want to arouse more suspicion by seeming unsure of her own address and phone number.

"Very good, Miss Jones."

The bellman led her up to her suite, on the third floor, with a patio that looked out over the dunes to the ocean itself. In the larger bedroom she carefully unpacked her clothes, no laundry marks, no unusual labels. She left three paperbacks in the small living room, some toiletries in the bathroom, and mussed the king-sized bed, pulling back the covers on one side and actually lying there for a moment with her head creasing the pillow, then pulling the covers roughly back into place.

There. Someone is staying here.

She had collected several scallop, a few mussel, and two turban shells when the security guard approached her on the beach. As far as she could tell, she was still a half-mile away from the houses at the end of Great Pond lane.

"Are you staying in this neighborhood, ma'am?"

She jerked her head up as if she'd been taken unawares. She'd actually noticed him some time back but had kept her head down, studying the sand and the shells with apparently unswerving attention.

She took a step back and put her hand to her chest. "Oh, my goodness! Where'd you come from? What's that you said?"

He was in a brown uniform that looked vaguely police-like and his belt supported all the usual law-enforcement equipment, ranging from nine millimeter automatic to nightstick to radio. "Are you staying in this neighborhood? This is a private beach and unless you're a resident or a guest . . ." He let that trail off.

"I'm at the Winnetu," she explained.

"Could I see some ID, please?"

She spread her arms wide. She was wearing a one-piece swimming suit, a sweatshirt tied around her waist, and capri pants. She was barefoot and the only bag she had was the plastic Ziploc holding her shells.

"You can't. I left my purse in my room—it's not the sort of thing I take beachcombing." She fished in the waistband of her pants. "I have my room key, see?" She showed him the Winnetu tag without displaying the room number stamped into the key. "And I can *tell* you my name—Jones, Millicent R. The R is for Regina." She looked at his uniform shirt with the name of the company, Island Security, plainly labeled on one of the shirt flaps. "And as a security guard, I didn't think you could ask for someone's ID." She pointed at his name on the other shirt flap. "Isn't that right, Bob?"

"One can always *ask*. You passed the Private Beach sign back there, ma'am." Bob pointed.

Millie made a show of looking but she'd already seen the sign. She'd just ignored it. She looked back at the guard and held up her bag of shells. "Sorry. Was looking down. Didn't see it."

"Yes, ma'am. You'll have to go back."

"I see. Do I have to leave the shells I picked up beyond the sign? I think I got one of the turban shells in this last stretch."

Bob shook his head. "I don't think that'll be necessary."

"I must confess I'm surprised they keep a security guard just to watch the beach."

He smiled slightly. "No, ma'am. I'm making my rounds. We watch this neighborhood." He gestured vaguely behind him, in the direction Millie had been walking. "Some of these houses sit empty through the winter so we keep an eye on them."

And some don't? "Must get pretty cold here in the winter. I sure wouldn't want to stay here then."

"Windy and cold."

"Do many people in this neighborhood stay through the winter?"

He ignored her question. "You can't miss the hotel, ma'am, if you just walk back the way you came."

She blinked. *Put me in my place, didn't you?* "All right." She smiled politely but not warmly and headed back down the beach the way she'd come, at the waterline, still looking for shells. At the border between the private and public beach she looked back.

He was still watching her from the same place. She waved and he raised his hand briefly, then turned away, walking back through the dunes. She went back to the hotel and rinsed her shells off in the kitchenette sink, then arranged them on the coffee table in the living room.

Someone might come see if I kept them or not.

EIGHTEEN

"Are you saying you found another Teleport?"

Davy came down to breakfast reluctantly, timidly. It had been three in the morning on the East Coast when they'd returned from Nigeria, and after Hyacinth had left his room, he'd felt limp with exhaustion. *Though not in the way I'd thought I would be.*

When sleep had finally come, it brought nightmares of small plane crashes and burning villages, towering natural gas flares bending from on high and torching house after house. At one point in the horrid stew of images, he'd seen Reverend Ilori bent over the coals of his burning church, cooking a large lizard on a stick. He turned to Davy and said, "Good eating!"

When he stuck his head into the breakfast room there was no sign of Hyacinth, but the room wasn't empty.

Conley was sitting at the table, alone.

"Well, the math is bizarre and nobody believes my data and I can't tell them the circumstances."

Davy blinked, relieved.

Bad enough that I've turned a monster loose, he thought, thinking of Roule. *I'm glad I don't have to eat breakfast with one.* He'd gone along with the recovery because the kidnappers really were bandits. He'd seen the newspaper reports about the attack—seven guards and a secretary killed during the abduction—and he'd thought he was actually doing a good deed.

Davy looked suspiciously at Conley. His recent encounter with Hyacinth made him reexamine the man's words. "What do you mean, 'can't tell them?'"

Conley looked up blinking, clearly engrossed in his physics puzzles. "Am not allowed to."

Davy jumped to the other side of the table, standing right behind Conley. With his right hand he grabbed the neck of Conley's shirt from behind and shoved down as Conley tried to scramble to his feet. With his left hand he ripped Conley's shirt open, exposing the man's left shoulder, collarbone, and upper chest.

The scars were there, both of them. He prodded with his finger and felt the hard lump under the skin.

Conley, realizing what he was doing, stopped struggling.

Davy released him and walked slowly back around the table.

Conley glared at him. "I really liked this shirt!" Pointedly, he popped a dangling button off its last strand of thread and dropped it in his shirt pocket.

Davy pursed his lips. "Your scars are older than mine, but not as old as Hyacinth's. How long ago did they put it in?"

Conley poured himself some more coffee from the thermos carafe. "You saw Hyacinth's scars? Wow."

Davy felt himself blush scarlet. "Is it everybody here? Everybody who comes in contact with Simons?"

Conley shuddered slightly like a horse twitching off a biting fly. He stared at the opposite wall and said, "Not only did I track your mass moving from station to station, but every time you jumped, the gravitational signature actually overlapped for one hundred and thirty to two hundred milliseconds. It was as if you were in two places at once, which is impossible, of course."

Davy sat down and shook his napkin out before placing it in his lap. "Must be anybody who knows Simons. Inner circle stuff."

Conley shook a packet of artificial sweetener into his cup. "So it confirms my previous hypothesis. You aren't really disappearing and reappearing. You're opening a gateway, a hole between the two space-time locations. Because the hole persists, I'm getting my doubled mass reading—through the door."

Davy poured himself coffee. "I think I know what you mean."

Conley looked up from stirring his coffee, the spoon dangling in his hand. "Really?"

"Yeah. For instance it seems like we're in the same room right now but from the conversation, we're actually a million miles apart."

"Think about it! Don't you know what this means? If you could open such a hole and leave it open? At the least, it means unlimited energy. You could end droughts by diverting flood waters from one part of the planet to parched riverbeds elsewhere. Add a hydroelectric generator and you'd get energy as well. Hell, open a gate between a low altitude reservoir and an upper one and you have perpetual energy."

"Perpetual motion?" said Davy, a skeptical look on his face. "Where does the energy come from?"

It was Conley's turn to blush. "Well, where does the energy come from for *your* jumps?"

Davy shrugged, "Ah, that. Well, each time I jump every hot beverage on earth loses a millicalorie of heat."

Conley stared at his coffee for a second before smiling. "Well, that's a thought. We should measure the net energy in your departure and destination environments."

"Yeah—imagine what global warming would be like without my efforts!"

Conley sighed. "I take it you don't really know where the energy comes from?"

"I take it you don't know which of the staff here have implants in their chest?"

Conley stopped talking and ate his breakfast. Davy glared at him for a moment before fetching his own from the sideboard. When he was done, Davy said, "I'm going to the beach if it's okay with you."

"Conley looked vaguely up at the ceiling and said, "Turn on the beach keys, please."

A wall-mounted intercom said, "All clear."

Davy shivered. He thought he was watched always, but it was nasty to have it confirmed.

Conley nodded at Davy. "Listen for the whistle—he wants to talk to you later."

"He? Your master? Simons?"

Conley looked away. "He's flying in. They'll want you locked down when he lands."

"Yes, Renfield."

Conley looked puzzled and raised his eyebrows.

"You guys need to read more. Go Google it. R, E, N, F, I, E, L, D. To narrow it down add the search term 'Stoker.'" He jumped directly to the beach.

It's an odd duck that doesn't know who Renfield is.

The wind was strong out of the east, parallel to the beach, tearing the long ocean swells to rags as they broke. Davy sat in sun-warmed sand in the lee of a rock, sheltered from the stinging wind-borne sand.

The tide was out. He stared at the smooth expanse of wet sand and thought about tramping out a message for passing spy satellites, DAVY HERE, in letters twenty feet on a side. It would be visible but, even if his jailers let him do it, what were the odds of the right SatIntel analyst reporting it to someone who was sufficiently in the know?

He thought about what Conley had told him, about keeping the gate open. He pictured putting his hand in a full bathtub in Stillwater and simultaneously putting the same hand in the cistern in the cliff house—holding the gate open—having the water flow through from bath to tank. *Would beat hauling buckets.*

The whistle blew and, reflexively, he jumped back to his room, in the square. Conley was already there, the padlock in his hand. "Time to put on the manacle, I'm afraid. They're on final approach."

Davy put the manacle on around his ankle. He let Conley examine it for snugness, snap the padlock shut, and check that the lock was definitely engaged.

Conley didn't stop there—he followed the chain to its floor anchor and verified every link. "Secure," he said to the mirror.

It was another half-hour before Hyacinth came in the door and double-checked the chain and lock. Only then did she hold the door for Lawrence Simons to enter, a file folder in his hand. After Simons was seated, just outside the radius of Davy's chain, she took up a station against the wall. She didn't speak and she didn't look at Davy.

"Good morning, Mr. Rice. Good morning, Dr. Conley."

Davy watched Simons's face. The man smiled as he spoke but it struck Davy that the politeness was a shell, spoken like some barely understood foreign language. *He knows when to use the phrases but he doesn't really understand why.*

Simons continued. "I don't think we'll be needing you at this time, Dr. Conley."

Conley blinked, then said, "Of course. I'll be in my office." He left quickly and, Davy thought, gratefully.

After he was gone Simons turned to Hyacinth and said, "If you'd see about that other matter, my dear."

Hyacinth nodded and left.

Simons put on the polite smile again and said, "Nice work there in Nigeria."

Davy nodded slightly. "Have you known Mr. Roule long?"

Simons tilted his head as if considering. "I've known *of* him for several years. But I don't think I've ever been in the same room with him. He's not a direct report."

"Ah, so he *is* one of yours?"

"He is unaware of the connection."

"What happened to the kidnappers?"

Simons shook his head. "Bit of a botch, really. The army leveled the island and pumped thousands of rounds into the surrounding mangroves but they didn't come up with a single body. Closer coordination was called for."

"To keep them from leveling the mission?"

Simons looked at Davy like he was from another planet. "To insure the destruction of the kidnappers."

Hyacinth came back in and nodded to Simons. "All off, sir."

"You're sure?"

"I unplugged the AV board. All video and audio feeds are dead until I plug it back in and I locked that room. I have the only key on site."

Davy remembered the day the welder had blown the circuit

breaker—how Hyacinth had talked to the mirror without response. He filed it away.

"Very good, Hyacinth." Simons shifted in his seat, turning his attention fully upon Davy.

"As I understand it, you can teleport to any place you've been previously."

Davy shrugged. "Within reason. I have to have sufficient recall of the place. If I haven't been there in a while, I need my memory jogged."

"Jogged? How jogged?"

"By going there again, by some more traditional means." He paused for a second then added, "Or images—photos or video."

Simons took a folded page from his file folder. "I see. How fresh is your memory of Caracas?" He handed the sheet to Davy.

Davy unfolded the sheet and studied it in silence. It was a color printout of the central areas of Caracas, major avenues only, with several points of interest highlighted and an overlay of the subway system.

Simons shook his head. "You were there last July for the NSA. You delivered several cardboard boxes."

Indeed? Davy looked up surprised. Simons knew that much. "All right. I have a site at the Metro station at Plaza Venezuela. Also at the *Parque Central*."

"Not Bolivar Plaza?"

"I wouldn't go there in an armored car."

"Surely in daylight?"

"Well, perhaps in a large group, in daylight."

"The airport?"

Davy shook his head. "It's been seven years. I had no business there and since the coup attempts and the strikes, it's not been one of my, shall we say, pleasure destinations."

Simons waved his hand and said, "Surely you didn't take the boxes to a public metro station?"

"Close. The agent-in-place parked a moving van in a nearby alley. I jumped the boxes into the back of the truck. Then I closed the padlock on the door and left. They picked the truck up twenty minutes later. They never saw me. They don't know how the boxes were delivered. They weren't supposed to." He looked at Simons. "Neither were you."

Simons ignored the last. "Did you know what was in the boxes?"

"You don't?" Davy had known. He also knew roughly what its purpose was, else he wouldn't have moved it. But he didn't want to share that with Simons.

"I know. Paper."

Hyacinth frowned. "Documents? They used him for *FedEx*?"

Simons shook his head. "Brightly colored paper. Venezuelan Bolivars. The price was falling even then. They sent several million."

"Why not dollars?"

"Traceability. They were setting up a network of informants on both sides."

Well, that's what they told me. Hope it wasn't another attempt to destabilize the government. He didn't *think* it was. "Do you work for the NSA?" Davy said.

Simons laughed. "Of course not, silly boy. Like Roule, they have no idea of the relationship."

"You don't work for them," Davy said slowly. "But sometimes—"

"Exactly. Sometimes they work for me."

Davy shuddered. He couldn't help it. Visceral—that's what it was, and Simons watched with a faint smile on his face.

"So, your NSA file—and let me tell you, it was *very* difficult getting a copy—says you're the only known teleport. What other lies are in the file?"

Davy raised his eyebrows. "Oh stop it. Am I still beating my wife? Don't you have better things to do with your time? Who came up with this approach—Conley?"

"The facts dictated it." Simons crossed his legs and tilted his head to one side, continuing to watch Davy steadily.

Davy stared back. He narrowed his eyes. "Are you saying you've found another teleport?"

"I am."

"I don't believe it. I've been actively looking for ten years. Who is it? Where are they from?"

Simons shook his head. "You're very good. You haven't shown yourself capable of this level of deception before. You had us all fooled."

"You think I'm lying?" He shrugged. "Okay, feel that way. There are really twenty-seven other teleports. My gang, and when they catch up with you you'll wish you'd never been born."

Simons frowned. "Now see? You're so clearly lying when you say that, that your ability to dissemble about the other teleport surprises me. How is it done?"

"The lying? Or the teleporting?"

"Who was the first to teleport? Was it you or was it your wife? We know from the file that she was held by the NSA during your first 'interactions' with them, yet she didn't escape. Either she couldn't do it then, or it was very deep cover."

"My wife?" Davy laughed, but it died almost immediately as the implications settled in. "What on earth makes you think she can jump?" Davy couldn't help it—he found his voice rising. If they thought Millie could jump she'd be an even higher priority target for Simons. Not just as a way to control Davy but as a spare.

"She was trapped in a hotel room in Virginia. My people were in the hall, outside the window, and in both adjoining rooms. They were monitoring her movements acoustically through the wall. When the point man went through the front door, the monitor heard a splash from the tub. Her clothes were there—she was gone."

Davy's eyes widened. "No way. Your people are hosing you." *Or you are hosing me.*

Simons had tilted his head to the other side. "Hmmm. We must consider the third possibility, I suppose."

Davy was there before him but he kept his mouth shut.

"That she couldn't jump before, but now she can."

What do they hope to gain with these lies? "What was she doing in Virginia."

"Looking for you." Simons took another sheet of paper out of his folder and pushed it across to Davy. It was a poster with Davy's picture, a shot he recognized from their stay in Tahiti. It gave the rough time and place of his disappearance and asked for anyone who had information to call the number below. However, the number had been cut out of the paper with a razor blade or X-Acto knife.

His intake of breath was sudden, surprising. The picture was from the cliff house bedside table. He felt tears well to his eyes and he blinked them away. He tried to make his voice light, uncaring. "Ah. Well, it's not a milk carton." *She made it out of the cliff house.* The relief was painful, overwhelming, and he knew it showed in his face. So what—Millie was all right and she wasn't in *their* hands.

Why are they trying to convince me she can jump? Maybe Millie had faked something. He'd seen magicians do some pretty convincing fakes in the past. "To the best of *my* knowledge, I'm the only jumper there is. You sure the NSA isn't spoofing you? Maybe your people were listening to a tape recorder?"

Simons's eyes narrowed for the barest second before his expression returned to its customary urbanity.

He isn't sure, Davy realized.

Simons turned to Hyacinth. "Please fetch Miss Johnson."

Davy didn't recognize the name.

"Yes, sir." She left.

"You trouble me, Mr. Rice. Your field test in Nigeria was quite promising. It is my hope that you'll continue to make yourself useful, but, in the event you choose not to, I want to make absolutely clear that the consequences will be severe."

Davy tensed. Was he about to be punished for supposedly concealing Millie's ability to teleport? *Well, if they activate it, I'll aim for his very expensive suit.*

When Hyacinth came back she held the door. His old friends Thug One and Thug Two came through the door, each holding the arm of a figure dressed in a short-sleeve, ill-fitting, dark green jump suit. The hands were cuffed in back and they had a black cloth sack over her head. Once the door was shut, Thug One pulled off the hood revealing the woman's face. She was a black woman who blinked rapidly in the sudden light and her lower lip was bleeding. She looked familiar to Davy. Then her eyes squeezed shut in a prolonged blink before reopening, and her tongue thrust wildly out of her mouth.

"Sojee?" It'd been over three months but the facial twitches were unmistakable. "What did they do to you?"

Sojee looked at him blankly, then smiled. "My angel!" Her face was transformed, bloody lip and all. She tried to step forward but her escorts pulled her back. Bitterly, she said, "They took my coat."

Thug Two, the redhead, was holding a bloody handkerchief to his beak-like nose.

Simons frowned. "What happened?" His voice was mild but both guards looked nervous.

Thug Two said nasally, "She head-butted me, sir. In the nose. I knocked her back, off of me."

Simons's voice was scathing. "You know what she did in D.C.! Did you underestimate her because she's a woman or black?" Simons looked at Davy. "I swim in a sea of incompetence. It's no wonder we haven't caught up with your wife."

Davy was watching Sojee. Besides the split lip she looked okay. Well, she looked like Sojee. Her facial spasms were as severe as ever and the way she stood there, her head tilted to one side, he suspected she was listening to voices. "What happened in D.C.?"

Sojee smiled again. "The Blue Lady and I whupped 'em when they came for us. I would've finished 'em 'cept the FBI pulled me off."

Davy looked back at Simons.

Simons closed his eyes and pinched the bridge of his nose.

Davy said, "Who is the Blue Lady, Sojee?"

Sojee frowned. "What? The Blue Lady! The one who comes from the sea to protect us." She pointed down at the poster on the table. "The lady who was handing out those. She *said* she was your wife."

"Millie?"

Sojee nodded.

"She *is* my wife. But why 'Blue Lady?' Was she sad or is it something else?"

"Yes and yes."

Davy shook his head, his mind racing. "How long have they had you? Are they mistreating you?"

"They lock me in a heated room with a shower and a toilet. They stick meals under the door on trays, three times a day. It's *horrible*."

"Enough!" said Simons. "Take her back."

Sojee looked down at Davy's shackle, then at Simons. Her mouth made a silent *oh*. "I see." She jerked her head over toward Simons. "Satan's minion, the demon king."

Simons waved his hand and Thugs One and Two put the hood back over her head and pulled her back out through the door. When it had closed again, Simons said, "She may think her conditions are bad now, but I invite you to consider how much worse they could be."

Davy had a hard time not laughing in Simons's face. Sojee hadn't been *complaining*—she'd been boasting. Compared to the streets, the cell was like heaven . . . for now.

Simons continued, "They're idiots. Brutal idiots." He looked into Davy's eyes. "But for all that, they'll do exactly what I say. And, after the head-butting incident, they'll probably enjoy it."

Davy felt his stomach roiling. "You'll have to spell it out."

"You're right," said Simons. "There should be no chance of misunderstanding. It goes like this: when I said the consequences of non-cooperation would be severe, I was talking about more than just for you personally. Ms. Johnson will also face those consequences and Hyacinth will deliver the results to you one finger joint at a time. Do I make myself clear?"

Davy made his face go blank. "You do."

Simons stared at Davy for a moment, silent, considering. Finally he said, "Very well. Let's talk about Caracas."

They served him lunch in his room, but Conley didn't come back in with the key until the afternoon was almost gone. As he removed the padlock, Conley said, "I've thought up some experiments to try, but we'll have to wait until they've finished with you. Day after tomorrow, perhaps?"

"I suppose." Davy rubbed his ankle. "So, they haven't told you?"

Conley held up his hands. "Apparently it's not my concern, so I'm happier not knowing."

Davy gestured at the shackle. "I take it Simons hung around for a while?"

"Golf, I believe. He flew in to play golf. Now he's gone, though."

Davy shuddered. Busy day for Simons. Fly to Martha's Vineyard. Taunt prisoner. Threaten torture to innocent victim. Eighteen holes of golf. Fly back to wherever. *A minion's work is never done.* He gave his attention to Conley. "Umm. Well, what kind of experiments?"

"Thought we might try jumping back and forth between two different places, quick as you can, oscillating so to speak."

"More like vacillating. Like I can't make up my mind where I want to be."

"Yes. We know there's some persistence of the phenomenon, perhaps we can actually get the gate to stay open."

Davy thought about this. "How will you tell? How can you measure it?"

Conley frowned. "By what flows through, I suppose. I might put a weak radio transmitter by one location and a field strength meter at the other. If we can get the signal strength to stabilize—"

Davy nodded. "Got it." His felt his heart pounding and a rush of adrenaline coursed through him. *Got it!* He wondered if Conley had thought it through. The impulse to glance at the mirror was almost overwhelming but he mastered it.

Conley nodded back. "Well, we'll try it when you're back, unless you want to try something right now."

Davy shook his head. Simons told him they were waiting for the electronic keys to be flown from Nigeria to Caracas. Apparently the soonest the KLM flight could get to Venezuela was six o'clock but there was serious doubt as to whether they'd made the connection in Amsterdam. There was very little chance they'd need Davy before tomorrow but he wasn't going to tell Conley that. "They told me to hold myself ready."

He felt safe in this lie. They'd turned off the cameras and the microphones after all. *Or they said they did.* He didn't really doubt it, though—it wasn't as if they'd been trying to get Davy to say anything revealing or incriminating. Simons had been the one doing all the talking.

What, then, was the point? What topic of the briefing did they not want on tape? *Well, they did threaten to chop Sojee's fingers off joint by joint.* He remembered other things said and done in this room, ostensibly when the cameras and microphones *were* operating. *No, it's something about Caracas.*

Conley was still looking at him, hefting the weight of the padlock in his hand. "You all right?"

Davy blinked. "Oh. Yeah. Just thinking about that stuff you said you didn't want to know about."

"I don't ask. Don't tell."

Davy exhaled. "You be nice to me or I'll start telling you everything I know. And, of course, I'll tell *them* I told you."

He'd meant it as a jest, something to get the conversation off of the notion of a gate, but Conley blanched and dropped the padlock to the floor. "Shit." He stooped to pick it up and when he stood again his eyes were wary.

Davy felt compelled to say, "Just kidding, man. Really."

Conley put the padlock on the dresser and said, "I'll go work on my notes. Later." He opened the door partway and sidled through.

That was weird.

He turned his thoughts back to Sojee. He hadn't gotten any sense of another prisoner in the mansion. They'd told him he had the run of the public rooms when he was allowed out of his room but he'd been warned away from any locked door. He'd also been told specifically never to enter the room behind the mirror again on pain of confinement to the square.

He couldn't get into the attic—the door was steel and locked. He was looking down the steps into the basement when Hyacinth showed up, an amused look on her face. "Miss Crazy Face isn't in the building, Lover. She was well away from here even before lunch." She spread her hands. "We're not *stupid.*"

No. Unfortunately.

"The keys made it to Caracas but we're giving the boys the

night off. Jet lag. We'll go oh-eight-hundred—that's nine in Caracas. Set your alarm or, if you want, you can leave a wakeup call with *me*. I'd be glad—"

Davy jumped away, back to his room, without letting her finish. He was hoping she'd find it as annoying as any other person who'd been cut off in mid-sentence. *But I doubt it.* Hyacinth would see his reaction as her victory.

Let her. If Hyacinth thought she was in the driver's seat, she'd be less vigilant.

Maybe I should *sleep with her. Let her have her way to put her off guard.* He felt his body responding to the thought. *You just want to get laid. Stop rationalizing.* He called up the memory of Brian Cox's blood splashing across his face in the rain and the scars above and below Hyacinth's collarbone. The ache subsided.

A shower is called for.

He started the water running before undressing. The boiler in the basement was huge, but it took some time for the heated water to run through the pipes to the third floor. Once it reached his bath, though, the supply was unlimited. Long showers had saved his sanity. After the messy and shameful episodes when they'd trigger the device, it took a long time under the water to feel clean again.

But another thing he'd noticed: when the bathroom door was open and the shower was running at length, it filled the bath with clouds of steam and coated the mirror in the bathroom with moisture.

It blocked the camera.

Before, he'd used that privacy to cry, to rage, and to masturbate. Now, it was time to use it for something else.

Slowly, to start. He began with a simple jump of a mere three feet, from one end of the tub to the other. He stood relaxed, his feet spread. There was a shower mat but it didn't extend the entire length of the tub and he didn't want to fall on his ass. He took a towel from the rack and spread it over the uncovered part of the tub. Wet, it clung to the enamel and he felt more confident.

He changed his orientation with each jump, always facing toward the opposite end of the tub. He stepped up the pace, jumping twice a second easily, three times a second. His vision spun. The two shower walls, one with the showerhead and controls and one with a towel rack, blurred together and then the figure appeared, like a ghost in the mist, facing him, there and not there.

"Shit!" He shoved his right hand out and recoiled away. The shower head banged into the back of his head, the water valves stabbed into his butt. The figure in front of him also threw an arm forward, flinching backward, and vanished.

Oh. Despite the scrape on his posterior, he started laughing.

It's like a Firesign Theatre record: "How can you be in two places at once when you're really nowhere at all?" He remembered a time right after they'd begun conditioning him when he couldn't face himself in the mirror. *No mirror. Can you face yourself now?*

It took him a moment to get it again. He was struggling and his knees were getting weak. Jumping had never tired him before, but this was draining. He was about to give it up again but there he was, blurred, two sets of features overlapping, like the showerhead and the towel rack blurring together. He reached out cautiously with his right hand—both of them—and his fingertips touched, solid, yet with an underlying vibration, a shaking. He dropped his hand and stared at the face.

Not a mirror. It wasn't what he was used to. He had regular enough features but apparently there was enough asymmetry to render the features familiar yet strange.

Push it. He changed his destination, trying to hold onto his original post at the showerhead end of the tub, while switching the other terminus to the Aerie.

His ears popped hard and the shower curtain swirled around him at a sudden gust of wind. The difference between the sweltering hot shower and the icy unheated air broke his concentration and he found himself standing completely in the Aerie. The governor kicked in and he was back in the bathtub, on his knees, vomiting up part of his lunch.

It had only been an instant—the device had kicked on in

warning mode. The bathtub had already been his intended destination and he counted it a great victory that he hadn't flinched back to the square to vomit in front of *their* eyes.

He cleaned up with the shower still running, the steam still swirling, washing the vomit down the tub drain. He hoped they hadn't heard the retching over the noise of the water. The tub clean, he stood with his head tilted up, his mouth open, letting the water run into and out of his mouth, rinsing the taste, soothing his throat.

When he bent over to turn off the water, the room swam, and he had to steady himself against the wall to keep from falling. He thought it was the heat at first, but realized quickly that he felt drained—exhausted. He did a sketchy job of drying himself and staggered, more than walked, into the bedroom. He stared at the dresser across the room but it seemed unimaginably far. He dragged the covers back on the bed and let himself fall.

He struggled to think. *Did they drug me?* It was nearly dinner time and he'd last eaten five hours before. He felt like he'd been awake for days and, despite an overt effort to keep his eyes open, he plunged into sleep.

NINETEEN

"Nerve gas?"

Padgett was sleeping, fully encased in the new sleeping bag, stretched out by the dying embers of the fire. She left another six-pack of water and a resealable bag of beef jerky near his head.

She found the night vision goggles at B&H Photo, the same place she'd bought her binoculars.

"That's over three thousand after tax."

"You're paying for sensitivity and resolution," the clerk told her. "This is third-generation technology—much more sensitive to infrared. Wildlife will show up against the cold background like a torch."

The wildlife she was concerned about walked on two legs, but what showed up looked like nothing human.

Beyond the PRIVATE BEACH sign, she saw a series of blotches in the scope, spread among the dunes. When she approached one of these from the land side, having jumped past it, she found it was a mostly buried video camera housing hidden in the dune grass, its little seven-inch antennae virtually invisible among the brown grass strands. She put one fingertip on top and found it slightly warmer than the surrounding air. *Enough to show up.* She was profoundly grateful she'd splurged for the best goggles in the store.

Hmph. No wonder Bob the security guard showed up to check me out.

She kept low and studied the surrounding dunes. She didn't see any more dots overlooking her current location but that didn't mean there weren't any more cameras. And they were probably all low-light devices, designed to pick up moving persons, day or night. She pursed her lips.

Tread softly. Take it slowly. Don't scare them off.

She jumped away, first to the Aerie to change clothes and leave the night vision goggles in their case, then back to the restaurant in the Winnetu, the Opus, where she ordered a ridiculously large dinner. She lingered over the meal, giving anybody who might be interested a chance to study her. When she was done she took the leftovers in a large takeout box back to her room.

She delivered them to Padgett followed by a fresh load of firewood. Five minutes later, when Padgett was hunkered down before the rebuilt fire and eating, the new sleeping bag wrapped around him like a shawl, she came back. "I particularly liked the bread with roasted garlic spread," she commented. She knelt down and extended her hands to the warmth, directly opposite him across the flames.

He glanced at her but didn't say anything. He went on to the Seared Langoustine and Foie Gras. At the first whiff of aroma from the Styrofoam box he froze, then looked up at her. "Nice. What restaurant?"

Oh, are we talking now? She studied him. His attitude had changed slightly. It was *more* casual and relaxed than just a moment before. *It could be the food.* No, the man had just started. Too early for a change in blood sugar. He looked like some of her clients when the topic on hand had strayed too close to something they didn't want to deal with. He was deliberately casual, *artificially* relaxed.

"*That* restaurant," she ventured. "On the south shore of *that* island. Just a mile down the beach from *that* house."

"I don't have the slightest idea what you're talking about," Padgett said, but it came too quick and he knew it.

She smiled broadly and Padgett threw up.

It was sudden and convulsive and titanic, seemingly everything in his digestive tract geysering into the fire.

Millie fell backward recoiling from the roiling cloud of steam and the smell. She scrambled back as the convulsions continued.

She stood, and came forward, hesitantly. *Epilepsy?*

Padgett was lying on his side now and his head was getting dangerously close to the fire. Rather than walk around him, she jumped to the far side and pulled his shoulders back. The spasms were continuing and, she realized, not limited to emesis. He'd voided his colon as well.

I've got to get him help. He's going to choke to death at this rate.

Unlike Davy, she didn't have a major trauma center jump site memorized. She'd never been anywhere near the one Davy used, the Adams Cowley Shock Trauma Center in Baltimore.

But I must've walked past the entrance to the ER at George Washington University Hospital a dozen times while I was putting up those stupid posters.

It took her a second to concentrate, no mean feat as Padgett thrashed at her feet, but she tried it and found herself on the sidewalk of New Hampshire Avenue, fifty yards away from the ambulance driveway where it cut through the building itself. She sprinted forward, up the drive, and went toward the door at the ambulance loading ramp. A hospital security guard stepped forward saying, "Whoa, Ma'am. You've got to go in the other—" But she dodged around him and twisted through the just-opening automatic door into the antiseptic smell of the trauma center. She heard footsteps as the guard hurried after her and a figure in blue scrubs positioned himself in her path, his hands raised.

She stopped, looking around, taking in the smell and feel of the site.

"Lady—you can't come in this door! It's for the trauma patients!"

She turned to face the security guard and gave him a level look that caused him to pause, one hand outstretched, apparently in the act of reaching for her arm.

She held up her finger and said, "Hold that thought, will you?" Then jumped.

Padgett had stopped vomiting but his breaths were coming in wheezes punctuated by short, barking coughs. She grabbed him under his armpits and jumped.

"Whoa—shit!"

In the few seconds she'd been gone, the security guard and the man in scrubs had walked forward to where she'd vanished. The security guard tripped over Padgett's legs and stumbled forward. The nurse or doctor dressed in scrubs fell backwards.

Other figures in scrubs came forward. Millie didn't know if they'd seen her disappear and reappear or any portion thereof but she didn't care. She just started talking.

"Five minutes ago he began vomiting and voided his bowels, accompanied by uncontrolled spasms. He just ate some seafood but he knew what he was eating and didn't mention any allergies. He's had a recent near-hypothermia experience but has been in a sleeping bag in front of a warm fire for the last eight hours. He was lucid and apparently fine right up to the first convulsion." She looked around at the staring faces. "Is anybody getting this?" She looked down at Padgett. "Oh, God—he's stopped breathing!"

That did it. Out came the masks and gloves. One shouted, "Possible code yellow!"

Millie stepped back and the whirlwind descended.

The security guard stayed with her, hovering, but he had put on one of the ear loop procedure masks just like the medical staff, and was pulling on latex gloves.

When she glanced at him, he flinched, so she said, "Let me guess, you'd rather I hung out in the waiting room?" She was feeling odd—disconnected.

The staff had lifted Padgett onto a gurney and one of them straddled Padgett's body on the table as he snaked an endotracheal tube down his throat, even as the others rolled the whole shebang into a room labeled "Resuscitation."

"The admissions clerk needs to get some patient info," the security guard said. It was hard to read his expression through the mask but he was still looking at her as if she had two heads and one of them would bite him. He gestured to a masked woman with a clipboard approaching from the door that led into the waiting room.

Millie made a soundless, "Ah," and turned to the clerk. "Do you want to do this in your office?"

"We've got a room over here."

She led Millie off to the side, a room with a chair—more of a booth actually—separated from an adjoining booth by a glass window. The woman took the chair on the other side of the window after shutting Millie's door. She took off her mask and smiled through the glass before she started asking her questions through a two-way speaker.

Millie was patient. "His name is Lewis Padgett. I don't know his address. I don't know his social. I don't know his insurance provider. I don't know if he has any drug allergies or allergies of any other kind—he is not and was not wearing a med-alert bracelet. No, I cannot give you permission to treat—barely know the man, but since he is unconscious, I don't think you guys have to worry about *that*."

The woman wore a pained expression on her face. "We really need more information."

"I know a number you can call—I believe that they'll be able to give you all sorts of information about him. They will probably assume responsibility for him, too."

"Financial responsibility?"

"I don't know about that but at the very least they'll have his social security number." With trembling lips she gave the woman Special Agent Becca Martingale's cell number and her name, but not her title and employer.

"And your name, ma'am?"

Millie looked up. There were at least four video cameras in the trauma reception area. *Shit, they've recorded me jumping!* For a brief moment she considered finding the machines that recorded the video feed but she knew nothing about the technology. The security office could be anywhere in the entire massive cluster of buildings or, worse, off premises. There was no point in lying. She wished she'd at least had time to put on the wig and glasses before bringing Padgett in, but she was the short-haired blond in contacts. *So much for* that *disguise.*

"Millicent Harrison-Rice. Mention my name if Ms. Martingale has any doubts about the identity of your patient."

"And your address?"

"I'm not the patient and I'm not assuming financial responsibility," she said.

"Ma'am, I need this information. Mr. Padgett may be contagious. You could be exposed, not only in danger of contracting his disease yourself, but also of spreading it. You are required by law to give us this information!"

Well, who doesn't know our Stillwater address? After all, it was where she'd found Padgett and certainly the NSA had been there. Surely the FBI could figure it out—it was a matter of public record.

She gave the clerk the Stillwater address and phone and her work phone at the clinic though she doubted she'd ever be able to work there again after this night's work.

"But you're staying here in DC, I take it, someplace? A hotel? A friend."

"Oh, no." *I commute.* "Just got here. No local address."

"I'll give Ms. Martingale a call, why don't I," said the clerk when she'd taken down the info.

Millie expected her to go back to the admissions office adjacent to the waiting room but she simply reached below Millie's line of sight, picked up a phone handset, and dialed.

I should go. But Millie stayed. She wanted to know how Padgett was. No matter that he was her enemy, that he was one of those who'd taken Davy. She felt responsible for Padgett's current condition. She also wanted to know *what* was wrong with the man. She found it odd that he'd gone into convulsions the moment he'd actually revealed something to her. And then there was the possibility Padgett was carrying some kind of contagious disease. She wanted that cleared up. *Typhoid Mary would have nothing on me as a disease vector.* Millie pictured herself jumping from city to city, coughing and sneezing and leaving loci of infection strung behind her.

Better to know.

She could afford to wait—they didn't have much chance of stopping her when she did decide to leave, but this thought, initially comforting, suddenly sent a cold chill through the very core of her being. *That's almost certainly what Davy thought right before they took* him.

The admissions clerk's side of the phone conversation came clearly through the grill. "Ms. Becca Martingale? My name is Sarah Lewinski. I'm with patient intake at George Washington University Hospital. We just admitted a Lewis Padgett and we were told you could help us complete our intake information. You do know Mr. Padgett?"

"Well, a Ms. Millicent Harrison-Rice told us you might know more about him than she did."

"Yes, Ms. Harrison-Rice is right here. She brought Mr. Padgett in."

"Sorry, they just arrived. I don't know what Mr. Padgett's condition is. Can you help me with any of Mr. Padgett's information—his social or employer or insurance provider?"

Special Agent Martingale had apparently finished asking questions and was now talking at length, for the admissions clerk had her mouth shut and her eyes open. Then she said, "Yes, ma'am. I'll tell security immediately." She hung up the phone and said in a mildly accusatory tone to Millie, "You didn't say Ms. Martingale was an FBI agent."

Without waiting for a response she stepped out of the booth and called the security guard over. Millie couldn't hear what she said to him but when she was done talking, the guard unhooked his belt radio and began speaking into it as he headed back for the treatment room where they'd taken Padgett.

Millie started to step back out of her side of the interview booth to get an update on Pagett when a siren, previously distantly audible, suddenly swelled to a nearly earsplitting level as the vehicle entered the ambulance driveway. Fortunately the driver turned off the siren almost immediately but Millie could see blue lights bouncing off the walls. Her first thought was that an ambulance was delivering a trauma patient but that scenario was dispelled when four soldiers in hooded gas masks and full chemical warfare protective gear came through the door.

A doctor came running from the treatment rooms to meet them. Talking rapidly, he gestured first back toward the treatment rooms and then pointed directly at Millie.

What the hell?

Two of the soldiers followed the doctor back to treatment and the other two turned to Millie. She stepped back involuntarily as they approached.

The one in the lead waved an instrument the size of a large hardback with an off-center projecting nozzle and an LCD readout. He stepped into the other side of the isolation booth, the room the admissions clerk had used, and waved it around, watching the screen. After studying it for a moment he lifted the gas mask and shoulder draping hood up, revealing mild looking eyes and bifocal glasses. He used the speaker. "Good evening, ma'am. How are you?"

"Well, until you guys showed up in your gas masks, I was fine. Then I almost had a heart attack. Who are you and why are you here?"

"Ah. Well, my name is Sergeant Ferguson of the C/BRRT—the Chemical/Biological Rapid Response Team. We're here because the trauma center reported a possible occurrence of nerve agent."

"Nerve gas? Like sarin?"

"Or tabun or soman or VX. Or the most common is organophosphate pesticide, so it doesn't have to be something sinister. I'm going to put my mask back on and use this," he held up the instrument, "to check you and your clothing for any traces of nerve agent."

"Have you detected any out there yet?" She gestured at the room beyond the glass.

He smiled. "Not a trace, thank God."

She gestured. "By all means, check away."

He redonned his mask, did a quick check on the seal, and came over to her side of the booth, pushing the instrument through the door first. When it was apparently negative, he came on in. She stood as directed and he checked her from head to foot. He had her hold up her shoes one by one so he could check the soles and then exhale as he held the instrument before her mouth. This close, she could hear a small fan sucking air in through the nozzle.

From a pocket he pulled a charcoal gray foam packet with pressed seams and a Velcro closure, and set it on the counter. His voice, muffled by the mask, said, "You seem all clear, ma'am, but I'm sure they'll want you to stay in here until they've totally ruled it out or any biological agent."

He exited, consulted briefly with his associate, and went back into the other side of the booth. His mask back off, he smiled and said, "On the very long chance you've been exposed, I've left an antidote kit on the counter there. If you start salivating and your nose starts running, if you feel a pressure in your chest, if you have trouble focusing on close objects, or if you feel nauseated, sing out. If we're not immediately available, there are two autoinjectors in there—one has 2 mg of atropine, and the other has six hundred milligrams of 2-PAM, pralidoxime chloride. Remove the protective cap and press them into your thigh about four inches above your knee. Don't worry about your clothes—the autoinjector will push the needle right through, all right? Atropine first, 2-PAM second."

"You're scaring me, here."

"To be perfectly honest, I don't think you have a thing to worry about."

"Then why are *you* here?"

He grinned. "To make *sure* you don't have anything to worry about." He gestured back toward the trauma center. "I see why they called it in—your friend had several of the symptoms of acute nerve agent exposure. He was crashing—respiratory and cardiac failure—but he responded pretty well to atropine, but since atropine is good for a host of different problems it's not a definite indicator for nerve gas. It's just that we're less than half-a-mile from the White House here. That's why my little unit is on detached duty here in D.C. instead of back with the rest of the team up in Maryland. Better we should overreact a little—we've all seen the consequences of under-reacting.

"I'm going to check with my boss, Captain Trihn—he's in with the trauma team—and we'll know more. Specialist Marco there," he pointed to the other soldier outside, "will stay here.

Let him know if you start experiencing any of the reactions I listed."

She nodded and he put his mask back on, then walked back up the hall toward the trauma theaters. The fact that he walked calmly, rather than trotted, reassured her more than anything he'd said.

A few minutes later Special Agent Becca Martingale entered the emergency room with a team of six agents—all neatly labeled F-B-I, in white letters across dark navy windbreakers. The medical staff apparently expected them, though her chemical warfare attendant, Specialist Marco, did a serious double take when he saw the shotguns three of them were carrying.

This is getting crazy. I should jump out of here. But she hesitated—there were things she wanted to know, both from the medical staff and from the FBI.

Becca gave Millie a nod as she passed, but clearly her first priority was securing Padgett. Millie almost wished she could be there when the different agendas of the medical staff, the FBI, and the C/BRRT all collided.

She stared at the packet Sergeant Ferguson had left with her. MARK I NERVE AGENT ANTIDOTE KIT. She shuddered. It didn't seem possible—not only had she been exposed to everything that Padgett had—they'd even eaten the same food—he'd been totally isolated. *He did have his clothes. The old suicide capsule in a hollow button?* She'd been watching him the whole time. The only thing he'd put in his mouth was the food she'd brought him—food she'd also eaten.

The walls of the isolation booth were closing in on her and she felt her heart beating faster. *Oh, my god, I've got it, or it's got me.* Her hand closed convulsively on the kit—then she forced herself to release it. Her hand was shaking.

Idiot.

She of all people should recognize the psychosomatic expression of physical symptoms. She wasn't salivating. Her mouth, if anything, was dry as a bone. *Though if I obsess about it long enough, I'm sure I could express most of the symptoms the sergeant listed for me.*

Her tension was relieved when the sergeant, himself, came

back from the trauma theater. He'd stowed his gas mask in its belt case and his chemical oversuit was zipped open to the waist.

He opened her side of the isolation booth and picked up the antidote kit. "All clear, at least as far as we're concerned."

"Not nerve gas?"

"No traces on our equipment. They found an implant—some kind of vagus nerve stimulator—it's going haywire, apparently. There was a scar and they palpated a hard lump," he tapped his upper chest, just below his collarbone, "so they took a chest x-ray. The device and a wire going up his neck showed up on the film. They're pretty sure that's the problem."

Millie blinked. She'd seen the scar on Padgett, but considering the man's history, she'd thought it a war wound, from his days with Executive Outcomes. "Why would he have something like that?"

"The trauma surgeon said it's a treatment for some kinds of epilepsy and there's also some experiments with it in treating depression. But he says there's nothing in the literature about one doing this. If it's the FDA-approved implant, from Cyberonics, it should've failed completely rather than give the over-voltages that caused these symptoms."

"What do you think?"

He shrugged. "Don't know. My boss likes it. Captain Trinh is an MD—a toxicologist. He says vagal stimulation would account for the symptoms the patient did express *and* the symptoms he didn't." He tucked the antidote kit back in one of his pouches. "So, we're standing down—the Secret Service was very relieved." He rolled his neck around. "We were ninety percent sure when we got here, actually, but we went through the whole nine yards, though, because of the hallucinations."

"Hallucinations? Padgett was seeing things?"

"No. The patient has never been conscious. Some of the staff seemed to be seeing things, though, so we thought there was some kind of nerve agent involved and enough *on* him to contaminate the first responders. They said you disappeared, then reappeared with the patient." He smiled. "Might be working too hard. Either that or admin needs to inventory the drug cabinets."

Millie smiled weakly. "So I can leave this booth?"

"As far as *I'm* concerned. The captain and the attending seem pretty sure it's not biological, either. But the FBI might want to talk with you. Wonder why they're here?"

"Didn't they tell you?"

"Maybe they told the captain. I'm just a working man."

"Padgett—the patient—was involved in the attempted kidnapping of two women here in D.C., last week. The FBI were watching and when they moved in, he shot an agent to escape."

"Get outta here!"

"No, really."

"I didn't read anything about that. How did you hear about it?"

"I was one of those women," she said. "What are they going to do for Padgett?"

"Pull the implant, I believe. They were prepping him and waiting for a neurosurgeon to come over from the next building."

"And if he's epileptic?"

"Doesn't matter. The thing will kill him if it keeps firing like it is. Better seizures than dead. He survives, he can get a new implant that works right."

Maybe it is *working right.* Millie shuddered. "Well, thanks for proving it *wasn't* nerve gas."

Sergeant Ferguson nodded and, as he turned away, he said, "I wouldn't have it any other way. I get nightmares as it is."

Special Agent Becca Martingale joined Millie shortly after the Rapid Response Team pulled out.

She looked Millie up and down and frowned. "So, changing the image?"

"The hair, you mean?"

Becca nodded. "Yeah, and you got rid of the glasses—contacts?"

Millie nodded. "They're still after me. That's how I got Padgett. They set a trap for me and it didn't quite work."

Now that the FBI had arrived, the security guard was back by the door and watching her warily. Millie wondered if he'd told Becca about Millie's odd arrival. Becca saw Millie glance at the guard and said, "You want coffee? I want coffee."

Millie waited until they were walking down the hall outside ER before asking her first question. "What about Sojee Johnson?"

Becca sighed. "Sojee? Ah, I get it. Still no sign of Ms. Sojourner Truth Johnson. It would be very nice if we got something out of Padgett."

"He wouldn't talk for me. Will you be able to talk to him? Last time I saw him, he wasn't even breathing on his own."

"He was conscious a minute ago—confused. They think he'll be okay. You know about the implant?"

She nodded. "The Chem Warfare guy told me."

"Well, they were getting ready to cut when they kicked me out. They decided not to wait for the neurosurgeon. Instead, the attending is gonna make a small incision and simply cut the leads between the implant capsule and where the electrodes wrap around the vagus nerve. Where did Padgett set this trap you speak of?"

Millie swallowed. "Remember that we didn't tell you what Davy—my husband—did for the NSA?"

"Indeed. Anders said it was burn-before-reading secret, though from some of the context, I got that he was some sort of covert ops insertion specialist."

Millie shrugged. "That'll do to tell."

"What's that have to do with my question?"

Millie inhaled and held her breath while she studied Becca's face, motionless. She felt like a deer, frozen in a car's headlights. Finally, in one explosive exhalation, she said, "Do you remember the last time you saw me?"

Becca tilted her head. "Sure, it was on Fourteenth Street after they tried to snatch you. I ran up the alley when Padgett shot Bobby—uh, agent Marino."

Millie shook her head. "No. You last saw me on the roof of that Medical Building over in Alexandria. The one near Bochstettler and Associates." She felt in her jacket pocket and found the sunglasses she'd been wearing that day. "I don't have the baseball cap with me," she said, putting the shades on, "or the green plastic chair, but surely you remember."

Becca's eyes widened. "That was some trick. I nearly had a

heart attack when you went over the edge. Want to tell me how you did that?"

I would love to. Millie felt like crying, suddenly. "Can't."

Becca stopped dead and looked at Millie with a sour expression on her face. "Did you ever hear the story about the blind men and the elephant?"

Millie nodded, not trusting herself to speak.

"How do you people expect me to do my fucking job! You won't tell me anything and then you stop trying and then I get pressure to shelve the entire investigation. Don't you want to find your husband and Ms. Johnson?"

"Are you talking about the NSA when you say 'you people?' " Millie felt her face go tight.

"Yeah."

"Well, I don't work for them, all right? Please don't lump me in with them. I know they've dropped the investigation—or at least they took Anders off of it. I won't go anywhere near them. I went to ground because whoever is behind this has somebody inside the NSA—they nearly got me again that same night, after I holed up in a motel out in Alexandria. The NSA delivered me to that hotel—they were the only possible leak."

Becca's normally calm demeanor was back in place and she began walking again. "You could've been followed."

"Cows could fly."

"So, who *are* you working for."

"Me, myself, and I. I'm looking for my husband, dammit!"

Becca looked skeptical. "Someone trained you, dear. That rooftop stunt was not the work of an amateur. We searched those stupid shrubs for an hour looking for your body."

Millie blinked, then her jaw dropped. "You think I'm an *operative*!"

"How else do you explain it?"

"Nerve gas?"

Becca was *not* amused.

"I've a master's degree in Psychological Counseling and I'm a Licensed Marriage and Family Therapist in the state of Oklahoma, which requires lots of ongoing professional development coursework. I also did a two-year stint of supervised counseling before becoming licensed. I took a Community Ed class in African dance last summer and I've read extensively in the novels of John Le Carré. *That* is the extent of my training."

They turned the corner to the cafeteria. A metal grill blocked the entrance. According to the posted hours, it had just closed.

"Shit!" Becca said. "Explain the rooftop thing, then."

Millie licked her lips and told the truth. "I jumped." She saw the sour expression return to Becca's face and said, "Wait." She looked up and down the corridor. It was empty. "Okay. I'm going to show you how I did the rooftop thing." She jumped to the other side of the hallway, about eight feet behind Becca. She watched the agent frantically swivel her head left and right, then up and down. Millie cleared her throat and Becca spun around, one hand diving into her windbreaker, then freezing again as she saw Millie.

Becca's mouth worked for a moment before she managed to say, "Hypnosis?"

Now that's *an idea.* She sighed. "No. Not hypnosis." *I am so tired of lying.* "You still want coffee?"

It was after sunset, but only just, in San Francisco. Millie jumped Becca to the Yerba Buena Garden outside of the Metreon, then caught her as the woman's knees gave way, guiding her to the grass. By the time Millie returned from the Starbucks on the first floor of the Metreon, Becca had mostly recovered, though she wasn't standing yet.

She accepted the coffee without comment.

"Do you recognize where you are?"

Becca pointed at the massive fifty-foot-high waterfall fountain of the Martin Luther King memorial at one end of the grassy plot, then north at Saint Patrick's Church. "I've been here before. Even this Starbucks." She stood, moving gingerly. "How do you do this?"

Millie shrugged. "I don't really know. It suffices that I can."

Becca's eyes narrowed suddenly. "Is this what Davy does for the NSA?"

"Right."

"But not you?"

Millie shook her head. "No."

Becca slapped her hand to her forehead. "Oh, my God. The foiled hijackings—ten years ago! Those airliners and the cruise ship. That was Davy? Or was it you?"

Millie's first instinct was to deny everything but she sighed instead. "Davy. Not me. This . . . is new to me."

"What *else* can you do?"

"I've given you my other qualifications. Are you in a relationship with problems? Do you have any childhood issues you want to work on? Then I'm your guy."

"Nothing else in a paranormal ability?"

"I can hang a spoon off the end of my nose."

Becca stood and took a pull on her coffee. Her brow was furrowed and she kept her eyes on Millie but didn't say anything for several seconds.

Millie said, "I wanted you to know so that when I started answering your questions, you wouldn't think the answers as crazy as they sounded."

Becca nodded. "So go ahead."

"I caught Padgett at my condo in Stillwater, Oklahoma. I think they suspect I can do this—teleport—because he filled my rooms with some sort of anesthetic vapor. I barely got out but I returned in time to see him check the trap." She neglected to mention how long ago that was. "I was asking him about Davy and he went into convulsions. It was weird—he'd just let something slip and BAM, like a spy taking cyanide or something, only, I swear, the only thing he'd put in his mouth was food I brought him."

"Brought him? Was he your prisoner?"

"He was my *guest*, briefly. Wait a second." She jumped to the Aerie.

As she wandered back to the low table where she'd examined Padgett's belongings, she unexpectedly slipped and dropped to one knee, to keep from falling. There was a puddle on the floor, its edges clearly drying, but a good half inch of water caught in one of the natural depressions in the floor. Her knee was soaked where she'd touched down.

She looked around, surprised. The cistern was thirty feet

away and it was certainly too much water to have come from a spilled glass. She looked up, at the ceiling, looking for some sign that the water had oozed in from the ridge above, from a rare desert thunderstorm, perhaps, or a subterranean aquifer, but the stone above was dry and unbroken.

The front door was latched and everything seemed to be as she'd left it, including the collection of Padgett's belongings. She gathered them up and returned to San Francisco.

Becca jerked as she reappeared.

Millie handed her the plastic bag. "You okay? You look a little pale."

"I was just trying to think how the hell I was going to explain this to my boss without getting sent in for psych review. Then I started worrying about what would happen if you left me here three thousand miles from D.C. What's this?"

"It's the stuff Padgett had on him. Wallet, some fake ID, his guns. I handled them." She'd left Padgett's cell phone back in the Aerie. She was going to hold those phone numbers to herself for now.

"What did Padgett let slip? You know, right before he started barfing?"

"A clue. Something that confirmed another lead—like saying 'hot' or 'cold.' Sort of 'getting warm.' I'm not going to tell you, though. I want Davy out of there, first. Besides—now that you have the guy who shot your agent, are you going to go any further? Don't tell me you haven't gotten any pressure. The NSA's doing their best to pretend Davy never existed. Are they telling *you* anything?"

"I had a brutally brief talk with Anders when they reassigned him. The only thing I've gotten out of his replacement is questions."

"Questions?"

"Well, one question, asked several times."

Millie waited. *You know you want to tell me.*

"They wanted to know if I'd seen *you*."

It was warmer in San Francisco than it had been in D.C., but Millie shivered.

Becca's cell phone went off, surprising both of them.

"National call plan?"

Becca nodded. She punched the button and said, "Martingale." She listened for a moment and her eyes widened. "Jesus! One second." She covered the mouthpiece. "Can you get me back to the ER?"

"Sure."

Martingale talked back into phone. "I'll be right there." She disconnected and looked at Millie. "Padgett's dead."

"Dead? They said he was stable! Didn't cutting the leads on his implant stop the convulsions?"

"They'll never know. When they cut the leads, the implant exploded."

She jumped Becca to the sidewalk outside the ER.

"I've been around here too long," Millie said. "The NSA will be here soon. Maybe Padgett's people. Hell, I'm not convinced that Padgett's people *aren't* the NSA."

Becca paused, looking back, obviously torn. "You've got my number, right? You're the one who gave it to the hospital?"

"Yeah. I got it from Anders, though it would probably get him in trouble if they knew I was still talking to him."

"You are?"

"Sort of. E-mail. On the sly."

"I understand. His last talk with me was like that: a little more frank than his employers would probably like. Call me in an hour?"

Millie nodded and jumped. She went back to the hotel room in the Winnetu and lay in her bed, kicking around until the sheets were well disturbed. For good measure she took a shower and changed clothes. She thought it was a long shot, but after her encounter with the security guard on the beach, they might check her out. They might slip a five to the chambermaid to ask if there was anything odd about her.

So, mess the bed and the bathroom, give them evidence of occupation. *And if they call the room when you're not there, say, in the middle of the night?* Let them think she was shacking up with one of the radiologists. Hell, let them think she was working her way through the entire roster of symposium doctors. Well, they'd have dirty minds, then.

She felt a stirring of desire. *It's been too long. Who really has the dirty mind?* She unplugged the phone and conspicuously coiled it on top of the bedside table. *Let them think I don't like having my sleep disturbed.*

The puddle of water in the Aerie was smaller when she checked on it. Again, except for the water, everything seemed untouched. She checked the door and scanned the canyon floor below. Nothing.

Could it have been Davy?

If he could jump as far as the Aerie, why wouldn't he have stayed?

She used a pay phone at D.C.'s Union Station. Becca, barely audible among a background torrent of other voices, asked Millie to hold a moment. When she spoke again, the background sounded different, much quieter.

"Sorry. Couldn't hear anything in there. Got the D.C. Metro bomb squad in and—you predicted it—two guys from the NSA. I've told them I don't know where you got to. It's the truth, after all."

"Thanks. How big an explosion was it?"

"Well, it only killed *him*, though the attending doctor's arm looks like it was hit by a ball-peen hammer. They found the remains of two U.S. Military M6 blasting caps among the fragments of the rest of the implant."

"You autopsied already?"

"No—the trauma team tried to save him, they were pulling the debris out of his chest as they tried to clamp all the leaks. They were gonna try and put him on a heart-lung machine. It was too much, though, even with them right there. He hemorrhaged like a sieve." She sighed. "Guy from the bomb squad recognized the blasting cap fragments—you can still see the leads. Some implant, huh?"

"Why?"

"Well, he'll never testify about his organization now. Myself, I'd prefer a simple nondisclosure agreement."

Millie felt like throwing up. "Puts a different meaning on 'cross my heart and hope to die.' I killed him, didn't I?"

"Whoa, girlfriend. You put that thing in him?"

"If I'd just left him alone—"

"Like he left *you* alone?"

Millie didn't say anything for a moment. "I wonder if all of his people have them. I don't suppose any of those other guys you arrested on Fourteenth Street have scars under their collarbones?"

Becca was silent for a moment. "Now *that's* a scary thought. I doubt it, though. When we processed them in they went through the usual metal detectors and wand scans. Still, I'll call over and see what got put in 'scars and marks' on their booking sheets."

Millie said, "They might not know enough to warrant the implant. Maybe only the upper echelon get it."

"People who know something worth telling?"

"Those who know who their boss is."

A name she thought she could supply.

TWENTY

"Oh, yes. She's naked."

It was six-thirty when Davy awoke. He put on his robe and stuck his head out into the hall. The window at the east end of the hall showed dim light without. *Morning, then. Not evening.* He'd slept thirteen hours straight through. His stomach rumbled and he remembered he'd missed supper.

When he walked into the breakfast room Hyacinth was wearing much the same outfit she'd worn in Nigeria—bush pants, sports shirt, and a photojournalist's vest.

She looked at Davy and raised her eyebrows. "Don't we look nice. What do you think this is, a dance?"

He was wearing khaki's, a starched white shirt, a blue blazer, and a pair of sunglasses perched in his hair. He ignored her and went to the sideboard. The smell of bacon was tantalizing—far more interesting than Hyacinth's comments.

"How are you going to keep your girlish figure?" Hyacinth asked as he piled the plate high.

"Skipped supper."

There was a single poached egg and a piece of dry toast on Hyacinth's plate. "So I heard. What was that about?"

"Tired. Nigeria." He shrugged. Let them draw their own conclusions.

"So, explain the outfit. Don't you think you'll stick out dressed like that?"

Davy paused with his fork halfway to his mouth. "You've never been to Caracas, I take it."

Hyacinth narrowed her eyes. "Why do you say that?"

"Strikes and killings notwithstanding, it's a modern city—subways, skyscrapers, the whole twentieth-century thing. And they dress up. Women tend to wear dresses. I understand—you have your own unique style. You like standing out in a crowd, having people look twice at you, having them remember your *face*." He resumed eating.

Before they left, Hyacinth went back upstairs and changed into a green dress and a matching, slightly oversized jacket. When he picked her up for the jump, he felt the gun in the shoulder holster.

Caracas was gorgeous. The weather was dry and warm and a brisk breeze whipping around the Avilas had swept the smog away. After chilly New England and sweltering Nigeria, it was like heaven. *Even when you're accompanied by the devil.* Davy remembered Sojee's words. *Correction: a minion of demons.*

They arrived standing on a nest of cardboard and torn blanket. Davy's jump site was a nook between the subway entrance and some bushes at the edge of the plaza. Apparently someone was sleeping there but, luckily, not at this moment.

The sidewalks were full and street traffic jerked along to the staccato beat of horns. A man on his way out of the subway watched Davy and Hyacinth come out of the nook and raised his eyebrows at Davy, then grinned. Davy shrugged and smiled back. *Well, we know what* he's *thinking.*

Hyacinth was blinking in the sunlight and looking across the road at the huge circular fountain in the middle of the plaza and the gold-tinted skyscrapers behind. She shifted her gaze up to the giant Pepsi globe atop a nearby twenty-two-story building.

Davy took her arm and pointed. "There. That's the bus stop where they'll pick us up."

"Yes. I *know*."

The stoplight changed and a stream of morning commuters flowed across the street, passing them left and right on their way into the subway. Davy felt Hyacinth tense.

He threaded his way through the crowd and stood behind a

group queuing up at the bus stop. Hyacinth took a moment to join him. She was visibly nervous. "I didn't know the environment would be so crowded."

"It's the end of rush hour. Five million people. Busy, busy, busy."

Hyacinth took the radio from her purse and inserted an earphone. She talked, then listened, briefly. "They're circling the park. They were here but the police chased them out of the bus stop."

Two traffic police in white pith helmets were trying to untangle a snarl of honking taxis at the entrance to *Paseo Colón*. At the far corner stood two soldiers in camo battle dress with slung rifles.

He let his eyes wander past the skyscrapers. The air was clear and he could plainly see the brown and red brick barrios on the lower slopes of the Avilas. Deathtraps, just waiting for another flood of '99. Deathtraps in other ways, too. Criminal attacks, disease, malnutrition, police, army, both pro- and anti-Chavez elements.

The high crime rate wasn't the only reason Davy avoided Caracas and, as usual, he felt guilty for it.

It took ten minutes for the car to make the circle. Davy hoped like hell that they hadn't screwed up the placement of the cars carrying the keys. At Hyacinth's direction he climbed into the back seat of the shiny green Land Rover with dark-tinted windows.

The driver was a local hired for his knowledge of city traffic—not, they found, for his English.

Hyacinth became dangerously still when the driver shrugged helplessly at her directions. Before she reacted badly Davy said, "A la Embajada de Estados Unidos, por favor."

"*¡Claro que si!*"

With no traffic, the trip to the U.S. Embassy would've taken less than fifteen minutes. It took forty-five. Davy wondered what it would've been like two hours earlier, at the height of rush hour.

Normally, he would've enjoyed the drive, but they were behind a diesel bus belching large clouds of noxious fumes and, combined with the jerking stop and slow traffic, it was making him carsick. *I hope it's car sickness.* He wasn't feeling the buzzing feeling in his throat that normally accompanied the device-induced nausea, but he was far more susceptible to motion sickness than he'd been before they'd done this thing to him.

He felt the anger rising again, the rage. It was hard not to lash out. He knew he could kill Hyacinth at any time, jumping behind her and striking her down with a blunt object or, if he chose, jumping her fifteen hundred feet in the air above Ground Zero, the place that used to be just outside the observation deck of the World Trade Center. He could leave her hanging in the air and jump away again, without having to see her impact. *A nicely sterile approach, like launching missiles against distant targets.*

Very brave.

The thought made him shudder as the anger mixed with shame. He leaned back and closed his eyes for the rest of the journey.

The embassy was relatively new, built back off the streets, designed to keep car and truck bombs at a safe distance. Hyacinth took off her jacket as they approached and Davy realized she was shrugging out of her shoulder holster at the same time. Below the level of the window, she removed the gun and harness from the folds of the jacket, wrapped the straps around the holstered gun, and slid it under the seat before her. After she'd redonned her jacket, she reached into her purse and took out a passport. "Here."

It was his and it wasn't. Even the number was correct, but it was shiny new. His passport, back in the Aerie and replaced two years before, was already worn and soft. While he rarely went through customs anymore, he always carried it when he was out of the U.S. *Unless I'm traveling on an NSA passport.*

"You put in for a replacement?"

"No. They change the number if your passport gets lost. We had his one . . . made up."

"It looks good." He was flexing the hologram and looking at the security threads and watermark. "I'm surprised you gave me one with my own name."

"They don't just *look* at a passport anymore. Not at a U.S. embassy. They scan the barcode and pull the record. The number has to be right and the face has to be right. Earlier this year there were bombings at both the Colombian and Spanish embassies. We have to go through this at least once, to get inside."

He jerked his chin toward the gun under the seat. "And I guess they must have metal detectors." At Hyacinth's raised eyebrows he said, "I avoid embassies in general. Too many video cameras."

The Land Rover pulled up to the curb and Hyacinth said, "Come on."

There was a crowd of Venezuelans at the gate, but they were being turned away, for the most part. Davy heard one of the marine sentries repeating the same lines over and over again in Spanish: "U.S. Visa services for Venezuelan citizens by appointment only. Pay your application fee at the *Banco Provincial*, then call the automated system at the embassy to obtain an appointment."

Their U.S. passports got them through the gate to a smaller line at the building entrance. When it was their turn, Hyacinth produced two cards, saying, "We've got pacemakers."

The marine raised his eyebrows. "Both of you?"

"It's how we met," she said, smiling. "In post-op."

Instead of making them walk through the main metal detector, they used a hand wand and Davy had to remove his belt and suffer his shoes to be x-rayed. Hyacinth's purse was completely emptied. When asked, Hyacinth said, "We're here to register for the Warden program."

"Ah, so you'll be in the country for a while?"

"Six weeks, hopefully."

"Citizen Services, second floor."

There, Hyacinth filled out the contact information and a photocopy was made of the main pages of each of their passports— "to expedite replacement if you're robbed or if you lose it."

Looking over Hyacinth's shoulder as she filled in the form, he learned that their purpose in visiting Venezuela was "educational." *For whom?* And that Hyacinth was not going under her own name.

Their ostensible business complete, Hyacinth said, "Is there a restroom on this floor?"

"Out the door and to your left. On the other side of the cafeteria."

"Thanks!"

There were video cameras in the hall, in Citizen Services, in the stairwell, and in the cafeteria but not, apparently, in the bathroom. Pursuant to instructions, Davy acquired an unmonitored jump site within, choosing the large handicapped access toilet stall.

The Land Rover pulled up as they exited the gate. Hyacinth said, "Go to the other side but don't get in." She climbed in and shut the door; by the time Davy opened the far door, she'd retrieved her gun and holster from under the driver's seat and slid across. She stepped out onto the pavement and shut the door behind her. The dark-tinted windows and the bulk of the Land Rover shielded them from the embassy.

"Back to the Vineyard," Hyacinth said.

Davy lifted her and jumped.

Conley joined them for lunch. "All done?" he asked Hyacinth.

Hyacinth inclined her head. "For now."

Conley's mouth twitched up. "All right." He looked at Davy. "This afternoon, then."

Conley put a milliwatt radio transmitter in Davy's room. He measured its output with a little handheld RF meter. "Right. I've got a signal anywhere in this room. Let's walk down to the beach."

The signal dropped to undetectable levels by the time they reached the courtyard. They went all the way down the boardwalk to the beach. It was cloudy again and the chill wind from the east made Davy sink his head down into the collar of his jacket. He thought wistfully about the weather in Caracas.

On the beach, Conley examined the meter again. "Zilch.

Okay, to start, I want you to jump back to the room, count to five, and jump back. Ready?"

"All right." He did it, using the five seconds to take a hat from the wardrobe. Back on the beach Conley was still looking at the meter. "Right. Pretty much what I expected. There was a transitory spike when you left and one when you came back. So, you want to try what we talked about—the jumping without jumping?"

Davy did *not* want to. Not in front of Conley or any of *them*. "Sure," he said. He jumped back to the room, waited a silent "one-one thousand" and jumped back. "Hmm. Jumping without jumping. Let me try again."

He just stood there and let his stare go vacant. After about ten seconds he jumped back to the room again, counted slowly to two, and jumped back. He shook his head in feigned frustration. "Sorry. Not working. Any suggestions?"

Conley pursed his lips. "How about you just try doing it as fast as you can? I mean, back and forth without any sort of pause?"

He put a doubtful expression on his face. "I can try, I suppose."

He jumped and after a beat he jumped back to the beach. He kept doing it without increasing the frequency—a jump and a jump and a jump and a jump. After doing this for twenty or so seconds, he began introducing more delay, waiting a fraction of a second more each time. He kept this up for another half minute and then stopped, on the beach, and staggered for effect.

"Dizzy. Got to sit down." He dropped to the sand, cross-legged and put his hands to his head. "It's not working."

Conley looked worried. "Okay—sit for a few minutes, we'll try again after you rest."

This was how they spent the next hour. Finally the combination of no results and increasing cold caused Conley to call a halt.

Davy jumped them both back to the room, then staggered across to the bed. "It's too big a drain."

Conley eyed him speculatively and Davy wondered if he

saw right through his pseudo-cooperation. Conley faced the mirror and said, "Turn the beach off, please." He turned back to Davy and said, "I'll have to rethink this. You looked wiped—perhaps you should take a nap."

"Good idea. I will."

And he pretended to, but his mind raced. On top of his list of concerns was, *why do they want a jump site inside the U.S. Embassy in Caracas?* If they just wanted to transport people back and forth to Caracas, his original site would do just fine.

It's about power. Somehow, it all comes down to that. They'd had him rescue Roule in Nigeria. Now they wanted him to do something in an American embassy. Was there a connection?

He had to do something about Sojee. They could already apply a surfeit of pressure with the implant but, bad as that was, it was on him alone. It particularly worried him that Simons hadn't hesitated to reveal his face to Sojee.

They don't mean to release her.

And finally, there was Millie. Millie who had at least gotten out of the cliff house.

He thought about their claims that she was jumping and dismissed them. *They're confused about her, that's all, or they're not confused and just messing with me.* But how could he get a message to her? She needed to stay hidden, to keep out of their reach. Davy needed her to be safe. *It would be the last straw if they had her.* The breaking point, so to speak.

And there were several things that could break.

Hyacinth came to dinner with her hair down, wearing a backless silk sheath dress so sheer that Davy would have been able to see the most minute seam and texture of her undergarments . . . had she been wearing any. As it was, he was able to see the outlines of . . . other features.

He tried to keep his eyes averted, but he found his gaze straying to her chest every time his attention wandered. It didn't help that his hands had been there once.

She held her shoulders back, tightening the fabric across her chest.

Sitting erect. Davy squirmed in his seat. *How ironic.*

"Aren't you cold in that outfit?"

She looked at him and the corners of her mouth twitched up. "Parts of me."

He avoided further clarification.

She followed him when dinner was over and gestured toward one of the smaller formal rooms near the foot of the stairs. "Why not come into the drawing room and sit a while."

"Why?" Davy said baldly.

She blinked. "I just thought you might like to talk. You know—" she gestured vaguely at her upper body "—one cyborg to another." The dress covered her collarbone scar but the faint line on her lower neck was visible.

He followed her in, watching the muscles in her back and the outline of her buttocks shifting under the silk.

Run far, far away.

There was a small log fire on the hearth of the marble-faced fireplace. Hyacinth stood on the bricks with her back to the flames.

"Parts," said Davy.

She raised the rear hem of her dress and let the heat warm the backs of her legs. "Ah. That feels good."

There were footsteps in the hall and Abney came in to offer them drinks. Davy asked for tonic water. Hyacinth requested a double martini and turned around to face the flames. The firelight shone through the silk and outlined everything.

Davy swallowed and looked away. He perched tentatively on the arm of the sofa. After a moment Hyacinth went to the opposite end of the sofa, kicked off her shoes and sat, her legs curled underneath her. It was a long couch and Davy felt safe settling onto the cushions at his end, a clear gap of four feet between them. He kept his eyes on the flames.

"Where are you, David?"

"Now that's a good question," he said. "We're on the south shore of Martha's Vineyard. Before you narrowed it down, I thought maybe the Cape or Nantucket. Now I'm just trying to decide whether we're closer to Menemsha or Edgartown."

She blinked and for an instant sat naturally. "Is that part of your talent? Do you always know where you are?"

Davy shook his head. "You told me not to talk to the men who welded the plate in my room. You should've told them not to talk to me."

"They didn't talk to you."

"No, just to each other. It's a regional accent—very distinctive."

"And knowing it's the south shore?"

"Even Simons can't order the heavens. The sun still rises in the east—it sets in the west."

Hyacinth smiled slightly and looked back at the fire.

Abney came back in with the drinks. After he'd set them on the respective end tables, complete with lace coasters, he said, "Anything else, Miss Pope?"

Hyacinth said, "Close the door, please, on the way out."

"Yes, ma'am."

The double doors were heavy oak and when they closed they blocked the hall lights, leaving only the light from the fire. Hyacinth took a large gulp of her martini. Davy squeezed his lime into the tonic water and swirled the ice around to mix it.

"So, as one cyborg to another," Davy started, "What behavioral change did they want to bring about with your implant? They didn't need to keep you confined to one location, like me. So what is it that they keep you from doing?"

Hyacinth's slight smile vanished and her face twisted for a moment into an expression so different from her customary mask that Davy had trouble identifying the emotion. Then the mask dropped back into place and Davy doubted his own memory of the expression. *Maybe it was the firelight. Shadows, not flesh.*

Hyacinth finally said, "Loose tongues."

"How the hell do you measure that? Is someone always listening to what you say, with a finger on the button?"

She shrugged. "Someone." She tapped her left temple. "It's a matter of conditioning. I don't know exactly how it's set off—there seems to be some sort of stress monitor but ordinary stress doesn't do it. After we recovered from the surgery the program took six weeks and half that time we were under drug-induced hypnosis. Seems like the rest of the time we were undergoing mock interrogations while vomiting or shitting ourselves. Make that vomiting *and* shitting ourselves."

Davy's imagination triggered a wave of nausea and he realized what the unknown expression on Hyacinth's face had been. "Yuck city."

Hyacinth looked away again. "Well, we signed up for it." She drained the rest of her martini and stood again before the fire, her hands outstretched to the flames.

Why is she being so forthcoming? Besides the obvious. She was dressed for seduction but was it her own idea or was she under orders? How many handles did they need on him? He took another gulp of tonic and his legs and arms started to tingle. Against all expectations he felt the corners of his mouth tug up. He stared down at the tonic water.

"What did you use?" He asked.

Hyacinth was watching his face carefully. "Half a tab of ecstasy. Half a tab of Viagra. You've been depressed. It shows, you know."

"You think?"

He jumped to the beach. As he thought, the beach keys weren't enabled and he felt the warning spasm in his throat but he steeled himself to stay still in the chill and windy dark until the implant kicked in full force. His supper sprayed across the sand and then, as he flinched back to his room without volition, also across the rug. He was profoundly grateful that he'd remained continent but the smell was causing reflexive gagging. He stumbled into the bathroom, dropped to his knees, and vomited once more into the toilet.

His limbs were still tingling and his mood felt grossly at odds with the situation. He flushed the toilet and rinsed his mouth out before drinking a tumbler of tap water.

Back in the room he sopped up the worst of the vomit on the rug with a towel, then rolled the rug and dragged it out into the hall.

Let them deal with it. As he turned to reenter the room he saw Hyacinth turn into the hall from the head of the stairs.

He paused and leaned against the doorframe. As she walked up the hall the walls seemed to vibrate around her, an undulation as if her personal gravity was so great that it warped space around her. *It's the drug. Don't invest her with any more power.*

Hyacinth looked at the rug, then her nose wrinkled as the odor reached her. "Upset tummy?"

He snorted.

"Come back to the fire. It's nice and warm."

"And no doubt you have another drink for me."

She shook her head. "It wasn't the drink. MDMA tastes too strong to put in a drink. It was in your dinner."

"Oh, that makes me feel *so* much better."

Even with the smell of the vomit in the hall, the Viagra was starting to take effect. He shifted his stance. He told himself it was just the drug—but part of him didn't believe.

"Believe it or not, I did it to help you."

"Oh, yeah? I'm not seeing much benefit."

She stepped closer and reached toward him. "You haven't given it time."

Before her fingers could touch his chest, he jumped away to the drawing room. He was chilled both from emesis and his moment on the beach. He stood by the fire and warmed himself until he heard her high heels on the stair. She closed the door again as she entered and walked out of her shoes. She reached behind her neck and undid the clasp. The silk slithered off of her like some living thing and she stood there, four feet away, naked.

He wanted to run his hands over her skin, through her hair—all of her hair. He hated himself.

You can run, but you cannot hide.

And they had the ability to keep him from running, too.

He thought of Millie, trying to direct the thoughts of arousal toward her and her body.

I've got to draw the line.

He stood still and waited. When she walked up to him he didn't resist when she kissed him. Her hands wandered down to his thighs, stroking up, then around. He stooped and lifted her, one arm under her knees, *like Rhett carrying off Scarlet.*

She gave a slight laugh and squirmed against him, playing with the nape of his neck.

He jumped to the boardwalk that led to the beach—the midway point where it stretched over the salt marsh and estuary. He shoved out and dropped her, staggering for a second as one of her hands clawed at his shoulder, but the warning tingling in his throat came and he let the reflex work, flinching back to his old friend, the green box, visible again on the floor since he'd removed the rug. He gagged once, but kept from vomiting.

He didn't know how cold the estuary was but it had to be below 50° Fahrenheit. The air temperature was within spitting distance of freezing. He counted to five, then jumped again to the same spot on the boardwalk, in time to hear feet pounding back up the boardwalk toward the house. He flinched back to the square again, then jumped downstairs to the kitchen and peered out at the courtyard through the little square panes of glass in the door.

At least she's not drowning.

Abney stuck his head out of the side pantry, his eyebrows raised. "May I be of assistance, sir?"

Davy looked at him. "Miss Pope is running up from the beach right now and will be here in less than a minute. She is soaking wet and very, very cold. She'll need a hot bath or shower." He looked out the window again and saw Hyacinth throw the gate open at the far end of the courtyard. Her arms were wrapped across her chest and she came forward at a stumbling run. "Oh, yes. She's naked."

Davy jumped away to his bathroom and returned with the plush terry cloth robe. He thrust it into Abney's arms. "Good luck."

After a while, the effects of the drugs seemed to fade, and he suspected he'd successfully vomited up a substantial portion of the dose with his supper.

Hyacinth didn't enter his room for two hours after he'd dropped her in the estuary. He suspected she'd spent most of the time in a hot bath. She was back in her traditional clothes, hair bound tightly into a bun, makeup gone. Her voice was strident. "*Did you think that was—*"

He jumped away, back to the drawing room, where the fire

had burnt to embers. This time, instead of following him, she put him "in the box." He felt the buzz in his throat and flinched back.

She was standing there, her mouth opening to speak, but he forestalled her.

"Don't you get it? I don't want you. I don't want you around me. I don't want you yanking my chain."

"Why didn't you say 'no'? Ever heard of that! *Just Say No.* Sound familiar? If I weren't under orders I'd shoot your dick off!"

"I thought I did—when we got back from Nigeria. Under what orders? To do what? To avoid shooting me or to seduce me? Were you under orders to make me more *manageable*?"

She swung her fist at his face, but he jumped two feet to his left, still in the box. The missed blow turned her and he shoved hard on her shoulder, sending her staggering three steps back. "I'll drop you back in the marsh," he said as she recovered her balance and started back toward him.

Hyacinth stopped where she was and held up her hand. "I told you before—I don't have to touch you to spank. I can do it from another room."

Go ahead, do it! Davy thought. *Counteract the conditioning.* His voice dripped with derision. "Talk, talk, talk."

She took a step forward, then took a deep breath and exhaled. The furrows around her eyes smoothed out and she smiled slightly.

He found that far scarier than her previous rage.

She turned away from him and walked to the door. Before she closed it, she said, "Have a good night."

They put him "in the box" several times an hour for the rest of the night. Finally, at three in the morning, after a ten-minute period in the box, he simply removed the blanket and pillow from the bed and lay on the floor, within the taped borders.

He didn't know if they kept turning it on the rest of the night, or not, but they didn't bother him.

Good thing. I would not submit tamely.

His back ached from sleeping on the floor. He dressed and jumped down to the breakfast room, only to find himself back in the room, gagging. He tested the border. He wasn't "in the box." He hadn't felt anything when he'd gone into the bathroom so he'd assumed he had his usual run of the house. He explored the edges of the room—again nothing—but when he walked a few feet out into the hall he felt the border effect, the tingle in his throat, the coughing, and some nausea. Backing into the room put him in the clear again.

So, confined to quarters, is it?

Abney stuck his head in ten minutes later and recited the offerings for breakfast.

Davy chose the cereal with fruit and nuts, coffee, and "none of Ms. Pope's supplements."

Abney said, "Yes, sir." When he came back with the tray, he said, "*Exactly* as ordered, sir." When Davy searched Abney's face, Abney added, "Ms. Pope was called out of town very early this morning."

"Ah. Am I confined to my room until she returns?"

"I was told to provide meals in your room—until further notice."

Davy felt a surge of anger and he was surprised. *You've been in their hands far too long.* "Thank you, Abney."

"You're welcome, sir."

He had no appetite but he made himself chew methodically. When he'd finished, he slid the tray out into the hall and withdrew to the bathroom. *Time for a shower.*

He still had the end pages from *The Count of Monte Cristo* hidden between the toilet tank and the wall. Shielded by the shower curtain, he pointed the showerhead straight down at the drain, before he took the pencil and stared at the blank page.

As long as they'd been married, they'd never written letters to each other. No matter how far afield Davy roamed, he could be back to Millie in the wink of an eye. The closest they'd come to letters were notes like "gone to the store" and "don't forget to buy milk."

What did he write? He didn't want to tell her where he was. She'd come to him and they'd get her. He didn't want her to tell the NSA. They seemed to be Simons's puppets.

Finally he wrote:

IMPORTANT YOU REMAIN FREE. AVOID NSA. GO INTO HIDING. THEY'VE IMPLANTED A DEVICE THAT PUNISHES ME IF I TRAVEL AWAY FROM SPECIFIC LOCATIONS BUT I THINK I CAN DELIVER THIS NOTE.

He visualized the condo—specifically the counter by the refrigerator—and extended his arm, holding the note between thumb and forefinger. He jumped, releasing the note, and flinched back to the bathroom, but the note was still with him, fluttering toward the bottom of the tub. He snatched it out of the air before it landed in the water.

He tried three more times, finally achieving success by perching the note on his fingertips and pushing it away from him as he jumped. When he stood, gagging, back in the bathtub with *no* note, he relaxed and stood for a moment, under the hot water, rubbing his ears.

Stillwater was a thousand feet above Martha's Vineyard. His ears ached from repeated equalizing, the cycling between decompression and recompression.

So pick someplace also at sea level.

He thought about a beach he'd visited on the Queensland coast, one hundred kilometers from the nearest town, deserted even during the day and, as it was on the other side of the planet, in darkness now.

It came easier this time. He did the mirroring thing again at both ends of the bathtub. When he switched to Queensland he kept his eyes closed to avoid the sensory overload, concentrating more on maintaining the two different places, but he still felt the sand under his feet, alternating with the wet enameled tub. He extended his awareness to the cooler, but not unpleasantly cold, air. The wind was from the land and there was no surf, just a slight sloshing at the water's edge. Finally he opened his eyes and took in a swath of moonlit water stretching across to a gibbous moon.

Water was splattering the dry sand before him but the sky

was clear. *The shower.* The same shower he felt on his back and shoulders was falling on this beach half the planet away. The breeze swirled around his legs and stirred the shower curtain.

He wiggled his feet and felt them sink ankle deep into wet sand. *Wet from the water in the tub.* A slurry of wet sand oozed between his toes and slurped as he shifted his feet.

He stooped, carefully, and put his hands down. For a moment, his fingertips touched the enamel tub but then his hand closed on a handful of fine coral sand. He stood again and his head swam. He dropped back to the bottom of the tub, grabbing for the spout to steady himself, no longer in two places.

A mound of sand at least ankle deep formed an island in the middle of the tub, eroding slowly from the flow of the shower. Lovely, fine coral sand, totally unlike the coarse quartz sand at the beach in Martha's Vineyard. While the steam still fogged the room, he transferred the majority of the sand to the toilet and, under the guise of normal bodily functions, flushed it away. The remainder he risked in the tub's drain, praying it wouldn't clog.

When he left the bathroom he wasn't as exhausted as the first time, though he did sit down in the recliner and close his eyes for a while.

But he was far from asleep.

TWENTY-ONE

"Like the one that *killed* Padgett."

Millie rented a bicycle in Edgartown and rode it past the hotel and west, toward Edgartown Great Pond. Temperatures were in the fifties and the sky was dotted with fleecy cumulus clouds. She had to fight the wind on the bike path south from Edgartown harbor but, by the time she passed the hotel, she was screened from the offshore wind by the dunes and brush. The turnoff for Great Pond Lane was only a few minutes farther along the road but a closed steel gate blocked the entrance and its guardhouse was occupied. She noted two pedestal-mounted cameras and kept pedaling.

It was only another ten minutes to where the road ended on the shore of the estuary. She skirted the reeds for a few minutes on foot and considered.

From what she'd been able to see, the gated community consisted of half a dozen homes of varying sizes. She'd only been able to see the nearest houses clearly but a three-story brick mansion at the farthest end of the lane had been visible in the distance. That was her chief candidate for Driftwood Hall, but it could really be any of them.

At the edge of the water she was no longer shielded from the wind, and the sweat on her skin quickly chilled. She returned to the bike. On her way back she passed a car headed toward Edgartown Great Pond. It had a police-style light bar on top but the lettering on the side said Island Security. She waved and the driver lifted his hand briefly from the wheel before passing on.

Checking on me?

Again, she didn't pause as she passed the gate. Once around the corner, and out of line of sight, she rolled off between two trees and selected a jump site in the brush. She thought about just jumping back to the hotel but the weather was beautiful and she liked the strain she was feeling in her thighs from the unaccustomed exercise.

Besides, the patrol car might return, to check on her again. She got back on the bike and kept going.

She regretted the exercise later, after dark. She dressed in ninja chic, took her night goggles and her binoculars, and appeared in the spot she'd selected on the bike ride. Her thighs burned and she was hard put not to groan as she moved quietly through the brush. She worked her way west, parallel to the road and screened from it by the scrub. When she was across from the gate to Great Pond Lane she lay down and wormed her way between bushes until she could see the guardhouse.

Like the other night on the beach, the cameras glowed slightly, their temperature just high enough that the night vision goggles picked up their IR signature against the cool night. Though the lighting was low in the guardhouse, it blazed in the goggles. She avoided looking at it after counting the two guards within.

She retraced her path to the east and, when she could no longer see any cameras, crossed the road. There wasn't a fence around the community. The brush was thick and it was a job to work her way through it. When it thinned again at the edge of winter-brown lawns, she picked out the cameras pointed out toward the brush line.

Through the goggles most of the houses were cold and dark, shut down for the winter, but three were occupied. Two of the houses glowed with IR warm spots and the big house on the end, which was well beyond the brush, blazed, with or without the goggles, since spotlights lit its grounds.

She switched to the binoculars and studied the cold houses.

Most of them were thoroughly winterized, temporary or permanent shutters completely covering the windows, but there was one without shutters. It was midway down the block on the near side of the street.

She studied a second-floor balcony on the back side, then switched to the cameras. None of them pointed *toward* the houses. She understood that. These people had all this security to protect their privacy. It wasn't private if the security also watched them.

She jumped to her chosen balcony and crouched against the sliding glass doors. After listening for a slow count of thirty, she switched back to the night goggles and looked through the glass into the house. The curtains were drawn over the first door but only halfway across the second and, with the goggles, she could see a stretch of empty carpet, a chair leg, a low couch. She concentrated and, an instant later, she stood inside.

Alarm time. She looked around the room, especially the upper corners, but there weren't any little boxes with blinking LEDs. Maybe there were motion detectors in the downstairs rooms but a quick survey revealed none on this floor. There were dust covers over most of the furniture and when she tried the tap in an upstairs bathroom, nothing happened. The air was an odd combination of dust and stale damp.

Excellent. Doubtless the house would come alive some time before Memorial Day but, for now, nobody home. Nobody expected home.

She moved from window to window, studying the neighborhood. There was a single-floor house near the guard shack that was occupied. When she switched to her binoculars she saw that the car parked in its driveway was the Island Security patrol car she'd passed earlier, or its twin.

A two-story house diagonally across the street from her vantage point was also occupied, five cars parked on the wide apron in front of the triple garage and three more on the street. While she watched, three men and two women walked up the street from the spotlighted mansion. Three of them went in the front door of the two-story house and two more, a man and a woman, got into separate cars and drove off, the steel gate at the end of the street opening as they approached.

Staff? The cars were older, not particularly fancy, but on the Vineyard that didn't mean anything. The rich drove rusty heaps and it was gauche to dress up. Still, she thought they would've parked closer if they weren't the help.

She turned her attention to the mansion at the end of the cul-de-sac. *Are you in there, Davy?*

She counted six exterior cameras on this side alone. *Something is in there.*

The mansion's many-gabled roof offered possibilities. None of the cameras she could see covered the roof, but the flood-lights on the grounds cast it into deep shadow. She used the night vision goggles but they auto-adjusted to the floodlights' glare and she couldn't get any detail in the shadows of the roof. The places she *could* study in sufficient detail were covered by cameras.

I need to see it in daylight.

She went back to the Aerie to put away the binoculars, the night vision goggles, and her dark clothes. She was still low on underwear. She thought about the condo and jumped there, holding her breath.

Though the doors were still taped and there was the faintest scent of the anesthetic, it was clear it hadn't been replenished. She grabbed her entire underwear drawer and dumped it into a clothes basket in the living room. She was looking around, wondering if she should take anything else, when she saw the note.

Davy had terrible handwriting—it was totally distinctive and instantly recognizable. She snatched it and jumped back to the Aerie.

She stared at the paper, trying to read the words, her head cocked to one side. There was a ringing in her ears and her lips were dry and she wet them with her tongue. She took a plastic cup and held it under the cistern spigot but she didn't realize it had filled until water ran across her fingers and splashed on the floor. She closed the valve.

He's alive.

The glass dropped from Millie's fingers, spraying water across the floor and bouncing with an echoing clatter. She dropped to her knees and burst into tears.

He's alive.

She'd never really thought about the alternative but it was obvious that a part of her had seriously considered it. The sobs were titanic, a flooding of grief released because it no longer had to be held back.

He's alive.

It was several minutes before she could stop and actually consider the information contained in the note.

IMPORTANT YOU REMAIN FREE.

Well, yes.

AVOID NSA. GO INTO HIDING.

Davy had never trusted the NSA, but did he know something more now, as she did? And did he really expect her to just sit on her ass and do nothing?

THEY'VE IMPLANTED A DEVICE THAT PUNISHES ME IF I TRAVEL AWAY FROM SPECIFIC LOCATIONS BUT I THINK I CAN DELIVER THIS NOTE.

Just like Padgett. Well, maybe not *just* like Padgett. That device seemed more about keeping Padgett from talking. But she bet it was still a vagal nerve stimulator. And apparently he *could* deliver the note. *At what cost?*

She remembered Padgett vomiting into the fire and shuddered. They were conditioning Davy, she thought. So they could use him.

To do what?

For the first time since Davy's disappearance she fell asleep without effort and, when she awoke, she lay there for a moment and actually smiled. When she left, she put a large cardboard sign on the counter in the condo, right before the spot Davy had left his note.

I'M SAFE. I CAN JUMP. ARE YOU IN THE BIG HOUSE ON MARTHA'S VINEYARD? I'LL BE RIGHT HERE AT 6 PM CENTRAL EVERY DAY. I LOVE YOU.

There was a guard on the gate of the Stillwater National Guard Armory but the building itself was locked up tight and unoccupied.

It took Millie a while to find the chemical and biological protection gear: the gas masks, protective suits, and what she really cared about: the Mark I Nerve Agent Antidote kits. She scavenged four atropine autoinjectors out of four kits and put the empty foam cases and the leftover 2-PAM injectors in the Aerie. She didn't want incomplete kits left in the armory where, God forbid, someone should need it someday. Nor did she want someone to run across the 2-Pam; it was just waiting for the wrong combination of touches to send the spring-driven needle into someone's unsuspecting flesh like some striking snake. The atropine she put in a fanny pack and buckled it around her waist.

Her next stop was the interior of the winterized house on Great Pond Lane. She stayed well back from the windows and used her binoculars on Driftwood Hall.

There were more security cameras than she'd seen the night before. *Why didn't I see them?*

She studied their positions, mounted near windows. *Ah. They were lost against hot backgrounds.*

One shadowed corner looked good, where a dormer window projected from the slanting shingles of the main roof. She stared at the dark gray squares. *Fiberglass shingles, like the ones Dad put on his roof.* They'd be gritty to the touch and, depending on their age, might smell like asphalt, especially when warm. Despite the slope, she'd have no trouble staying in place. She'd want to creep very slowly, lest someone in the room below should hear her movements.

She took fast food back to the condo and ate there, next to her sign, next to the spot Davy had left his note.

He might come back at any moment.

Her sign looked forlorn and pitiful on the counter. As she chewed her food every rustle of sandwich wrapper, every smack of her lips echoed off the walls and floor tiles, and made her feel completely and utterly alone.

"He might," she said aloud. It sounded even more unlikely spoken aloud.

She wanted to touch base with Becca Martingale. She wanted to buy some pepper spray. She wanted to take a shower at the bath house in Santa Fe. But she found herself unwilling to move, unwilling to leave that spot.

"This is ridiculous!"

She jumped to the twenty-four-hour drugstore in the Virginia suburbs of D.C.—the one next to the Comfort Inn where they'd kicked the door in while she was bathing. She snatched a container of talcum powder off the shelf and rushed it to the counter. The cashier scanned it and said, "Two fifty-three." Millie threw a twenty down and rushed for the door. "Your change!" the clerk called after Millie. Millie yelled, "Keep it!" over her shoulder. She jumped back to the condo as soon as she was through the door.

He *probably* hadn't been there in the seventy seconds she'd been away.

"Probably." Never had a spoken word carried so much doubt.

Holding the talcum at arm's length, she sprinkled it liberally, letting it drift down to evenly coat the tiles before the sign. Then she took several steps back and repeated the process on a smaller patch. She walked across it and turned to study the result.

Her footprints were clearly evident in the talc, like tracks in dust.

What if he jumps into some other part of the condo?

Only a great effort of will kept her from sprinkling talc on every floor in the dwelling, but when she got back to the Aerie, she spread some there, too.

Becca Martingale's number switched directly to voicemail and Millie hung up before the message tone. *She could be on the phone. She could be in a meeting. She could be out of range of the nearest cell.* Twenty minutes later it was the same. On the next try, after five more minutes, Becca answered.

"It's Millie. Any developments?"

There was the barest hesitation and Becca said, "Sorry, Judy, I know I said I'd set up an appointment, but I'll have to do it later. Things are too hectic for a haircut right now."

Millie blinked. "You can't talk right now. How about in an hour?"

Becca responded doubtfully. "I'll want to take more off the sides."

"A half-hour?"

"Probably."

Millie looked at her watch. "I've got seven after. Call you at twenty-three till, uh, ten. Eastern daylight."

"Right. Bye."

She disconnected.

Millie went back to the condo. There weren't any tracks in the talc. She jumped across town to the University area, and found a shop that specialized in alarms, locks, and personal security devices.

"The best thing is pepper foam," the clerk told her. "It lets you know if you're hitting your target, it clings, and there's less chance of getting blow-back or hitting innocent bystanders."

He showed her a small one-ounce keychain model in the case, but sitting next to it was a larger four-ounce model. "I want *that* one."

"Oh . . . kay. That's the pro model, for cops and mailmen. It's a bit big for the pocket."

"I have large pockets."

"You're the customer."

She bought two.

Becca answered on the second ring.

"I was in a meeting with my boss and *his* boss. It seems that, now that we've got Padgett, the man who shot one of our own, we get to drop the investigation."

Millie's upper lip wrinkled. "Indeed. With two kidnappings ongoing?"

"What kidnappings? Mere innuendo. Ms. Johnson probably

went back to the streets as is her wont and as to Davy, the NSA is saying they were mistaken. He is abroad, on assignment."

"Just like that? You drop it?"

"No. We don't. Not if you still maintain that your husband was kidnapped. We still have the witnesses from the restaurant and a dead NSA agent."

"And the two kids who saw the killing."

"What! What kids?"

"The ones who identified the angel on the ambulance. They saw Davy put in the ambulance."

Becca was silent for a beat. "The NSA didn't tell us there were witnesses to the actual murder. They just gave us the angel."

"Ah." Millie told her quickly about her interview with the Ruiz family and the subsequent analysis of the conversation by Dr. Henri Gautreau.

"So, the waitress, huh? It's *so* nice when we're kept in the loop."

"They told me they'd tell you what you needed to know."

"Oh, yeah. I've heard that before. Shit. So, yeah, we have lots of reasons to keep the investigation open. My boss sent a message back up the chain—he's about to retire and he has family money even if they yank his pension—he's threatened to go straight to the press if they pull the plug."

Millie felt her eyes water. "Good for him."

"Yeah—not bad for a *male*. As to developments, you tell me."

"What do you mean?"

"Everything we have is negative. Bochstettler and Associates claims Padgett was fired months ago and has produced paperwork to that end. We followed the money on the credit card you gave us and it comes from an account in the fake name started three months ago with cash. The IDs are forgeries, but good ones made with stolen official stock in the case of the license. His apartment in D.C. was furnished, but it was about as lived in as a hotel room. The ambulances haven't led to anything specific. The thugs under Padgett don't know anything though they fingered Padgett as their control and paymaster. They're willing to talk about stuff they've done for him but it's old and, except for that day of following you around, irrelevant." She took a deep breath. "But you, my dear, said you had something, but you didn't want anybody flushing the prey."

"Flushing the prey? Did you actually say that? I can't believe you actually said that. I never said that."

"So sue me. It's what you meant."

"I don't care if they run. I just don't want them to take Davy with them . . . or worse."

"It's not the usual kidnap situation. They can't use him if he's dead."

"They can't do anything to him if I get him back before they know I'm onto them."

"Are you that close?"

Millie bit her lip. "No comment."

"What if they kill you? Or capture you? I know what you can do, but the same was true of David, right? And they caught him. Shouldn't you have some form of backup?"

"This is your cell phone, right?"

"Yes."

"Jesus! I'm *such* an idiot. You want to talk to me, meet me where I last dropped you off."

"At the—"

"*Don't* say it. How long?"

"Forty-five minutes."

"You'll be followed, but it won't matter." Millie hung the pay phone up and jumped away.

Still no footprints in the talc.

She found a waiting room on the second floor of George Washington University Hospital that overlooked the sidewalk on New Hampshire Avenue, where she'd left Becca the night Padgett died. The sun was bright and unobscured and the windows were mirrored so she was effectively invisible inside.

Becca was dropped by a car with government plates that then drove on. Millie grabbed her without warning, jumping directly behind, lifting, and jumping. It was so fast that Becca's gasp came only after Millie released her in the Aerie.

"You might warn a girl!" Becca looked around, adjusting to the dimmer light. She reached up to touch the rough stone ceiling then looked at the crude stone masonry wall and the windows. "Where are we?"

"This is our place, Davy's and mine. Our private place. It's a bit of a mess right now."

"But *where* is it?"

"Well, it's in the northern hemisphere but I'm afraid that's as far as I'm willing to go." She put a piece of piñon on the coals in the stove, leaving the door open. "You want some tea?"

Becca blinked. "Why not. Why is there talc on the floor there?"

Millie looked. The talc was trackless. "I told you, the place is a mess." She walked around the talc to put the kettle on the propane burner and handed Becca Davy's note.

Becca dropped into the big chair in the reading nook and took out a pair of reading glasses. She held them up, still folded, to look at the note through them, then jerked her head up, eyes large. "He's *been* here?"

"To our condo, in Stillwater, but here, too, I think. There was a water puddle here where none should be."

"A device implanted? Like Padgett!"

"Yes. Like the one that *killed* Padgett."

Becca put the glasses on properly and reread the note. She looked up blankly, her mind clearly racing. She gestured at Millie's sign on the counter. "What big house on Martha's Vineyard?"

Millie tilted her head to one side. "What will you do if I tell you?"

"Is it where he is?"

"Don't know. But I followed a lead from Bochstettler and I checked it out. It's guarded like a fortress and it's the Northeast—the ambulances, right? And you said something about Hyacinth Pope traveling to Logan. She might've connected to the Vineyard."

"Whose house is it?"

"Again, what are you going to do?"

"What do you want me to do?"

"Not 'flush the prey.' "

"I can't believe you said that."

"Sue me. I'm willing to tell you, in the interests of backup, but I don't want you to go in until I've got Davy."

"And how are you going to deal with the implant?"

Millie bit her lip and decided not to mention stealing the atropine. Behind her the kettle started whistling. She said, "I've got to *find* him first. But I'm working on it."

"So you have no *evidence* that Davy's in this house, right?"

"It's very tenuous. You couldn't get a warrant, even if it was just some ordinary guy and from what I understand, he's not at all ordinary."

"Okay. I'll leave it alone unless you don't come back."

"It could mean his life, Becca."

"Oddly enough, I know that. What I'm concerned about is *you*. You don't exactly have the training for this. Don't you think you could be endangering him or yourself?"

Millie jumped the intervening ten feet, to appear inches away from Becca's face, like she did the night she'd scared Padgett off the balcony, only she didn't yell. Still, it was a good thing Becca wasn't on a balcony. The chair would've fallen over if it hadn't been next to the wall. Millie jumped back to the kettle.

"You've got to admit I have certain advantages."

"I nearly peed myself!"

Millie took the cups down. "You promise?"

"Swear on a Bible. I won't move unless you go missing. But I won't know if you're missing unless you check in with me before you go in."

"Deal." Millie took a deep breath, let it out, then said in a rush, "The house is called Driftwood Manor and it's on Great Pond Lane on the south shore near Edgartown." She felt a weight come off of her shoulders. *Burden shared, burden eased.*

Becca pulled out a notebook and was writing the address down. "And it belongs to?"

"Lawrence Simons."

Becca's pen froze. "Oh, fuck."

Millie finally took the whistling kettle off the burner. "Well, at least you've heard of him."

The talc was undisturbed in both places when she returned from dropping Becca near Interrobang. Her overwhelming desire was to stay by the patch and wait. *Sitting on my ass.* Instead she located a Laundromat several blocks from the condo in Stillwater and took all her dirty clothes there.

If she kept jumping back to the Aerie and the condo to check the talc, at least she wasn't frozen there, immobile. She was proud of herself, of her resolve and fortitude, but when all the clothes were dry, she jumped them back to the condo before folding them.

You aren't fooling anybody.

She jumped onto the roof at twilight while she could still just barely see it through the binoculars. She was wearing her ninja outfit and she flattened herself against the tiles to blend in. Almost immediately the floodlights came on, below, as if in reaction to her presence, but she discounted that. It must be dark enough at ground level to trip the photocell that controlled the lights. In the resulting shadow she felt invisible.

Then why is my heart pounding so?

The air was cool but the roof was warm to the touch, residual heat from the sun, or, more likely, the house's furnace. She lay there, a shadow within a shadow, as the sky darkened in shades of gray-blue. She turned her head and pressed an ear against the shingles, closing her eyes. There was a humming, probably from the central heater blower in the attic. She didn't hear any voices but at one point she heard something that might be a distant door shutting. She didn't know whether it was on her floor or lower.

She jumped back to the Aerie and stripped the tee-shirt mask off of her head. By the time she'd left, the air was positively cold, but her neck was wet with sweat.

She wanted to go straight back, to enter the house, but it was too early. The residents would be active, dealing with dinner and its aftermath. When she'd seen the servants leaving the night before, it had been after nine. She would wait a good hour after that before she went further.

She stripped off the dark clothes and hung them, to air, then drank deeply from the cistern. She stepped outside, onto the ledge. Here, two time zones to the west, the sun was still up, though blocked from Millie by the ridge above her. The sky was still crystalline blue, with a contrail drawn across the expanse far above like a knife slash. Her skin cooled immediately and a breeze went through her hair like a caress. Oblivious, the moment before, she became acutely aware that she was standing outside in just panties and a bra.

So? There's no one to see.

And that was the trouble.

She shivered and went back in, wrapping herself in a robe. She left the door open and lit a fire in the stove, enjoying the combination of cool air and warm radiance. She kept her eye on the counter. It was nearing six in his time zone but, like a watched pot, Davy neither appeared or boiled.

At nine-thirty she put the dark outfit on again, wrapped the tee-shirt around her head in the ninja mask, and put on the fanny pack with the atropine autoinjectors and pepper foam.

The belt's pressure made her aware of her bladder. She used the composting toilet in its closet at the end of the dwelling. As she came out again there was a flickering near the counter, and for a moment she thought she'd seen someone but there was no one there.

Wishful thinking.

When she went to get the night vision goggles off the shelf, there were footprints in the talc. Two prints, left and right, bare. Facing away from her sign, dammit!

She had seen him. Had he seen her, coming out of the bathroom? Had he run from her?

She waited another forty minutes, staring at the spot before the counter, then, swearing, snatched up the night vision goggles.

She called Becca's cell from a pay phone in Crystal City, the night vision goggles tucked under one arm, the mask pulled down around her neck like a rumpled scarf.

"Martingale."

"I'm going in."

"Call me after?"

"Yes."

The roof creaked when she appeared back on it, in the shadow of the gable. She held her breath and froze, staring up, ears listening for an approaching guard. The cold stars glittered down like distant, uncaring eyes.

When she did move, she thought, *Like glaciers creeping. Imperceptible in the short term, covering distance over time.* Far better to err on the side of caution. There would be no second chances.

It took her half an hour to move the four feet to the edge of the dormer windows. She never moved more than an inch at a time and she rested and listened between each movement. It was cold and a sharp breeze had sprung up as the sun went down but she was sweating.

The floodlights on the grounds below cast the shadow of the gutter across the window, lighting the peak of the dormer above and the very top of the window frame but not the glass panes themselves. The room within was dark. She lowered the night vision goggles over her eyes and, shielding the lenses from the glare with her hands, peered through the glass.

Blinds. Closed.

She examined the window itself, an old-fashioned sash. When she tugged at it, it didn't budge.

There were perhaps three feet of slanting shingles between the window and the edge of the roof. She eyed the lip and decided to go around, instead, moving up the slant of the roof, over the top of the dormer, and then down again, to the next window. She even turned to do it but stopped herself.

Idiot! You can teleport, remember?

She studied the next window and jumped across the twelve-foot gap. This window was also tightly closed but the blinds had been raised. The room was unlit but a thin line of light coming under the door was like the noonday sun for the night vision goggles, letting her see into a small garret bedroom. There was a twin bed beneath the window, a desk on one wall, a freestanding wardrobe opposite, and a dresser with a television next to the door opposite. The bed, though made, had a crease on it, as if someone had been lying atop the covers.

They could come back at any minute.

She jumped within and pressed her ear to the door. She heard nothing, no footsteps, no voices, just a slight hum from the central heat. She checked the wardrobe. Women's clothes, mostly semi-casual, with several maid's uniforms—gray dresses with white aprons. The top drawer of the dresser held bras, panties, hose, nightgowns, and two clips for a 9-mm automatic pistol.

Turn down the beds and shoot out the lights.

She took out her dental mirror, flipped up the night vision goggles, and eased the door to the hallway open.

TWENTY-TWO

"You should've left me chained."

Davy was on his bed in a tee-shirt and pajama bottoms, ignoring a DVD, when his throat tingled and he found himself standing "in the box."

It was late at night and Hyacinth entered without knocking. She held the door for Thug One and Thug Two as they each carried in a large aluminum case. Both of the cases were dented and battered and the olive-drab anodized coating was scratched. They were clearly heavy, for both men leaned to counteract the weight. Clear of the door, they lowered them to the floor as if they were made of glass.

Hyacinth turned off the TV without speaking. She jerked her head toward the door and Thug One and Thug Two left. Davy thought they looked relieved at the dismissal.

"I hope that's not your trousseau," Davy said.

She looked at him in silence for a moment before saying, "It's just a quick delivery. Two quick trips to the embassy in Caracas." She took a handkerchief from her pants pocket and wiped the handles carefully, then polished the top of the case.

Davy looked down at the tips of his own fingers. "What's in them?"

Hyacinth shook her head. "No need for you to know. Just leave them in the bathroom and our contact will collect them."

Davy felt a chill. *You knew this time would come.* He leaned out of the box to peer at the cases. They were padlocked shut. A large pink Post-it note was stuck to each with the word FIRST on one and LAST on the other. There was a line of lettering on a metallized label and when he squinted he saw lines of Arabic.

"Should I dress? Do I take you to the embassy first?" he asked, testing.

She shook her head. "Not necessary. Just leave them in the bathroom and . . . come right back." Her eye contact broke.

"Open them," he said.

"Are you deaf?"

"You're not going to open them?"

"Hell, no!"

"Right." He'd gone as far as he could. More specifically, as far as he *would*. He dropped down onto the floor, cross-legged. "Deliver them yourself."

Hyacinth's hands clenched into fists. "Mr. Simons told you what would happen if you didn't cooperate. Is it time to bring Ms. Johnson over from—" She shut her mouth with a click. "Let me rephrase. Is it time to bring Ms. Johnson up here . . . one piece at a time?"

It would be so easy to break your neck. Davy visualized the act, jumping behind her, grasping her chin, and jumping sideways without letting go. He felt a stir of arousal. He wanted his hands on her, all right. *For what?* His stomach heaved but it wasn't the implant.

"Are they on a timer or are you going to radio-detonate them?"

Her posture shifted subtly, less forward, slightly smaller, and she unclenched her hands. "What on earth do you mean?"

He licked his lips. Might as well be as clear as possible. "Well, it's not drugs, not with Colombia next door. That would be like taking sand to the Sahara. It could be money, like I carried for the NSA, but if so, why not show me? Unless you know it's something I won't touch."

Hyacinth waved her hand. "Why would we want to take a bomb into Caracas? That's like your sand and Sahara thing. Plenty of bombs. Fifteen explosions in the last two years."

Davy crossed his legs. "On the streets of Caracas, yes. But inside the security cordon of the U.S. Embassy?"

Hyacinth didn't move for a moment. Then, "Why on earth would we do something like that?"

"Can you say 'regime change?' I don't know if you guys want the oil, or want to keep this administration in office with a timely little foreign adventure, or if you want to give them a reason to go directly after drugs in Colombia or, hell, perhaps it's an excuse to go someplace else. I can't read Arabic. Does anything else in that case point to a particular country? Say, Syria? Iran? For all I know, you guys are heavily invested in the defense industries and just want another war." He steepled his fingers. "Syrian bomb blows up U.S. Embassy in Venezuela. U.S. sends troops? Crashes stock market? Street price of cocaine skyrockets? Maybe you've stockpiled against a shortage."

"That's ridiculous." Her affect was flat, eyes watchful.

"Indeed." Davy's lips went tight. "Which scenario?"

"All of them!" She half-turned to the door. "I'll just go get Ms. Johnson, then? Is that what you want?"

He felt cold inside. "I can do the math. Ms. Johnson dies. Perhaps I die, too. But how many people die in the explosion? How many die in the subsequent military actions?"

"It's *not* a bomb, so none of that will happen. Except Ms. Johnson will die and you'll wish you'd never been born."

He watched her, his tongue on his lips. The last time they'd talked about Caracas, the cameras and microphones had been disconnected. And she'd just sent the two Thugs out, as well, as if they weren't to hear this conversation. *So the cameras are probably* off *now.*

He said, "When you're lying in the dark, trying to get to sleep, do they visit you? The people you've killed and hurt?"

She wrinkled her nose and said, "I sleep like a baby."

He exhaled sharply through his nose. "With colic?"

She turned toward the door. "I'll be back with some part of Ms. Johnson."

Davy tilted his head forward and narrowed his eyes. "I don't think so."

His knee struck her in the stomach before she'd had time to react to his disappearance from the square. As she doubled over he kneed her once more in the same place and then was back in the box in time to watch her drop to the floor, unable to breathe, her nervous system temporarily overloaded.

He was bent over himself, trying to avoid tossing dinner. He gasped out, "You turned off the cameras, didn't you, dear? Lest you leave any evidence of this plot." He jumped again, took her by the collar, and jumped back into the square. Each excursion out of the square hit him with a jolt.

Hyacinth thrashed, striking out with her elbow, but he avoided it easily. She was making little half-choking, half-gasping noises, still unable to draw a breath. Davy switched his grasp to her arms, lifted them over her head, then lowered them. The first gasping intake of air rushed through her vocal chords in a protracted moan. To Davy it sounded like a caricature of sexual pleasure.

You're sick, kiddo.

"You should've left me chained," he said.

He grabbed her shirt collar again, and jumped her to the midnight darkness of the pit, fifty feet above the water, and released her. Unlike times past, he was unable to stay, to see or, in this case, hear her impact the surface. He'd taken too long.

He doubled over, back in the square, first vomiting, then coughing, then vomiting again. A part of him watched, detached. *Been here, done this.* He wondered if Hyacinth was too weak to make it to the shore of the island.

The smell and sight of his earlier night's dinner kept him gagging. He turned away from the lumpy puddle and drew deep breaths though his mouth. His throat burned. *I am so tired of this.* He eyed the two cases, halfway to the door, and wondered what would happen if he threw them against the wall.

How long before they check on Hyacinth? And what could he do with the period of unobserved time?

He thought about moving the cases to the island in the pit. *Make them* her *problem* but, for all he knew, they'd already put them on a timer. He looked at the Post-it notes again. Why was it important to take one before the other?

He presumed both contained explosives. Perhaps the second one contained the detonation device.

But why would it matter?

He thought about knocking the locks off and opening them. *What if they've boobytrapped them?* What if opening them set them off?

From the size of the things, and their apparent weight, he felt sure they didn't expect him to carry both cases at once. So, they wanted to make sure one was in place before the other got there. Again, why?

The answer chilled him.

Because it's designed to go off once it's been moved?

He shook his head. If they did that, how could they re-use him?

Maybe they've decided they don't want to re-use him. *Maybe their concern is, how can they let me live, if I know who arranged for the bomb to be put there in the first place?*

That had to be it. How could they possibly risk his revealing the guilty? It would undo anything they hoped to accomplish.

So, move one case, then, when the second one was moved, it would go off, blowing the first case in sympathetic detonation. And, incidentally, silencing Davy. At ground zero, there probably wouldn't be much left of him.

And what would set it off?

Obviously movement wasn't the thing. Thug One had brought it in, after all. What about some sort of GPS receiver? Perhaps it was programmed to go off when it found itself in the right location?

He thought about that and rejected it. He'd used GPS receivers and it usually took them some time to reacquire enough satellites to determine position after he jumped. If they were counting on GPS, he'd be long gone before the detonation and their delivery order wouldn't matter.

He thought about the embassy. There'd been a lot of concrete in its construction and, though the radio keys for the implant had reached within, Davy doubted they could count on getting *any* satellite signal into the middle of the building.

So maybe it detonates from the absence *of a signal?*

After all, this was how they controlled Davy. But it couldn't be the *same* signal, otherwise they couldn't count on him getting it to its destination. They'd need to be transmitting the keys in Caracas for him to jump there. If they used the same signal, the second case wouldn't detonate until they turned it off. *Calls for too much coordination.* Far simpler this other way.

They were, he decided, transmitting a simple signal here, at the house, and the minute the detonator in the second case stopped receiving it, *boom.*

You're going to feel really stupid when it turns out to be fresh shirts for the Ambassador.

He didn't think he could stand another kick from the implant so he didn't leave the square to get the cases. Instead, he twinned himself, like in the bathtub, both jumping to the cases, yet staying behind.

It's a gate, really, between two places. I'm just a Davy-shaped hole in the universe. And a Davy-shaped hole that leaked even weak radio signals, keeping his implant happy. He picked up the cases, one at a time, untwinned, and set them down in the square.

He looked at the door, at the two-way mirror, and back at the cases. *Better not wait* too *long.*

He picked up the first case and twinned to the beach in Australia, the deserted stretch on the Queensland coast, where the dry sand met the wet.

His vision was distorted, the bedroom overlaid on the sun-drenched beach, but the beach was so bright the fluorescent lights couldn't compete. The room was a dim ghost overlaid on the sea and sky. The light hurt his eyes, but, as he turned slowly in place, he couldn't see anybody. He wasn't surprised—the nearest road was miles away. He'd gotten there originally by teleporting in jumps down the coastline. He scanned the horizon. There was a distant triangle of sail but it was far enough away that the hull itself was below the horizon.

He lowered the case but it seemed to float just above the sand. He tried twice more before it settled, not on the oak floor of the room, but on the beach. He let go and untwinned.

There was only one case in the room with him now and a dusting of sand on the parquet.

He twinned again, back to the beach. The case was still there, listing slightly to one side in the sand. He untwinned, back to the room.

He looked at the second case. The word on the Post-it seemed horribly significant: LAST.

The last thing I do? Last thoughts?

He wanted to see Millie—at least once more. He twinned to the Aerie and looked around, hoping she was there but almost immediately he heard the faint sound of a distant footstep and thought it was *them*, coming to check on Hyacinth.

He flinched back to the room, took hold of the last case and twinned again, to Queensland, his heart thumping.

He blinked in the bright sunlight, holding his breath.

Well, it hadn't blown up yet, as he stood there in both places. He set it down beside the first case, getting it onto the sand at his first try and removed his hand from the handle. It leaned slightly to once side, contacting the other case and he froze at the slight click of contact.

His chest hurt and he exhaled, relieving the discomfort. With an effort, he took his eyes off of the case, to look around once more, to make sure the beach was still deserted.

It was. Even the distant sail was shrinking, dropping lower behind the horizon. He noted with amusement that the sun shone through him to light the oak floor about his feet.

"All right."

He knelt and put his hand on the oak floor, concentrating on the furniture and the walls and the ceiling of the room. When he untwinned, he did not want to be on the beach. If he was right, the consequences would be . . . significant.

He found himself wholly back in the room, kneeling on the hard oak parquet.

It was quiet. The distant footstep he'd heard wasn't the first of more. He swallowed and then counted slowly to thirty. When he twinned back to the beach, it was not where he'd left the cases, but by the tree line, well back from the water.

The air was hot and full of chemical-smelling smoke, dust, and falling bits of sand. Where the cases had been now stood a smoking crater thirty feet across and several feet deep. It was slowly filling from the ocean. The trees around him were shredded, the leaves stripped from their limbs and, in some cases, entire trunks felled, broken in splintered fractures a foot off the ground.

Not *the ambassador's shirts.*

A knock sounded on the door and he flinched, untwinning back into the room. He wrinkled his nose, annoyed with himself. They wouldn't have knocked if the cameras were still on. They would've done something more drastic, like sending him into convulsions. He wished he could lock or block the door. He had a feeling that his "most favored guest" status was about to come to an end. *Never mind. As the lady said, if they want to, they can spank me from off-site . . . with a button.*

"Come in."

Thug Two, the hook-nosed redhead, stepped into the room. "Excuse me, Hyacinth, but—" He stared around, looking at Davy, where the cases had been, the puddle of vomit, and then Davy again.

"Where is Miss Pope?"

Davy smiled grimly. "She had to leave." He wondered if he could grab the man while twinning. Regretfully, he decided it would take more practice than he had time for.

He broke Thug Two's magnificent nose with a heel strike and was back in the square, with only the slightest dry heave.

Thug Two staggered back, his hands to his face, blood dripping over his chin. He kept one hand to his nose and groped for the door with the other, his eyes streaming tears.

Davy took a deep breath through his mouth, then grabbed Thug Two and dropped him in the pit.

This took too long. Though he flinched back to the square he lost motor control and dropped to the floor, coughing, vomiting, and defecating, and, though he *was* back in the square, it didn't stop.

Must've turned the cameras back on, he thought, and passed out.

The first thing he noticed was the smell, an awful penetrating mix of odors that was becoming far too familiar. He gagged and the resulting movement tugged at his leg. The manacle was back on his ankle, the padlock firmly latched to the chain.

He wanted to clean off more than anything, to get this taste out of his mouth and the smell off his body, but they'd put the padlock well up the chain, with only a few feet of slack between his leg and the anchor ring. He couldn't reach any of the furniture, much less the bathroom.

This can't be good.

Lawrence Simons came into the room and shut the door behind him.

Definitely not good.

Davy pushed himself up to his hands and knees. His head felt heavy and drooped. He settled back on his shins and braced his hands on his thighs. With a decided effort, he balanced his head upright, eyes level. "Have to come far?"

Simons's nose wrinkled and he took a chair at the edge of the room, as far away as possible. "Far enough."

Davy said, "You should smell it from over here."

Simons's urbanity, his smooth polish, was completely gone. "Where are the cases?"

"Is that your priority? I would've thought you'd be more concerned about Thug Two and Miss Pope." He worked saliva into his mouth. "I don't suppose I could have something to drink, to rinse my mouth out?"

"Answer my question and I'll consider it."

Davy shrugged. The truth wouldn't particularly help Simons and he was too tired to make up lies. "The cases, or what's left of them, are in and about a crater on the northeast coast of Australia. It was right at the water's edge and filling rapidly with seawater when last I saw it."

Almost sadly, Simons said, "You didn't take them to the Embassy?"

"Surely you've checked to see if the building is still standing? But, no, of course I didn't. Someone might have been *hurt*. May I have that glass of water?"

Simons took a radio from his jacket pocket and raised it to his mouth. "Bring Ms. Johnson over."

Over? Like from another building? "No water?" *He's got the cameras and mikes turned off, too, or he wouldn't need to use the radio.*

Simons held the radio antenna against his chin. "I'm considering it. Why aren't you dead?"

"Ah." Davy nodded slowly. "Did you want me dead? I was wondering about that. You've gone to an awful lot of trouble, after all, and, while I'm sure the payoff for your little embassy explosion was probably considerable, it seemed a waste of a valuable resource to just *flush* me in the process. Not to mention, it *hurt* my feelings."

Simons stared at him, unmoving, unmoved. "We tried, Mr. Rice. We tried. But we came to the conclusion that you aren't really biddable. Not *dependably* so. We gave Hyacinth one more chance to secure your cooperation but then you dropped her in the salt marsh. That was a mistake. You should've just fucked her and cooperated."

Davy blinked. *So* that's *what she was doing.*

"But our analysis is that you're just too *rigid*. Your self-interest is insufficiently paramount over your value system. An uptight little prig, really."

Davy didn't know whether to be pleased or offended.

Simons continued. "So, why aren't you dead?"

"In the explosion? You should listen to Conley," Davy said. "You're paying him to do all that research, right? Didn't you know about the persistence of the portal?"

Simons's eyes narrowed. "Vaguely. He said something about it."

Davy lied. "I jumped the second case and dropped it and jumped back. There was enough portal latency for your detonator to receive its signal until I was safe back here."

Simons's lips pulled back from his teeth. "Why would you do that? I mean, what made you think to do that?"

"You know my mother died from a terrorist's bomb?"

Simons's eyes narrowed. He nodded warily. "Well, yes, it's in your file. So you knew they were bombs?"

"A deduction." Davy tilted his head to one side. "Why? Did you think Hyacinth told me?"

Simons shook his head. "Not really. Nor Mr. Planck. They *are* biddable, after all. They are well aware of the consequences. *They* have self-interest. But something told you?"

"She wouldn't let me see in the cases. They were labeled 'first' and 'last.' She told me to take the cases to Caracas, but not her, and then she hesitated before adding, 'and come right back.'" He spread his hands. "She didn't expect me back."

Simons scowled. "I see. It was badly handled. Where are Ms. Pope and Mr. Planck?"

Davy laughed. "They're at the bottom of a sinkhole. There's plenty of fresh water, but they'll starve in a couple of weeks unless one of them turns on the other. My money is on Hyacinth. She's a survivor. *Her* self-interest is paramount." He clicked his teeth together. "I wonder if she'll sleep with him first?"

Simons's eyes narrowed. "You'll tell us where, of course?"

Davy shrugged. "Perhaps we can reach an accommodation."

"Involving?"

"Ms. Johnson."

Simons smiled nastily. "Oh, I'm sure we can."

"Let her go and I'll fetch Hyacinth and Thug, uh, Mr. Planck, back for you. You'll be well ahead of the game. No chance of them spilling any of your secrets. Ms. Johnson doesn't *know* any of your secrets or where she is and she'll be dropped far from here with no way to trace where she's been."

"Oh. You'd drop her somewhere, you say?"

"Of course. I'm afraid I don't trust you to do it."

"I'm hurt." Simons didn't look hurt. He looked . . . well, cold as ice. Like steel. Anger controlled. Anger harnessed.

Davy spread his hands. "No offense, but it's not *my* life I'd be gambling, after all."

Simons leaned forward. "But it is, my boy, it is."

Davy shook his head. "No gamble there. I'm not expecting to get out of this alive. You assholes have too much to lose with me out of your control. Far as I'm concerned, I'm already dead." He paused to lock eyes with Simons. "I just don't want Sojee to die, too."

"Before we're done with her, that's *exactly* what you'll want. There are worse things than death."

Davy sighed. Well, at least he'd ditched the bomb.

There was a knock on the door, and someone said something, but Davy didn't catch it.

Simons said, "Enter."

The door opened, and a man Davy hadn't seen before held the door for one of the maids, who carryed a silver tray with a coffee service. There was only one cup. The maid turned abruptly and set the tray down on the table, then asked Simons how he wanted his coffee.

Davy stared at her back. The voice didn't sound right. *And she doesn't know how he takes his coffee? Maybe she's new.*

Simons kept staring at Davy as he said, "Cream, one sugar."

The door opened again and Thug One pushed Sojee into the room, then jerked her to the right, away from Simons. Though her wrists were cuffed behind her, she looked all right—no overt signs of mistreatment—but her tardive dyskinesia was in full bloom, a chorus of facial twitches, tongue thrusts, and lip smacking.

Davy tried to smile reassuringly at her but it felt weak on his face.

Thug One gripped Sojee's short Afro and wrenched her head back sharply, causing her to cry out, but Davy thought it was more from surprise than pain. Davy readied himself. There was a chance Sojee would survive this. Again, he wished her hands were free.

"Your coffee, sir," said the maid, handing him the cup.

Simons finally took his gaze off of Davy and looked up at the maid. "You may g—" His eyes widened and Davy tilted his head. *Simons is surprised.*

The maid picked up the silver coffeepot and disappeared.

Then she was splashing the entire pot of coffee onto Thug One and the blonde was slapping at his clothes and falling to one side. Sojee screamed again, but this time it was cut off abruptly as Sojee, and the figure in the maid's uniform, vanished. The empty silver coffeepot fell to the floor with a clank.

Davy staggered, fell off his shins to the side. The room seemed to whirl. *I guess she* can *jump.*

He shook his head hard. *Or it's a psychotic break.*

He felt packed in cotton, distant, as if he were watching things through thick glass.

But the others were reacting as if it had happened, too. In fact, Simons reaction warmed Davy's heart.

Simons was on his feet, the chair falling back to thump against the wall and fall, sideways, to the floor. "Oh, shit! Shit, shit, shit!" He pulled a gun from inside his jacket and backed into the corner by the two-way mirror. He held the gun out, one hand bracing the other and swiveled his head back and forth, scanning the room.

Thug One climbed to his feet, holding the hot cloth of his shirt and pants away from his skin.

Simons yelled at him. "Get in the other corner and get your gun out! No, not that corner—you want to shoot me? She'll be back for her husband. For God's sake, shoot to kill!"

Millie? It was Millie. They'll shoot *her!*

He clenched his fists and staggered to his feet. The room reeled. *This ends now.*

He twinned to the beach, by the trees where the water-filled crater in the sand was still visible. He saw the ghost Simons react to the sudden flood of sunlight across the oak floor.

Simons jerked his gun up and pointed the gun right at Davy.

Fire blossomed from the muzzle and the sound was palpable. Davy gasped, expecting to die, but he heard the bullet hit a branch behind him and tumble, ripping through the underbrush with a harsh buzzing sound.

How could he miss?

Davy shifted several yards out into the ocean and splashed neck deep in water.

But he was also still in the room.

The wave of salt water rushed out of his body in every direction, a torrent flowing through the Davy-shaped hole. The circuit breakers blew as the salt water filled the electrical outlets and the high-mounted emergency light cast a garish glare over the rising water. It filled the room neck deep in two seconds despite pouring out through the open door. The heavy oak wardrobe toppled and bobbed, then wedged against the door. It flooded and sank, damming the door and raising the water higher. Davy moved to deeper water, kicking off the bottom, and the water level in the room rose too.

He saw Simons open his mouth in a scream but it was inaudible over the rushing water. Simons pointed his gun and fired and this time the bullet burned across Davy's shoulder. Then the rising water swept Simons off his feet.

Davy was tugged and pulled, but almost mildly since the water flowed through his body, not against it, completely unlike the cascade of water that swept Simons and the blonde off their feet and squirted them through the doorway into the hall.

Davy ducked his head under and heard the house groaning, shifting, as tons of water filled the third floor hallway and cascaded down the stairway. He put his head back out of the water and shuffled to deeper water, floating higher in the room until only a foot of air space remained below the ceiling. The emergency light showed from below the water for a few seconds then flickered out, shorted by the salt water. He heard something crack and the water dropped abruptly.

The Australian sunlight still poured through him, making the water around him glow and this light, refracted by the dancing surface, flickered across the ceiling. Between the bathroom and the square, the floor had opened up and water was draining through it in a whirlpool, like a toilet flushing.

Into the room where my electronic leash lives. He took a deep breath. *At least Sojee is free.*

The implant triggered. He doubled over, flinching wholly back into the room, into the unlit dark. His body, now subject to the roaring waters, spun and jerked as the water drained through the floor, but the manacle and chain tethered him, wrenching his knee and hip but keeping him from the hole.

His convulsing body settled to the floor as the last of the water receded, but he wasn't conscious and he wasn't breathing.

TWENTY-THREE

"I guess they shot me."

There were video cameras in the hall, one at each end. She saw them in the dental mirror she stuck out into the hall.

She frowned. *So who's watching? And where?* She pulled the mirror back and hoped it hadn't shown on the camera.

She felt intensely frustrated—all the work she'd done to get this far and it was a dead end. She thought about going back onto the roof but every window she could reach on this level would still open out onto the hall and its cameras.

She heard steps on the stair and then in the hall. Her first impulse was to jump away before the person got to this room— if they were coming to this room—but then she'd have to come back. She'd need to know if the room was empty or not.

And maybe you can find out something.

She positioned herself against the wall, behind the door. The person *was* coming to this room. They weren't. They were. Hope and fear collided, grappled, surged back and forth like sumo wrestlers. The doorknob rattled and turned and the door swung in.

A woman in one of the gray uniforms flipped on the light and, when she then turned to push the door shut behind her, saw Millie. She jumped, startled, and took a sharp intake of breath to scream or cry out.

Millie fired pepper foam directly into the woman's face and open mouth. The incipient scream never emerged, instead she produced a desperate choking sound. Still, the woman kicked out toward Millie and Millie jumped away, to the Aerie, just in time to avoid the foot. Teeth set, Millie jumped back to the room.

The maid was on her knees now, groping for the doorknob. Tears were streaming down her face, cutting the white foam, but she clearly couldn't see and, from the wheezing noise, could barely breathe. Millie felt sorry for her but she couldn't let her alert the household. She grabbed her by the collar and jumped to the inky darkness of the island at the bottom of the pit, then pushed her to splash ankle deep into the shallows.

"Wash it off," she said.

From behind Millie a woman's voice cried out, "Who's there?"

Millie flinched away to the Aerie.

What the hell?

She jumped to the rim of the pit, above the island, and flipped the night vision goggles down. There were three figures down there. The maid on her knees in the shallows, splashing water over her face, and two others huddled on the other side of the island. She jumped back down to the island, to the center, crouching in a small gap in the brush, screened by a mesquite bush.

She stood enough to see over the brush but couldn't really see the man's face. He sat, both hands covering his mouth and nose, but now she could make out the other woman's features clearly—it was the woman from the National Gallery, the one Becca Martingale had identified. She had a gun in her hand and kept it pointed across at the splashing sounds, though the arms shook visibly.

Davy put them here.

She felt sobs trying to surface and she ruthlessly choked them back. *Cry after he's home!*

The maid stopped splashing and the woman with the gun tried again. "Who's th–there?" The woman was shivering so badly it distorted her voice.

The maid's voice was a weak rasp. "Is that you, Miss Pope?"

"Who are you?"

"It's Agnes, Miss Pope. The upstairs maid."

"Wh–what's wrong with your va–voice?"

"They used pepper spray on me."

"Who di–did? David?"

Millie held her breath.

"No ma'am. It was someone else. They were in my room when I got there. They wore a dark mask and they had night vision goggles flipped up on their forehead. Not Mr. Rice."

He is *in that house!*

"And they pu–put you here."

"Yes, ma'am. It was a woman's voice."

"Oh. Right. I heard her. D–do you have a lighter, Agnes? We're soaked. It's been hours and we n–need a fire."

"Uh. No, ma'am. But I have my Beretta," Agnes wheezed. "One could start a fire with the muzzle blast, if the kindling were prepared."

"I d–didn't think of that."

Pope . . . that's right—Hyacinth Pope. She doesn't sound like she's thinking too clearly. Chilled—on the edge of hypothermia. Davy dropped them into the water—just like old times.

Millie studied Agnes. The maid had climbed laboriously to her feet and she pulled up her skirt. She had a holster strapped to her thigh—the skirts were full enough to conceal it—and she drew her gun. Her hair was cut long along her jaw line and got shorter in back and she was about Millie's height and weight.

Millie studied Agnes's hair again, then jumped away before they started firing their guns about, trying to make fire.

In the Aerie, she took her brown wig, the one she'd bought to make herself look like the old Millie, and trimmed, cutting quickly, doing a rough approximation of Agnes's hair. Then she jumped back to the maid's room and, door locked, changed into one of the clean uniforms, arranged the white apron, positioned the wig, and stowed the atropine autoinjectors in the apron pocket. Clenching the pepper foam in one hand she stepped out into the hall.

She walked placidly along, trying to match the tempo of the

footsteps she'd heard when Agnes had come down the hallway. It took an enormous effort not to look up at the camera as she passed into the stairwell. *They'll see what they expect to see.*

I hope.

She took the stairway all the way down to the basement, thinking about dungeons and manacles and dank, dark cells. With every step her heart pounded harder and her breath came in shallower and shallower little gasps. Instead of cells she found storerooms and pantries, a walk-in freezer, and a small apartment.

Occupied.

A man in chef's whites lounged in a recliner reading the paper. He glanced up as the door opened. "Yes, Agnes? Why didn't you knock?" His eyes widened. "You're not Agnes!"

Millie nearly flinched away, taking a step back.

The man reached for an intercom phone beside his chair.

Millie jumped across the room and kicked the side table aside, crashing the phone to the floor. The man in white struggled to rise but the recliner was locked back. Millie lifted the footrest and the chair tilted easily and inevitably back, spilling the man over on his neck in a crash. As he struggled upright, she coated his face with pepper foam.

Ten seconds later he was splashing in the shallows of the island in the pit.

Millie didn't tarry. The previous prisoners had managed their fire and Millie jumped away from its flickering light like a vampire fleeing the sun. But she returned immediately, to the rim above, to watch them investigate the new arrival—hoping they wouldn't shoot him by accident.

The voices drifted up, thin and distant.

"It's Harvey," said Agnes. "The cook."

A man's voice, nasal, as if he had a bad head cold, said, "Don't touch his face, you'll get it on you!"

Hyacinth had found Padgett's sleeping bag and clutched it around her, Indian style. She crouched before the fire and said listlessly, "Go on, Harvey. Rinse it off." She barely looked up.

Millie tried to return to Harvey's apartment but couldn't picture it well enough. After taking several deep breaths and feeling her heart slow, she finally managed the basement hallway at the foot of the mansion's stairs.

So, if Davy's not in the basement, he's probably not on the ground floor either.

She took one step past the first floor and turned back. *Better be sure.*

This floor matched the exterior, everything she imagined when she thought of mansions—high ceilings, chandeliers, antique furniture, broad expanses of space. She didn't run across anyone until she entered the smaller hallway off the main wing.

The man wore a cutaway coat, a picture out of a depression-era film or an MGM musical, and he carried himself like the king of the world as he walked out of the kitchen.

He took one look at her and said, "You've put the apron on wrong. The lower edge should be two inches above the dress hem. And we don't carry objects in that pocket. It's *decorative.*"

Millie blinked and stopped while he was still eight feet away. Her palms sweated and she shifted her grip on the pepper foam, concealed behind a fold in the skirts. She wondered if he had a gun and where he kept it.

He bowed slightly. "How may I assist you, Madam?"

"I'm looking for—" *my husband* "—Mr. Rice. What floor is he on?"

His face didn't change an iota. "I'm sorry, Madam, there's no one of that name here. May I show you the door?"

She shook her head. "I've already talked with Harvey and Agnes and Hyacinth. I know otherwise."

"Well," he said, and moved like a striking snake.

Apparently this man didn't need a gun. For Millie it felt as if something exploded in the region of her stomach and she found herself flying through the air. She suspected she was still rising when she jumped away.

She fell to the floor in the Aerie, her mouth gaping. Something was terribly wrong with her lungs. *He'll raise the alarm.* She jabbed her fist into her own diaphragm, then raised both her arms. The pepper foam clattered on the floor and she snatched at it.

The first breath wheezed back into her lungs and she jumped.

He wasn't in the hall and she thought he'd run to some other part of the house, but then she heard footsteps from the kitchen. She jumped down the hall and saw him through the kitchen door, going across toward an intercom.

She was already spraying the foam when she appeared five feet in front of him and he *still* almost got her. This time, though, she was ready. His foot passed through empty air and she appeared three feet to his other side, still spraying. His head began to look like a white puff ball. He lashed out again and she jumped to the far side of the room, willing to wait for the foam to do its work.

The butler was made of sterner stuff than Agnes and Harvey. Instead of collapsing to all fours, as they had, the man in the cutaway extended his hands and moved calmly toward the sink.

He's holding his breath. Millie didn't want to get into range of him again but she didn't want him washing off the foam. She threw the kitchen trash can into his path and he went down. She jumped to the other side, kicked him in the stomach, and it was over.

Five minutes later, when she jumped him to the island, she left him to the others to guide to the water.

She rested for a moment, bent over, in the Aerie. She was having trouble standing upright. Her midsection was screaming and her skin burned as her fingers traced the foot-shaped bruise on her stomach.

The pepper foam container felt light. She'd used a lot of it on the butler. She discarded it and got the second can. *I should've bought a case.*

Back in the mansion's kitchen, she put the trash can back in its corner and hurriedly picked up the spilled garbage. While she was doing this, she heard a door open and footsteps. Lots of footsteps. When she used the dental mirror to peer down the hall, four men, grouped around a fifth, entered through the main door to the house.

She thought she recognized one of them, from the National

Gallery in D.C., a blonde who walked closer to the man in the middle.

"Jimmy—go back to control and stand by. I'll probably want that woman, Johnson. If I do, bring her and don't let her head-butt you like she did Planck."

Sojee? For a brief second she considered following him but she was more worried about Davy. She felt guilty about it, but Sojee probably didn't have a device surgically implanted in her chest. *I hope.*

"Yes, Mr. Simons." The blonde turned back to the door and left.

The man himself.

Simons pointed at one of the remaining men. "Desmond, find Abney and ask him to send me up some coffee, then wait down here with Trotsky. Graham—you're with me."

"Yessir." Simons and Graham moved down the hall. Millie heard an elevator door.

Trotsky took out a pack of cigarettes and said, "I'll be on the porch."

Desmond, the man detailed to find Abney, said, "Don't let him catch you off station."

Trotsky said, "Worry about your own butt. Go on, fetch the coffee." He spun on his heel and went back out the front door.

Desmond came up the hallway toward the kitchen.

Millie suspected that Abney was the butler who was so handy with his feet. She pursed her lips. Desmond wouldn't find Abney.

Not without assistance.

She helped Desmond find Abney but doubted very much that Abney would be able to bring the coffee.

Afterwards, as she was straightening her apron (and putting it two inches above the hem of her dress), she froze.

But I could.

The industrial-sized coffeemaker was a Bunn with a constant reserve of preheated water. A gleaming silver service sat on the counter beneath the china cabinet. It took only minutes to fill the silver coffee urn and arrange the creamer, sugar bowl, spoons, and cups on the heavy silver tray.

Abney probably knows what he takes in his coffee. Tough.

The indicator above its door showed that the elevator was parked on the third floor. *So that's where they went. That's where he is.*

There was a small framed mirror in the elevator and Millie noted her wig was crooked. She wedged the tray against the wood paneling and, one-handed, straightened the wig and removed a smudge from her jaw. The door opened on the third floor and she caught the corner of the tray on the frame as she exited, nearly spilling the coffeepot. It rocked precariously on its heavy silver feet, then settled back.

Calmly, calmly.

The elevator whined to life, heading back down. Graham, the man detailed to follow Simons upstairs, was leaning against a wall down the hallway to the right. As he saw her, he stood and knocked on the door next to him. His voice, a surprising tenor in such a large man, said, "The coffee, sir."

Millie expected him to look at her, to know she wasn't on the staff, but he'd studied her face without reaction. *Maybe he isn't familiar with the staff here? Maybe Simons brought him from New York?*

At some command from inside Graham opened the door and held it for Millie. She kept her eyes down and walked into the room. He closed it behind her.

The smells hit her, feces and vomit, at the same time she saw Davy, seated on his knees, and the chain running from a floor-mounted steel ring to his ankle. He looked horribly thin to her eyes.

Can't snatch him and go.

She turned. Simons was sitting by himself, to the left of the door. She put the tray down on the small table near him and faced the wall, away from Davy. She poured coffee into a cup.

"Cream or sugar, sir?" It was a horrible strain to make her voice emotionally neutral.

Simons didn't even look at her. "Cream, one sugar."

The door opened again and Sojee was pushed into the room,

wearing a dark green jumpsuit and handcuffs. The blonde followed her and pushed her, none too gently, to the right, away from Simons. There was no mistaking Sojee—her lips were smacking and her cheeks kept twitching.

Millie's first impulse was to spill the coffee cup onto Simons's lap, but just then the blonde grabbed Sojee's hair from behind and wrenched her head back. Sojee cried out.

"Your coffee, sir." She handed Simons the cup and saucer.

He took it and finally looked at her. "You may g—." He froze.

Took you long enough.

She took the handle of the heavy silver coffeepot in one hand, flipped open its hinged lid, and jumped ten feet to the side, her arm swinging.

The blonde screamed as the scalding coffee poured onto his side and back. He fell away, clawing at his clothes. Sojee yelped when Millie put her arms around her, but then they were in the Aerie and she stumbled away when Millie released her.

"It's okay, Sojee. It's okay!"

Sojee's eyes were wide open and she was trembling.

"It's me—Millie!"

Millie still had Padgett's handcuffs and their key in the Aerie. She found the key and held it up. "Here, let me get you out of those cuffs."

Sojee looked confused and disoriented. She was muttering to herself, disjointed snatches of meaning. ". . . could be a demon. Could be the Blue Lady. No, I don't want to do that. Leave off . . ." She started when Millie took hold of her wrist.

"Easy. It's okay." She unlocked one of the cuffs, then pressed the key into Sojee's hand. "It's okay. I've got to go get Davy, all right? I'll be back soon. Just rest, right? No one can get you here."

Sojee rubbed the freed wrist. "Millie?"

Millie took Sojee's hand and pressed it against her face. "Yes. Millie. I've got to go get Davy, all right?"

Some of the tension went out of Sojee's posture. "It *is* you!"

"Yes. Look, don't go outside. There's a cliff and you could fall, okay? I'll come back for you."

"Uh, I guess."

Millie took a deep breath. She wanted to go straight to Davy but those men probably had their guns out by now. *I'll risk the hallway.*

The water struck her entire lower body from the chest down but she felt it most where the butler had kicked her. It roared in her ears and she lost her footing and fell, dropping under the surface. It stung her eyes and stung her nostrils. *Sea water? Warm sea water? On the third floor?* When she struggled upright, the wig had shifted around, hanging sodden across her face. She spat hair out of her mouth, then swept the wig from her head with her hand, letting it go in the current. Her hands were empty—she'd lost the pepper foam.

She grabbed a doorframe as she swept past it and her shoulder screamed, but she held on and struggled to her feet. The noise had increased. Still holding on carefully, she looked behind her. One emergency light set high in the stairway shed a harsh glare on the water and she saw the water drop abruptly away in a cascade.

The stairway had become a waterfall. Above the landing, several feet below her, she saw Lawrence Simons clinging to the banister with both arms. He still gripped his gun tightly in one hand. His eyes were wide and his beautiful suit was ruined.

She couldn't blame him for holding on so desperately. Just below him the landing window had torn out, frame and all, and the bulk of the water shot out onto the grounds, two-and-a-half stories below. As Millie watched, the hole was widening, as bricks were plucked out singly and in groups by the raging torrent.

She wondered what had become of the blonde and the guard outside the door.

Simons gun flared and suddenly she was on her back in the water, blinking, stunned. The current took her.

It was like a waterpark ride. She kept her feet before her and her face above the water. As she swept down the stair she saw Simons swing his gun toward her, and she lashed out with both feet. Her left heel crashed into Simons's shoulder; his grip broke and he was in the current flailing his arms and then they were both shooting out through the wall and into the bright spotlights, which, perversely, still shone on the exterior of the mansion.

Simons screamed and the sudden drop got to her in a way the current hadn't. She flinched away to the Aerie.

Gallons of water cascaded to the stone floor around her.

Sojee, still standing where she'd left her, jumped back from the splashing water. "Who the hell are you?" she asked.

Millie, her heart pounding, wiped water from her face. "Huh? It's me, Millie."

"Did they scalp you?"

"Oh. It was a wig."

"And the blood?" Sojee gestured toward the left side of Millie's head.

Millie put her hand to her face and stared blankly when her fingers and palm came away covered in red. "Oh. I guess they shot me."

She felt for it and found a furrow above her temple, three inches long. When she touched it the nerves screamed to life and she nearly fainted.

Sojee snatched up the dish towel hanging from the refrigerator handle and folded it into a pad. She held it against the side of Millie's head and pressed.

"Ow!"

"Hold still!"

Millie lifted her own hand. "I'll hold it. Get me something to tie it on. I still have to get Davy."

"Won't they shoot you?"

"No. Not anymore." Millie pointed to the pink button-down shirt lying draped over a chair. "Rip that."

Sojee tore it lengthwise into three pieces, then helped her use the longest piece, tail to collar, to secure the dishtowel over the wound.

Millie caught a glimpse of herself reflected in the window. *Like the fife player in that painting,* "Spirit of '76." "Thanks!" She jumped.

She jumped back to the hallway, braced for the water, but it had dropped substantially and she staggered forward, in a knee-high current. By the time she'd splashed down the hall to Davy's door, it was swirling about her ankles. The room itself was a dark cavern and some furniture had come to rest across the lower half of the doorway. Only the emergency light at the end of the hall provided any light and it didn't reach within.

She jumped back to the Aerie and picked up the night vision goggles, started to lift them to her head, then realized the headset would rest on her head wound. She looked around wildly.

Sojee was staring at her, backed up against the wall, her lips smacking, her eyes blinking.

Millie tried to smile. "Need a light."

Sojee pointed at the old electric lantern Davy kept for backup or when they wanted to turn off the generator.

Millie's smile became genuine. She jumped across the room. "Great!" She took it, and left.

When she climbed over the wardrobe lying across the door she found Davy on his side stretched lengthwise between the chain and a five-foot gap in the floor. His face lay in a puddle of water and he wasn't breathing, though Millie swore she saw his hand twitch.

She groped for the atropine. Two of the autoinjectors were gone, washed out of the apron pocket in the flood, but two remained. She yanked one out of its holder, arming it, then jammed the opposite end into the outside of Davy's thigh. The pop as it activated was quite loud, startling her. The internal coil spring plunged the needle through pajamas, skin, and muscle. She waited, as the instructions said, counting, "One elephant, two elephant, three elephant," giving the spring time to drive the dose into his body. She pulled it straight out, then threw it aside.

Davy still wasn't breathing. She tried for a pulse and wasn't sure if she could feel one or not. She wanted to take him to the trauma center but the manacle still circled his ankle—the chain still stretched to the floor bolt. The last of the water drained through the gap in the floor and she heard a motion in the corner of the room. She jerked the lantern around.

A foot-long flying fish wiggled and flopped across the wet floor. She wondered if she was hallucinating.

Gotta get him breathing, she thought, and checked Davy's mouth for obstructions and to see if he'd swallowed his tongue. As her fingers swept his mouth, he began breathing again, ragged, irregular breaths. He was still unconscious. She presumed his heart was beating.

Tears started and she blinked them away.

No time.

She jumped to west Texas, to the rim of the pit. The desert air, bone-dry, turned her soaking wet maid's uniform into an evaporative cooler, sucking heat from her body. She shook herself, like a cat, heard water drops hit the rock around her, and, after a few seconds, splash the water below.

She was regretting that she'd given Padgett's guns to Becca but there were lots of weapons down *there*.

Her prisoners had found the old fire pit and the piñon logs she'd brought for Padgett. Their fire was now a staunch blaze before which Agnes, the butler, the chef, and the man with the injured nose couched and warmed their hands. Hyacinth sat with her back to the fire, her gun in her hand, swiveling her head from side to side, staring out at her own shadow cast across the water and onto the limestone wall across the water.

Millie, more desperate than calculating, just snatched the weapon from Hyacinth's hand, grabbing it from the side as she appeared and jumping away immediately, back to the rim. She nearly dropped it then, but managed to shift it around until she held it by the grip.

And all without shooting myself.

Millie *hated* guns.

Down in the pit a string of curses floated up, but she didn't wait to make sense of them. In Davy's room she crouched low, held the gun with both hands, and aimed it at the chain just short of the floor-mounted anchor loop. She squeezed the trigger.

She ended up on her back, her ears ringing. A line of bullet holes crossed the floor and climbed halfway up the wall. It was, she realized belatedly, set on full auto. She didn't know guns this size could *be* full auto.

A chain link had parted, bent and distorted. She put the weapon down on the floor and slid it away. It came to rest under the toppled dresser, in the wet shadows.

Davy's breathing was worse, ragged, stopping for seconds, then resuming with a catch.

She put her hands under his shoulders, pictured the George Washington University Medical Center's Trauma Center, and jumped.

TWENTY-FOUR

"Dating tip."

There was a mask over his mouth and nose, and his lungs were rising without effort, inflated like a party balloon. The pressure stopped and he could feel the air rushing back out. Then the positive airflow began again. Whatever he was lying on felt like it was spinning slowly and his scalp tingled. His mouth felt like a desert, desiccated and granular, as if all the water had been baked out of it.

Several people were talking at once and someone shouted over the babble, "Where are those flack vests?"

"Coming!" a distant voice called.

He felt someone holding his hand and, with great effort, opened his eyes. He immediately closed them again. The light was blinding and his eyes weren't working right. Everything that wasn't a glaring light source was an over-bright, blurred mass of white, blue, and skin tones.

Something stabbed into the skin of his upper chest, burning, and he flinched away from the pain and the light into soothing darkness.

He was "in the box" sprawled across the floor but he didn't feel right. The room was dark and the floor was wet and cold. He smelled salt water—low tide—and remembered something about the ocean and Simons and bombs. The oxygen mask was gone and it took forever to take a breath. There was a light shining on the floor beside him but it was nowhere as painful as the lights in that previous room. He had a stabbing pain on the inside of his right elbow.

Then someone was crouching over him. He wanted to push them away but his body wasn't working right. All he managed was a weak flop with one arm.

"Davy. Oh, Christ! You can't do that. We'll *never* get the damn thing out if you jump away in the middle of the operation."

He knew that voice. He tried to speak but it took several tries. "M—Millie?"

"Yes, heart. I'm jumping you back to the trauma center." She knelt and put her hands under his shoulders. "They were getting ready to pull the vagus stimulator when you jumped away."

"Stop!" His voice was a rasp, half groan, half gasp.

Millie stopped lifting. "Did I hurt you?"

"It's wired . . . it's booby-trapped. The implant."

"Yes. We know. We've got the pieces from the other one and multiple x-rays. There seems to be a light sensor and we learned the hard way that if you cut the leads it will blow up."

The other one?

He opened his mouth again and she said, "I love you and I want to hear everything you have to tell me, but for the moment, just *shut up and trust me*! Jumping."

They were back in that bright room on the floor and his eyes squeezed shut against the brightness.

There was a collective gasp and a sharp voice said, "Will he stay *put*?"

Millie took Davy's hand. "If you keep him conscious and rational. Talk to him. Tell him what you're doing so it doesn't surprise him. He woke up just as you stuck him with that needle. What do you expect?"

The man's voice sounded both exasperated and amused— almost stunned. "We don't get that many people who can do that. I got it, though. Let's get him up on the table, people!"

Through his eyelids the light dimmed slightly as several people bent over him.

"And . . . lift!"

The table felt hard and cold. The mask went back over his face and the doctor said, "I'm Doctor Sullivan, Davy. We're bagging you to help you breathe. We've been continuing the atropine your wife administered to counteract the effects of the vagal stimulator. Do you understand what I just said?"

Davy lifted a hand weakly, thumb extended up.

"Good. We're going to make an incision to pull the implant itself. It's going to be pretty long—we have to get enough play in the electrode leads. If I'm talking too fast hold up your hand, flat, like you're saying 'halt.' "

Davy extended his thumb again.

"Great. Fortunately, the thing is only subcutaneous—we won't have to cut through any muscle. You'll end up with a nice scar but hopefully nothing worse. Where's that pipe?"

A woman's voice said, "I have it, with the sandbags."

"All right. I was numbing the skin over the implant but you jumped away before I injected more than a fraction of the lidocaine. I'm going to do it again but if I got any in the first time, you probably won't feel this. *Don't* bug out on me again, all right?"

Davy squeezed Millie's hand and she squeezed back, saying, "I've got your back, Davy. I'm not losing you again."

Davy held up his forefinger and thumb in a circle.

"Right," said Doctor Sullivan. "First shot."

Davy did feel it but he stayed, squeezing Millie's hand until the lidocaine stopped burning.

"There. Okay. We'll wait a minute for it to numb. You all right?"

Davy tried to speak. The mask was lifted. "Mouth. Dry."

"Ah. That's the atropine. Bet the light hurts your eyes, too. They call that side effect 'photophobia.' "

Davy nodded as the oxygen mask lowered again.

"We can't give you something to drink just yet. You could choke. Give me fifteen minutes and it'll all be over." ·

Someone else muttered quietly, "One way or the other."

Sullivan cleared his throat, then spoke again. "We'll put your IV drip back in. It's just saline for drug transport. You ripped it out when you jumped away but it looks like the needle came out the way it went in, luckily." Aside he said, "The back of the hand. *That* lovely vein."

There was a stab in the back of his hand and he almost jerked it away, but Millie was holding the wrist down. "Easy, Davy. Let's get this over with," she said.

Davy's nausea seemed to be increasing and he coughed, then a female voice said, "Heart rate dropping again."

"One milligram atropine, IV. No, half that. We don't want him so disoriented he teleports again."

Someone muttered, "I wonder what we'll get in here next. Little green men?"

The nausea dropped back again and the female voice said, "Pulse is back up."

"Okay. Do you feel this?"

Feel what? Davy shook his head. The table felt like it was bucking now, as well as spinning.

"Good. We're cutting. Sponge that. Good. There it is. Clamp that little bleeder. Good. Okay—let's avoid nicking the leads. Who's got the lightproof bag?"

"Here," said a pleasant alto.

"Okay. I'm going to extend the incision two centimeters on either side then we're going to turn off the lights. Did we fix the emergency lights so they won't come on?"

A nasal tenor said, "Yeah. I disconnected the battery—both terminals."

"So, Erin, show me where you're going to hold the bag open."

The alto said, "I thought *here*. I'll rest my wrist on his collar-bone for reference—you'll be able to feel my fingertips on the rim of the mouth. I'll cinch it up at your command."

"Okay. Ready?"

"Ready, Sully."

"How about you, Davy? It's really important you stay with us on this. You teleport away while we're holding onto this device and it could rip out your vagus nerve. Trust me, you don't want that."

Davy gave him a thumbs up.

"Right. *Lights.*"

The blessed darkness was a relief, holding Davy like the womb. He heard a sound like someone pulling their shoe out of the mud.

"There. In the bag. Cinch it. Double check. We're sure it's inside?"

"I confirm," said the alto.

"Lights on."

Even through his eyelids, the light was like a blow.

"Okay. Jerry, put in a drain and close it. Staples."

"Right—speed."

There was pressure and tugging and the sound of the surgical stapler was an odd little "chunka, chunka, chunka." He tried to look but the light still hurt too much and everything was blurred. He squeezed his eyelids together.

"Okay. Throw a temporary dressing over that and let's have the flack vests."

For who? He made an agitated sock puppet talking motion with his free hand.

Millie said, "*Talk* to him, Doctor. Tell him what's going on!"

"Oh. Right. Sorry. Feel that, Davy?" They placed something heavy across Davy's lower chest. "We're draping body armor over you. This one's over your stomach and groin. This one's going over your upper chest and face."

Something cast a shadow over Davy's face lessening the palpable beat of light against his eyelids. He had a sense of something tented over his face, a heaviness across his shoulders.

"The electrode leads from the implant are sticking up between the two Kevlar vests and we've got the device in a lightproof bag." The voice lessened in volume. "Pipe, please." The volume increased again as the doctor turned back toward Davy. "I've got a nice piece of half-inch steel pipe here, six inches in diameter, two feet long. We're putting the implant inside it then . . ." Davy heard the sound of duct tape being ripped off a roll. "We're taping a plywood board over the bottom of the pipe—the leads are pinched between the pipe and the board. Sand, please. Okay, Davy, while I'm holding the implant through the open end of the pipe, we're filling the pipe up with sand."

The weight over Davy's chest increased and he could hear the sand whispering against the pipe. He coughed.

"Support that! It's putting too much weight on his chest."

The weight lessened.

"Good. There, the implant's buried in the sand. Now we're putting another board over the top of the pipe." The duct tape sound repeated. "And we're wrapping the pipe in more body armor—just a precaution." More duct tape. "The last device had two blasting caps in it. If so, the sand alone will suffice. The device is mostly battery, so it can't have much of an explosive."

Davy thought there was an underlying quaver in the doc's voice. *What last device?*

"Rig an instrument stand to support the pipe."

There was a clatter and the sound of rolling wheels across the floor.

"Oh—kay. Who's got the wire cutters? Thank you. Right, then. Everybody out."

There was the sound of footsteps. Millie squeezed Davy's hand but didn't let go.

"You, too, Mrs. Rice."

"You already tried that, remember? If security couldn't keep me out, what makes you think you can?"

Davy let go of her hand and pushed it away. Then he pushed the Kevlar vest aside and the oxygen mask off his mouth. The anesthesiologist lifted it up. "Back up at *least*, Millie. You can't watch my back if you get . . . hurt." The anesthesiologist started to put the mask back over his face and Davy pushed it away again, "You, too. I can breathe on my own for this."

Millie leaned over and kissed his forehead. It felt odd and he realized she was wearing a surgical mask. "Okay," she said. "I'll back up to the wall."

"Whatever!" said the doctor. "But do it!"

The alto voice said, "Pulse dropping again. You want to hit him with some more atropine?"

"No. Get behind me!" Feet shuffled across the floor. "Stay with me, Davy. I'm cutting the wires—now!"

There was a muffled "THUD" and sand stung the back of Davy's hand, then drifted across his face. He felt it then, like being back in the box, the cessation of the nausea, a background feeling so faint he noticed it only in its absence. He tried to open his eyes but the light still hurt.

"Je—sus," said a voice. "Maintenance is gonna freak about all the sand."

Footsteps approached in a rush. "Pulse rising. Respiration strengthening. Wow—it's like you threw a switch. See his color improve?"

Millie took up his hand again. When she spoke he could tell she was crying.

"Shhhhhh. It's okay," he said.

"It is *now*."

They put the wire back under his skin, sterilizing it as best they could. "I grounded each lead to the other. Even if you got a transient because you walked through an electromagnetic field, it shouldn't shock the nerve. But I don't want to go near the vagus without a neurosurgeon and I wouldn't be surprised if a neuro would say just leave it. Less risk."

They hooked the drain tube up to something that looked like a clear plastic cylinder with accordion-folded sides. They opened a cap in the end and compressed it vertically to squeeze the air out, then sealed it again. As the accordion folds tried to expand, they pulled a vacuum on the drain, sucking Davy's stapled skin down over the void left by the implant. Clear reddish liquid started up the tube. It felt odd now, under the numb skin, but he suspected it would hurt later.

"We've got vacuum bottles and pumps, but this one you can take to the bathroom."

Davy approved. He'd had it with being attached to *things*.

They rolled him down to a recovery room and turned the lights off. They gave him water—lots of lovely ice water with a straw—and the desert in his mouth was slowly greening.

In the dim light he tried his eyes again and fared better. Things were fuzzy, but not impossible. The new Millie, the one with the short hair bleached blond and the gauze dressing on the side of her head, asked, "Is there an antidote for the atropine? Something to clear it out?"

Doctor Sullivan said, "For extreme atropine intoxication—yes. But that would mean he was in a coma or extreme delirium, perhaps with tachycardic arrhythmia. But physostigmine is a *nasty* drug. The atropine metabolizes quickly on its own. He'll be symptom-free by the time we've moved him to a regular bed—two or three hours, tops."

Davy locked eyes with Millie. She nodded and said, "Yes, I know."

The doctor blinked. "Know what?"

That there's no way we're staying here a minute longer than necessary. To the doctor, Davy just smiled and shook his head.

"You guys don't read minds as well, do you? I mean, then you'd know why I came back just now?"

Millie laughed at the man's expression. "No, Doctor. Just married ten years, you know? The one talent is more than enough to deal with."

Sullivan's look of mild alarm faded. "I came in here to tell you that some men from the National Security Agency want to talk to you. I've put them off. I thought for a moment that they were going to force their way back here anyway, but the FBI showed up and the two groups started arguing."

Davy saw Millie's eyes narrow and the corners of her mouth turn down. Then she smiled. "Thanks, Doctor Sullivan. For everything. Tell accounting I'll drop payment by soon."

Realization dawned on the doctor immediately. "Ah. Well, you're welcome. It's been . . . surreal. Watch the drain—it could get infected easily. You need to have it pulled in, oh, two days, after the reservoir stops collecting fluid. We can do it, but so could any clinic."

Davy held out his hand and shook Doctor Sullivan's. "Don't let the Feds push you around."

"Do you want me to stall them?"

Davy shook his head. "Doesn't matter. We're going *now*."

He didn't bother getting up. One moment he was on the hospital bed, the next he was in his own bed in the Aerie. It was cool and dark and comfortable. But though he lay back against the pillow, his body tensed and anxiety clawed at him.

Then Millie appeared, over by the counter, and the tension dropped away from him like water flowing off a hillside. *Like seawater draining from a room.*

When Davy awoke, light was filtering in through the windows. His chest hurt and his eyes didn't. There was a creaking sound that he realized he'd been aware of for some time, a constant through the slow journey to consciousness. Millie was sitting beside the bed, in the rocker. He looked around.

"Where's Sojee?"

"I put her in a hotel in Baltimore under a fictional name and left her five thousand dollars. She's going to buy some clothes and rest and when she's ready, she'll go see her sister in the 'burbs. It was her choice."

Davy licked his parched lips. "You think they'll go after her?"

She handed him a glass of water. "I don't know. I said I'd check on her daily. I offered to let her stay here, but she's had enough with being under the control of others."

Davy winced. "I know that one. Tell me about *that*." He pointed at the gauze pad on the side of Millie's head.

She blushed. "It was Simons."

Davy raised his eyebrows.

"He, er, shot at me."

Davy took a deep breath and held it.

Something about his expression alarmed Millie. She said quickly, "It's just a graze. I kicked him right after that and he let go of the banister and fell two stories, washed through the side of the house in that weird flood of seawater. What *was* that, by the way?"

Davy exhaled. "He shot you. During the flood. Perhaps you should begin at the beginning."

Millie tilted her head to one side. "Perhaps we *both* should."

Catching up, even in summary, took them through breakfast and most of the way until lunch.

He told her everything up to and including Nigeria. He hesitated then and his mouth twisted. Then, in a rush, he told her about Hyacinth, about the moment after Nigeria, when he'd almost succumbed and why he hadn't.

Millie stared over his head for a moment, gaze focused a million miles away.

"I'm sorry!" he blurted. "It was just—."

She put her hand over his mouth. "Shhh. I'm not angry at *you*. Under those circumstances—well, I won't say it wouldn't hurt, but I wouldn't have blamed you."

He looked away, blinking water from his eyes.

She hugged him, pulling his head into her shoulder. Then, she told him about her dealings in D.C. and in Stillwater with the NSA and Padgett.

Davy said, "The bastards!"

And later. "So, we've got prisoners?"

"Yes," said Millie. "They were all asleep, this morning, when I dropped off a bunch of happy meals. Most of them still have weapons, but I took Hyacinth's to shoot the chain off your shackle. It's a wonder I didn't shoot myself. It was set to full auto."

"*That* gun. Yeah." Davy blinked. "Do you still have it?"

"I left it in the mansion. It's under the dresser."

He pursed his lips. "Shit. It's probably the weapon that killed Brian Cox."

Millie vanished.

Davy swore and gathered the tubing and suction reservoir to him, but she appeared again, holding the gun, before he jumped. "Don't *do* that!"

She put the gun carefully on the top of the refrigerator. "It's okay. They cleared out last night. When I went back after Simons, after we got home, they were all gone."

"You didn't tell me you'd gone back after Simons!"

"We hadn't got that far. We'd just gotten to the prisoners, remember?" She looked at the coiled tubing and the reservoir in his hand. "Were you going to come after me *naked*?"

He lay back, his heart pounding. "I'm not sure I can take being married to a teleport."

She lowered her head and looked at him over her glasses. "So now you know what it's like."

"Oh, shut up and get over here."

Then, "Glad to see you're not blond *everywhere*."

"You've lost too much weight."

"You, too. Is it true? Do blondes have more fun?"

"Shut up," she explained.

When they dressed, two hours later, they both felt better than they had in a very long time.

Davy squirmed on the ledge. He had wound the tubing behind him and tucked the suction reservoir into the inner pocket of his black leather jacket but movement still tugged at the spot where it exited his skin. Below them, in the pit, the fire had died to coals and most of the prisoners were sleeping. Thug Two—Planck, was it?—was trying to get mesquite branches off the brush without impaling himself on the thorns.

Davy whispered, "I've got his right side."

"Just like we practiced," said Millie.

"Three, two, one—"

They each took one of Thug Two's arms and jumped again, into blinding floodlights. Millie and Davy simply stepped away as the man recoiled away from the light and their grasp.

The FBI agents waiting were not so easy to avoid. They threw him against the wall and cuffed his hands behind his back. They were wearing latex gloves and had evidence bags standing by for the gun they removed from his belt holster.

"One down, four to go," Becca said.

Davy rubbed his eyes. "Don't forget Simons."

Becca said, "We won't. He's back in his New York townhouse. He flew by private jet from the Vineyard. We lost him for a while but it was because he popped into Mt. Sinai. Seems he's got a broken arm."

Millie and Davy looked at each other, then both smiled.

Davy said, "You da man."

"Why don't you pick him up?" asked Millie.

"I don't dare move on him until we've got evidence." Millie started to speak, but Becca said, "I know, Davy will testify, but

Simons is political dynamite. He makes one phone call and the White House Chief of Staff calls the Attorney General and the Director of the FBI and they come down on me like a ton of bricks. The evidence has to be hard, irrefutable, and the right people have to be briefed before we take him into custody."

Becca jerked her thumb toward the prisoner, now on his feet and still being frisked. Peripheral bleeding from his broken nose had blacked both eyes and now, in the second day, the discoloring looked like sunset over Newark. "One of your birdies might sing."

Davy said, "But you better pull their implants first."

"There's a legal issue. If they won't consent to the surgery . . ."

Millie said, "But you could pull it to save their lives, right? If the damn things were triggered and your prisoners were unable to refuse consent?"

Becca nodded.

"In that case, I wouldn't ask them a single question until you have a prepped medical staff standing by," Millie said. "Otherwise, they're all going to be dead."

They saved Hyacinth for last. When they'd taken the chef, he'd yelled, waking Hyacinth to find all four of her companions gone. Now she paced back and forth across the island, nervous as a cat. Davy remained still and watched from the shadows, well away from the dying flames of the fire.

A light appeared on the other side of the island, a battered electric lantern perched on a rock. Millie sat there on the green plastic chair, hands held down in the glow of the light, polishing the surfaces of Hyacinth's Glock eighteen with a soft cotton cloth.

Hyacinth slowly stood, straightening from a crouch, but her shoulders remained rounded and she was still hunched over. She shuffled toward the lantern like someone who is pulled in two directions. Hyacinth was ten feet short of the light when Millie spoke.

"I'm afraid I dropped it in salt water." Millie held up the gun and peered at it. "It's rusting a bit." She rubbed at a spot on the trigger guard with the rag again.

Hyacinth spoke slowly, reluctantly. "What did you do . . . with the others?"

Millie looked up from the gun. She had the coldest expression in her eyes, one that didn't go at all with the little smile on her lips. "They have been . . . dealt with."

Davy blinked. He had no idea his wife could be such a hardass. He knew she was faking, that is, he *thought* she was faking. Well, he *hoped* she was faking.

Hyacinth looked less sure of herself than any time Davy had seen her. "Dealt with how?"

Millie just smiled and kept polishing at the gun.

Hyacinth turned away. "I won't talk, you know. I can't."

Millie blinked. "Who wants you to? Though I suppose I could do a spot of interrogation—just recreational. Eventually your implant will kick in, I'm sure, just like poor Padgett. Poetic justice, really."

Hyacinth turned back again. "So, it's revenge, is it?"

Millie, holding the grip of the Glock with the cloth, sighted down the barrel toward the lamp. She worked the slide and one cartridge flew through the air. "Oh. There was a round in the chamber already." She picked it up and threw it out into the darkness. A wet ker-plunk reverberated from stone wall to stone wall.

Davy knew that had been the only round in the gun. He'd worked with Millie over and over until she could work the slide naturally, with authority. Davy hated guns as much as Millie but he'd handled more of the damn things over the years.

Hyacinth backed up a pace.

Davy didn't blame her. He would've jumped away himself, especially since Millie was untrained in their use.

"I had Padgett on this island for seventy-two hours. *He* died in the ER when his implant detonated." Millie extended the gun toward the ground between Hyacinth and herself, and sighted down the barrel. "Bad enough that you kidnap Davy, that you put that device in his chest, that you tortured and beat him."

Hyacinth clenched her teeth together. Then, with an effort, she said, "Now I get it. *You're jealous!*"

Millie laughed. "Of Miss Damaged Goods? He saw right through you from the beginning. Dating tip: When trying to establish a rapport with someone, don't kill their friends in front of them." She sneered. "You might've worn him down, eventually—Davy's only human—but it would've been just because he was tired. It would've been like throwing a bone to a yapping dog to get it to *shut up*."

Hyacinth's eyes narrowed and when she spoke Davy could tell the fear was gone, washed away by anger. "Oh, really? Didn't seem like that when his hands were all over me!"

Millie smiled. "Yes. Right before he found your scars, yes? Are you going to tell me he found that a turn-on?"

Hyacinth looked away.

"Exactly," Millie said. She teleported the fifteen feet between them and stuck the gun right in Hyacinth's face.

Hyacinth reacted as Davy had said she would, an initial flinch, then going for the disarm. She swept the barrel offline and grabbed Millie's wrist, going for the arm bar but Millie jumped away before her elbow locked, leaving the gun in Hyacinth's hands.

Hyacinth swiveled about, both hands holding the gun extended, always pointing it in the direction she faced.

But unable to see anything.

The dim light from the lantern only served to make the rest of the island darker, an almost palpable blackness surrounding the faint puddle of light by the dying coals of the fire.

Davy jumped back to the Aerie where Millie was waiting, pulling and twisting at the polishing cloth. "What a piece of work!"

"She's all of that," Davy said. "You okay?"

Millie shuddered. "Couldn't we interrogate her *just a little*?"

Davy felt a wave of nausea at the thought. "I'd sooner kill her."

Millie's eyes widened. "But you don't—"

"Of course not," he said. "I could've killed her a hundred

times over. If I didn't do it then, I won't now. Did you leave any prints on the gun?"

"No. I was holding it with the cloth. She didn't really notice. The only prints on it now are hers."

"Right, then." He pulled on a pair of latex gloves and threaded his fingers together to push the plastic all the way down over his fingers. "Shall we?"

Millie took a deep breath and threw the cloth down on the counter. "Sooner done, sooner over."

Back in the pit, Davy took the gun from Hyacinth, a twisting motion that took the barrel back in toward her stomach and bent the wrist, forcing her fingers open. When Hyacinth lashed out with her foot, he was gone, but Millie wasn't. She reached out from behind Hyacinth and jerked down on the woman's shoulders. Hyacinth hit the ground hard.

Davy took the chair. Millie stood slightly behind him, her hand resting on his right shoulder.

Hyacinth rolled to her feet, her teeth bared.

Davy worked the slide on the Glock. A brass gleam flickered against the darkness.

Millie jerked, squeezing Davy's shoulder. "I thought we—"

"We did. Apparently she had a spare magazine." He ejected the clip, then worked the slide once more. Another brass and lead cylinder tumbled through the air, to thud to the ground. Davy took a large plastic bag from his back pocket and put the gun, the clip, and the two cartridges from the ground into it.

Without taking his eyes off of Hyacinth he handed the bagged gun to Millie. He sensed, rather than saw her departure, an absence made manifest, an area of warmth replaced by the chill desert air.

Hyacinth twitched.

Davy peeled the gloves from his hands and dropped them to the ground. Hyacinth inhaled sharply and Davy smiled.

"Right—your prints only, which the FBI will pull off. They'll get a ballistic sample and compare it to the bullets that killed Brian Cox. You might want to consider a plea bargain. No death penalty, perhaps, if you turn in Simons."

She wrinkled her lips. "You know that's impossible! And even if I did, you'll never be able to touch him."

Davy began unbuttoning his shirt.

Hyacinth's brows came together. "You're coming on to me *now*?"

He didn't say anything. Instead, he pulled the shirt over to show the dressing and the suction tube.

Hyacinth's eyes opened wide. She hardly flinched when Millie reappeared.

Millie looked from Davy's open shirt to Hyacinth. "Ah, told her, did you?"

"Why aren't you dead?" Hyacinth said.

"I am getting really tired of that question," Davy said, looking up at Millie. "Never underestimate the power of a determined woman."

Hyacinth raised her hand to her left collarbone. "How did you get it out?"

Millie, deadpan, said, "Love will find a way." She looked down at Davy. "Ready?"

"Ready."

The waiting FBI agents handcuffed and frisked a subdued, ashen-faced Hyacinth. Becca began the litany, "You are under arrest for the murder of Brian Cox and the kidnappings of David Rice and Sojourner Johnson. You have the right to remain silent—watch it!" Becca took a quick step back.

Hyacinth doubled over and began vomiting.

Davy flinched away, unable to watch. He waited, his forehead against the cool stone of the Aerie, and took deep measured breaths. Millie finally came and he looked at her, expectantly.

"They started her on atropine and called Sullivan. He'll have his team ready by the time the ambulance arrives." She sat down suddenly, like a puppet whose strings had been cut. "You were right. Kinder to kill her." After a moment, she added, "Becca said, 'I didn't mean it this way when I wanted one of them to spill their guts.'"

TWENTY-FIVE

"It's time."

"None of them will talk?"

Becca's voice on the phone sounded tired. "None of them who are still alive."

Millie winced.

She was at a pay phone in a D.C. Metro station. She kept her eyes on the platform and the approaches. Cell phones were killing the pay phone business. It was getting harder and harder to find a working pay phone, but the subways were good bets—any place where it was hard to use a cell phone because of transmission interference.

"I thought all the surgeries were successful!"

"Yes. Sullivan had it down to a science by the time he pulled the last implant. But the only one who was willing to plea bargain was the chef."

"And?"

"Somebody poisoned him."

"In custody?"

"Yeah, in maximum security. A guard's missing."

"The one who took him his meal?"

"Yes."

Millie was silent for a moment, watching two suits come down the escalator. They turned away from her, though, and one began reading a magazine he'd been carrying under his arm. "He wouldn't be dead if I didn't take him from that house."

"And Davy might be dead now. *You* didn't poison him."

"Do the others know? Hyacinth, the rest?"

"Well, we didn't tell them, but we couldn't keep the lawyers away. I'm pretty sure they spilled the beans—the prisoners were quieter than usual afterwards."

Several high-school-aged kids came down the escalator and accreted into two separate clusters, boys and girls, each talking only to the members of their own sex but oh-so-aware of the other group.

"And who is paying for the lawyers?"

"That's privileged, apparently, but the firm's done business for Bochstettler and Associates in the past."

"So, barring Davy's testimony, I take it you don't have enough to move against Simons?"

Becca sounded angry. "No. Even the link to the house is iffy. I know he said this was one of his houses but he doesn't own it, not directly. Its owner of record is a real estate holding firm in Boston and it was leased, on paper, to Abney, the butler, who's saying even less than Hyacinth. I say on paper because there's no record of any rental payments. The record you told me about at the Edgartown Golf Club is gone, too. There's no sign of the physicist, Conley, or the other household staff who left before you got there. Even the security company has been stripped of anyone who worked out at Great Pond Lane and the computer hard drives from the security video station are gone."

"And Simons?"

"Still in New York. We've got a wiretap on the townhouse and he's still taking calls but if he's discussing anything of note, it's well coded. We're sniffing his DSL connection, too, but his e-mail is encrypted and we're not sure we want to go to that *other* organization for help."

And the NSA could be listening to this, too. "I understand your reluctance."

"We'll keep digging. We'll keep watching."

"At least until the ton of bricks lands."

Becca sighed. "Well, Mom always wanted me to be an accountant, anyway."

Two days later, Millie went with Davy as he got a randomly chosen Family Practitioner in Portland, Oregon, to pull the suction tube. "It still aches," he said. "But I feel less . . . *infected*." He swiveled back and forth, twisting at the waist, then rubbed his wrist. "Less tethered."

The ton of bricks arrived later that same day.

"Suspended, pending investigation into departmental malfeasance. My boss is tarred with the same brush—several thousand dollars in seized RICO cash has gone missing."

Millie closed her eyes tight and leaned against the wall next to the phone booth. "Are you in any danger?"

"I doubt it. A disgraced agent is one thing. A dead agent is something completely different. Besides—it's a balancing act. If they push too hard, we'll go to the press. It's an election year and there are too many photos showing . . . that man with senior administration members. They want to quiet this down, not blow it up."

"I need to talk to Davy about this. Watch your back, okay?"

"Twenty-four/seven."

"All the windows are shuttered. You can't see anything of the interior. Even before, when I was watching people go in and out, I never saw inside the door. It's got that awning."

They were on the roof across the street and down the block from Simons's Manhattan townhouse. Davy was eating a chicken kabob on a bun, bought from a street vendor at the edge of the park.

Millie glared at him. "Are you listening to me?"

He licked one of his fingers. "Sure. No jump site inside. But we don't want to go *inside* that building." He gnawed at the bamboo skewer, getting the last bit of chicken off the shaft. "It's a death trap." He wiped his fingers on the napkin before reaching over, and took the binoculars from her. "*Nice.* You buy these while I was, uh, gone?" He peered through them.

"Yes."

"Nice flat roof. The parapet is three feet high or so with drains to downspouts. Maybe interior plumbed drains as well." He gave the binoculars back to Millie.

"We'll need about a cubic yard of fast-setting cement."

Millie watched from the distant building as Davy dealt with the video surveillance system, smashing each of the roof cameras with a thirty-three-inch Louisville Slugger baseball bat in maple, bought especial. He took out all four cameras in less than three seconds.

She jumped to join him. He was spinning the bat and grinning like a fool and she said, "Very nice, dear. Don't tear your stitches."

He stuck out his tongue. "Take a peek at the front door."

She stuck her head over the parapet and looked down. There was no activity below. She wondered what they were thinking inside or if they'd even noticed.

"No activity," she reported.

He put down the bat and said, "Back in a second."

When he returned he held two galvanized buckets, each half full of wet cement. He worked his way around the edge of the parapet, filling each through-the-wall rain drain with the thick glop. He made several trips back to the cement yard. By the time he'd blocked all sixteen spouts, the first one was hardening to the touch. There were four more, through-the-roof drains out in the middle of the expanse. He used a bucket over each, letting it squeeze in among the gratings.

He whistled cheerfully as he worked.

She couldn't help smiling.

"Well," he said, tossing the buckets to one side. "It's not too late to stop. We do this and they'll chase us the rest of our lives."

Millie stopped smiling. "And this changes things how? As if they're not going to keep chasing us if we don't? Let them understand the consequences."

Davy nodded briefly. "Yeah, but now *we've* crossed the line as well. You want the front or the back?"

She said, "I'll go across the street and watch the front." She jerked her thumb directly across the street to a building one story higher.

Davy nodded. "Got your horn?"

She held up the compressed air can with the boating horn attached.

"Be off with ya, then." He picked up the bat and wandered back toward the rear of the building.

Millie jumped across the street to the fire escape she could see and climbed to the roof. She watched Davy lean over the rear parapet and glance below, at the rear garden. He turned back to her and waved. She waved back.

He'd described it, of course, when he told her what he'd done back on the Vineyard, but she was unprepared for the sheer volume of water. The roof was approximately sixty feet by sixty and it was knee deep in under half a minute.

About one hundred and sixty-two tons of water.

She was wondering if it would hold the full three hundred and twenty-four tons that water all the way to the parapet would entail when the question answered itself. The roof caved in near the front of the building, and the water flowed down into the gap.

Almost immediately water smashed through the glass and geysered between the bars of the windows on the fourth floor.

Up on the roof Davy kept the water coming. He was holding onto the rear façade and the roof under him was apparently still solid.

Now water was coming out of the windows on the third floor. The front door banged open below and Millie focused the binoculars. They mostly seemed to be servants—at least they wore livery, wet, in some cases, to the waist.

Three more men *washed* out the door and down the steps, as the water began to flow in earnest on the first floor, turning the stoop into a cascade of rapids. An end table, a lamp, a coat rack, an attaché case, and a padded bench followed in the flood. One of the two garage doors started to creep up, then stopped, with a gap of three feet. Several bottles and gallon jugs washed out onto the driveway, then a mechanics creeper, and a bundle of rags.

The electricity is out. That's why the garage door had stopped rising. It's also why Davy had used—was *still* using seawater.

A man crawled out under the garage door, then reached back to drag, well, *float* another man out on his back. A man wearing a cast and sling.

Bingo. She squeezed the horn button and winced at the noise, a thousand balloons being rubbed together, then threw it aside. Before her ears stopped ringing, Davy was at the front edge of Simons's building perched on the parapet like a gargoyle. He looked down at the street and vanished.

She jerked her head back down to the sidewalk but Simons was already gone.

She went to the Aerie first, and picked up the handheld metal detector she'd purchased that morning. It was a black and yellow "wand" unit like those used at airports.

Davy, as arranged, had jumped Simons to an empty stretch of desert some fifty miles east of the Aerie, northwest of the town of Terlingua. He was worried about tracking devices. They were smaller and smaller, with satellite transceivers using the global positioning system to fix location. And knowing Davy and Millie were alive and active, Simons might have taken precautions.

Simons was face down in the sand and Davy was kneeling on him, one knee in his back, while Davy patted him down with one hand. Tossed to one side were a cell phone, a wallet, a set of keys, and two clips for an automatic pistol. The gun that went with the ammo was in Davy's hand, the muzzle pressed quite hard against the back of Simons's head.

The expression on Davy's face frightened her. She was half afraid he'd kill Simons.

And half afraid he won't.

She switched on the wand and swept it over Simons's legs. The shoes beeped and she pulled them off before throwing them into the growing pile. His back was negative but his watch set it off. She stripped it off.

Simons's right forearm was in a fiberglass wrist cast stretching from the base of his fingers to just short of his elbow. When she passed the wand over it, the speaker shrilled.

"There's something in his cast," she said. "Strong signal."

Davy ground the gun muzzle into Simons's head. "What did they put in your cast?"

Simons said slowly, "They put two pins in my wrist."

Millie shook her head. "They can't put a hard cast on after surgery until the swelling goes down. He's lying."

With his free hand, Davy picked up a large rock the size of a small cabbage and held it close to the ground, before Simons's face. "Let's just break it open, and see."

Millie said, "Won't exactly help his broken bones."

Davy laughed. "And your point would be?"

"I suppose one could consider that a benefit," she said, hoping she was playing along with an act.

Simons pulled his cast in to his side, trying to hide it with his torso.

Davy dropped the rock, took his knee off of Simons's back, and rolled him face up. "Don't move," he said, pressing the gun to Simons's forehead. "See what other toys he has." Davy smiled, but the expression was neither kind nor reassuring.

Millie swept the wand over the front of Simons's limbs, then up over his torso. It screeched at his belt buckle and at some change in his pockets, which she added to the pile. She swept higher. At his left shoulder it screeched again.

Davy's face stilled. He ripped the shirt open, popping buttons. The nasty smile dropped from his face.

"Oh," said Millie.

Simons was tan under his shirt but it only highlighted the two scars, the larger one below the collarbone, the other above, on the neck. Old scars, years old.

Davy took the gun away from Simons's head and yelled at the sky. "Where does this stop?"

Simons flinched.

Davy looked down at Simons. "I thought your reach was . . . enormous, but it wasn't *your* reach, was it?"

"Another implant zombie," said Millie. "Then who heads your organization?"

Simons rolled away from them and they let him. He sat up and scooted away, coming to a stop against a large boulder in the shade of a mesquite bush four yards away. He sneered at them

Millie eyed him warily. "What do you think is in his cast? Could it be a weapon?"

Davy shook his head. "A tracer perhaps, or some sort of bug. Almost certainly electronic."

"How long do you think we have until they come for him?"

Davy looked at Simons. Simons pointedly covered his mouth and yawned.

"We have forever." Davy picked up the rock again. "We can jump away from here before they come and when they do, we'll have removed whatever is in his cast." He turned toward Millie and winked at her. He turned back to face Simons.

"This might sting a little."

"You can't touch me," Simons smiled. He raised the cast, like he was cradling it, up and across his chest, but there was an awkwardness as he pushed it even higher.

Getting it up to the—"Davy! Don't let—"

It was as if Simons been shot from behind, the way his upper chest exploded. The cast diverted much of the blood but the spray reached several feet and Millie felt warm droplets strike the back of her hand.

The heart beat on, blood fountaining in pulses, once, twice, three times, and then mere seepage unaided by the contractions of the heart. Simons's eyes went from wide-opened and surprised to half-closed and distant and, finally, absent.

Millie thought for a moment that it had been the cast that had exploded, but while the fiberglass was covered in blood, it was intact, still covering his wrist, lying across the sand, the projecting fingers slightly curled.

She swallowed convulsively.

"So, that's what they put in the cast," Davy said. He swayed slightly on his feet and his eyes were glazed.

Millie took a quick step to his side and grabbed his arm. "Steady."

He bent over and took several deep breaths. When he stood again, his color was better.

"What was it?" she asked.

"Something to make his implant detonate. A magnet,

maybe, or something more sophisticated. I guess he believed me, about the rock. He didn't want me to remove the cast."

Millie spoke more to herself than Davy. "He did it to himself. To keep us from interrogating him about his masters."

Davy licked his lips. "Masters? More than one? God, I hope not. I had this picture of *him* sitting at the center of the web, pulling on the strings. What if he's on the periphery?"

Millie shook her head. "Layer upon layer. Circles within circles. We may never know. From the way you described him—from what I saw of him—he wasn't the sort to relinquish control. Maybe that's why he did it. *His* choice to the last."

"I didn't try to save him. If I'd jumped him to a trauma center—"

Millie stroked Davy's back. "Padgett was on the operating table when his went off and they couldn't save him. And—" She looked away from Simons. "I wouldn't have killed him. I know you wouldn't, either. But he can't hurt anybody else now and prosecuting him has just become moot."

Davy finally nodded.

"What are we going to do with his body?"

Davy looked at his watch. "It's only been fifteen minutes since he 'left' his townhouse. Let's put him back."

She frowned at him. "You're sending a message."

"I hope so."

"And the text is?"

"Leave us alone. Pursuing us is not worth the price." He gestured at Simons. "He was very highly placed. They lost far more than two houses and several agents. Hopefully, they lost influence."

Millie was doubtful. "Maybe. Or perhaps they've already got someone primed to step in."

Davy nodded slowly. "Maybe."

They took a cab from BWI. It was to a high school just outside the District on the Baltimore side. It wasn't their high school, but both kids were participating in the swim meet. They found the kids' mother in a shadowy, empty section of the upper bleachers.

Davy offered his hand. "Hello, Mrs. Cox. My name is Davy Rice. This is my wife, Millie."

Cindy Cox stared at him, wide-eyed. "I never thought I'd meet you. I know about you, but I'm not supposed to. Brian was pretty good about not bringing his work home, but—" She shook his hand belatedly.

"Did you know I was there when Brian died?"

She blinked and the color drained out of her face. "You couldn't have been! You wouldn't have let him die! Not with what *you* can do."

Davy's mouth went flat and tight and Millie saw his eyes tear. "I—I wish that were so."

Millie said, "Davy was drugged, Mrs. Cox. Brian died trying to keep him from being kidnapped. He failed. Until last week, Davy's been a prisoner—a subject of experiments."

Cindy looked at him. "I'm sorry. It's just that you were one of my 'if only's.' If only he'd been sick that day. If only he'd stayed home that night. If only I'd insisted when early retirement was an option. If only Davy had been with him, to take him to safety."

"The NSA didn't tell you?"

"They only said he'd been killed in the line of duty. Greater love hath no man and all that."

Down in the pool the starter was preparing a heat of fifty-yard freestyle. Cindy said, "Excuse me. That's Billy, our eldest, in lane five."

The starter tone echoed in the closed quarters of the indoor pool and the bodies arched through the air to slice into the water. Billy wasn't the fastest swimmer in his heat but his dive and turn were both so clean that he won anyway.

His mother cheered and waved and cried.

When she turned back to Davy, he said, "Did the NSA tell you that your husband's murderer is in the custody of the FBI?"

She took a deep breath and exhaled. "Not the NSA. But a friend in the agency did."

"Anders," said Millie.

"Yes, when he asked where you could meet me. I don't know if it helps or not. Even if they convict her, Brian will still be dead." Cindy rubbed her nose with the back of her hand.

Davy took a deep breath and said, "Brian's last words were, 'Tell Cindy she's the best thing that ever happened to me. Her and the boys.'"

Cindy Cox stared at him and the corners of her mouth hooked sharply down. Millie slid over and held her upright as the woman dissolved into tears and sobs.

When she stopped she seemed drained. Four heats had been run but the cheers echoing through the building had easily covered the sobs. She pushed herself away from Millie. "I'm all right. Zachary is in the next event. I need to watch." She held out her hand. "Thank you for giving me his message. I'm sorry I said what I said. I know you would've saved him if you could. It must've been awful, watching him die."

"It was. But I owe him, so I owe you." He handed her a card. "You need anything, place that in the Wednesday *Washington Post* Classifieds and I'll come running." He paused. "Is there something I can do for you now? Before I go?"

Cindy looked around, then said. "Just one thing. When you go, could you go *your* way? I've always wondered—"

"My way? Oh. Okay."

They jumped.

"Christ, it's freezing!"

The cabin was a sprawling two-story log house at five thousand feet in the Yukon Canadian Rockies, one hundred miles from the nearest town. It had been built by a millionaire as a fly-in hunting lodge, but the lack of safe flying weather in the area, even in the dead of summer, made him give it up. Davy purchased it and the surrounding four hundred acres for thirty thousand Canadian dollars.

Even now, in May, snow lay heaped around.

Davy said, "But there's a hot spring under the bathhouse."

"But the cabin is freezing! I'm turning blue!"

"Wait." He closed his eyes.

The gust of wind made her stagger. The front door blew shut with a bang and her ears popped. Davy *glowed* and hot air streamed out of him.

"What are you doing?" she said. She walked up to him and held her hands out, as if to a fire.

"Twinning. To Terlingua. It's a couple of thousand feet lower and a *lot* warmer so the air pressure differential gives us forced air heating. Feeling better? I'm sweating." He stopped glowing and walked over to the window. "There," he said, pointing. Water was dripping off the eaves as snow melted. "Besides, the radiators are plumbed to the hot spring. The pipes were drained when the building was mothballed."

"And no one will bother us here?"

"Who knows? I bought it under one of my old NSA fake passports as a Canadian national. The deed's registered in a closet down in the provincial courthouse in Whitehorse. I mean, the weather's so bad that you can't even *get* here most of the time unless you go *our* way. We're closer to the Arctic Ocean than we are to the lower forty-eight. And we own it, unlike the Aerie. If someone stumbles on it, we can tell them no trespassing, private property, *arrivederci.*"

She looked out the front window. She could see fifteen miles down the valley and caribou grazed the bottoms, where the snow was beginning to melt. She twitched her lips into a smile. "Well, use *our* way to go get some food. I'm hungry."

She built a fire while he fetched Indian takeout.

"Where?" she asked.

"One of those we've never been in, chosen randomly on St. Mark's Place in the East Village. No more 'favorite' restaurants," he sighed. "No more predictability."

Millie looked down at the floor. "No more clients. No more condo. No more classes, no more books. No more teacher's dirty looks."

Davy turned to her, his mouth a tight line, a piece of chicken tandoori forgotten on his fork. "No. I guess that follows. You aren't just a potential handle on me, now, are you? You're a target in your own right—another jumper."

"Yeah. Another. Why is that?"

"Maybe it's catching," he said.

"And maybe it's learned. For the past twelve years you've taken me all over the world, teleporting me thousands of times. Nobody else—barring you, of course—has experienced the phenomenon that much."

He nodded. "Yeah—that's pretty much what I thought. I know it's screwing up your life, but I'm *so* glad not to be the only one."

"You going to start a school for jumpers? You know, jump them a hundred times here and there, then push them off a cliff?"

He shuddered. "I don't want to think what the graduation percentage would be."

She shrugged. "They don't have to actually die—they just have to *think* they're going to. That's my guess."

"And if it works, then they become the targets, right?"

Millie stirred her chai. "You're right. For now I guess we'll keep it in the family." She smiled suddenly and Davy looked at her, eyes narrowed.

"Family."

She nodded.

"You and me."

She smiled again. "*Et cetera.*"

"What do you mean?"

"And so forth. And so on." She took another gulp of chai, then put it down and braced her hands on her knees. "I stopped taking birth control the day you disappeared."

His eyes widened. "I'm not sure—"

"No," she said. "I know you're not, but it's time. I know you're afraid you'll turn into your father, that you'll treat your own children like he treated you. But look, dear one, if you resisted killing and punishing the people who imprisoned and tortured you, I'm pretty sure you won't raise your hand to your own children—even when they start throwing food or tearing pages out of your precious books."

She waved her hand at the cabin. "And this is a much better place for kids than the Aerie. More room—no cliff. You must've been thinking about that a little."

He blushed. "Well—"

She took his hand. "It's *time*." She took a paper napkin and wiped the corner of his mouth, then led him out into the cold, through the snow, to the bathhouse.

"In more ways than one."